ALSO BY
ROMAIN GARY

The Colors of the Day
The Company of Men

# THE
# ROOTS OF
# HEAVEN

by

## Romain Gary

TRANSLATED FROM THE FRENCH

BY JONATHAN GRIFFIN

19 58

SIMON AND SCHUSTER
NEW YORK

LIBRARY OF CONGRESS CATALOG CARD NUMBER: 56-6679
MANUFACTURED IN THE UNITED STATES OF AMERICA
BY AMERICAN BOOK-STRATFORD PRESS, INC., NEW YORK

*With gratitude to*
HENRI HOPPENOT
JEAN DE LIPKOWSKI
LEIGH GOODMAN
*and*
ROGER SAINT-AUBYN
*this book is dedicated*

## AUTHOR'S NOTE

*Inasmuch as the English text departs from the French original, the responsibility for the alterations lies with the author, not with the translator.*

*The alterations will be incorporated into future French editions.*

# PART ONE

~~ I ~~

EVER SINCE DAWN the track had followed the hillside across a tangle
of bamboos and elephant grass in which horse and rider sometimes
disappeared entirely; then the Jesuit's head would reappear above
the yellow sea, with his big bony nose set above virile and smiling
lips, and with those piercing eyes that carried in them far more
suggestion of limitless horizons than of the pages of a breviary. His
stature was ill suited to the proportions of the Kirdi pony which
served him as a mount; his legs formed an uncomfortable angle
under his cassock, in stirrups much too short for him, and he sometimes swayed dangerously in his saddle as he observed, with abrupt
movements of his conquistador profile, the landscape of the Oulé
mountains, in which it was difficult not to sense a certain air of
happiness.

Three days ago he had left the site where he was conducting excavations for some Belgian and French foundations of paleontology, and after a day's journey by jeep, for the last forty-eight
hours he had been following the guide on horseback through the
bush, toward the mountain place where Saint-Denis was said to have
pitched his tent. He had not caught sight of the guide since morning, but the track did not branch, and sometimes he could hear,
ahead of him, a rustle of grass and the sound of hoofs. Occasionally
he dozed off, and this put him in a bad humor—he did not like to be
reminded of his seventy years. But the fatigue of eight hours in the
saddle sometimes caused his thoughts to end in a reverie that his
priest's conscience and scientist's mind disapproved, both for its

sweetness and its vagueness. Sometimes he stopped and waited for his boy to catch up, with the horse that carried—in a field chest—a collection of fragments from his last excavations, and his manuscripts, which never left him.

The hills were not so high, and had gentle slopes; sometimes their flanks began to move, to live: it was the elephants. The sky was, as always here, impenetrable, both luminous and woolly, clogged by all the sweat of the African earth. Even the aimless birds seemed to have lost their way to it.

The path continued to climb, and at one turning the Jesuit saw, beyond the hills, the plain of the Ogo, and its close, crinkled bush which he disliked so much. Compared to the great Equatorial forest, the bush was, he thought, what the coarseness of fur is to the nobility of hair. He had reckoned on reaching the summit at noon, but it was not till after two that he emerged from the sea of grass and saw the administrator's tent and the boy busy cleaning saucepans with earth, crouching before the remains of a fire. The Jesuit poked his head inside the tent and found Saint-Denis asleep on his cot. He did not disturb him, but had his own tent put up, washed, drank some tea and slept for a while. Then he woke up, feeling weariness in every part of his body.

He remained for a while stretched on his back. His thoughts too were weary, and he felt a little sad to be so very old; it meant he had not much time left and would have to content himself with what he knew already. When he emerged from his tent he found Saint-Denis smoking his pipe, facing the hills which the sun had not yet left entirely, but which seemed already to be touched by a premonition of darkness.

Saint-Denis was rather short, bald, with almost half his face caught in a black untidy beard, with strong cheekbones and burning eyes that took a lot of room under a lined forehead; his narrow, rounded shoulders suggested sedentary work, not the job he did as last official guardian of the great African herds. The two men talked for a while of people they knew, of war and peace, of the North African rebellion, and then Saint-Denis questioned Father Tassin about his scientific work, asking him if it was true that since the latest excavations in Rhodesia it could be said with certitude that Africa was the cradle of the human race.

Finally the Jesuit asked his question. Saint-Denis showed no surprise that an eminent member of the Most Illustrious Society, aged seventy and with a reputation among the brethren in the missions for taking rather too much interest in man's scientific origins and not enough in his soul, should not have hesitated to do two days on horseback only to question him about a girl whose beauty and youth were unlikely to loom large in the mind of a scientist accustomed to counting in millions of years and in geological epochs. He therefore replied frankly and without restraint and spoke with increasing abandon—and with such a sense of relief that he began to wonder whether Father Tassin had not come all this long way simply to help him rid himself of that weight of memories which was oppressing him in his solitude.

But the Jesuit listened in silence, with a sort of distant politeness, not once attempting to offer one of those consolations for which his religion is so justly famous.

Night overtook them thus, but Saint-Denis went on talking, breaking off only once to order his boy, N'Gola, to light a fire. The fire immediately drove away what was left of the sky, so that they were obliged to move a little away from the flames in order to regain the company of the hills and the stars.

## II

"No, I can't claim to have really known her; it's rather that I thought a good deal about her, which was one way of keeping her company. Certainly she fell short of frankness and simple honesty with me. It was thanks to her that the administration of a land I loved was taken away from me and I was put in charge of these great reserves of African herds, on the ground, no doubt, that the trusting naïveté which I had shown with her proved me better qualified to deal with wild animals than with human beings. As for Morel . . . Everything has been said about him. I believe he was simply a man who had gone even further into loneliness than others

—and that's a real exploit, by the way; where breaking records in loneliness is concerned, we're all champions in the field. He often comes to visit me during my sleepless nights, with that angry look of his and the three deep lines on his forehead, obstinate, under that shock of hair, and carrying his famous briefcase—it never left him, even in the jungle; and I often hear him repeating to me, in that rather common voice of his, so unexpected in a man who has received what we call an education, 'You see, dogs aren't enough any more. People feel so damned lonely, they need company, they need something bigger, stronger, to lean on, something that can really stand up to it all. Dogs aren't enough; what we need is elephants. . . .'

"He says that to me always quite seriously, without a trace of irony, in that tough, bad-tempered manner of his, and each time he slaps that briefcase full of petitions, statistics and resolutions, as if to add weight to his words.

"It's been claimed that he hated his fellow-men because of the years he had spent in a concentration camp, that he had become like a rogue elephant who attacks anyone in sight. . . . It's been said that he was crazed by loneliness and that he took up his gun to defend the African herds, because they were the only company he kept. And as if there weren't enough of all this nonsense, I've just come across an even deeper explanation in an old newspaper. It seems that the elephants Morel was trying to save were purely imaginary and symbolic, a parable, as they say, and that the poor bastard was really defending the old human rights, the rights of man, those noble, clumsy, gigantic, anachronistic survivals of another age—another geological epoch. . . ."

Saint-Denis shook his head and uttered a brief laugh, without a trace of gaiety.

"But let's stop at that. Everything has been said, or rather printed, on the subject, and I wonder why you bothered to come here at all. Unless, Father, you need a little company, like all of us on earth; there's no better reason for a long journey over the hills. My own opinion on Morel is simpler: he loved nature and all that was part of it and defended it with all he had. I have no better explanation to offer. I too have often felt the need to understand it all; but I

know my limits. In my life I've done more suffering than thinking
—though I believe one understands better that way.

"So don't ask me for any deep thoughts on this great adventure.
All I can do is to place some fragments before you, myself among
them, and accustomed as you are to digging things up and piecing
them together, I trust you to do the rest. I did hear, however, that
in your writings you've been giving our old Christian notion of
salvation a scientific meaning: salvation as a biological mutation
that will bring our species to a new spiritual horizon; and that you
announce this salvation as coming 'soon'—though I suppose that in
the language of paleontology, which is not exactly that of human
suffering, the word 'soon' means a few trifling hundred thousands of
years. And I confess I don't see very clearly what place there can be
in so grandiose a vision for one wretched girl whose principal
destiny here below seems to have been to satisfy certain needs that
are not exactly spiritual. But even leaving Minna aside—I'm not
unaware of the humble but necessary part played by the prostitutes
in Scripture—what place can there be in your theories and your
studies for a man like Habib? What significance can one grant, with
the best of will, to that enormous, silent laugh which several times
a day and for no apparent reason would shake that jet-black dyed
beard of his as he gazed at the glittering waters of the Logone, sunk
in a deck chair on the terrace of the Hôtel du Tchadien, a white
yachting cap on his head, fanning himself ceaselessly with one of
those paper fans that bear the purple trade-mark of a famous lemonade, and chewing a sodden, extinguished cigar? If it was, however,
to find the reason for that entirely carefree laugh that you under-
took your journey, your two days on horseback will perhaps not have
been in vain. I can give you my explanation. I've thought a great
deal about it, and—would you believe it?—I've even sometimes lain
awake in my tent, all alone under the most beautiful landscape in
the world—I mean the African sky at night—and wondered what
could make a scoundrel like Habib laugh in such a carefree manner
and with such pure delight. I wondered—and I finally reached the
conclusion that the Lebanese was a man who was in love with life,
and that his carefree, enormous laugh—head thrown back, eyes
closed in a grimace of mirth—celebrated a perfect, a total under-

standing between the two, an agreement which nothing ever managed to disturb: happiness, in fact. A beautiful affair: life and Habib were inseparable. It was difficult not to marvel at that aura of health and happiness which Habib always had around him, at his herculean strength, at the extremely earthly solidity of his calves, and at those friendly winks he addressed to the desolate landscape, the buzzards, the steaming river; it was impossible to see him remove his cigar from his lips, close his eyes and give way to a happy laugh, and not to make certain deductions. Earth was his kingdom, his place, his field—he *belonged*. . . .

"You must have known him, as I did, presiding over the destinies of the Hôtel du Tchadien at Fort Lamy together with his young and fair protégé De Vries, after the establishment had changed hands for the second or third time—business was not brilliant. That is to say, it wasn't brilliant until the arrival of Messrs. Habib and De Vries, who installed a bar, sent for a 'hostess,' rigged up a dance floor on the terrace overlooking the river, and soon exhibited all the outward signs of a growing prosperity whose real sources came to be known only much later.

"I met De Vries only once—more exactly, our paths crossed in the bush near Fort Archambault. He was coming back from a safari, in a jeep which he was driving himself, followed by a small lorry. He was very thin, very straight, with wavy fair hair and a face rather handsome in a strange, flat way. He turned a pale blue gaze on me, and I was struck by the tiny features of his face even though our encounter was so brief—he was filling up with petrol from cans, and had just finished as I came up. I remember, too, that he had a rifle that shone like a mirror in his hands—the butt was encrusted with silver. He started his jeep without answering my greeting, leaving the lorry behind, and I stopped for a chat with the Sara driver. He explained that they were on their way back from an expedition into the Ganda District and volunteered the information that the master 'he hunt all the time, even when rain.' I don't know quite why I lifted up the lorry's tarpaulin.

"I must say I was rewarded. The lorry was literally stuffed with 'trophies': tusks, tails, heads, skins—an orgy of butchery. But the most astonishing were the birds. There were birds of all colors and all sizes—hundreds of them. And that fine sportsman, De Vries, was certainly not collecting for museums, because most of them had been so riddled with shot as to be unrecognizable and in any case unsuitable for the pleasure of the eye. Our hunting regulations are what they are—I'm not the one to defend them—but there was no permit that could justify the ravages the 'sportsman' was wreaking. I questioned the driver a bit, and he explained to me proudly that 'the master, he hunt for pleasure.' I loathe pidgin French, which is one of our great disgraces in Africa, so I talked to him in Sara, and in fifteen minutes I knew enough about De Vries's sporting exploits to land him with Hell's own fine—which I did, on my return to Fort Lamy. I don't think this bothered him much: there are people who are always ready to pay the necessary price for satisfying the intimate urges of their soul, as you must know, Father. I also had it out with his protector on the terrace of the Tchadien, begging him to moderate his young friend's extravagances a little. He seemed amused. He removed the cigar from his lips and made a broad gesture toward the river, the water birds, the pelicans that were settling, as always, on the sandbanks at twilight, and the caymans imitating dead wood on the Cameroons shore.

"'How can I help it, my friend? A noble soul, a terrible need for purity—hence violently up against nature, it can't be otherwise, a sort of perpetual settling of accounts. Member of several cynegetic societies, holds several records, a very great hunter in the sight of the Almighty—Who, most luckily, is out of range . . .'

"He laughed. 'So he has to limit himself to an intermediate sort of game—bits and pieces: hippos, elephants, birds—things like that. The really big game remains invisible, out of range, very wisely. A pity—what a shot! The poor boy must dream of it at nights. Have a lemonade, my friend, it's on the house.'

"He went on fanning himself, sprawling in his deck chair, and I left him there; the place was his—he belonged. . . . As I moved away, he called after me.

"'And don't worry about the fines: I shall take care of that. Business is good.'

"It was good indeed. The explanation of that prosperity, surprising as it was to anyone who had witnessed the financial struggles of the Tchadien's successive owners, revealed itself soon in an unexpected manner. One of the lorries that carried Habib's lemonade into the bush had an ill-timed accident to the east of the Ogo; there was an explosion not entirely explicable by the gas content of the lemonade. It was discovered that Messrs. Habib and De Vries were taking an active part in the contraband of arms along the old routes of the slave merchants into the recesses of French Equatorial Africa, starting from certain well-known bases in Egypt and Tripolitania. You are not unaware of the muffled strife of which our continent is the stake: Islam is increasing its pressure on the fetishist tribes, from overpopulated Asia a new dream of expansion is slowly rising, and the lesson of the issueless struggle which the British have been carrying on for years in Kenya has not been lost on everybody. Morocco, Tunisia and Algeria have been torn by bloody strife. Habib was installed at the heart of all that even more comfortably than in his deck chair, and his police record, when somebody at last thought of having it fetched, turned out to be a perfect hymn of triumph to this world. But by that time he had already vanished, together with his handsome associate, the enemy of nature, warned no doubt by one of those mysterious messages which in Africa always seem to arrive in time; while nothing, ever, betrays haste or anxiety on the impassive faces of certain of our Arab merchants, as they sit in the well-aired half-light of their shops, dreamy and gentle and apparently altogether apart from the noises and agitation of this troubled planet. And so they vanished, and were only to reappear, in an entirely unexpected and yet, come to think of it, natural way, at the moment when Morel's star was at its height, in order to gather upon themselves a few last rays of that glory which so well suited their earthly kind of beauty."

## III

"ANYHOW, IT WAS Habib's idea, as soon as he had acquired the Tchadien, now transformed with the aid of neon lighting into a *café-bar-dancing*, to grace the somewhat desolate atmosphere of the place—this was particularly noticeable on the terrace, with its view

over the Cameroons shore across the river all bristling with the loneliness of petrified reeds, and in the immense sky, which seemed to
have been conceived eons ago for the sake of some prehistoric beast
proportioned to it and now gone forever—it was his idea to 'pep up,'
as he said, this rather nostalgic atmosphere by a feminine presence.
He disclosed his idea to the customers well in advance, to whet
their interest, and repeated it every time he came to sit at one of
the tables, fanning himself with that tiny billboard of a fan which
looked particularly frivolous in his enormous hand. He would sit
down, give you a pat on the shoulder as if to comfort you, help you
to hold out a little longer—he was looking after you—he was going
to bring someone out here—it was all part of his plan for reorganiz-
ing the place—not a tart, mind you—simply a nice piece—he could
understand perfectly well that the fellows, especially the ones who
trek three hundred miles to get here from the bush, are sick and
tired of perching in front of their whisky—all by themselves—they
need company. He would then get heavily to his feet and go and repeat his patter at some other table, and it must be admitted that he
succeeded pretty well in creating an atmosphere of curiosity and
expectation. People wondered with a certain amount of pity and
irony what sort of girl was going to fall into the bag; and I'm sure
there were a few poor fellows among us—you see that I'm quite
frank about it—who dreamed about her secretly in their corners.

"So Minna had become a subject of conversation in the most forsaken spots of the Chad long before she made her appearance, and
the time she took to materialize gave some of us a chance to realize
once more that years of isolation in the depths of the jungle have no
power against a tenacious hope, and that a hundred acres of land
at the height of the rainy season are easier to clear than are certain
little intimate nooks of our soul. So much so that when, one day, she
stepped out of the plane, with a beret, a suitcase, nylon stockings,
a large impressive body and a fairly inexpressive face—apart from a
trace of apprehension, which, heaven knows, was rather understandable in the circumstances—it can be truly said that she was
expected.

"Apparently Habib had written to Tunis, to a friend who owned
a night club where Minna was 'stripping' at the time. He had ex-

plained exactly what he wanted: a well-made piece, with all it takes where it counts, preferably a blonde, who could look after the bar, do a song perhaps, but above all be nice to the fellows—yes, a nice girl who'd do what she was told and with whom she was told—he didn't want any trouble—no trouble whatsoever—that was the thing. He didn't want a whore either—it wasn't that sort of place—simply a girl who would sometimes give it to a fellow whom he, Habib, would recommend to her particularly. At Tunis the night-club owner must have looked at his girls one evening a little more attentively than usual, must have observed that Minna was a blonde, probably remembered that she was a German, that her papers were not in order, which was obviously a guarantee of obedience, and made her the offer.

" 'And you accepted, just like that, without thinking twice?'

"It was Major Schölscher who asked her this question during the inquiry that followed the disappearance of Messrs. Habib and De Vries and the revelations of the interesting activities in which they indulged. He had sent for Minna; he had to weigh certain accusations made against her by Orsini. The inquiry was being carried out by the police, but the military had for some time been preoccupied by the appearance of the first bands of lavishly armed fellahin on the Libyan border, and the ramifications which the Habib enterprise might have at Tunis and elsewhere seemed to deserve the greatest attention. Few men knew the border better than Schölscher, who, at the head of the camel-corps companies, had ranged the desert from the Sahara to Zinder and from the Chad to the Tibesti for fifteen years, and whom all the nomad tribes rushed to greet from far and wide when the whirlwinds of dust raised by his camels rose on the horizon. For nearly a year now, and for the first time in his career, he had been occupying an almost sedentary post, acting as special adviser to the governor of Chad, who was worried by the stealthy flow of modern weapons which seemed at that time to be spreading over the territory from the south, reaching into the depths of the forest.

"Minna had arrived in the major's office between a couple of Senegalese soldiers, utterly terrified by the grilling the police had just put her through, and convinced she was about to be deported from a corner of the world to which she appeared to have grown curiously attached.

" 'I like it here, I don't want to be kicked out!' she had cried tearfully to Schölscher with that heavy German accent that made you blink in spite of yourself. 'When I open my window in the morning, and see the thousands of birds standing on the sandbanks of the river, I feel happy. That's all I ask for. . . . I like it here, and besides, I've nowhere to go.'

"Schölscher was not a man to allow himself irony in the presence of any human distress whatever, but he was unable, all the same, to avoid a certain flicker of humor; it was the first time in his experience that someone had compared a possible ban on residence in French Equatorial Africa to expulsion from the Garden of Eden. That obviously implied a past—well, not a very happy one. This was as near as he was prepared to come to pity, even a long time afterward, during our last interview. It was immediately apparent to him that Minna had known nothing of the secret activities of her employer, whom she had served as part of a façade, as a blind, along with the rest of the establishment—the two dwarf palm trees in their tubs on the terrace, the bottles of lemonade, the gramophone, the scratched records, the moths whirling around the lamps, and the rare couples who in the evening ventured out onto the dance floor. He had some coffee and a sandwich brought to her—she had been hauled out of bed at five in the morning—and he asked her no more questions; but she kept on trying to convince him, looking at him anxiously, her lips trembling, her face crumpled, at the same time vehement and humble, sometimes raising her voice almost to a scream in her passionate desire to be trusted. Perhaps she had read in Schölscher's eyes, as we all did, something different, something she cannot often have met with in men's eyes, and she needed sympathy. She was absolutely set on telling all she knew, she insisted; she had really nothing to hide, and she did not want to leave even a shadow of suspicion hanging over her. She could very well understand that she might be suspected. People might well wonder, indeed, how she could have fetched up in the depths of French Africa—she, a German, without an entry permit, with papers that were not in order. . . . It was true that Habib had helped her to get the papers. But from that to an accusation of aiding enemies of France, of having abused the hospitality with which she had been received at Fort Lamy, at a moment when she had literally nowhere else to go . . . Her lips trembled, heavy tears ran profusely over her cheeks, and Schölscher leaned forward and laid his hand gently on her shoulder.

"'Come, come,' he said. 'No one's accusing you. Just tell me why you came to the Chad and how you got to know Habib.'

"She raised her face, her handkerchief to her nose, and stared for a long time at the major, as if she were wondering whether she could make such a confession to him, whether he would understand. She had come to Africa, she explained slowly and gravely, because she could bear it no longer—she had such need of warmth—and also because she had always loved nature. She had wanted to go away from the ruins of Berlin, away from people, to some distant place where there would be warmth and peace and . . . She hesitated a moment. And nature, she added, with an air of finality, as if the word explained everything. She didn't bother to clarify what she meant by 'nature,' but the way she pronounced the word carried an echo of some almost desperate longing. Of course, she understood perfectly well how unconvincing this sounded, but she couldn't help it: it was the truth. Schölscher showed neither astonishment nor disbelief. That a human being should have need of warmth and nature—there was really nothing in that to surprise him. But she must have been well and truly destitute to be content with the warmth of the African earth and not dream of any greater marvel than the herds of elephants sometimes glimpsed on the horizon. In this there was an image of humility, and he was not altogether insensitive to it. He considered her totally defenseless and even more lost upon earth than any other nomad it had been given him to encounter.

"'And Habib?'

"Well, she was ready to explain that too. But to do it properly she had to go back several years. Her parents had been killed when she was sixteen, in one of the air raids on Berlin, and she had gone to live with an uncle, whom her family had always refused to see, but who took charge of her as soon as she was alone, and even had the idea of making her sing at a night club, although, as she immediately confessed, she had no voice. She therefore exhibited herself for a year at the *Kapelle*—the war was already as good as lost and the men had need of women. Then came the storming of the capital by the Russians, and she suffered the fate of many other women of Berlin. That had lasted, as it turned out, for several days, until the fighting was over and the command got the troops in hand again. After that . . . She looked embarrassed, almost guilty, and for a moment stared silently out the open window. After that, something quite unexpected had happened. She had fallen in love with a Russian officer.

"She broke off again and looked at Schölscher as though to ask his forgiveness. Oh, she could understand very well what he was thinking. She had had it thrown in her face often enough. 'With a Russian?' people would exclaim, giving her a look . . . well, he knew what sort of a look. How could she fall in love with a Russian after all that had happened to her? She shrugged her shoulders with a trace of irritation. That had nothing to do with it, of course. But her compatriots seemed to feel very deeply about it. Neighbors passed her in the street without greeting, looking straight ahead with cold, set faces. The braver ones told her what they thought— when they met her alone. How could she fall in love with a man who had, so to speak, taken her at the head of his troops? I imagine the people who made this sort of remark to her did so figuratively, but she seemed to have taken it literally. That, of course, wasn't at all certain, she explained to Schölscher, warmly. It might have happened. She discussed it once or twice with Igor—that was the officer's name—but neither of them knew or, frankly, cared. He had certainly gone into one of those villas—he had been at the front for three years, his family had been shot by the Germans, and he wanted peace, even if it was only a few minutes of it. As for her, she didn't even see the soldiers' faces; the only thing that had soaked into her memory forever was the brass buckles of their belts. So maybe he had been among them, and maybe not. And anyway, you can't judge men by their sexual behavior, particularly in the thick of battle, when they're scared and crazed and all in. . . . She raised her eyes toward Schölscher again, but the major said nothing, because there was nothing to say.

"So she went on, telling him about her Igor. He had won her heart straightaway. There was something gay and nice about his face, as in many Russians and Americans—and Frenchmen too, she tactfully corrected herself. She had met him in her uncle's house— he was billeted there—and he courted her shyly, bringing her flowers, sharing his food rations with them. . . . He was very gentle and considerate. Then one evening, he kissed her awkwardly on the cheek—she smiled, pressed her hand to her cheek and kept it there, at the place of that first kiss. 'It was my first kiss,' she said, raising her clear eyes once more toward Schölscher."

## IV

SAINT-DENIS PAUSED and breathed the air in deeply, as though he suddenly needed all the chill calm of the night. "After all," he said, "I suppose there are things that nothing can kill and that remain forever intact. It's as if nothing could ever happen to human beings. They're a species over which it's not easy to triumph. They've a way of rising from the ashes, smiling and holding hands."

The Jesuit bent toward the flames, caught hold of a branch and lit his cigarette. The firelight wandered for a moment over his long white hair, over his shining cassock, and over the bony face that seemed carved with an ax by one of those prehistoric cave-artists whose traces he pursued indefatigably in all the recesses of the earth. Since nightfall he had appeared to be devoting all his attention to the stars, and Saint-Denis was grateful to him for that remote gaze which seemed to be telling the rosary of the infinite in the sky.

"Yes, Father, you're right to suggest detachment. But, I confess it's become increasingly difficult for me to state facts instead of asking questions, and the nights, even the most starry nights, are capable only of beauty, not of an answer. But let's get back to Minna, since it's to her, apparently, that we owe the appearance among the Oulé hills, in the heart of this reserve of wild life of which I am now guardian, of an eminent member of the Society of Jesus whose sole earthly curiosity seems to have been—up to now—his labors on pre-history. But perhaps the Illustrious Society has been requested from above to conduct an inquiry into the matter and has ordered you to put together a file—one is told so many things about the Jesuits!"

He laughed into his beard, and Father Tassin smiled politely.

"So let's get back to Minna. She said that they lived in perfect happiness for six months; then the officer was posted back home. Neither of them had thought of this possibility, easy to foresee though it was. But their happiness had about it a quality of perfection that seemed to exclude any danger that it might end. The officer had been given forty-eight hours in which to make his arrangements, and he did so immediately. He decided to desert and to escape with her to the French zone. She explained that they had chosen the French zone because the French had the reputation of best understanding matters of the heart. Clearly they had to have some assistance. They made the great mistake of letting the uncle know of their plans. As he was deeply involved in illegal deals, and had contacts everywhere, he seemed the obvious person to help them. He hid Igor at a friend's house, then denounced him to the Russian police. It was impossible to know his exact motives. Perhaps he had done it out of patriotism—after all, it made one Russian officer the less; or, on the contrary, to buy himself credit with the Soviets; or perhaps he was jealous of her physically. . . . She made this last remark as though in passing and without appearing to have the least suspicion of the abyss she was opening under his feet. Schölscher did not flinch. I can imagine him—tall, with his serious face and crew-cut hair, the attentive, quiet eyes, sitting there in his white Saharan uniform—the sandals, his stick and the blue kepi in front of him on the table—forever a man of the desert wastes. He continued to smoke his pipe—he merely encircled it with his fingers, the better to feel its friendly warmth in the hollow of his hand. It's probable, indeed, that his decision was then already taken—that de-

cision which caused such surprise even among those who knew him
well, with the exception of Haas, who had always foreseen it: 'All
those men from the Desert Camel Corps are obsessed by Père de
Foucauld,'* he used to say, during his rare, brief appearances in
Fort Lamy. 'Schölscher is no exception.' She said with a sigh that
Igor was arrested and she never heard any more of him. She had
gone back to the *Kapelle*. Her absence had cost her a week's salary.
She had also gone back to live with her uncle. It was almost impossible to find a place to live in the ruins of Berlin at that time, and it
seemed to her natural to return to her old room. Besides, nothing
mattered to her any longer. If she had anything left it was her
horror of cold—and the uncle had coal through his contacts. But she
found the atmosphere of Berlin hard to bear. She dreamed of escape,
of going to live under some more clement sky, far, very far away
from it all, closer to nature. And the sight of every Russian soldier
wrung her heart. She must also have been short of vitamins; she
sometimes felt as though she were going to die of cold. Mind you,
she added this with an obvious desire to render everyone his due,
her uncle had treated her quite kindly: in her room he had installed
a big stove which burned day and night. But she dreamed of leaving the ruins around her, fleeing to Italy or to France—the soldiers
on leave during the war had often spoken of those distant lands with
enthusiasm, and shown her photos of blue sea and orange groves.
As in the song:

> *Kennst du das Land wo die Zitronen blühen,*
> *In dunkeln Laub die Goldorangen glühen,*
> *Ein sanfter Wind vom blauen Himmel weht,*
> *Die Myrthe still und hoch der Lorbeer steht.*
> *Kennst du es wohl?*
> *Dahin, dahin*
> *Möcht ich mit dir,*
> *O mein Geliebter, ziehen.*

She had often sung those lines from *Mignon* in public, until the day
near the end of the war when an S.S. officer had come down onto

---

* A French officer who became a famous missionary in the desert.

the floor and slapped her; she had then been questioned by the Gestapo, and accused of satirizing the German Army's reverses in the Mediterranean. So she looked for a job in the South and spoke of this to all the soldiers of the occupation troops. In the end, it was the pianist at the *Kapelle* who helped her to realize her dream. He had been through the Tunisian campaign with the Afrika Korps and had made friends there—he felt sure he could get her something. The hardest part was to find the necessary papers—all her savings went on that, but thank God she had a little luck and three months later she was in Tunis, doing a strip-tease act at the *Panier Fleuri*. She stayed there a year, more or less comfortable, except that the winter was colder than she had expected and of course there were customers who were troublesome. But she still felt that this was not quite the place, she still had that longing to escape, to go on still further in her search for warmth. She suddenly laughed—a kind of small, guilty laugh, as if asking forgiveness, and looked at Schölscher. 'You see that I really didn't know what I wanted. But that's how it was: a craving for something, a longing to be away from there.'

"One evening the owner of the night club, a huge Tunisian who had behaved quite kindly to her—he didn't like women—took her aside and asked if it would interest her to go and work as hostess in a hotel at Fort Lamy. She would have to run the bar, sing a bit— there was no need to have any voice—and above all, be nice to the customers. No, it wasn't that sort of a joint, he replied indulgently to the question she had immediately asked him. On the contrary, it was a very decent place. Only there were a lot of lonely men in the Chad, who came in from the bush and needed company. She knew that Fort Lamy was a long way away, on the other side of the Sahara, in the middle of Africa—another world. Another world— and that was exactly what she needed. There at last she would be able to satisfy her need for warmth—even at Tunis there were moments when the cold was more than she could take. So it was that, without quite knowing how, she found herself one fine day a hostess at the Tchadien, on the terrace of that famous establishment, from which she could see, on the sandbanks, thousands of birds every morning—it was the first thing she did when she woke up: she ran to her window to look at the birds.

"She took care of the bar and of the dance floor and, contrary to what she had feared at the start, Habib had never insisted on her sleeping with anyone—except once, she added quickly, and it was clear that she had completely forgotten. Schölscher had asked no question, but she hastened to give details. Yes, once Habib had come to the bar and had muttered to her: 'You'll say yes to Sandro if he asks you,' and Mr. Sandro had in fact asked her, and she . . . well, she said yes, of course, what else could she do? She didn't even have a work permit. She waited a moment, and although Schölscher said nothing and remained impassive, without a trace of disapproval perhaps because of that, she raised her eyes toward him rather challengingly, and declared with a shrug of her shoulders: 'To me, you know, these physiological things are no longer important. It isn't that that matters.' But she did not say what did matter."

V

"Sandro had a carrier business which served the out-of-the-way places where larger companies refused to commit their lorries. It was only too clear to Schölscher why Habib would want to please a man who, even if he did charge up to ten per cent more per kilometer, was always the first to launch his lorries after the rains upon ground from which the water had only just ebbed and over wooden bridges that had not been tested since the preceding dry season. His drivers were fairly often to be found dreamily settled in front of a watercourse which 'wasn't here last time,' or sunk up to the windshield in a mud before which even the sun seemed to recoil. But in the end, the load was always delivered where no other carrier dared go at that time of year, and reached tribes reputed to be out of range by road—the Diboons of the Cameroons, the Kresses of the Sudanese border, or even the Oulés. Such an 'opening' on the bush was obviously very valuable to Habib; he was thus sure of seeing his merchandise—covered by the same lemonade trade-mark

which adorned that eternal fan of his—find its way safely into the
hands of some friend in the depths of Africa; and for him the pio-
neering spirit of a man like Sandro was the cause of many a happy
silent laugh. The carrier had been completely ignorant of the real
nature of his consignments until the day one of his lorries exploded
in a ditch. Given the remoteness of the place, it took the investigators
over a fortnight to reach certain conclusions; and had they still been
at Fort Lamy, Messrs. Habib and De Vries would have paid Sandro
dear for the death of his Massa driver. But by then they had already
vanished, and all Sandro could do was have it out with Minna, whose
obvious innocence and bewilderment left him disgusted and disarmed.

"So she had not known Habib at all before her arrival at Fort
Lamy—she had even had to send him her picture—snapped in the
last stages of her strip—before she was accepted for the job; and
she had never even thought of coming to French Equatorial Africa
till the owner of the Tunis night club suggested it.

" 'And you accepted, just like that, without thinking twice?'

"Yes, she had accepted without hesitation. She had heard tales
of Lake Chad when she was still a little girl—her father had been a
schoolmaster; she volunteered this last piece of information with a
certain insistence, staring at Schölscher in a meaningful way, as if
to emphasize that she had known better days. It was a place a long
way from everything she knew, a very long way, in a still untouched region of Africa—and she had immediately thought of all
the great herds which still wander peacefully in the savanna. She
had nobody left in the world—well, except her uncle in Berlin—
and she had accepted without hesitation. . . . 'I'm very fond of
nature and animals,' she concluded as if to explain everything.

" 'It's an odd idea to come to the Chad simply for that,' said
Schölscher gently. 'You could have bought yourself a dog.'

"But she took this remark very seriously and grew animated. It
was clear that Schölscher had touched a sensitive spot. It was difficult for her to have a dog, she explained, with the sort of life she
led. At Tunis she was paid weekly and was always in danger of
finding herself once more on the streets, so she could not allow herself to accept responsibilities. 'Besides, you know, dogs have a lot

of pride,' she remarked. She had often noticed it. In Berlin one of
her neighbors had been an old man who used to go in full daylight
to rummage in the garbage cans, accompanied by his dog. 'Well,
you should have seen that dog's expression. I swear to you he used
to look the other way, as though he simply didn't notice that his
master was rummaging in the refuse, and I'm sure he was ashamed
for him. It's partly for that that I've never been willing to have a
dog.' She began to laugh, with a sudden gaiety which suited her
well. Schölscher noticed for the first time that she could be pretty.

"'I haven't dared. But that doesn't prevent me from loving them
at a distance. I'm the kind that strokes other people's dogs. Besides,
at Tunis the customers never left me alone—you know what it is
when you show yourself naked at a night club. And I really believed that the Chad was in some ways a place where one could
take refuge among the animals—all those great herds that range
over the plains. And the birds. That's why I came. I haven't been
disappointed, you know: it's enough for me to go to my window in
the morning. I look at the waterbirds and I feel quite happy.' Such
an explanation, given by a girl of whom it was often and, I think,
quite unjustly said that she was 'always willing for a price,' would
have seemed absurd and suspect to any man but Schölscher. When
repeated on the terrace of the Tchadien, it did not fail to provoke
a few grins and a few sardonic shakes of the head. In any case it
delighted Orsini, who later, during what everyone in the Chad
called 'the events,' would quote it with a connoisseur's jubilation, as
an example of the major's naïveté. But you knew Schölscher: he
was a man who could form his own opinion, and it took more than
a few sneers behind his back to disturb him. He had believed
Minna immediately when she described her need for warmth and
her love of animals and nature, and after some checking up at
Tunis and in Germany, he left her in peace.

"I should add, though, that the only animals she was able to see
from the terrace of the Tchadien, where she spent hours leaning
against the balustrade, were, after the departure of Messrs. Habib
and De Vries, a few caymans on the sandbanks, thousands of waterbirds, and the tame antelope belonging to the municipal vet, which
wandered freely in the streets and generally came to visit her at
twilight, before the first customers.

"I once saw her in the waning daylight, holding the beast's muzzle in the hollow of her hand, holding it with such an expression of youthfulness and absolute delight that, to use a phrase of Colonel Babcock, who was walking with me, 'You'd have thought you were a hundred thousand leagues away from all that'—he didn't say from what, exactly, but I'm sure you'll understand."

The Jesuit's face remained impassive, and Saint-Denis, after a moment of silence, resumed his story.

"It was indeed the same Colonel Babcock who, a bit later, when Minna had already become something of a legend at the Tchadien, and her memory a sort of private possession of the place, came perhaps as near the truth as is possible for an officer and a gentleman —which obviously presupposes certain limitations. He had remained all alone at the bar for a good while—he hadn't mentioned Minna at all or indeed addressed a word to anyone the whole evening—then he put down his glass, paid the bill, told the barman he could keep the change, and stated abruptly, looking him sternly in the eye, but very likely without seeing him: 'Well, she was just another animal who needed protection. . . .'

"Nobody even turned; he wasn't the only one who was secretly haunted by this matter. So much for Colonel Babcock. I'm sorry that the Society of Jesus can't question him about 'all that,' to use his own expression; unfortunately it takes more than a good horse and a very resolute Father to reach him where he is now." The Jesuit smiled: what the Colonel had to say had not been wasted.

"So you see there are quite a few of us who ask ourselves your question and continually relive that adventure in its smallest details. It sometimes seems to me that it's still going on somewhere around us, in another dimension, and that the heroes of it, in the grip of eternity, are condemned to go through it forever, forever to endure the same suffering and commit the same errors, until they are at last set free from that infernal cycle by a sudden and fraternal flash of our comprehension. It seems to me that they make us despairing signs, trying desperately to attract our attention, sometimes with a striking lack of modesty, as though they had to win our sympathy at any price. I'm sure you see them all as clearly as I do, and that they haunt your nights as they do mine; that's no doubt one reason why you came here."

Saint-Denis fell silent and turned toward his companion as if he expected a reply, a confirmation. With his arms crossed on his chest, the Jesuit raised his head. Moonlight wandered the hills; stars sparked along the ridges, flashing a remote, indecipherable lesson in detachment. Sometimes they could hear the sounds of a passing herd. Father Tassin took a cigarette and lit it. He wondered, with some annoyance, whether he would finally learn what he wanted to know, or if he would have in the end to content himself with what he already knew. He felt that, at his age, patience was ceasing to be a virtue and was becoming a luxury he could less and less afford. He therefore listened to Saint-Denis attentively, alert to the slightest hint; but at the same time he pored over his own memories, trying to settle accounts with them once for all; and, aided by the almost contagious peace of those hills and by the warm voice at his side, he strove for one last time to look at the affair with all the detachment and all the serenity suitable to a man of science.

# ～ PART TWO ～

## ～ VI ～

HE DID NOT LOOK at all "amok"—that was the nickname he had been given, "amok" or "rogue," in allusion to the elephant that lives alone, usually bears a secret wound, and in the end becomes bitter and dangerous, attacking everyone in sight. He was strongly built, with a rather somber face, dark eyes, and curling chestnut hair which he would sometimes brush aside with an energetic gesture—he did everything quickly, abruptly; he seemed to dislike hesitation. Very little had been seen of him at Fort Lamy. Later it was discovered that he had lived there for some time in the native quarter—no attention had been paid to him. Not, indeed, that he sought to pass unnoticed. On the contrary, he had found some way to bore practically everybody with an involved and ridiculous petition to the government. "The matter is one which concerns us all," he would say, pull a sheet of paper out of his briefcase, carefully unfold it, and point to where you were supposed to put your signature—he seemed sure you were not going to refuse, although there was not a single name at the bottom of the text. Generally, at the first mention of the word "petition," people turned their backs on him, saying that they were not interested in politics.

"But this has nothing to do with politics," he would at once exclaim with irritation, "it's a matter of simple humanity."

"Of course, of course," they would mockingly answer, giving him a friendly tap on the shoulder and getting rid of him with the minimum of politeness due, after all, to a white man in the tropics. He did not insist, but picked up his briefcase and went out in silence, without a glance, with the impassive face of a man who feels perfectly sure of having the last word. Those who took the trouble to glance through his "petition"—Orsini indeed knew it almost by heart, having kept a copy of it to read again and again with morose delectation, nourishing thus his hatred for what he detested, as he proclaimed often, more than anything else in the world, that is, a certain type of "dribbling idealist"—those who had read his petition had spoken of it once or twice on the Tchadien's terrace, glad to find a subject of conversation other than the drop in cotton or the latest atrocities of the North African fellahin. Minna, who was sometimes invited to join them, would listen to these remarks as she kept an eye on the boys who came and went with trays on the terrace, in the twilight that was rapidly carrying the world away—there was soon nothing left of Africa but the immense emptiness of a sky which seemed to be coming down, down, drawing nearer as though to get a better look at them, to see more clearly what all this noise was about.

"I say, I've had a visit from a sort of mad hatter who expected me to sign a petition to ban the hunting of elephants in Africa . . ."

Above the river, Minna watched a vulture slowly circling. Every evening it seemed thus to sign the sky, as if to allow eternity to turn one more page. A horseman appeared for an instant among the reeds on the opposite bank of the river, crushing them in a furious gallop: it was the American major, who always seemed to be fleeing some implacable pursuit at the hour of twilight. He galloped by before sunset almost every evening (except when he was too drunk) as if he were part of some inexorable minute hand dragging him mercilessly across that vast clock-face whose every feature Minna knew so well: a few trees, the three huts of a village of fishermen, a few pirogues, a line of horizon blurred by the grass, the loop of the Shari toward the Logone and, further eastward, the solitary palm tree of Fort Foureau, then again the immense sky, filled with absence.

"Anybody know that crackpot?"

Kotowski—Koto to his friends—the police commissioner, a meticulous, not very talkative Pole, who bore on his face scars from his Foreign Legion days, scars like the ritual brands of certain Himé tribes of the Cameroon, said that the crackpot was named Morel, that he had been living in the colony for over a year, but that he spent the better part of his time alone in the bush. He had written "dentist" on the police form he had filled in, but his great passion seemed to be the elephants; the brothers Huette had met him one day right in the middle of a herd of four hundred beasts, in the eastern district of the Chad. He had come and bothered them too with his petition. Clearly the man was a gentle maniac of the "our-dumb-friends" type, completely harmless.

It was at that moment that there arose among the shadows an extraordinarily vicious and aggressive sneer of hatred and contempt—and all those who knew Orsini saw clearly before their eyes, in spite of the darkness, his sarcastic, restless face, a face that signified to all the world that no one had ever managed to catch him napping—him, d'Orsini d'Acquaviva—"Call me simply Orsini," he used to say, "it doesn't matter a damn to me"—that he had seen through them all, hauled them into the light, smelled them out from the very first second; in short, judged them for what they were, which was very little. It was a cry that had a strange vicious power to reduce the whole human horizon to the dimension of a pin-point. To Minna that triumphant sneer seemed to proclaim that all one could expect of life was permission, afterward, to clean your teeth and rinse your mouth, that everything men do is destined to end in some slimy mediocrity. From the first glance she had refused to have anything to do with him. She had immediately and categorically rejected his advances with a sort of fierce, exasperated determination. After that he no longer called her anything but "the Boche woman," but generally, when Minna's name was mentioned in his presence, he fell abruptly silent, withdrew from the conversation, and looked in another direction with an air of studied indifference. His whole attitude seemed to suggest that he knew more than enough about her but was not going to waste his breath—at least, not for the moment. Sometimes this stratagem was successful with a newcomer, who then plied him with questions. Orsini would let himself be pressed for a bit, then burst out. Did they really believe —he lowered his voice, with a glance toward the bar, where Minna was counting out change to a waiter—did they really believe that such a girl had fetched up at Fort Lamy for no reason at all, simply because it suited her mood? Did they imagine that a **handsome** piece like that—he himself had no taste for the female Boche as a type, but still one had to admit that she had it all in the proper places—did they really imagine that a girl with her looks had come to French Equatorial Africa simply and solely to serve as barmaid at the Hôtel du Tchadien and to sleep with certain people—certain people, if you please, and not others—people chosen with somewhat particular care? It really took Koto to be as naïve as that—or perhaps it was something worse than mere naïveté. And what was she doing in the Chad, in his opinion? Orsini shrugged his shoulders, buried himself even deeper in his armchair. He preferred not to speak of it. It didn't concern him in the least. He was not in charge. The whole thing couldn't matter less to him personally. Which didn't mean of course that when the time came he would not speak up, that he would not put certain responsibilities on certain shoulders, where they belonged—but for the moment he would merely say this: he had never, in his life as a hunter, abandoned a trail, he had always followed to the end. That was all he was disposed to say for the time being.

Koto, to whom these remarks were regularly reported, received them with indifference, but a few days later, meeting Orsini at the market, he said to him casually, "By the way, I've a piece of news that may be of interest to you. I think I'm going to have little Minna deported. The wives are beginning to take notice. It's getting a bit conspicuous. I'm telling you because I've heard you too have complained about this situation—quite rightly, I hasten to say. So I'm going to ask her to take her charms elsewhere."

He said this while continuing, together with Dr. Terrot, to inspect the hands of a group of women who crouched in their black draperies in front of the heaps of peanuts they were offering to the passers-by. They were carrying out this examination because it had been reported that one of the women had leprosy, with sores on her hands, and what with peeled peanuts . . . Orsini had turned pale. His Adam's apple moved spasmodically. He tried to smile.

"Ah, good," he said. "Energetic measures, I see."

"Well, it took us some time, I admit," said the commissioner good-humoredly. "You've bought some peanuts? It's been reported to us that one of these old girls has leprosy."

"To hell with that," said Orsini. "It isn't contagious. I've been twenty years in this country, you know."

"Yes, I know."

Koto took a handful of peanuts and began nibbling them. He knew they would not find the leper, either because she had made off when they arrived or because, more likely, it had been a rumor put out by the Syrian shopkeepers at enmity with the open markets. Orsini left him without a word, but next morning Koto found him installed in one of the waiting-room armchairs.

"Can I have two words with you about a certain matter—although it doesn't concern me at all?"

"Sure. I'm always ready for advice, especially from an old hand."

"Look here, Koto, why not leave that girl alone?"

The commissioner did not raise an eyebrow. He understood perfectly well. A white girl in the heart of Africa, a German into the bargain, might resist for a time, but one day or another she would be obliged to give in, especially when the man was a friend of her employers. And the sort of rancor she inspired in Orsini could only be appeased in one fashion.

"Well, well," said Koto, his scars turning pink, "so you're among the happy chosen."

"You're wrong to treat this matter lightly," said Orsini with a sudden outburst of hatred. "Have you often seen a handsome piece like that at Lamy?"

"I've seen many things, you among them, Orsini," said the commissioner.

"She comes from Berlin, doesn't she?" said Orsini. "I happen to have some information about that. She used to sing in a night club in the Russian zone. She was mistress to a Russian officer. If you believe our troubles in North Africa started all by themselves . . ."

"All the more reason to get rid of her, I suppose."

"Allow me to tell you that that would be a rotten way to do a job," said Orsini. "What you must do, on the contrary, is keep her here, but under close watch. Stop her from moving, hem her in on all sides. Sooner or later, with the aid of the climate and frustration, she'll blunder. Then you'll be able to rope in all her little pals."

"I see," said Koto.

"In any case you can count on me to keep you posted. I have my sources."

"Thanks."

He gave Orsini a steely stare.

Orsini paled slightly; his narrow lips attempted a smile. "You seem to be making a diagnosis," he said. "What is it? A case of a first-rate swine?"

The commissioner said nothing, but bent his eyes to a paper on his desk. Orsini was silent for a moment; a puff of wind seemed to fill the room.

"Twenty years, Koto, I've been living in Africa . . . alone. You can't spend all your time killing elephants . . ."

The commissioner was still looking at his papers.

"You won't expel her? Let her rot here, till she gives up . . ."

He picked up his Panama and waited a moment for an answer; then his lips tightened and he went out. The commissioner remained bowed for a moment, then sighed briefly and rang for his corporal. The corporal was a Sara with a round, serene face, compounded of manioc and rice and a soft, dreamy, peaceful gaze. He stood at attention while Koto looked at him fixedly without a word. He showed no surprise, asked no question, simply stood there with his little finger on the seam of his trousers. The commissioner's gaze fed for a time on that simple, good-natured, reassuring being in perfect harmony with himself. After a while, when he felt better and was able once more to breathe deeply and freely, he sent him away.

## ⚋⚋ VII ⚋⚋

AND SO IT WAS Orsini's voice that rose in the shadows—the moment for lighting the lamps, which drew storms of insects, was always delayed as long as possible—to utter a cry almost lyrical by sheer force of cutting irony and scorn, a cry that seemed to enrich the

African fauna with a new kind of nocturnal bird—when the commissioner had described as "harmless" this man Morel. Instinctively everyone turned toward that corner of the night from which
the familiar sound had risen: he had a real gift for those flaring exclamations, those raucous outbursts, like wounds suddenly opened
in the flanks of silence. They waited. Then, from the depths of
darkness, arose a quivering voice, almost a song, with indignation
as its keynote—a limitless indignation, which always went far beyond its immediate object and always had room for more, in which
men, planets, each grain of dust, each atom of life, could always be
received with the honors due them. Harmless? He had his own
opinion on this matter, and no one could make him change his mind.
Of course to the pure all things are pure—he paid the homage of this
thought to Major Schölscher—but as for him, he cherished no excessive claim to purity. He, like everyone else, had been honored by a
visit from Morel, and he had read the petition with lively interest.
After all, elephant hunting concerned him somewhat. He had five
hundred, duly confirmed, to his credit. Not to mention rhinos, hippos
and lions: the total must be getting on for a thousand, a conservative estimate. Yes, he was a big-game hunter and proud of it, and
he had every intention to go on hunting big game as long as he
had enough breath in his body to follow a trail and enough strength
in his hands to hold a gun. So he had read the petition, as could
well be imagined, with particular care. It recalled the number of
elephants laid low in Africa each year—thirty thousand, so it
claimed, in the course of the last year—and bewailed at great length
the fate of these noble giants, pressed back more and more toward
the marshes and condemned by man to disappear one day from
the earth. It said—and he was quoting almost word for word—*"that
it was not possible for a free man to catch a glimpse of the great
elephant herds roaming the vast open spaces of Africa without taking an oath to do whatever was necessary to preserve forever this
living splendor, this image of liberty whose sight will always bring
a smile of happiness to the face of every man worthy of the
name . . ."* "Every man worthy of the name," Orsini repeated, almost with despair, with a last outburst of rage and scorn; and he
was silent for a long time, as if to emphasize the enormity of such

a claim. It proclaimed, also, he then went on, after taking a deep breath, that *"the time for pride is finished,"* and that we must turn with far more humility and understanding toward the other animal species, *"different, but not inferior."* "Different, but not inferior," Orsini repeated again, with a kind of exasperated relish. And it went on like that: *"Man on this planet has reached the point where really he needs all the friendship he can find, and in his loneliness he has need of all the elephants, all the dogs and all the birds . . ."* Orsini gave vent to a strange laugh, a sort of triumphant sneer, entirely devoid of gaiety. *"It is time to show that we are capable of preserving this gigantic, clumsy, natural splendor which still lives in our midst . . . that there is still room among us for such a freedom."* He fell silent, but they could feel his voice lurking in the blackness, ready to hurl itself on the first prey that offered.

A few people laughed. Someone remarked that, if this was indeed the content of that Homeric document, its author should obviously be considered a mild kind of eccentric, but that it was hard to see how he could be dangerous. Orsini ignored this observation, purely and simply excluded its author from the rank of mortals who had a right to his attention. There you had a man, he resumed, who for months had been going about the bush, who penetrated to the remotest villages and who, having learned several dialects while he fraternized with the natives, was devoting himself to an obstinate and dangerous work, undermining the good name of the white man. Western civilization was obviously being represented to the Africans as an immense bankruptcy from which they must at all costs try to escape. They were not far from being begged to go back to cannibalism as a lesser evil than modern science with its weapons of destruction, or from being encouraged to worship their stone idols, with which indeed, as if by chance, people like Morel were stuffing the museums of the world. Ah, it was all about elephants, indeed! Those who had seen in the Mau-Mau in Kenya a spontaneous movement of insurrection without any organization beforehand could go on shutting their eyes if they liked. As for him, d'Orsini d'Acquaviva, he proposed nothing, he suggested nothing, he merely refused to be taken in. Once more, he was not paid to watch over the security of French Equatorial Africa. Whatever he might say, it would be quite useless. Morel's petition would run its course un-molested across the territory, adorning itself with all sorts of signa-tures which he could see, so to speak, with his eyes closed. . . . He spoke a little more slowly, in a less irritated and more bantering tone of voice, and they could guess that the folds of skin about his mouth were creased in one of his narrow smiles. Yes, when Morel pre-sented the piece of paper to him, there had already been two names at the bottom—naturally, that was the first thing he had looked for. Two names: that of Major Forsythe, an American outcast dishon-orably discharged from his Army—one might wonder, indeed, why the authorities of the Chad had thought fit to offer hospitality to such a man, a traitor unwanted by his own country; and as for the second name, he left it to others to guess whose it was . . . He stopped. And in the enigmatic silence that followed, his presence could be felt, suddenly discreet, a gentleman to his fingertips, a man, as they say, who keeps his hands off that sort of thing. . . .

Then Minna's voice was heard, saying calmly, "It was my name. I too signed the petition."

~ VIII ~

He had appeared in front of her at the Tchadien, at the end of one afternoon, when she was behind the bar choosing the records for the evening.

He had emerged swiftly onto the empty dance floor and stopped, stood still, fists clenched, looking about him as if he had a score to settle. He seemed at once threatening and rather lost on the deserted terrace where the sky itself appeared to be waiting for the first cus-tomer.

She had given him a smile, first because that was more or less what she was there for, and then because she had never seen him before and she had a prejudice in favor of people she did not know. No, he had not offered her his famous petition, at least not immediately. He had come toward her and she had noticed then that his shirt was torn, his face covered with cuts and his curly, untidy hair sticking to his temples and to that obstinate, straight forehead of his, furrowed with three deep lines. He seemed both fresh from a fight and in search of another. He had an old leather briefcase under his arm.

"I'd like to speak to Habib."

"He's not here."

He seemed put out and looked about him again as though to make sure she was not lying.

"Monsieur Habib is at Maidaguri. He won't be back till tomorrow evening. Can I do anything? . . ."

"Are you German?"

"Yes."

His face cleared slightly. He laid his briefcase on the bar. "Well, we're almost compatriots. I'm almost German myself, by naturalization, if you can put it that way. I was deported to Germany during the war and I stayed for two years, in various concentration camps. I nearly stayed there for good. I became attached to the country."

She had bent over her records to hide her face; and yet, on the whole, they were kind to her at Fort Lamy, with only that sudden, rather ironical attention that came into people's looks when her nationality was mentioned. Abruptly she felt his hand on hers.

"There I go again, saying something I shouldn't. Living among the elephants I've lost the habit of talking to people. Not a bad thing to lose, either."

"You're a planter?"

"No, my business is elephants."

"You know Monsieur Haas, then? He works for the zoos and the circuses. He specializes in elephants. At Hamburg all Hagenbeck's animals are supplied by him."

"I know Haas," he said slowly—his face had darkened again. "Of course I know him. I've been on his track for a long time. . . . One day or another I'll catch up with him. No, mademoiselle, I don't capture elephants. I content myself with living among them. I like them. I like looking at them, listening to them, watching them on the horizon. To tell you the truth, I'd give anything to become an elephant myself. That'll convince you that I've nothing against the Germans in particular: they're just men to me, and that's enough. . . . Give me a rum."

She did not know if he was joking or serious. Perhaps he himself did not know. But she could feel that behind his words there was something nice and rather odd—kind people are often odd, she had explained to Saint-Denis, and she had added, rather mysteriously: it can't be otherwise.

"Since Habib isn't here . . . can I leave him a message?"

"Of course."

"Come with me then."

She followed him outside, wondering what it could be. In front of the triumphal arch forming the entrance to the Tchadien she recognized De Vries's station wagon. Morel opened the door. The sportsman was sprawled on the back seat. His pretty features were swollen; one of his arms looked limp. He had a blood-stained hand-kerchief around his head and seemed incapable of motion. He gave her a dazed look.

"I caught him to the east of the lake, just bringing down his fourth elephant of the day. I took a shot at the bastard at forty yards, but I'd been running too much and my hands were shaking; I missed."

He looked as if he were excusing himself.

"Then I had a little chat with him, using my rifle-butt. You can tell Habib that if I ever catch that piece of human dirt around a herd again, I'll make such a nasty mess of him that the elephants themselves won't be able to improve on it. That's all. *Au revoir.*"

"Wait."

He turned back.

"You haven't paid for your rum; you haven't drunk it, either. Finish it, at least. Please."

He followed her to the bar without a word. She gave orders to the boys, who went off to look after De Vries. The two were silent for a while. She had leaned against the bar, with her arms folded, and was looking at him. He kept his head bent, his glass in his hand. She seemed to be waiting for something with an extraordinary assurance, and he struggled for a while against this silent summons, then raised his eyes to her and began to talk. He did not tell her who he was or where he came from, but began to talk to her about elephants, as if they were the only thing that mattered. It was by tens of thousands that the elephants were killed in Africa every year—thirty thousand, to be exact, only last year—yes, thirty thousand—and he was resolved to do everything in his power to stop this murder. That was why he had come to the Chad: he had undertaken a campaign for the defense of elephants. Whoever has seen these giants on the march across the last great free spaces of the world knows that this is something that must not be lost. A conference for the protection of the African fauna would be meeting soon in the Congo, and he was ready to move heaven and earth to get the necessary measures taken. He was well aware that the herds were not menaced only by hunters, for trophies; natives hunted because they didn't have enough proteins in their diet, and there was also deforestation, the advance of the cultivated lands, progress, in fact. But hunting for the sake of trophies was obviously the most ignoble aspect of it, and it was the first thing that had to be stopped. As for the rest . . . did she know that an elephant fallen into a trap often lay in agony, impaled on stakes, for days and days? That hunting by fire was still practiced by the natives on a large scale, and it had been his lot to stumble on six baby elephants, victims of a fire from which only fully grown animals had managed to escape thanks to their size and speed? That whole herds of elephants sometimes escaped from the blazing savanna with burns up to their bellies, and that they suffered for weeks? Many a night he had lain awake in the bush listening to their cries of agony. That the contraband traffic in ivory was still practiced on a large scale by Arab and Asiatic merchants, who drove the tribes to poaching? Thirty thousand elephants a year—was it possible to think for a moment of what that meant, without shame? Did she know that a man like Haas, who was the favorite supplier of the big zoos, saw half the young elephants he captured die under his eyes? The natives, at least, had an excuse: they needed proteins. For them, elephants were only meat. To stop them, they only had to raise the standard of living in Africa: this was the first step in any serious campaign for the protection of nature. But the whites? The so-called "civi-

lized" people? They had no excuse. They hunted for what they
called "trophies," for the excitement of it, for pleasure, in fact.

He had raised his voice and clenched his fists, and his eyes had
taken on an expression of distress which explained much better
than his words what was involved. For she had understood at once,
from the first syllable and without the least hesitation. He must have
suffered a great deal in his life. That was it: he knew a lot about
suffering.

She did not move, leaning against the shelves of bottles, her arms
crossed, trying not to interrupt him, not to smile, either, at the idea
that never, surely, had a man spoken like that about elephants to a
woman. She thought, too, that he had luck and that he had come to
the right person with his petition. At one point she took a bottle and
poured herself a cognac, while he went on talking. Not once did he
speak to her of anything other than the African giants, but she was
to say later to Saint-Denis—during that long night when she had
come as near as possible to an explanation—that never had a man
told a woman more frankly everything about himself. "I wanted to
help him," she concluded, with a slight shrug, and Saint-Denis was
struck by the contrast between what she had so evidently felt and
the poverty of the words she found to express it. He had questioned
her then at some length, almost aggressively, but she never went
further in her explanations. "I just wanted to help him." She inhaled
the smoke of her cigarette and threw Saint-Denis one of those long,
insistent glances with which she often accompanied some of her
phrases, as if to prolong them, suggest that they had a hidden meaning though she left it to you to search for it. "I know how it is, after
all . . ." Saint-Denis had suddenly the impression that those thread-
bare words, that German accent, that glass of brandy, that eternal
cigarette at the corner of her rouged lips and those bare thighs
crossed under her scanty bathing wrap—that all this was only a way
of protecting herself aggressively, suiting her pace to the world's
pace, getting into step. "Yes, I know how it is. I'm sure you know
too, Monsieur Saint-Denis, since they tell me you've been living
alone in the bush for thirty years. He needed company. Sooner or
later a human being can't do without it any longer, Monsieur Saint-
Denis, and then for one it's the elephants, for another a jumping

bean or a dog, or the stars and the hills—they say that's enough for you. But he—I could see he couldn't bear it any more."

The Jesuit sighed and Saint-Denis, who had quoted Minna's words with some bitterness, nodded briefly. "Yes, Father, I understand you. That he should have turned to the animals just shows the destitution we have fallen into. You, no doubt, would have advised him to seek something larger than our excellent pachyderms. Perhaps he was at bottom a man lacking in boldness or with a limited imagination, a soul in search of God and so far gone in solitude that it didn't even know what it was seeking. I share your dismay entirely." The Jesuit raised his eyebrows with some astonishment at this interpretation of a simple respiratory phenomenon.

"There is a great space to be filled at our side, but all these African herds would not do it. The human soul, Father, is not, after all, like the African continent, which is unquestionably vast, but still limited, shut in as it is between seas and oceans."

Father Tassin lowered his eyes slightly. He was always embarrassed when people talked to him about the human soul with such assurance. "I felt I wanted to help him . . ." He understood that explanation much better.

Shadows were descending rapidly as they stood there in that amazing silence which seemed always to choose this moment of twilight to come and settle on the river and the reeds, among the last birds. He went on speaking to her a little longer in that muffled, rumbling voice full of restrained passion. Then he broke off and raised his eyes.

"But I'm boring you with all this . . ."

"You're not boring me at all. That's not how one is bored . . ."

"I first began thinking about the elephants during the war, when I was a prisoner in Germany, probably because they were the most different thing I could imagine from what surrounded me: they were the very image of an immense liberty. Every time we looked at the barbed wire or were almost dying of misery and claustrophobia in solitary confinement, we tried to think of those big animals marching irresistibly through the open spaces of Africa, and it made us feel better. Barely alive, starved, exhausted, we would clench our teeth and follow our great free herds obstinately with our eyes, and see them march across the savanna and over the hills, and we could almost hear the earth tremble under that living mass of freedom. We tried not to speak of it, for fear the guards would notice, and sometimes we would just look at each other and wink, and then we knew that it was all right, that we could still see it, that it was still alive in us. We held on to the image of that gigantic liberty, and somehow it helped us to survive. Maybe it all sounds crazy to you, mademoiselle—you're very young and I hope you haven't suffered much in your life—but that's one of the reasons why I came to Africa, why I started my campaign for the protection of nature, and why, when some scum of a hunter kills an elephant, I get such an itch to send a bullet through his ass that it keeps me awake at night. And that's also why I'm asking the authorities to take what is really a most moderate step . . ."

He opened his briefcase, took out a sheet of paper and spread it carefully on the bar.

"I have here a petition which calls for the prohibition of elephant-hunting in all its forms, beginning with the most ignoble, hunting for trophies—for pleasure, as they call it. That's the first step, and it isn't much. Really it's not much to ask of them. I should be happy if you felt able to sign your name there . . ." And of course she had signed.

## IX

THAT WAS the first step of an adventure which was to supply the Chad with something that might well become a legend with the help of the years. "I knew them both very well" was a phrase which never failed to gain a moment's undisputed attention for whoever managed to drop it into a conversation with just that degree of non-chalance required to sharpen curiosity.

But the truth was that Morel had no friends, that he spent the better part of his time in the bush, and that no one had paid any attention to him during his comings and goings with that ridiculous petition in his briefcase—no one, that is to say, but Orsini. For if ever there was a man whom events proved right, a man who was not "taken in," it was Orsini the old hand, Orsini the hunter, who had the knack of scenting big game in his neighborhood as if he were only living for that scent. Had he not from the beginning said openly that the business was one which might easily set the territory ablaze? Had he not vainly uttered his warning cry, both despairing and sneering, that astonishing cry, almost a song, which seemed somehow to have always been part of the Chad's nocturnal voices and was like the eerie echo of a pathetic aspiration? Had he not, above all, distrusted the "Boche woman"? Yes, Orsini experienced his hours of triumph, but they were short-lived, and though he is part of the legend, it is certainly not in the way he would have wished. He made one grave mistake: he identified himself too much with the issue. The flame that attracted him so irresistibly burned him in the end. He was the first to recognize the enemy and to cry tally-ho, and he had gone on the attack with all the passion of a man who feels himself challenged by everything that makes too-noble demands upon human nature, as if humanity began somewhere around thirty thousand feet above the surface of the earth, thirty thousand feet above Orsini. He was determined to defend his own height, his own scale, his own smallness.

Apart from him the only one to take notice of Morel was Father Fargue, a missionary whose primary interest was the lepers. He was a Franciscan who had the violent tongue, irascible kindness, and tendency to bang the table with his fist, of a man who had no patience with atheists. With his red beard and bull neck, his language of a naïveté sometimes near to blasphemy, he looked like a ribald half-soldier, half-monk— "It isn't my fault," he would roar, smiting himself mightily on the chest, "it's only the carcass"—but led an exemplary life in the depths of the bush to the northeast of Fort Archambault. He was known for the bricks he dropped, the most famous of which is sure of an eternal place among the legends of the colony. It made its entrance into history at Bangui, aboard the

Congo steamer which maintained the link with Brazzaville, and its enormity was due precisely to the desperate and imposing effort which Father Fargue had made to avoid dropping it. He had borrowed from his years as an Army chaplain the habit of calling each person he addressed *cocu*,* and for him men were divided into good *cocus* and bad *cocus*. "*Bonjour, cocu*" was his agreeable greeting. It happened that when Father Fargue appeared on deck, the usual group had already formed, and that it included a certain Ouard whose reputation was firmly established throughout the country, thanks to his young wife who was unfaithful to him in a grand, open, generous way. Fargue had approached the group and had begun shaking hands all round with his usual greeting: "*Bonjour, cocu*," he repeated as he passed from one to the other. "*Bonjour, cocu; bonjour, cocu; bonjour, cocu; bonjour . . .*" He suddenly realized that he was holding in his huge paw the fingers of the wretched Ouard. He then showed what he no doubt believed to be great presence of mind. "*Bonjour, Monsieur* Ouard," he bellowed, enchanted at being able at last to show that he had tact, and without a pause he went on, as he passed to the next man: "*Bonjour, cocu; bonjour, cocu*," and so on down to the last man present. Such was Father Fargue, the favorite missionary of the lepers and victims of sleeping sickness, one who had lived too long in the jungle, in the black heart of suffering, to be able to show anything but impatience when a man appeared before him at the Fort Lamy mission and shoved a ridiculous petition for the protection of elephants under his nose.

"You can stuff those elephants of yours up your—" the reverend father roared, displaying an incontestable breadth of vision. "On this continent there are I don't know how many people suffering from sleeping sickness or leprosy, not to mention the yaws, not to mention that they all do more fornicating than gobbling, and that the kids die as quickly as they're born—and did you ever hear tell of trachoma? And spirochetosis, and filariasis? And you come here belly-aching to me about elephants?"

The man—Fargue had never seen him before; he seemed indeed to have come straight out of the bush, bedraggled as he was, with

* Cuckold.

his dirty shirt, and a stubble of several days' growth on his cheeks—
the man looked at him with a trace of sympathy. Even Father
Fargue, in whom sensibility was not exactly the dominant trait, was
struck by those vehement, almost violent eyes of his, in which, nonetheless, there lurked a spark of irrepressible gaiety. The Franciscan
adjusted his glasses on his nose and repeated, for form's sake but
without too much conviction: "And you come here belly-aching
about elephants?"

Morel did not reply immediately. He clenched his fists, then took
a tobacco pouch from his pocket and remained silent for a while,
rolling a cigarette. One could feel that he was doing it to calm the
rage in his hands. At last he raised his eyes.

"Listen to me," he said. "All right, you're a priest. A missionary. As
such, you've always had your nose right in it. I mean, you have all
the sores, all the ugliness before your eyes all day long. All right. All
sorts of open wounds—naked human wretchedness. And then, when
you've well and truly wiped the bottom of mankind, don't you long
to climb a hill and take a good look at something different, and big,
and strong, and free?"

"When I feel like taking a good look at something different and
big and strong and free," roared Father Fargue, giving the table a
tremendous bang with his fist, "it isn't elephants I turn to, it's God!"

The man smiled. He licked his cigarette and stuck it in his mouth.
"Well, it isn't a pact with the Devil I'm asking you to sign. It's only
a petition to stop people from killing elephants. Thirty thousand of
them are killed each year. Thirty thousand, and that's a small estimate. You can't deny it . . . And remember—" there was a spark of
gaiety in his eyes—"and remember, Father, remember: they haven't
sinned."

"Who hasn't?" roared Fargue.

"The elephants, man, the elephants—who else?"

Fargue remained gaping. "Well, I'll be . . ." He stopped just in
time and crossed himself. Then he said, "Sit down."

"The fellow sat down," Fargue later told Father Tassin, who had
come to see him and had surprised and worried the good Franciscan by the extraordinary interest he was taking in the matter—it was
indeed the first time he had taken an interest in anything under a

hundred thousand years old—"the fellow sat down and we stared at each other angrily for a while. You see, it was a stab in the back he was giving me, blast him, with his elephants that hadn't sinned. He was stabbing me in the back, aiming straight at my faith. Original sin, and the whole thing—you know all that better than I do. You know me, I'm a man of action: give me a good case of galloping syphilis and I'm all right. But theory . . . this is between ourselves. Faith, God—I've got all that in my heart, in my guts, but not in my brain. I'm not one of the brainy ones. So I tried offering him a drink, but he refused."

The Jesuit's face lit up for a moment, and its wrinkles seemed to disappear in the youthfulness of a smile. Fargue suddenly remembered that he was rather frowned upon in his Order; he had several times been forbidden to publish his scientific papers; it was even whispered that his stay in Africa was not entirely voluntary. He had heard tell that Father Tassin, in his writings, represented salvation as a mere biological mutation, and humanity, in the form in which we still know it, as an archaic species doomed to join other vanished species in the obscurity of a prehistoric past. His face clouded over: that smacked of heresy.

"I told him that if he felt the need of another company, the need to forget men and turn toward something different and truly great, he was wrong to stop at elephants and would do much better to defend a bigger animal, one that was even more threatened with extinction in the hearts of men—that is to say, the good God."

Fargue said that with such innocence and simplicity that the word "animal" did not sound at all like a blasphemy, but like some rather rough and naïve expression of deep filial love.

"He let me rip, and then he gave me a sort of smile. 'That may be, man, but tell me, what's to prevent you from signing? It isn't your soul you're being asked for. All I'm asking is that people should stop killing elephants. There's nothing very wicked about that.' I must say, there he had me. I was struck dumb. I opened my mouth, but could find nothing to say. And when he kept shoving that rag of his under my nose, I ended by really losing my temper and I bloody well threw him out, him and his elephants. But the thing went on nagging at me. Why hadn't I signed? It wasn't in the least important, it wasn't politics, the Bishop couldn't object . . . I couldn't get a wink of sleep, half the night, for searching after the reason, and at last I think I put my finger on it."

Fargue cast a sly glance at the Jesuit, as though to say to him: "You see, my friend, I'm not, after all, such an ass as they say I am."

"It was because, the way that *cocu* put things, it seemed a bit too much as if he was spitting on a species for which Our Lord died. I don't know how it happened, but I even had the impression he was asking me to betray it, to turn renegade. He made me feel that he wasn't really asking me to sign for the elephants, but against man. I don't know if you see what I mean . . ."

The Jesuit saw perfectly.

"I thought of all the friends I had in the war who gave their lives for something that really mattered, and it seemed to me he was piling it on, really he was, with his elephants. As if they were the only thing . . . I don't like misanthropes and atheists . . ."

Fargue's face grew purple and he banged his fist on the table. "Every time I see one, I lose my temper. They're a dirty crowd, the lot of them."

Father Tassin broke in gently. "I'd very much like to meet that young man," he said.

"You'll meet him all right," the Franciscan growled. "He must be still hanging around Fort Lamy, and he's sure to come and shove his petition under your nose one of these days."

## X

BUT HE WAS no longer "hanging around" Fort Lamy.

As for his petition, he had torn it up, keeping only a scrap of paper bearing a signature in a feminine handwriting which he often looked at with a smile. Minna continued to look after the bar, the sun continued to mark the time upon the white dial of the African sky, beating down always on the same landmarks—the fishermen's huts at

ten in the morning, a brown cliff overhanging the Shari at noon, the
solitary palm tree of Fort Foureau at four; and then, toward half-past
five, the American major would go by on horseback on the opposite
bank, at a crazy gallop, disappearing toward the sun as if doomed
to some frenzied, desperate pursuit, his red hair flashing in the last
rays which seemed to seize them like a fist.

Minna sometimes met the major at the market or in the native
village, a turbulent, shaggy giant in his old airman's leather jacket;
and one evening she came across him in the middle of the Maidaguri road, where he lay, his face in the dust, in the midst of a group
of natives who were laughing with that light, eternal laughter which
is their way of enduring all things. She had him placed in her jeep,
and arrived in his inert company at the house of Colonel Babcock,
with whom she was dining that evening. The colonel was extremely
upset by the American's presence and condition: he had been impatiently awaiting this evening alone with Minna, whom she invited
to dine regularly every three months. They stretched him out on
the terrace under a rug; but when, after dinner, they came back to
see how he was, they found him on his feet, gazing at the night
which lay about the lonely bungalow like a soft, almost gentle presence beneath which even the herds felt peace and safety . . . He
turned toward them with a grin.

"The next time you find me in the gutter, leave me there," he said,
"or better still, come and join me; it's very nice there. You'll feel at
home."

The colonel's eyes flashed. "My car's outside," he said. "Take it
and get out. This young lady has probably saved you from an attack of pneumonia, and the first thing you do, of course, is to insult
her."

The American burst out laughing. "And you, of course, consider
that my remark can only be addressed to her, and not to you, don't
you, Colonel Babcock? I don't know where the English dug up all
that damned self-assurance, but I imagine it's just part of their sense
of humor. Don't worry, colonel, I had you in mind too; you aren't
excluded from the great fraternity of the gutter. The difference between the English and the rest of mankind is that the English have
long known the truth about themselves—which makes them always

able to evade it discreetly, to slip round it. There was a time when I had illusions too. But I was unlucky enough to get taken prisoner by the Chinese in Korea, and they made it their business to enlighten me about myself. No doubt you know that I was dishonorably discharged from the Air Force because over the Communist radio I protested against bombing the Chinese population with plague-carrying flies, after they 'proved' to me that my country was waging bacteriological warfare. Two hundred of the world's distinguished scientists and noble personalities had accepted the evidence as true, they vouched for it with their honor, and I was naïve enough and idealistic enough to believe them. I was ashamed and angry and shouted my anger and my shame into a microphone. But it wasn't true. The evidence was faked. All those honorable men, including that white-haired Dean of Canterbury, who had accepted it were just working for the Communist cause. It wasn't true, the evidence was faked, but the odd thing is that, whether it's true or not, the consequences are the same: one large group of human beings or another turned out to be triple-distilled sons-of-bitches, which proves that we all have it in us. Whether the Communists staged a diabolical lie or the Americans sowed plague in China, the one thing that matters is that, as a man, you're in the gutter, Colonel Babcock. There's one merit nobody will ever be able to take away from the Communists: that of having looked man in the face. They didn't send him to Eton to learn protective coloration. Maybe the West is a civilization, but the Communists are an ugly truth about man. Don't accuse them of inhuman methods: everything about them is human. We're all one great, lovely zoological family, and we shouldn't forget it. That's how you came to be in the gutter, Colonel Babcock, and it's no use your taking refuge on an island and behaving like an ostrich—being English I mean; the gutter is there, it's you, or rather in you; it flows in your veins. Now that that's off my chest, my name's Forsythe, of Charleston, South Carolina—pleased to meet you officially. When we're all in the same boat it's better to be acquainted. Sleep well."

He stumbled down the steps and disappeared in the night. The colonel let him go some distance, then took Minna by the arm and said softly, "Poor chap. How mistaken he is . . . about England."

From then on whenever Minna saw the tall horseman at twilight galloping past on the other bank of the Shari, as if trying to leave the very earth behind him, she followed him with friendly eyes. She tried several times to get news of Morel, but he had not been seen at Fort Lamy for a long time. And when one day she rode to the mud hut in the native village where the Frenchman was said to have lived, all she found was a toothless old woman who shook her head, held out her hand and knew nothing.

## XI

AND THEN THINGS began to happen in a startling crescendo, and the whole territory passed first from incredulity to stupefaction, then to indignation, and finally to a sort of reluctant pride: such a thing could happen only in the Chad, people began to say complacently, and even those for whom adventure had long ceased to be anything but a taste of quinine in their mouths and the faces of Mother Ostrich and Mother Garlic—two black women who did the rounds of certain bachelor quarters at siesta time—felt a vague familiar longing awaken in them.

Langevielle, who had been hunting the herds of elephants which regularly ravaged his plantation, was brought to Fort Lamy in the ambulance plane with a bullet in his leg. He had seen nothing, heard nothing; only, just as he was about to shoot the finest male in a herd of some forty animals methodically devastating a field, his left leg was pierced by a bullet.

Everyone took notice. At Kano, in British Nigeria, political strife had just broken out between the partisans and opponents of the Federation; in Kenya the Mau-Mau were putting to fire what had for a long time been the most peaceful and prosperous part of Africa; from the north could already be heard the threatening rumble of Islam once more on the march down the ancient routes of the slave merchants; and to the south the Africa of the Boers was salting the oldest wounds in the black man's soul. Terrorism was reaching for the very heart of Africa: that was the unanimous decision.

Then Haas, his six foot six of man half eaten by mosquitoes during his twenty years among the reeds of Lake Chad, whence he had supplied half the zoos of the world with pachyderms, was brought into the Assna medical post on a stretcher. The Dutchman was yelling, in his native tongue, oaths of a length without precedent in the history of the colony, rich though it was in this resource. His buttocks were ploughed up deeply by a projectile of the same caliber as the bullet which had so inopportunely interfered with Langevielle's fine shot.

Haas was an eccentric who knew probably more about the ways of elephants than anyone on earth. He was in such a state of rage and indignation that it took Schölscher ten days to get a coherent answer from him and even then it didn't make much sense.

Lying on his belly—with a nurse attending to his behind which she powdered, sprinkled and painted with the devotion of a severe angel—and cursing Schölscher who kept trying vainly to offer him a cigar of the particularly abominable brand he fancied, the Dutchman, in the end, growled out a few vague explanations.

He was visiting, as he did every evening, the enclosure where he kept his captured baby elephants. He had taken a new one that morning, a real nursling who stood motionless, pressed sidewise against the bars in spite of the other captives' incessant invitations to play, and kept his trunk curled round a branch as if he hoped that his mother would suddenly materialize at the tip of this imaginary tail. That same morning he had been trotting behind his mother in this familiar position, hand in hand so to speak, when Haas caught up with them and let off his fireworks display, which had so frightened the big animal as to make her for a few moments lose all feeling of maternal duty. The herd had fled in all directions, leaving on the field the youngest one, who had remained stiff, with his feet dug in, urinating from terror. Haas had slipped a rope over his neck and dragged him away, aided by two boys on horseback. At first the mother had fled with the herd, but she returned later and for hours charged blindly through the bush, bellowing in anguish and frustration, her trunk raised high, trying to pick up the scent of her young one in the air.

At this point, Haas broke off his story and looked up at Schölscher darkly, saying, "You know, there is such a thing as an elephant language. Every time I've heard a mother crying after a young one I'd captured, I've always recognized the same sound. Three notes. Something like this . . ." He raised his head and emitted an astonishingly lifelike, heart-rending bellow.

The sister rushed into the room like a cannon-ball. "Poor Monsieur Haas, do try to have a little patience," she begged him. "I'll give you an injection for the night." Haas said a few words in Dutch, and the sister fled precipitately.

"Well, on that particular occasion I could hear the mother trumpeting in the bush for hours, and she sounded to me very determined, so I took my precautions around the enclosure. The camp was ten kilometers from the place of capture and I was uneasy. I placed two of my boys up acacia trees with orders to keep their eyes open. Toward sunset I went along to see for myself that they weren't napping. They were napping, of course. The baby elephant was still clinging to his branch and whistling dolefully, something like this . . ." Haas whistled dolefully through his nose.

"I gave him one or two taps on the behind and was getting ready to go home, when I heard the endearing sound a hurricane makes trundling in your direction at a hundred an hour."

Haas smiled radiantly.

"I've heard it a good thousand times in my life and dreamed of it even more, but each time its effect on me is terrific. You feel a longing to rise vertically into the air and to stay there, sitting on a cloud, watching the whole thing from very high up. It's a noise that makes the world a better place when it stops. Practically at the same time, I saw the elephant tower over me with all the grace of a mountain getting ready to bury you. I took aim, but just as I was going to fire I got a bullet in the ass."

Schölscher was looking at the Dutchman pensively.

"The mountain went by, ten feet from me, without paying me the slightest attention," Haas continued. "She treated me with contempt. She didn't seem to care the least bit for my reputation. She had only one idea in her head—her young one. She crashed through the barriers, the young one stuck onto her like a flea, and they trotted off gaily."

"Who fired that shot?" asked Schölscher.

The Dutchman's face assumed a sly expression.

"It was that idiot Abdou," he grunted. "It's the last time I trust him with a gun. The idea, I suppose, was to save my life. But shaking as he was . . ."

"I've spoken to your boys," said the major severely. "You've taught them their lesson well, but you underestimate the prestige of my uniform. All they know is that you were found on the ground, covered with blood, unable to move and swearing like a trooper."

Haas looked at him cunningly.

"All right, old man, I'll tell you the truth, but keep it under your hat. If the story gets about, I'll be a laughing-stock."

Schölscher waited.

"The truth is, when I saw the elephant on top of me, I lost my head, aimed badly, and lodged a bullet in my own behind."

Schölscher stood up.

"Very good," he said. "It's as I thought. What I don't understand is why you're trying to shield him."

The old Dutchman raised his head. His eyes were suddenly full of deep, unremitting sadness.

"Look here, Schölscher," he said slowly. "I too love elephants—I even think I love them more than anything in the world. If I make this my trade, it's because for thirty years it's enabled me to live among them, to get to know them; and I know—I do—that every elephant I take means one less for the hunters, tics, sores and mosquitoes—yes, mosquitoes: elephants are particularly sensitive to them. But I caused the death of dozens of baby elephants before I learned how to feed them—before I understood, for instance, that without the muddy water of the Chad at a certain temperature they died . . . They died. Have you ever seen a baby elephant lying on its side, with its trunk inert, gazing at you with eyes in which there seem to have taken refuge all those so highly praised human qualities of which humanity is so largely devoid? Yes, I too love elephants —so much so that when I fall to praying—everyone has his moments of weakness—it is that I may go one day wherever dead elephants go when the moment comes. So get this properly into your head: I saw nothing and heard nothing. As for that bullet in my ass, well, I haven't stolen it. Besides, who told you it was a bullet? It might have been a fart that got out of control."

He threw Schölscher a challenging glance. The major was thinking of the motives that could drive a man like Haas to live alone for twenty-five years among the elephants of Lake Chad. It was again that spark of misanthropy which most people carry in them, a presentiment of some different and better company than their own kind, a spark that sometimes blazes up and takes astonishing, unpredictable and explosive forms. He thought also of the old Chinese who never move without their pet grasshoppers, of the Tunisians who take their caged birds to the café with them, and of Colonel Babcock who spent hours with his eyes fixed on a jumping bean, which kept him company. He was slightly astonished to hear that Haas believed in God—there seemed to be a contradiction there; it's true, he thought, taking a pull at his pipe, that God hasn't got a cold muzzle a man can touch when he feels lonely, that one can't stroke Him behind the ears, that He doesn't wag His tail at the sight of you every morning, and that you cannot catch sight of Him trotting over the hills with His ears flapping and His trunk in the air. One can't even hold Him in one's hand like a nice warm pipe, and since a spell on earth after all lasts fifty or sixty years, it's perfectly understandable that people should end by buying themselves a pipe or a jumping bean.

He had spent five years in the Sahara himself, at the head of a Camel Corps unit, and those years had been the happiest of his life. It was true that in the desert a man felt less lonely than elsewhere, perhaps because he lived there in constant, almost physical contact with the sky, and so had all the company he needed. For what remained, a pipe was enough.

He wanted to say all this to Haas, but his years in the desert hadn't made him very talkative, and he also noticed that certain things which he felt deeply changed their meaning at the touch of words, so that he could no longer recognize them himself as he spoke. So that indeed he often wondered whether thinking were enough, whether thoughts were not a mere groping for something that was forever out of reach, whether days of real vision were not still ahead, and whether the mysterious cells which lay still unused in man's brain would not, one day, lead toward light. He did, all the same, say, "I'm not so sure that elephants are the real issue in this business."

"What is the real issue then, according to you?"

Schölscher was on the point of replying that men needed another company than their own kind, that they craved it desperately, like an almost physical presence, and that nothing on earth seemed big enough to satisfy that urge, those roots of heaven, as Islam called them, which were forever gripping and torturing man's heart, but he felt that this sort of talk, and indeed of thinking, ill became the Army uniform he was wearing. The feeling dated probably from the time when, as a young cadet at Saint-Cyr, the thin stripe of a sub-lieutenant had been all the horizon to which he aspired.

He smiled faintly at the memory of his youth. For a long time the Army uniform had remained for him the very symbol of what he had most fervently desired from the first metaphysical stirrings of adolescence: fidelity to a rule. This forbade certain attitudes, certain states of mind. So he kept his reflections to himself—all the more so since, these last years, he felt less and less need to exchange ideas with other men, because essentially they no longer came to him as questions, but as certainties. He had thus nothing left but minor curiosities. Sucking at his pipe, he gave the Dutchman a very friendly glance.

"What is the issue, according to you, if it isn't elephants?" Haas repeated, in a slightly menacing tone.

"Loneliness, I suppose," said Schölscher vaguely.

The Dutchman observed him with an extreme mistrust, one eye half closed.

"Do you know what they call you here?" he asked. " 'The soldier-monk.' "

Schölscher shrugged.

"All right, all right. But you'll end up yet as a Trappist monk, *mon Commandant.* Indeed, every time I see a Camel Corps officer, with his white burnous, his naked feet in sandals, his shaven head, and his hurry to go back into the desert as soon as possible, I say to myself: here goes another child of Père de Foucauld. But about Morel you're on the wrong track. You're recruiting him for your own intimate legion, that's all. Why do you want to go complicating a thing as simple as a man's love for animals—I mean, for his betters?"

Schölscher stood up. "The best service you can do that poor fellow," he said, "is to help us lay hands on him before it's too late. If not, he'll kill someone next time, and we shan't be able to do anything for him."

With that he left him, and went home, asking himself how far men were capable of going in their wish for another company than their own.

~~~~ XII ~~~~

HE SPENT THE NEXT few days in the bush, on the track of Morel, whom rumor reported of course everywhere at once. The hunters who came back swore that they had caught sight of him in a village, that they had barely escaped his bullets, and each district chief was sincerely convinced that he was hiding in his sector and busy preparing some sinister coup.

Schölscher began indeed to wonder if Morel was really working alone, if he was not helped by accomplices who used him for their own purposes: it was hard to imagine that a white man alone could move about so easily through the bush. But every time he mentioned Morel to the natives, in the villages and on the jungle tracks, he met with blank faces: they shook their heads and seemed not to have the least idea of what he was talking about.

He returned to Fort Lamy two hours before dawn, but he had hardly gone to bed when he was dragged from it by an urgent order from the Governor of the Chad to come and see him at once. He dressed hastily, swallowed a large cup of scorching coffee, jumped into his car and drove shivering through a silent, star-beleaguered town.

He arrived in the midst of a council of war. The Governor—in full dress but unkempt, haggard and tired, the high, stiff collar un-

buttoned, having come no doubt from some official reception, with
a wet cigarette butt stuck in the middle of his tobacco-soiled beard
—was dictating telegrams in the company of Foissard, the Secretary-
General, whose liverish face looked like a pillow that has been much,
but badly, slept on. The three other men were Colonel Borrut, the
military commander of the Chad, who was bending over a map and
studying it with a concentration so obvious that it looked much more
like prudent withdrawal than genuine interest; the duty officer of
the garrison, who had a tiresome tendency to spring to attention as
soon as any of the eminent persons present raised his voice; and,
slightly to one side, Laurençot, the chief warden of the game reserves, who was rarely seen at Fort Lamy and was always knocking
about somewhere in the Oulé hills: a black colossus from Marti-
nique, who was the only man Schölscher knew who could talk about
lions without seeming ridiculous, and who now appeared sometimes
anxious and sometimes exasperated.

The Governor greeted him impatiently. "Ah, Schölscher . . . here
you are, after all. I suppose you know nothing of what's going on, as
usual? Foissard, tell him what's happening on his beat."

The Secretary-General began to speak with the staccato rapidity
of a man who had spent his life among telegrams. It concerned
Ornando.

"Perhaps after all you have heard the name of Ornando?" asked
the Governor, putting the maximum of sarcasm into his tone.

Schölscher grinned. For the past three weeks the whole of Equatorial Africa had been ringing with the name of Ornando. His arrival had been preceded by so many official telegrams, recommenda-
tions, circulars and confidential instructions that the very mosquitoes
seemed to be buzzing his name in the ears of the exasperated
officials.

Ornando was the most popular columnist in America, read, heard
on the radio and admired on television by more than fifty million
Americans every week, and the formal orders from Paris were to
make a good impression on him at any cost. It was hoped that on
his return he would influence American public opinion on the
French Union favorably. It therefore emerged clearly from the
coded telegrams that Mr. Ornando must not catch dysentery, get too

hot, be too much shaken about on the roads, or miss his game—for big game hunting was the principal object of his trip to Africa. Although the instructions did not say so explicitly, one could nonetheless feel the almost pathetic desire of the people in Paris to arrange that springs of cool water should gush out at Ornando's feet, that a gentle breeze should caress his curls, and that not a single mosquito should assault his august person.

He was a tall, obese man with a milky complexion and crinkly hair like white astrakhan, who had himself transported across the difficult places of the bush in a sort of litter and always turned the same strangely motionless stare upon the streams, hills and precipices over which he was trundled. It was difficult to imagine what obscure urge had driven this flabby, trembling mountain of flesh to come hunting big game in Africa, when he could reputedly kill a man with a word. Protected and guided by the brothers Huette, the most experienced professionals in the territory, he had already killed two lions, a rhino, some admirably graceful antelopes—and finally, at dawn of the third day, on the bank of the Yalou, a magnificent elephant with tusks weighing seventy pounds, which crumpled at his feet with all the humility of death. But half an hour later Ornando, who had taken a few steps out of his tent to urinate, received a bullet in the shoulder, and was transported with all haste to Fort Archambault, where he lay silent and morose, his eyes full of brooding hate.

"Well, there you are," said the Governor, pushing away the pile of telegrams. "It happened five days ago, and since then the only more or less coherent conclusion to emerge from all the messages from Paris and Brazzaville is that they aren't very pleased with me. It's an unforgettable experience. I'd never have believed that official telegrams could rise to such heights of lyrical invective, but you have only to pick one at random . . ." He indicated the pile on his desk. "I've been given forty-eight hours to arrest Morel. Our version was, immediately, that he is a sort of madman who went over to the elephants out of sheer misanthropy. Nothing political, of course."

"What about the bullet?" asked Schölscher.

"It's from the same gun as with Haas and Langevielle," said Foissard. "As good as a signature."

"I may just as well tell you that at first our explanation was rather ungraciously received," said the Governor. "In Paris they wanted, at all costs, a local version of the North African rebellion. Nationalism and all that. People's right to self-determination. When I stuck to my explanation, they really began to get sore. They told me that if it wasn't an organized terrorist movement I really had no excuse. In the end, I swear, they've managed to give me the feeling that I've failed in my task because I haven't organized a terroristic independence movement in the Chad. You see, deep in their hearts they're convinced that a colonization that doesn't end in a seditious movement and massacres is not a successful colonization. Perhaps they're right, in a way."

Schölscher knew that behind this old African's irony there lurked a lot of bitterness and great weariness.

"But I must say they're beginning to change their minds. We've been much helped by the press. I think it's the first time in the history of the territory that the Chad has at last attracted the interest of the world press. We've even been honored by special correspondents. Our madman seems to have captured people's imaginations—which proves that misanthropy, hatred of mankind, is the order of the day. They've even found some very pretty names for our friend. If you glance at the press reports, you'll see that the papers now speak only of 'the man who changed species' and of the last 'fighter for dignity.' I must say I don't see clearly what they mean."

"It's obvious enough, though, isn't it?" said Laurençot.

They all turned toward him, except Schölscher.

"Perhaps you will have the kindness to explain to us the full depth of your thinking, Laurençot?" asked the Governor. "It's three o'clock in the morning and you mustn't ask too much of bureaucrats."

"All I mean, *Monsieur le gouverneur,* is that up to now the elephants have had no modern weapons at their disposal. They had only their tusks. It was therefore possible for some thirty thousand elephants to be exterminated last year in Africa."

"Go on, go on."

"Thirty thousand elephants: three hundred tons of ivory, if that. And as the aim of a good government is to increase production, I'm sure that this year we shall do better. Let us not forget that the Belgian Congo alone has supplied more than sixty thousand elephants in the last few years; their last official figure is seven thousand a year—but would you hesitate to say it's closer to ten thousand? I'm sure we shall all put our hearts into surpassing this record. With a little good will, we shall certainly manage, taking Africa as a whole, to kill a hundred thousand elephants a year, and so on till the ceiling is reached, if I may put it that way. It will then be necessary to pass to other species. Ours, I suggest."

Cigarette in his mouth, the Governor stared at his lighter. Schölscher noticed that it was of ivory. Behind him elephant tusks chosen with a collector's love covered nearly the whole wall. But that was the work of one of his predecessors. Colonel Borrut was bending studiously over the military map of the Chad with the absorbed expression of a man who minds his own business. The lieutenant was standing to attention so perfectly that he seemed practically to have vanished. Laurençot alone appeared to be thoroughly at ease. He observed with interest the desperate signs the Secretary-General was making.

"Go on, please," said the Governor, with exquisite politeness.

"And of course I'm only speaking of fresh ivory; the old tusks, hidden by the natives, were long ago extracted from the village chiefs by the merchants. Indeed you know as well as I do that colonization has been based partly on the corpses of elephants: it was ivory-hunting that made it possible for the businessmen and colonists to meet the initial costs of establishment."

"Well?" said the Governor, evenly.

"Well, it's time to have done with elephant hunting, *Monsieur le gouverneur*. This Morel may be a lunatic, but if he manages to rouse public opinion I shall go and shake hands with him in his jail."

The Governor was sitting bolt upright behind his desk. It's better to hold oneself straight when one's short, thought Schölscher. It was not only in connection with the Governor that he thought this. The Secretary-General had the anxious, unhappy face of the man who knows he will still be there when this is over for the others. But when at last the Governor replied, it was without a trace of anger, in an almost friendly way.

"Don't you think, my dear Laurençot, that there are in the world, at the present time, causes, liberties, well . . . let's say values, which have a rather better claim than the elephants to that admirable devotion with which our friend and you yourself seem to be overflowing? There are still some of us who refuse to despair, to throw up the sponge and go over to other species for solace. There are men fighting and dying at this very moment, in the streets, on the barricades and in the prisons . . . One may still be allowed to prefer to take an interest in them."

He fell silent, fixedly contemplating his lighter, which he kept turning in his hands. The room was brilliantly lit by a chandelier but the light, as it flooded the window, stopped short before the African night, against which it seemed unable to make headway. The Governor had lost his only son in the Resistance, and Schölscher wondered anxiously if Laurençot knew or remembered.

"I know, *Monsieur le gouverneur,*" said Laurençot gently, almost sadly. "But the elephants are part of that fight. Men are dying to preserve a certain splendor of life. Call it freedom, or dignity . . . They are dying to preserve a certain natural splendor."

There was a silence. The Governor worked his lighter but it would not light. Schölscher smiled and was immediately astonished at the stupid pleasure he felt at impotence in the actions of men, even the most insignificant ones.

"I've something else to say to you, Laurençot. Humanity has not yet reached that degree of defeatism or—or of loneliness, which makes it so necessary for the old ladies to console themselves with Pekingese. Or with elephants, if you prefer. Love of animals is one thing, but hatred for men is another, and that is what we are dealing with in our friend. That's why I intend to put him under lock and key as quickly as possible, and with a certain pleasure. Not because I'm getting myself unpopular in Brazzaville or in Paris, but because I don't like people who mistake their private neurosis for a philosophical outlook."

He observed Laurençot steadily, with the severity of an old schoolmaster.

"For once it seems to me the journalists are right. That fellow is trying to tell us what he thinks of us, to show his scorn for humanity,

and he uses elephants as a means of expression, that's all. Formerly
the anarchists were against society; our friend has merely gone one
step further: he is against mankind itself. Only, you know, I'm an
old liberal who's getting on for sixty but hasn't yet learned to detest
human beings. It can't be helped; it must be some basic flaw in me.
My generation has never fed on that dish. Probably we're outmoded.
Well, that fellow who's come to the Chad to show off his misanthropy and to spit in our faces, to proclaim his scorn of us and of all
our achivements, I'm going to throw him into jail, with that beautiful soul of his. Colonel, you will kindly set your battalion searching between the sixteenth and the eighteenth parallels, where our embittered friend last showed up. Schölscher, you will set your in-
formers on the job, and tell 'em I want results this time, for a
change."

"It would be much more courageous to ban elephant hunting,
*Monsieur le gouverneur,*" said Laurençot. "That fellow is only saying in his crazy way what I've written to you in dozens of official
reports."

"You should write poems, Laurençot, I'm sure it would bring you
relief." He stood up. "Meanwhile, gentlemen, I shall go to Canossa,
that is, to Fort Archambault. I have to present excuses from the government to Mr. Ornando. A pleasant mission. Our distinguished
visitor, who after all this uproar isn't even dead, has quite literally
summoned me. Incredible, but true. I shall see you in an hour's time
at the airport."

Schölscher and Laurençot left together. The night was still intact.
They walked for a while in silence along the roadway; the wind
from the desert enveloped them in its eddies of sand. It was cold.
From time to time they passed a silhouette which seemed to float
in the dust. Green eyes gleamed strangely in the darkness, but the
flashlight transformed them into a stray dog which slunk away with
its tail between its legs. Peasant women were making for the market
with their queenly gait, carrying a few eggs or vegetables on their
heads. Schölscher knew they sometimes did twenty-five miles during the night to sell a handkerchief full of onions at Lamy. But he
knew also that this was not only poverty; it was also Africa. What
progress requires inexorably of human beings and of continents is

that they should renounce their strangeness, that they should break with mystery; and somewhere along that road is inscribed inexorably the end of the last elephant. The cultivated lands must encroach upon the forests, and the roads will bite more and more deeply into the quietude of the great herds. There will be less and less room for natural splendor. A pity. He smiled, grasped the pipe in his hand rather tightly, enjoyed the feeling of the cold air around him—which increased the friendly comfort of that bit of warmth he held in his hand—that cold air which went so well with the stars. He suddenly remembered Haas's words, "Sometimes I even pray that I may go wherever dead elephants go when my time comes," and for a moment he wondered what he would do without his pipe. But perhaps it would be possible to keep it.

A lorry caught them in the glare of its headlights, coming from far along the straight road, and two enormous shadows began dancing in the eddies of dust before them. At the exit from the native quarter a gigantic silhouette emerged suddenly onto the road, rose up into the sky in the light thrown by the truck upon the screen of dust, then reduced itself to the more human dimensions of the American major, who passed by them, leaning forward and muttering.

"Poor devil," said Laurençot. "He's come to Fort Lamy to find a burrow, a place to lay his head. No doubt another one who prefers the elephants . . . Do you think I was wrong, just now?"

"No."

"I was trying simply to talk as a naturalist. After all, that's what I'm paid for."

Schölscher listened absently. It was impossible for him to see this business simply as a question of conservation. Under that clear sky, before that horizon where the only limits were those of sight, he felt the presence of a different stake. He raised his eyes toward the stars. The white ample *seroual* made his silhouette take strange forms in the darkness. He puffed pensively at his pipe. But perhaps he was wrong and the sole issue at stake was the preservation of nature, after all.

It was obviously a matter in which each person saw mostly his own heart.

He was convinced that if the attack on Ornando had caused such interest in the world it was not so much because of the victim's importance, but because fear, resentment and repeated disillusion in the age of slavery and radiation death had in the end branded the hearts of millions of human beings with an edge of misanthropy, which made them follow with sympathy, and perhaps some feeling of personal revenge, the story of "the man who had changed species." He turned toward Laurençot with sympathy. It was difficult not to like that generous, slightly sing-song voice, not to like that black giant who spoke so frankly about himself when he thought he was speaking only of the African fauna.

"I'm merely trying to do my job. God, Schölscher, how can we talk of progress when we're still destroying, all around us, life's most beautiful and noble manifestations? Our artists, our architects, our scientists, our poets, sweat blood to make life more beautiful, and at the same time we force our way into the last forests left to us, with our finger on the trigger of an automatic weapon, and we poison the oceans and the very air we breathe with our atomic devices. Perhaps this madman Morel will succeed in rousing public opinion. By God, I feel I could join him in his *maquis*. We've got to resist this degradation. Are we no longer capable of respecting nature, or defending a living beauty that has no earning power, no utility, no object except to let itself be seen from time to time? Liberty, too, is a natural splendor on its way to becoming extinct. I'm speaking for myself to get it off my chest, because I haven't the courage to act like Morel. It's absolutely essential that man should manage to preserve something other than what helps to make soles for shoes or sewing machines, that he should leave a margin, a sanctuary, where some of life's beauty can take refuge and where he himself can feel safe from his own cleverness and folly. Only then will it be possible to begin talking of a civilization. A utilitarian civilization will always go on to its logical conclusion—forced labor camps. We must leave a margin. And besides, let me tell you . . . There's nothing to be so proud of, is there? There isn't anything any longer, really, except the Eiffel tower, from which we can look down on the rest of creation. You'll tell me, like the Governor, to go off and write poems, but just remember that men have never had more need of company than they have today. That fellow Morel said it straight out, in his famous petition. We need all the dogs, all the cats, and all the birds, and all the elephants we can find . . ."

He spat on the ground, suddenly and violently. Then he said, with his head bent as though he dared not look at the stars, "We need all the friendship we can find around us."

<center>~~~ XIII ~~~</center>

ORNANDO RECEIVED the Governor in his room at the hospital. He could hardly speak. He lay flat on his back, staring at the ceiling with an eye that recovered some of its habitual venom only when he saw the Governor effecting his entry in full dress uniform with decorations. His secretary, who acted as interpreter, was to say, later, that this glance of hatred was the first sign he had given of returning health.

Ever since he had been picked up, Ornando had uttered no complaint, had said not a word, and had contented himself with bleeding in silence; most of the time there was a strange expression of satisfaction on his face. One would have thought that what had happened to him was normal, or even pleasant. When someone at last had the courage to speak to him of Morel and of his campaign, he did not appear particularly surprised and continued to contemplate the ceiling fixedly. Then he sent for the Governor. Now he observed him closely, after listening with indifference to that high dignitary's expressions of regret and wishes for his recovery.

"Be sure to tell him, monsieur," concluded the Governor, "that the culprit will receive the punishment he deserves."

The secretary translated and Ornando suddenly came to life. He made an effort to sit up and said a few words rapidly. The secretary looked stupefied.

"Monsieur Ornando asks you to leave the man in peace," he translated. "He absolutely insists."

The Governor smiled knowingly.

"That is most generous of Monsieur Ornando, and you will please thank him," he said. "We shall inform the press of this gesture of his, and I am sure his public will much appreciate it. Nonetheless, justice will follow its course. Monsieur Ornando is, indeed, not the only man to have been attacked by this lunatic . . ."

Ornando suddenly began to yell. He had contrived to raise himself on one elbow in spite of the bandages, and yelled with impotent rage wagging his head.

"Monsieur Ornando reminds you that fifty million Americans listen to him every week," the terrified secretary translated. "He asks me to tell you that . . . that if you touch a hair of that man's head he will carry on, for years if necessary, a campaign against France which your country will not forget for a long time. If that man is not left in peace, he will devote his whole influence to destroying the prestige of France with his compatriots . . ."

He said, very quickly, in a supplicating voice, "*Monsieur le gouverneur,* I don't know if you are aware what influence Monsieur Ornando wields on public opinion in his country . . ."

Ornando had raised himself a little higher still. Drops of perspiration had formed on his face and were running down onto his fat neck. His eyes had grown larger, and were full of a suffering which seemed to have nothing to do with the pain of his wound, but to be as permanently at home there as their very color. The Governor stood by the bedside, gaping. In the short silence which followed they could hear the voices of children reciting verses of the Koran in the hospital yard. Then Ornando said a few words more.

"And Monsieur Ornando offers you personally twenty thousand dollars if you leave the man in peace," stammered the secretary, completely appalled, no doubt because he had not yet his master's limitless faith in human degradation.

The Governor started to shout in his turn. He began by shouting something about his son killed in the Resistance. Then he shouted something in the name of France, and then he just shouted, striking his Legion of Honor with his fist and stamping his foot.

"In any case," stammered the interpreter, who showed unmistakably that he would have liked, if he could, to hide under the bed, "in any case, Monsieur Ornando is starting, now, a fund of fifty thousand dollars for the defense of the man, should he be caught—which he hopes not, for everybody's sake. Monsieur Ornando is making a personal issue of this . . . a very personal issue."

Ornando had fallen flat on his back again.

The Governor of the Chad shouted more words that had to do with human dignity and honor, then turned on his heel and charged out into the street in his white helmet, beard foremost. He was seen going by, pale and very stiff, "sticking up like a bristle" as one sergeant of the escort put it, in the back of his limousine as it sped through Fort Archambault in a cloud of dust. The cloud seemed to be raised much more by his indignation than by his car and floated behind him for a long time with a sort of servile respect. At the airport, in a peevish tone that was unknown in him—he was a courteous and somewhat courtly man, inclined to a gentle skepticism which usually sufficed to protect him both against excessive illusions about human nature and against excessive doubt of it—he announced to the colonel in command that he had forty-eight hours in which to lay hands on Morel and bring him handcuffed to Brazzaville—"That bandit, do you hear me?" he repeated, raising his voice and staring the colonel in the face, with extreme severity, as if he were accusing him of a secret sympathy for the man.

In the plane he remained silent, with his arms folded on his chest, gazing through the porthole with a challenging air, as though he suspected Morel of being hidden behind each tuft of jungle, gun in hand, ready to deny the dignity of man. He frowned, champing at a soaked cigarette-butt which he had completely forgotten, and aiming thunderbolt looks at the jungle, the Shari river and all the wild life it might contain, all present and past species from the ancient pterodactyl to the wild artichoke, while he sent his cigarette-butt hurrying from the right side of his mouth to the left and back, his beard stiff with indignation, with all the fury of a humanist who indeed believes also in democracy. He swept the jungle with fiery looks and endeavored to think of Michelangelo, Shakespeare, Einstein, of technical progress, of penicillin, of the suppression of excision among the pygmies, for which he had made himself personally responsible, of the achievements of the French genius in painting and sculpture, of the third act of *Rigoletto*, sung by Caruso, of which he had the record at home. He thought of Goethe, of the Salk vaccine, of parliamentary institutions; and at each of these thoughts he triumphantly sent his cigarette-butt hurrying from one junction of his lips to the other and shot a thunderbolt glance down at the jungle below him and at Morel the misanthrope, skulking among his wild elephants; "wild"—he dwelt on the word. In short, he joined in terrific single combat with him, and pronounced himself victor. There he was, very high in the air, with folded arms and his cigarette-butt getting more and more soaked, and he scored point after point. He summoned up a great display of general culture and was glad he had received a good classical education. Petrarch, Jaurès, Johann Sebastian Bach—everyone took part. It was truly the battle for honor. With much address and discipline, with the astuteness of an old militant of the Radical Socialist party, he contrived to avoid the traps which Morel, though invisible, was obviously laying for him. He contrived to avoid thinking, even for a second, of that matter of the hydrogen bomb, of the maiming of Marshall Island natives, of the Japanese fishermen of the *Happy Dragon*, of Stalin, et cetera; he merely sent his cigarette-butt rushing across his beard with astonishing velocity, and he skillfully turned the tables by attacking the enemy in his own entrenched position: he thought of the benefits of atomic energy when it would enable Africa in particular to fertilize its deserts. His extremely elevated situation—they were flying at nine thousand feet in the clear blue, above the Bongo Mountains—was a great help to him in his fight for the good name of man, against the misanthrope lurking somewhere in the jungle below; so much so that, when he stepped from the plane at Fort Lamy, he had recovered his good humor and was humming an aria from the garden scene of *Faust*, of which he was very fond and whose inspired beauty was itself an answer to all detractors of humanity like Morel and Ornando.

He told the journalists who awaited him—three special correspondents had arrived from Paris that very afternoon and Air France reported there would be more next day—that they were faced with a case of banditry in which it would be a great mistake to look for political implications: a misanthrope who was acting alone, a man who had "run amok" or, if they preferred, gone "rogue" like the elephant that parts from the herd because of an incurable wound and becomes particularly aggressive and dangerous.

The journalists noted "rogue elephant" and assailed the Governor with questions. Could he give them some information about this man Morel? What exactly was known about him? His life history? Was it true that he had been a member of the French Resistance and had been deported by the Germans for his love for freedom?

The Governor glanced at Schölscher, who confirmed this with a nod. He had just received a telegram from the Ministry of the Interior where there was a file on Morel. But the Governor thought it more prudent to ride off on a few jokes. All he could say for the moment, he declared good-humoredly, was that the man was a dentist, and the explanation of this whole ridiculous business was perhaps that Morel had an obsession with ivory. A few people laughed, but the Governor realized that he had adopted the wrong tone, and his expression became slightly peevish.

He took a step toward the car, but the journalists still pressed around him. Was it true that Morel had tried to present his petition to him before taking to the *maquis*, but that he had always refused to receive him? This business was arousing extraordinary interest throughout the world, and it certainly seemed that the sympathy of the public was veering more toward the side of Morel, the side of the elephants, than toward that of . . . well, of the authorities. Was it true that about thirty thousand elephants per year were killed in Africa, all to supply billiard balls and paper knives? Was it true that the present game preserves were not large enough? And could the Governor also say a few words about the standard of living of the black peasant in Africa? Is it true that they had to shoot elephants because they simply didn't have enough protein in their diet?

This time the Governor answered very carefully: he realized that he was on slippery ground. He said that France was traditionally and firmly attached to the elephants. She intended to guarantee them all the protection of which they might stand in need. He was himself a great nature-lover and he could assure the journalists —and they in turn could assure their readers—that the necessary steps would be taken to protect these attractive beasts which we had all learned to love from our childhood. He managed at last to get into his car, followed by Foissard and Schölscher. He was so disturbed by the journalists' unexpected assault and by the importance they obviously attached to the matter that he did not even notice that the Secretary General looked sallow and ill, with, at the same time, the touching and scandalized expression which good civil servants have when faced with earthquakes, tidal waves and other losses of important files.

"Ouf!" said the Governor, mopping his brow. "Well, *mes enfants,* how do you like it? And mind, not a question about Ornando! The one and only thing they're interested in is Morel."

"The papers speak of nothing else, it's true," said Foissard with an effort. "The public always takes a passionate interest in anything to do with animals. The journalists do all they can to make the business even more romantic in their eyes."

"Yes. Well, I don't intend to give them what they want, damn them. Which reminds me . . . As I shall no doubt have to receive the journalists in my office, you will do me the kindness of removing those elephants' tusks all over the walls."

Schölscher smiled.

"You may smile, my friend, but after their questions one can see very well which way the sympathies of the public are going. Not that I'm after popularity—that's not my worry—but I'm not anxious to be represented as a heartless brute without a trace of sensibility, either. You'll see: if we don't lay hands on that lunatic quickly, he'll become a sort of hero. What are they saying in Paris?"

"They seem to have said everything, for the moment, *Monsieur le gouverneur.* On the other hand . . ."

They were passing in front of the vaccination center. The Governor gave the buildings a proprietary glance: since he had been there, infant mortality in the Chad had fallen by twenty per cent. He always felt better when he passed in front of the Center. He experienced something like the feeling of having been a good father. His face cleared. After all, much will be forgiven them, he said to himself, thinking of the natives. Foissard took advantage of the smile to present his bitter pill.

"On the other hand, there's fresh news of Morel."

The Governor started—but perhaps it was merely a jolt of the car. "Well? What is it now?"

"He has attacked a plantation. The Sarkis plantation. The Syrian was away but they burned his farm to the ground. And he is no longer alone. He has a whole band with him."

Oddly enough, the Governor appeared relieved, almost reassured. Schölscher observed him with interest. He thought at the same time of what was said about all true creators: the great works are the ones that in the end always escape them.

"Well, I prefer it that way," said the Governor slowly. "At least now it's sharp and clear. The man is a common bandit. If he were really defending elephants, it would be very difficult to deal with. You cannot fight a legend. But now, it's obvious. A desperado, probably the last white adventurer in Africa . . . Nothing political, of course." It was rather moving to see a man defending his achievements so desperately. "We had all that in France, during the occupation. There were scum who, under cover of the Resistance, practiced organized banditry."

Schölscher looked up; he had not expected that comparison.

"That's exactly it, *Monsieur le gouverneur*," said Foissard eagerly. "He has also attacked the Banerjee ivory shop in Bangassa. He had the Indian tied to a tree and read him the text of his petition. Next, he condemned him to six strokes of the rod in the name of the World Committee for the Defense of Elephants or something like that. He also announced his intention of going to the defense of elephants in Asia, where, he said, they are also in mortal danger. Banerjee—he's in a hospital suffering from a nervous breakdown—is convinced that the man is a lunatic who believes sincerely in his mission but is being maneuvered by someone. In any case they did a good job of destroying his shop. They took all the money they could find, also some weapons and ammunition. One of the Sara women was raped. The men he had with him were all Oulé, and the servants recognized two or three convicts among them, including the notorious Korotoro, who escaped three weeks ago from the Bangi prison."

"So . . . nothing political, after all," the Governor repeated heavily.

The Secretary General cleared his throat, but said nothing and nodded.

Schölscher watched the two civil servants trying so valiantly to struggle against the hideous phantom leaning over their shoulder. They could not help seeing in this affair all their deep-seated obsessions, their sleepless nights, their dreads and—almost—their superstitions. They were too proud of their African achievement not to feel threatened. But their achievement was not perhaps as complete as they feared, and their work not great and fine enough to come suddenly to life under their eyes and to start living an independent life of its own. They were anticipating. They were seeing too far and on too large a scale. But suddenly, with a warm, and as it were brotherly, impulse, he felt grateful to them for this.

"I think we mustn't try and look too far, *Monsieur le gouverneur.* We should take a more modest view of the events, if I may put it that way. Perhaps the fault is ours, but it is premature to look upon the Chad too politically. I believe it's much simpler—and much more fantastic. This Syrian, Sarkis, is the biggest elephant hunter in the district. He's been fined several times for having organized 'punitive expeditions' against the herds that were trampling his fields and for having done so without the supervision of a game warden. Banerjee is a big ivory dealer . . . I don't think we should look for another motive. We have to deal with an extraordinary man—and with an extraordinary adventure."

Foissard gave him a disapproving glance.

"Yes, and the Oulé are the simplest and most primitive tribe in the whole of Africa," said the Governor. "I agree with you, Schölscher. We're getting a bit too impressionable. It's ridiculous to look for political implications. All the same . . ." He smiled gloomily. "All the same, things didn't start much differently in Algeria."

"What I don't understand," Father Fargue thundered to the Jesuit, who was dining with him that evening, "is why everyone in this affair behaves as if he were personally involved, or personally insulted. For some reason they all make disgusted faces, as if that wretched Morel had spat on them in person. What can you make of it?"

The Jesuit could not refrain from teasing his host a little. "Pride, pride," he said, shaking his head.

Father Fargue looked uneasy: if there was anything he hated, it was talking shop. "That's true of course," he said hastily, bitterly sorry that he had set the other going on this tiresome subject. "Have a little more chicken."

Father Tassin smiled. They understood each other perfectly. "They feel insulted, because our friend has, as they say, 'changed sides' and seems to prefer other species to ours. Pride, but pride for the species, which is already an improvement. I'm sorry my Order looks upon my ideas on this subject with such . . . let's say, prudence. Anyhow, I hope my manuscripts will be published after my death. It will be interesting to see humanity emerge as a living whole some day from its two thousand million individual cocoons, with one conscience, one dignity, one soul."

Fargue did not like this at all: he knew the Jesuit traveled everywhere with a whole case full of manuscripts. Another word and he would be forced to read them, and God only knew what that would lead to. "Prayer's enough for me!" he declared gruffly, with his usual tact, and went for the chicken with a violence that excluded any other topic.

## XIV

FORT LAMY was never a place where tongues were idle; but this time gossip really rose to the occasion and soon assumed truly epic proportions. "He" was in liaison with Egypt and the North African terrorists. "He" had attacked a military outpost at the head of a band of natives, massacred the officer in command and taken the soldiers with him into the *maquis*. "He" was forming an African Liberation Legion: "My dear man, after all, you don't believe it has anything to do with elephants, do you?" But strangely enough people *did* believe it. They even seemed astonished that nothing of the kind had happened before. In general, Morel had the sympathy of the women: they were sorry they had paid no attention to him; it was most romantic, most moving; why not leave the poor elephants in peace? It was no use explaining that this was not a matter of elephants but of a terrorist who set himself up as the enemy of mankind—the ladies refused to see Morel otherwise than as a handsome young man with burning eyes, a sort of Saint Francis of Assisi, only more energetic, more dashing, more muscular. At the Tchadien, Minna went from table to table, her shawl over her shoulders, alert to the smallest fragments of conversation.

"Yes, that's just what she was doing," said Colonel Babcock, smiling slightly to the Jesuit who came to visit him at the hospital, a few days after the heart attack which had struck the officer down. "She was going from one table to another with the mechanical steps of the possessed, of people who have only one thought, one single aim. She listened for a while to the news—of course no one knew anything, but there were plenty of rumors—stood there without saying a word, her hands clasped over her shawl; then she would move on to another table. She didn't ask questions. But she seemed to be waiting for something, anxiously, impatiently—a fact, a guess, a titbit of information. I was far from suspecting what was going on inside her pretty head: this sort of thing was well outside my experience."

The Colonel's face again took on that helpless, drawn look which suggested heartbreak much more than mere heart trouble. "I suppose I had better get it off my chest once and for all. The men of my class, of my circle, received a certain upbringing—or rather, I should say, a certain outlook on the world. This outlook is what it is—for better, for worse. I suppose I shall make everyone smile if I say that we were brought up to take our place in a world of gentlemen. We knew, of course, that there was the risk of sometimes being hit below the belt, but we were brought up in the belief that the blow below the belt was outside the law. The idea had never entered our heads that the blow below the belt might be the law, that that was how the game of life was played. You can, if you like, consider me an out-of-date old fool, but men of my kind simply never come in contact with the sort of circumstances that can produce a Morel or a Minna. I confess that even today I'm practically incapable of seeing in Morel anything but an eccentric. The rest . . ." He shifted laboriously in his bed, as if he hoped at last to find a comfortable

position. "The idea that it was perhaps a deliberate gesture—a gesture of spite and even hatred for the human species, a sort of—break,
a slap in the face—that this man was deliberately siding with animals against human beings—you know as well as I do the things
people have said about it—has always been, and still is, completely
incomprehensible to me. Those are morbid, unworthy ideas, and it's
hard for me to believe that there are circumstances in life that
might fully justify them. But apparently such circumstances exist."

He gave the Jesuit a glance of distress, a look that owed nothing to
his physical exhaustion. "All I mean to say is that I was lacking in
the experience required to understand a person like Minna. I
lacked a certain intimacy with the real truth about ourselves, like
many of my compatriots—we have remained an island to this day.
I knew, of course, that the girl had suffered a great deal, but I
hadn't the least idea of the total of resentment against mankind she
had piled up in her heart. In any case I could not possibly have
foreseen the insane gesture she was to make—a plan which was
probably already in her head as she came and went with her quick
steps among the customers of the Tchadien.

"She had come to sit down for a moment at my table, and I must
say she smiled at me as usual—she always smiled when she saw me;
I suppose I must have seemed to her a comic figure. 'Well, Colonel
Babcock, what do you think of this adventure?' I replied that I always felt a certain sympathy toward a man who loved animals, and
that it was perfectly true that the elephants had been practically
exterminated in certain districts of Africa, but that Morel was really
setting about it in a rather exaggerated way. 'In England,' I told her,
'the whole thing would probably have been settled by a letter to the
Times, after which, under pressure from public opinion, Parliament
would simply vote the necessary laws for the protection of the
African fauna.' She didn't seem to listen, but was following her own
thoughts. 'Obviously they'll soon get him,' she said, as if expressing
an established fact. I said that in truth Morel's chances appeared to
me practically nil. I shall never forget the look she gave me then:
bewildered, drowned, supplicating. I hastily added that he would
no doubt get out of it with a year in prison, unless he killed somebody meanwhile—which, of course, was quite possible. I asked her if

she would have a drink with me—which was, I admit, a discreet way
of reminding her that I had been there a good while and that no
waiter had come for my order. But I think she didn't even hear what
I said. She stood beside me, shivering, wrapping herself in her gray
shawl, and she was busy thinking of something that was certainly
not my whisky. Very attractive she was—I realized it each time I
saw her—very attractive." The Colonel fell silent. "A pity," he said,
without indicating more exactly what he meant. "A thousand pities."
He fell silent again. "I grasped the fact that she was preoccupied. I
told her she seemed worried. She gave me a surprised look. Then
she smiled and do you know what she did? She took me by the
hand. I may say—regretfully—that I'm not the kind of man with
whom women generally hold hands in public. Twilight was indeed
beginning to fall, but for once that famous African twilight, which
always seems in such a hurry, did not appear to be hastening at all.
People probably weren't looking at us, but all the same I was rather
embarrassed. I didn't know how to get out of this. I coughed and
gazed around me sternly, in case they should take it into their heads
to smile. But the most disagreeable thing was still to come. As I sat
there with my hand in hers, not daring to withdraw it for fear of
seeming brutal, suddenly I felt something wet on the back of my
hand—tears! She was crying. She was holding my hand clasped
tightly between hers and she was crying. I opened my mouth to say
something, anything, to try to help her, to comfort her, when I saw
her smile through her tears and say, in a broken, shaken voice which
everyone on the terrace must have heard: 'Oh, Colonel Babcock,
you're such a darling!' and then, abruptly, the girl—Minna—raised
my hand to her lips and kissed it." The Colonel took a laborious
breath. "What she meant by that, what I had done to cause such a
gesture, remains a mystery to me until this day. But there are times
when I wonder whether my bad heart doesn't date from that moment."

He broke off and looked at the Jesuit reproachfully. "I can't remember very clearly what I did or said. In spite of everything she must
have realized my situation; she let go my hand. Or perhaps her
thoughts were already elsewhere. I believe that was it, more likely,
and she wasn't even thinking of me. 'But there's still a little time

left, before they get him, isn't there?' she asked. By then I hadn't
the least idea what she was talking about. I was completely dis-
concerted. The lamps had just been lit, and I had the impression
that everybody was watching us. You'll say: why worry so about
other people? Well, no one likes ridicule, old English retired
colonels no more than anyone else. You'll say, too, that at my age
those things hardly matter any longer. But perhaps there are points
about which one never grows old. And it is no more agreeable at
sixty-three to feel that a young woman no longer considers you a
man than it is at sixteen to feel that she still considers you a child."

The Jesuit indicated that he understood. He was sorry the world
should have passed by the Colonel without paying him a little
more attention. Decency: a quality of a man obviously without
great ambition, without genius, without any magnificent possibilities, yet all the same a quality before which humanity ought to
have hesitated longer than it had. Also he had the greatest respect
for humor, because it was one of the best weapons ever forged by
man for the struggle against himself.

"In the end, all the same, I realized that she was speaking of
Morel," the Colonel went on. "I told her that our man could escape
the search for some time yet, but that it was a question of days at
most." The Colonel shifted slightly in his bed. "She listened to what
I was saying with extreme attentiveness. She had leaned over toward me, holding herself very stiff, tense, with her hands clasped,
almost biting each other. She didn't hide her feelings, you see—not
with me; she must have known that with me she was in no danger, I
wouldn't understand. She must have said to herself that one can
always rely on a gentleman when it's a question of *not* understanding a woman. She listened to me with the same passion others put
into talking—if I may use such an expression, she listened to me with
volubility."

The Colonel fell silent. "I don't know if you remember her eyes,"
he resumed after a while. "They were big and clear, and they always seemed to be questioning you sadly. There was a sort of contradiction between her eyes and all the ugly things that had
happened to her. But after all, in the darkness, no doubt the soldiers
hadn't seen them. . . . They had an extraordinary innocence, per-

haps it was just their color—they were eyes that had seen everything, but victoriously. I should add that the voice was very different from the eyes, perhaps because of the German accent. It was a sort of heavy, sort of . . . experienced . . . Also, she smoked a lot. Well, I was busy explaining to her that Morel's arrest was only a matter of days, and that he hadn't a chance of escaping it, alone as he was in the bush, when she interrupted me. 'But he isn't alone,' she said. 'I've talked with the journalists, and they've all told me the same thing: he has the public on his side. If only someone could let him know . . .' Then she got up and went away.

"I stayed there alone, with my pipe, trying to look indifferent, but I was always sorry when she left me. Since I've grown old I've had more and more need of company. I stayed there a while longer, because she was moving from table to table and it was possible she might come back. Sometimes she did come back, sometimes twice or even three times in an evening—I used to get there at about six o'clock, and if I didn't feel like going home I dined there; she would generally come when I was ordering dinner, and later, at the coffee stage, but that of course depended on how many people there were. I could never be sure beforehand. I never went there on Saturday evenings, she was then very busy. . . . I mean, it was impossible to get attention. Monday was the best day, she was much freer. During the next half-hour, all I could do was to follow her with my eyes, from a distance. I looked at her frequently—not at all because she was pretty or graceful, although she was, she certainly was, but to see if she was coming back in my direction—I had the impression she was feeling a bit lonely and I didn't want to seem to be neglecting her. So I gave up the whole evening to her—I stayed and had dinner on the terrace—I had a vague feeling that she needed a friendly presence. I don't much like the Tchadien, if only because the prices there are so scandalous, and then you always see the same faces there, but I used to go there, all the same, nearly every evening, because of her—she used to smile when I came in. I think she cared for me, in her way, and she needed company. But the place itself is dreadful, what with its insects and its gramophone records, always the same ones—there's one that's called 'Remember the Forgotten Men' which I'd have loved to smash—and that sinister fellow Orsini whose voice was always the first thing one heard as one came on the terrace.

"I must say I always make a great effort to be particularly nice to him, because I consider one ought to be tolerant, and that it isn't the fault of a polecat if it smells bad. One hasn't the right to show people that one finds them beastly. So I always made efforts to behave to him in a friendly way. In the end he came to look on me as one of his great friends—once he even told me that I was his only friend, with a sort of dampness in his voice that was absolutely disgusting—which forced me to invite him home from time to time so as not to hurt his feelings, and I came to detest him so much that the mere sight of him gave me a headache. This made me feel a little guilty and forced me to still greater efforts to hide my real feelings—feelings which to my mind I had no right to have or to show toward any human being whatever. The result was that we often spent evenings together, at my place or at his, on the terrace, gazing at the stars, and I must admit the wretched man was so distasteful to me that he ended by making me loathe the stars, simply because he was there, at my side, gazing at them. He even seemed to like them and to find them beautiful. In that too there was something that seemed to me loathsome. That a man like Orsini could love the stars seemed to prove that they aren't what they're generally thought to be. So we often spent our evening together, and I was obliged to hear him pouring out his venom over everything and everyone, and when he was sitting there at my side, gazing silently and dreamily at the stars, one had the impression that he was merely wondering how to reach them with his slime. Up to a point you may even say he succeeded in that, because he spent his time covering Minna with slime by attributing to her all sorts of physical adventures with all sorts of people—it goes without saying that when I speak of stars in connection with Minna it isn't out of any ridiculous romanticism—I'm too old for that—but simply to indicate that for Orsini she was as inaccessible as any distant luminary in our firmament, and that he consoled himself for that by denigrating her. I never could bear people speaking ill of women. You'll ask me, therefore, how I could bear to let Orsini do so in front of me, and for my benefit alone, on the terrace of my own house, three miles

away from the nearest neighbor. But suspicious and malevolent as
he was, if I had called him to order he'd have suspected me of
heaven knows what absurdity—I mean, of some sort of tender feeling for that young woman. He was a creature who saw everything
in the basest terms. What's more, if I had forbidden him to talk all
his nonsense about her, since he couldn't talk about her in any
other way, he wouldn't have talked about her to me at all. There
were moments when I asked myself whether I didn't tolerate his
presence under my roof two or three times a week simply and solely
because he was the only man who talked to me about her. And anyway that stopped him from pouring out his torrent of filth elsewhere,
in the presence of people who might have shown themselves more
disposed to believe it than I was. You can see the painful situation I
had got myself into. All the more since I ended up by feeling I was
being very dishonest with Orsini, and that forced me to be doubly
nice to him, especially in public, to avoid the reproach of hypocrisy
which people are so prone to make against us English—so much so
that in the end everyone believed we were friends, although in the
whole of Fort Lamy I must have been the one who loathed Orsini
most.

"That evening he was at the other end of the terrace, engaged in
abusing—in front of the black boys, who understood every word he
said—the natives, who, according to him, had certainly been helping
Morel, simply in order to let the world believe there were political
disorders in the Chad as in Kenya. It was the sort of silly talk that
has done us such harm in Africa. I was so irritated by his nonsense
that I had actually lost sight of Minna, when I saw her again in
front of me, close to my table. I stood up. I can even remember, now I
come to think of it, that my heart suddenly began beating faster
than usual—which proves that there was already something wrong
with it, and that an abrupt movement was enough to quicken the
pace abnormally. She sat down in the wicker chair and remained
motionless for a while, absent, staring beyond me at some point on
the other bank of the Shari—I nearly looked around to see what
was fascinating her so. 'Orsini says the natives help him. If only
it were true.' I told her the idea seemed to me absurd. 'The one
thing the natives see in an elephant is meat,' I told her. 'Believe

me, the beauty of the African fauna leaves them perfectly indifferent. When the herds devastate the crops and the administration has a few of the animals shot, the bodies are supposed to be left where they are, to rot, as an example to the others. But as soon as the *lieutenant des chasses* has turned his back, the blacks fall upon the meat and leave nothing but the carcass. As for the beauty of elephants, their nobility, their dignity, et cetera, those are purely European ideas, like the right of peoples to self-determination.'

"She turned toward me with a fire, a passion that left me speechless. 'Here's a man who believes in you, Colonel Babcock, who appeals to you to try and save something, and all you can do is theorize, coldly, as if the whole thing were no concern of yours. He believes in some beauty in life, and all you people do nothing but pour scorn on it; he thinks it's possible to do something, to save something, to be generous and kind—that everything is not irremediably doomed to ugliness.'

"I was so surprised by this unexpected outburst, by such talk coming, above all, from her, you understand, after all that had happened to her, all that she had . . . er . . . er . . . seen, with her own eyes, that my pipe fell out of my mouth. 'But, my dear child,' I stammered, 'I don't see how the desire to preserve the African fauna . . .' She broke in on me: 'Oh, to hell with the African fauna! Can't you see what the real question is? The question is simply whether you have confidence in yourselves, in your good sense, in your reason, in your ability to prevail, yes, to prevail. Out there in the bush is a man who believes in you, a man who believes you're capable of kindness, of generosity, of . . . of a . . . of a great love, in which there'd be room even for herds of elephants, and . . . and even for the most wretched dog alive!'

"Her eyes were full of tears, and what with her extremely fair hair and the beauty of her face it really seemed to me she was right. 'If you English don't understand what the question is, that means that England is just another lie they told us—*ein Wintermärchen*,' she finished in German. Then she got up, walked away across the terrace, and I didn't see her again that evening.

"*Ein Wintermärchen? Ein Wintermärchen?* I suppose that means a fairy tale. I couldn't exactly see what she meant. Was she really expecting England to rush, with Sir Winston Churchill at the head perhaps, to the defense of the elephants? To place itself on Morel's side as if it were some immense society for the prevention of cruelty to animals? Besides, she seemed to be saying that it wasn't only a question of animals—then what was it all about? I couldn't exactly see what she was reproaching me with, and yet at the same time I felt vaguely in the wrong. After all, old retired colonels of my kind aren't exactly made for coping with situations of this sort. I didn't shut an eye that night. I turned over and over in my bed; I could see her face in front of me and I was sure she was right, because she was so obviously suffering. I could feel that in some mysterious way I had not justified her confidence, and as I had no one but her in that part of the world—I've still got one distant cousin in Dorset—I naturally felt rather sad. All the more so since I had, a little bit, the feeling that she was perhaps being unjust to me. After all . . ." The Colonel raised his eyes. He seemed tired, his eyes looked deeper, his features sharper. But his gaze, in spite of its suggestion of pain, held firm and to the last took refuge in humor. "I don't really know how to put it. After all . . . It seems to me I've always respected the elephants in my life, if I may put it so."

## XV

AND THEN, when rumors were at their peak and everyone was trying to embellish his secret fears with some new terror—it was being said that African nationalists were openly helping Morel and using him for their political aims—just then, Saint-Denis, rising up out of the forgotten hole where he carried out his duties as administrator of the Oulé hills with a devotion which had made him dwindle year by year until nothing was left of him but a bald head, a black beard and a pair of eyes devoured by some ravenous dream of hygiene and universal health, came and gave the affair more humble, human proportions. He announced that he had run across Morel in the bush, and that Morel was half-dead with fever and exhaustion, alone and helpless. When asked where he had met him, he gave his questioner a long, straight look that conveyed some surprise but not the least trace of anger—then sent him packing in a manner so calm that no one insisted. Yes, he had run across him in the middle of the bush, and Morel had asked him for quinine. "And you gave him some?" Yes, of course, he had given him some, he didn't know then who he was. Nothing, he assured the journalists frankly—staring at them with that burning, feverish, mystical gaze of his, in which there lurked heaven knew what loneliness, what absence of God—nothing in Morel's appearance made it possible to guess that this was not a human being. Then he waited for the abuse to die down, and added, with the swagger of a diminutive cock that has shed feathers in a thousand fights but is still game: "I even gave him some ammunition." There was a sound of oh! and ah! and Saint-Denis looked pleased. "Yes, I gave him ammunition. How was I to know that the man was dangerous? I had been cut off from all news for six weeks, on a tour of inspection in one of the zones we're disputing with the tsetse fly. Out comes a white man from the elephant grass and tells me that in crossing the Obo he's lost his hunting ammunition—and can I give him some? I did. He told me he was a naturalist, studying the African fauna. I said it was a noble enterprise. And then we went our ways."

Later, when he was reduced, like everyone else, to debating endlessly the whys and wherefores of the affair, and when nothing was left of all that but the long starry nights of Africa, which always have the last word, Saint-Denis was to tell the Jesuit with what an almost physical sharpness he had felt at that moment, beside him, an anguished woman's presence. She was listening to him—but with an attention that made him turn his head in her direction as if he had felt he was being questioned.

"She was standing in shadow, with her two hands gripping her gray cashmere shawl, and her passionate stillness had in it all that I remembered of the Greek tragedies. As soon as I saw her, bolt upright and rigid, at the back of that miserable little rabble busy abusing me as hard as it could, as soon as I met her gaze, I felt at once that she was part of it, that this thing concerned her deeply, in one way or another, and that in her heart she was on the side of Morel. I remember thinking 'Well, well, well' like an idiot, but not so much in irony as for self-protection against that wave of pity which swept over me and could not be ignored. Then, of course, like all of us, I had no idea what was going on in her pretty head— I say 'then' although we're hardly any further along today. All I can say is that the affair is one with plenty of room in it, room for you and for me, and for the herds of elephants, and for a thousand things still unborn . . . But at that moment, of course, I suspected nothing."

He threw some twigs onto the fire, the flames leaped up, crept nearer, then crouched down again. The Jesuit was gazing into the dark. Saint-Denis remained quiet for a moment, in order to regain contact with the silence of the night and with the herd of hills massed at their feet and extending to the frontiers of the moon.

"People must have noticed where I was looking, because heads turned toward Minna, some people laughed and a voice said ironically: 'You know, of course, that Minna signed the petition?' I didn't know. 'Come and have a drink with us,' I said to her. She excused herself. She hadn't the time, she must keep an eye on the boys, change records . . . She turned her back on me and moved away. I had, I don't know why, the idiotic impression that I was losing her forever. She went and put on a new record: 'Remember the Forgotten Men' or something like that. But she came back almost at once and sat down at our table, as if in spite of herself. The talk was still about Morel, of course. That he had no ammunition except the few cartridges I had given him, that he could hardly last in the forest, that he was bound to give up. 'Yes,' someone added, 'he's done for, and it's hard to see what the elephants can do to help him.' I had had enough of it: I felt in the air an atmosphere of a manhunt and God knows what dark settling of accounts between each person and himself in his own tight little stinking hole.

"You could feel it especially in Orsini. He wasn't at my table—I believe he despised me, accusing me, from the full height of twenty centuries of lily-white civilization, of having 'gone native'—but his voice pursued me from the other side of the terrace, that voice which you couldn't hold against him—you had to learn to take it along with all the other voices of the night. He was talking to the journalists.

They formed a circle round him, because after all he was the first
man to have 'seen clearly through it all.' He was busy declaiming
against 'the criminal negligence of the authorities' and about 'the
irreparable damage to the prestige of the white man in Africa.' He
spoke also of collusion in certain high places and in this connection
he uttered an astonishing phrase about Morel, a phrase that really
went far. In that sharp voice, filled with an exalted sense of injustice—my God, here I am, still talking about his voice—he exclaimed at one point, in an astonishing tone of combined triumph
and mockery: 'And don't forget, gentlemen, that he's what you call
an idealist!'—and never have I heard hatred strike so close to truth.
For in a certain obscure way, tortuous and hate-filled like itself, it
seemed to me that Orsini's thinking had scored a bull's-eye, and
that in some manner hard to explain and yet irrefutable, his voice
had rung the knell and downfall of those other clumsy, touching
giants who desperately pursue a certain ideal of human decency,
call it tolerance, justice or liberty, and that, from lost cause to lost
cause, from failure to failure, one of them had run amok and, no
longer knowing where to lay his head, had come to black Africa to
die side by side with the last elephants. In this there was an image
of despair and of downfall which Orsini could not let slip. I can still
remember his final remark, thrown out with a ringing emphasis that
made it heard from one side of the terrace to the other: 'With the
authorities incapable of doing their job, there'll soon be some old
African hands taking over.'

"I moved off. I was in a hurry to be no longer there, at the mercy
of that voice, that mediocrity which grew to be so grandiose and to
engulf the whole world within its pettiness. It was one of those moments when you need all the immensity the eye can find, on earth
and in the sky, in order to feel reassured; a moment when weight
and the very existence of matter make you dream of some all-
powerful friendship and help. I was in a hurry to be outside, to
get back at last to my stars, for that's what this old Africa of ours
is made of, when you know how to look at it in the right way."

Saint-Denis raised his face slightly toward the sky, which was
everywhere, so vast that it seemed near. "You could stretch out
your hand and touch it," he said, with a calm which his voice appeared to derive from the very source of all tranquillity. "I felt sad,

and I believe that, ever since that evening, each time I've thought of Orsini it has been without animosity but with an understanding which in the end brought me nearer to him. I can still see him, in white, with his lips viciously twisted in a sort of total knowledge of the world—an ignoble comprehension—you can't call that a smile— yes, I can still see him, and shall no doubt always see him, with his eyes pathetic in their rancor, brandishing his fists in a gesture which expressed, more than anything else, the impotence of fists." Saint-Denis fell silent. Perhaps he had himself felt keenly what a contradiction there was between the sympathy and pity betrayed by his words and the cold lesson in remoteness which was coming to them from the stars. He sighed. "But no doubt I'm boring you with Orsini. I'm sure he doesn't interest you, and that too was part of a fate against which he never ceased to protest. So let's leave Orsini alone. He's out of place on these heights.

"I left the terrace and made for the way out. I was under that ridiculous triumphal arch which forms the entrance to the Tchadien, when I felt a hand on mine. I growled: sometimes the black girls come as far as there with their humble offers of services rendered among the empty stalls of the market. But it was Minna. 'May I speak with you a moment?' I hesitated. Ever since I had first met her, I had avoided speaking to her when I came to Fort Lamy, or even looking at her too much. I live alone in the bush, without memories, and it's very bad to go back to your solitude with the image of a girl like Minna in your mind. It needles you, it aches in you until you have the impression that you've not freely chosen your life but missed it. Still I followed her. I hope you won't conclude that I'm one of those strong souls that aren't afraid to flout danger."

## XVI

"SHE TOOK ME up to her room. The Hôtel du Tchadien was built in the most handsome style of the 1937 Colonial Exhibition, and her room was at the top of a corkscrew staircase, inside one of the two towers on which rested the triumphal arch I mentioned before. I must say she had arranged her room with a good deal of taste. I could easily see what she might have made of a real house—a 'home,' as the English call it. However . . .

"'They never come here,' she said, 'never.' She was probably referring to the customers below—we could hear a faint echo of their voices and laughter. She looked at me attentively, rather challengingly, ready to defend herself, to justify herself, but I was absolutely determined not to embark on that sort of discussion—it really was not very important. I remember I was chiefly struck by the drawings pinned to the wall: dogs, cats, the usual nursery trash—they awoke in my mind some vague memory of childhood. It was all very *gemütlich*. Yes, I thought, she was right not to bring them up there. It might have embarrassed them in their transports. As you see, I was not particularly well disposed. I turned and looked at her: a tall woman with a helmet of fair hair, a German—there was no mistaking it—with a very pale face and with eyes that—how shall I put it?— that had nothing to do with all that. I suddenly longed to ask her: But, after all, what are you doing here? Why are you where you are? It's a question, of course, one can ask a lot of people in the Chad—or anywhere else on earth, for that matter.

"It seemed to me also that she had been drinking a bit. Her eyes were shining, her hair undone, there was no trace now of submissiveness in her attitude, and she no longer huddled in her shawl as though it were all she had to protect her in the world, but held her head high and looked triumphant—yes, and defiant. I don't know why, but I felt a sudden antipathy toward her, a sort of almost physical animosity. She moved up and down the room quickly, abruptly, rather mechanically. She seemed in a hurry. There was a bottle of brandy on the table, and a single glass. I observed her rather more attentively, but she shook her head, with an almost contemptuous smile.

"'Oh no,' she said, 'I'm not drunk. Of course, I sometimes have a drink with myself.' Her French wasn't very good. Anyhow, her accent was very strong; she almost said *che* instead of *je* and her voice lacked discretion—she talked much too loud.

"'But this evening I had one with somebody who isn't here.'

"I confess that at that point I made the mistake everybody had made. It was so easy to be wrong, so convenient, too. I knew, roughly, the girl's story, and anyhow I knew quite well the part about Berlin, the war, a town taken by storm, the rape, the ruins, the difficulty of keeping alive, and again and again the men who had made use of her for their sweet needs. I imagined her embittered and full of rancor. I said to myself that this girl at twenty-three had seen everything spectacular that humanity, when it makes a slight effort, can offer in the way of beastliness, and that she must now be feeling an evil joy at the idea that in the depths of the bush there was a man who had gone over, gun in hand, to the side of the elephants. I had a sudden vision of that . . . that Berlin girl locking the door of her room and saying *Prosit* as she raised her glass to the health of the terrorist who had taken a stand against the common enemy. It was not possible to be more completely mistaken." The man who was listening to Saint-Denis in the tranquillity of the hills could feel from the bitterness of that old African's voice that that error was with him forever.

"I don't know if I shall ever manage to get it straight. There was in my reaction, first and foremost, a feeling of guilt. A sort of instinctive distrust of human beings who have suffered too much. The irritation you feel, in spite of yourself, when cripples offend your sight a little too cruelly. The idea, too, that people who have suffered too much aren't any longer capable of . . . of complicity with you, for that's what it amounts to. That they aren't any longer capable of playing ball with us. The idea that they've somehow been *spoiled* once for all. It was partly on account of this idea that the German theorists of racialism preached the extermination of the Jews: they had been made to suffer too much, and therefore they could not be anything after that but enemies of the human race. That, then, was my first reaction—with, to be fair, a twinge of pity. I sincerely believed that the only link existing between that girl and Morel was a common rancor and contempt. Yes, it wasn't possible to be more mistaken. But I must say she didn't make things easier for us, that girl, Minna.

"'I wanted to thank you,' she said with a kind of solemnity, as though she were recording some official link between us. *Ich wollte Ihnen danken,* I translated mentally, and in spite of myself, aggressively. She took a cigarette and lit it. 'I wanted to thank you for helping him. For giving him quinine and ammunition and not betraying him to the police. You at least have understood.'

"No, by God, I hadn't understoood." Saint-Denis' voice filled out with a mocking fierceness. "No, I hadn't understood anything whatsoever—but I'm telling you, that girl didn't make things easier. Do you know what she did, all of a sudden? Perhaps she had read something in my look—it was difficult not to follow her about with one's eyes . . . In any case, she smiled at me—the worst of it is, I swear to you, that she had tears in her eyes—she smiled and undid the belt of her dressing gown. Then she opened it. 'If you like?' she said. She stood there with her hands on her hips and her dressing gown open, offering herself, looking at me with her head held high. That's what she thought of men, and she was anxious to let me know that I was not excluded. 'If you like,' she said. 'For me, that doesn't count, it doesn't exist, it never has existed. So if it can give you any pleasure . . .' She smiled at me again, like a kind of nurse, a sister of charity. . . . They do say these women from Berlin have all gone sexually off the rails, hysterical." Saint-Denis shook his head, angrily.

"Just you try and sort that out. You should have seen that superiority of hers, so characteristic—isn't it—of the Herrenvolk. 'For me, that doesn't count, it doesn't exist, it never has existed.' I can still hear her declaring that, calmly and in a tone of triumph, as if no one had ever had her. What did she mean by it? That those things can't defile you? Was she trying in this way to wash herself clean of her past, to recover a kind of virginity? To liberate herself from the memory of it? Was she trying to recapture Berlin from the Russians? Was she merely a child trying to defend herself, trying to minimize that which had most wounded her and most tortured her? In any case, there she was in front of me with her dressing gown open, and . . ." Saint-Denis clasped his hands violently together, as though to crush the void.

"I did not touch her. I think I was chiefly taken by surprise and was lacking in quick reactions, that's all. Anyhow, I did not spend an unforgettable night in her arms, not even the five minutes which a man requires in order to be completely happy on this earth. I even believe my expression must have shown a certain pity, because she rather nervously shut her dressing gown and poured herself a brimming glass of brandy, just like all young girls set on showing you that they're tough.

"'You're drinking too much,' I said to her sternly. She put down her glass. Of course she was crying now. 'Where is he? Please, tell me where is he?'

"I don't know what that voice had in it, what sudden passion, but I remember vividly thinking: Some people have all the luck. I'm fifty-five, but I'd have given a lot to be in Morel's place, and at that moment, believe me, his place wasn't three hundred miles away in the depths of the bush, in the Oulé hills, but in that voice. And she asked me where he was!" Saint-Denis glanced at the Jesuit with an almost scandalized expression, and Father Tassin shook his head quickly as if to indicate that he shared his amazement.

"'Mademoiselle,' I said to her with, God forgive me, a pinch of irony, 'I know you're ready to rush into the heart of the forest to take him by the hand and try to save him, but you must be reasonable. I'm going to confess something to you. I didn't meet him at the edge of the woods by accident. I've moved heaven and earth to find out where he was, to get in touch with him, to try and argue him around.' She said nothing, but smoked her cigarette and observed me with those gray eyes of hers, which took good care not to make me aware of what she thought of me—she must have been telling herself that I was an idiot." The Jesuit nodded curtly.

"For weeks the tom-toms in the forest had been speaking of nothing but Morel, and I am the last white man alive who understands the language of the African drums. What they were saying boded no good for the peace of Africa. A legend was busy establishing itself; the drums were speaking the language of hatred, and I can assure you that they said nothing of elephants. That's why I wanted to meet Morel, although territorially speaking—either you're a bureaucrat or you're not—he didn't come within my jurisdiction. In my region the tribes are intact, and I swear to you that as long as I'm there no one shall come and contaminate them. There are still places, in my part of the world, where the natives live in trees: I'm not the man who'd force them to come down. All I can do is keep a few branches free for the survivors of the atomic age. It happens, too, that I've more belief in the fetishes of my black people than in the political and industrial trash in which others want to submerge them.

"Those were some of the things I wanted to tell Morel, but for my urge to meet him there was, of course, a much more intimate reason: I wanted to find out if the man was sincere, if there was really someone at last to raise an angry cry against our species, to find out if he was a man after my own heart.

"I hadn't the least idea where he was, for the excellent reason that he was reported everywhere at once—in every marketplace the gossips boasted of having seen him, usually on a horse with wings, and holding a fiery sword. There's nothing like legend for building up a man—we've learned that only too well in Europe. In the end I sent my boy, N'Gola, who is the son of the biggest, and no doubt the last, fetishist chieftain of the Oulé, to see his father and ask him to help me. Dwala is an old friend, a great performer of miracles—he can make it rain when necessary, raise certain people from the dead, and exorcise demons for you when they haven't been in you for too long and you haven't called them in yourself. He's a great man who'd have done honor to any country. I've a deep respect for him. I was sure he would understand, and I wasn't wrong.

"Three days later, N'Gola returned and told me that his father wished me to come.

"I went to see my friend Dwala."

 XVII

"HE RECEIVED ME in the shade of his hut—an old, wrinkled, short man, seated, legs crossed, eyes closed. His body and face were covered with blue, yellow and red. I knew from this that he was just back from some magic ceremony. He appeared completely exhausted. N'Gola told me that he had just raised a little girl from the dead."

Saint-Denis broke off, pursed his lips and cast an irritated glance at the Jesuit. "Father, I think you smiled. You can if you like—you won't be the first priest to lack imagination. If you like, you may think me very simple, and perhaps later whisper to some of my young colleagues in the administration that Saint-Denis has gone completely native, that having lived among his blacks for so many years he has adopted their superstitions. I know that's what they say about me. But it happened that I was myself raised from the dead by Dwala, when I had been dead quite a long time—two hours —after a bad bout of fever. He told me he had had to make a terrible effort to get me back, because I was already a long way off, and I can't see at all what's extraordinary about that. They have their secrets, we have ours, and I—I believe in Africa." The Jesuit quickly made a sign of approval.

"Anyway, the girl, Minna, listened to me attentively and didn't smile at all. She seemed even to be very friendly toward me. She had sat down on the arm of a chair, crossing her legs, and I felt a longing to tell her everything about my life and the things I had seen. But for the moment, of course, I could only talk to her about Morel. Otherwise I had no reason for being there. Perhaps afterward she would ask me about myself. She seemed interested and well disposed. She never took her eyes off me, and nervously smoked one cigarette after another.

"I told her how I had talked to Dwala, and how he had sat there with his eyes invisible under their lids, motionless, his arms inert; he seemed not to be breathing. I didn't even know if he was listening to me. Perhaps he had already gone off in search of Morel and was busy traversing thousands of miles of forest to find him. Usually he was a small, energetic man with rapid movements, always gesticulating and busy, with gray hairs on his skull and chin which made him seem to bristle. But this time he appeared really exhausted. I went on talking nonetheless; he might be hearing me in spite of everything.

"I didn't have to explain very much to him.

"We had known each other a long time. We trusted each other. We had both of us the same love for our land of Africa, for our tribes, and the same attachment to their beliefs, their traditions, the

same desire to guarantee them peace. We had also the same distrust of civilization and its poisons. The only difference between us
was that I knew better the peril threatening our pastoral world, a
peril of which Dwala had only a confused premonition. I often
talked to him about it, but it was difficult to explain the full horror
of what we used to call technical progress. In the Oulé language
there were no words strong enough to express it. There were no
words for our technical terms, no names for our inventions, and I
was obliged to have recourse to traditional images which always had
a magic meaning, in order to express something that was so totally
devoid of magic. I therefore did not say much, and simply asked
him to help me. He still kept his eyelids lowered, but at that point
I uttered the name of Waïtari and at once he came to life. He
opened his eyes, his head shook, and he began to speak angrily, in
jerky phrases, and sometimes waved his fists in the air. Waïtari was
a traitor, he said—he used the word *gouanga-ala*, which means
literally: 'he who changes tribes and leads his new tribe against
his own'—our Western tribes call the thing a quisling. He shouted
at me that Waïtari was no longer an Oulé, and when he came into
the villages he came with white men's ideas, foreigners' ideas. He
wanted to abolish the power of the elders in the councils of the
tribes, to suppress the fetishist monasteries, to ban the magic ceremonies, to punish parents who still forced their daughters to submit to removal of the clitoris—he was poisoning the minds of the
peasants with the ideas he had learned among the French. But
above all, Waïtari was disturbing the sleep of the whites. He kept
waking them up violently and alarming them badly, and the whites
would move, would try to change Africa, break with the past, give
her a new aspect. My old friend was trembling with rage, his fists
were high in the air, and the magic lines drawn upon his body—
yellow, red and blue—were running with sweat, and blurring. He
had come back to earth with a vengeance, there was no trace in
him now of fatigue or remoteness, he was with us. What were the
French doing, then? he groaned. Why did they let men like
Waïtari have their head? Why did they encourage them, why did
they negotiate with them? Had they not promised to respect the
tribes, their customs, their ancestral gods?

"I pointed out to him that Waïtari no longer had the ear of the authorities and had joined Morel in his campaign. He was cleverly making use of him for his own aims. I tried to bring the conversation back to Morel. But he listened impatiently. It was Waïtari that interested him. I don't think he understood the Morel business at all. To him it was one more affair between whites and whites. When I tried to explain, he interrupted me: 'Our people have always hunted elephants, they're good to eat.' But in the end I got him to understand the advantage Waïtari could derive from Morel—he knew as well as I did what was being said in the markets and where the armed attacks on plantations were leading. And I was convinced that he knew, day by day and in the minutest detail, the movements of the armed band. He detested Waïtari, but he was certainly trying to maintain good relations with him: you never could tell what the future had in store. Tomorrow perhaps Waïtari would have his say in the councils of the French. The thoughts of the French are inscrutable, and the fact that they didn't hang Waïtari long ago shows that they may do anything. 'And is it not a sorcerer's business,' I said to him with a grin, 'to entertain correct relations with the demons, so as not to be taken by surprise?'

"To my old friend's face there came a sort of smile—something like the trace left by an extremely long experience of this world, not merely the world of magic—in our land it would have been called cynicism, but we were very far from our land. We understood each other—a hint was enough: we had been playing hide-and-seek together for twenty years. I told him I had no doubt about his real feelings toward Waïtari, which were very close to mine, but that I was sure, also, that he was in constant touch with him and was no doubt regularly sending him millet and chickens. Perhaps there were even one or two boys from the village in the small group with him and Morel? Dwala half closed his left eye—an admission —then celebrated with a few minutes' silence our old and complete understanding. Then he assured me of his hatred for Waïtari, upon whom he had several times cast the evil eye—unfortunately the man was a miscreant, and curses had no effect on him. But it was true that a young lad from the village was in his troop to keep an eye on him, and that Dwala's son was in constant touch with him. He advised me to go home and wait. His son, N'Gola, knew all the tracks, he added, and I knew that this was a formal promise.

"And that is how, a week later, I found myself in N'Gola's company, somewhere on the edge of the Galangalé, in the Bongo Mountains.

"I knew the district: it was where, a few years before, I had had to deal with the Kreich bandits who were raiding—and still are—from their territories in the British Sudan, massacring elephants in the reserves and carrying off the ivory.

"I had not been expecting to find Morel in that direction. According to the last report, he had been operating farther south, where he had last been seen at the time of the attack on the Sarkis plantation. That he should be able to move with such rapidity and ease across a region where there was no lack of villages showed clearly what prestige Waïtari still enjoyed. For the first time it seemed to me that Morel was not such a dupe as the sometime deputy for the Shari perhaps believed, and that he had something to gain from being with him.

"I confess I went to the rendezvous with great curiosity and even some excitement. I tried hard to imagine what he looked like. I felt a passionate need to see him, and this need was, perhaps more than any other consideration, the reason for the efforts I had made to get in touch with him. A man can't spend his life in Africa without acquiring something pretty close to a great affection for the elephants. Those great herds are, after all, the last symbol of liberty left among us. It's something that's fast disappearing, from more points of view than one. Every time you come upon them in the open, moving their trunks and their great ears, an irresistible smile rises to your lips. I defy anyone to look upon elephants without a sense of wonder. Their very enormity, their clumsiness, their giant stature, represent a mass of liberty that sets you dreaming. They're . . . yes, they're the last *individuals*. Add to this that we're all more or less misanthropic and that Morel's gesture touched, in me at any rate, a particularly sensitive nerve. Such were my thoughts when, after we had left the road, N'Gola made me do two days on horseback along the wilderness paths of the Bongo Mountains. Then, one morning, as we were picking our way slowly through the thorny undergrowth and over the volcanic rocks of the Galangalé, a man emerged from the thickets and seized my horse by the bridle. We had arrived."

 XVIII

"Morel came toward me all alone, in the middle of a clearing surrounded by rock walls, but I had only to raise my head to see, near a waterfall, a group of armed men standing beside their horses. He walked quickly, pushing his way through grass that came up to his chest, with his head bare and his slung rifle pointing at the ground, holding in his hand the briefcase that was to become so famous, and made toward me with an air of almost menacing resolution which I found irritating, but which no doubt would merely have made you smile indulgently, as a member of a Society well known for its lack of illusions about the airs we give ourselves. My first impression of him was one of smallness and insignificance, perhaps because the sky was vast and tumultuous above the basaltic rocks piled there by the ages, and suggested a quite different scale. Above all, I believe I had, in spite of myself, let myself be impressed by his legend. Deep in my heart, I was expecting to meet a hero. Someone larger than life, if you see what I mean. Instead of which, I found myself facing a stocky, slightly vulgar man with an obstinate, scowling face under untidy hair tufted by sweat; his cheeks were covered with several days' growth, and he gave an impression of strength and even brutality. But the eyes were rather amazing—large, dark and violent—eyes literally blazing with indignation. He had in him also something unpolished, something simple, a kind of seriousness, a look of real belief in what he was doing. And of course he held tightly under his arm that almost legendary briefcase stuffed with melodramatic appeals and blank petitions. I don't know why, but that briefcase particularly provoked my hilarity—perhaps because it suggested some conference room at Geneva or a

trade union meeting in a Paris district much more than the wild
thickets of the Galangalé. And then I understood that that was it,
that was precisely it: he had come to parley with the enemy and he
had brought his files. I nearly burst out laughing, but something in
him made me want to spare him. Perhaps his obvious lack of humor:
it has often seemed to me that above a certain degree of seriousness,
of gravity, a man in real life is a cripple—one always wants to help
him cross the road. That's how I described him to Minna, insisting,
in spite of myself, on his slightly ridiculous side. She smiled, and I
was weak enough at first to take that smile as a tribute to my sense
of irony. But that was not it. I understood almost at once that it
was an expression of tenderness and that the image I was evoking
met with her entire approval. There was even a trace of superiority,
of condescension toward me, as though to point out to me that this
was obviously something I could not understand, a private and
secret world which I was not permitted to enter. You know that
feeling which a woman is so well able to inflict on you: you feel shut
out, excluded." The Jesuit indicated that he did in fact know it.

"As I kept silent, thrown out of countenance, she recalled me to
order: 'What did he say to you?' I explained to her with some irritation that I was the first to speak. I began by asking him if he had
taken arms to serve the cause of African nationalism. I asked him
if it was true that he was preaching revolt to the Oulé tribes. I told
him that I knew Waïtari and his ambitions. I asked him if he
wanted to throw the white man out of Africa and, if so, what elephants had to do with it. He listened to me with visible impatience
and irritation.

" 'Is it to tell me that that they've sent you?' he growled in a low
voice—I could feel he was holding himself in. 'It really wasn't worth
tiring your horse. Yes, there are some among us who are fighting for
the independence of Africa. But why? To protect the elephants. To
take the protection of African fauna into their own hands. Perhaps
for them elephants are only an image of their own liberty. That
suits me: liberty always suits me. Personally, I have no patience
with nationalism: the new or the old, the white or the black, the
red or the yellow. You can tell them that at Fort Lamy; I hope it
will reassure them.'

"Suddenly he spat, as if to free himself of an excess of contained violence. His way of talking was curious—he passed from rather careful language to barracks slang, sometimes with coarse, common intonations, a sort of intentional vulgarity. Since then I've had time to think about him a great deal, and I've come to a conclusion about his way of speaking. He had spent a good many years in places frequented by the so-called 'common people'—barracks, prisons, *maquis*, concentration camps—and every time he felt something deeply, he spoke like them. But perhaps I've thought too much about him, and let him assume almost epic proportions.

" 'But I know that the first thing our black friends will do when they are masters in their own house is to guarantee the protection of the elephants; they're ready to include it, in so many words, in their platform, and even in their constitution.'

"I gave him a searching glance to see if he was making fun of me: but no, nothing of the kind—he merely seemed angry.

" 'They always say that,' I remarked.

" 'Yes,' he agreed calmly, 'they always say that. But meanwhile, what is there to stop the French, British, Belgian and other governments from showing the way? The new conference for the protection of African fauna is meeting soon at Bukavu.'

"There he was again, talking to me about the African fauna: was that really all he had in mind? I gave him another searching glance —but it was in vain that I sought, deep down in his eyes, some gleam, some glimmer of pitiless humor. Or if only he had consented to give a wink of complicity to the misanthrope whom everyone to some extent carries about in himself, one would have immediately felt at ease—which of us has never been seized by a hatred, as sudden as it is momentary, for our species? But no, nothing of the kind—he merely seemed angry.

" 'The bastards,' he said, his face hardening, and slightly lowering his voice. 'They aim between the eyes, just because it's big, free and beautiful. That's what they call a fine shot. A trophy. We've found females among the animals that have been shot, and don't try to tell me it's not true.'

"It was true.

" 'All the same, your friends have burned a plantation,' I said to him, without too much conviction. 'That begins to look a little too much like banditry pure and simple.'

" 'We have, in fact, burned a plantation up north,' he said. 'The Sarkis plantation. But that was a particularly clear case, and we shall not hesitate to do it again. You know what's going on as well as I do.'

"Yes, I did know. Under the pretext of driving away the elephants that were trampling their fields, certain planters indulged in a systematic extermination of the herds. According to the law, this sort of punitive expedition was supposed to be carried out under the supervision of a game warden. But in actual fact the planters hadn't the time, nor often the desire, to inform the authorities, and they took the matter into their own hands, being only too glad of the chance for a pleasant outing.

" 'Those are quite exceptional cases,' I said, rather weakly.

"It wasn't true, and I knew it. I knew, for example, that at the very moment, the authorities of South Africa, Rhodesia and Bechuanaland were systematically exterminating a herd of eight hundred marauding elephants which, hemmed in on all sides by the inexorable advance of cultivated lands, were ravaging crops in the Tuli region, at the confluence of the Limpopo and the Shashi. It was one of those conflicts which are impossible to avoid in the march of progress, and no amount of good will could save the elephants. There could no longer be enough room in this world for such freedom.

" 'After all, those are exceptions,' I repeated.

"For the first time, he allowed himself a somber smile. 'Well, we don't propose to burn *all* the farms,' he said, almost good-humoredly. He opened his briefcase and handed me a sheet of paper.

" 'Give them this list: it enumerates all the species threatened with extinction, whose protection is necessary.'

"I took the list and saw immediately that man did not figure on it, and I was so disgusted with the word and the thing that I heaved a sigh of relief and immediately began to like him better. Besides elephants, the table included the mountain gorilla, the white rhinoceros, the yellow-backed bushbuck and, in general, all the species slowly disappearing from our earth in spite of the warnings of our scientists and naturalists. But, as I've told you, Father, the one chiefly concerned did not figure there, and I was seized with mild hilarity at the idea that this time man was about to receive what was coming to him: he will not be missed. . . . I glanced at Morel with a meaningful smile, inviting him to share my misanthropic humor, but it was in vain that I looked for some sign of collusion in his face. He seemed very sincere and earnest and angry; there wasn't a trace of sardonic purpose in him, and my good humor changed to exasperation before such a refusal to co-operate. He was clearly one of those well-intentioned, dead-serious men who haven't the slightest sense of perspective and who see no further than the ends of their noses. He stood there in front of my horse, in the elephant grass, with his legs apart and with a stupid expression of firmness, of obstinacy, of confidence on his unshaven face.

" 'All I ask of them,' he said, 'is a decree banning the hunting of elephants. I shall give myself up at once. They can put me in jail, I don't care. I know there isn't a single French court that would condemn me.'

"I was indignant. Yes, I was really scandalized, outraged, seized by a formidable exasperation, by a terrible longing to bash his face in, to rough him up, if only to remind him of the facts of life, to show him who we were. For it was obvious that he still trusted us, that he had kept his damned confidence in us intact. He obviously believed it would be enough to draw our attention to the plight of the last elephants, and that we would immediately take the necessary measures to guarantee their immortality, their eternal presence among us. The most revolting part of it was that he appeared calmly convinced that we could do something in the matter, that we had our destiny and that of the elephants in our own hands, that there was no fatality about it, that we could still endure, escape, prevail. Obviously he was an ass, a pathetic idealist, a stubborn dreamer, a cuckold, in fact one of those eternal cuckolds who notice nothing even when they assist at the ceremony. You must excuse my language, Father, but if there's one thing that drives me mad it's those little smart alecks who think human destiny is a mere matter of organization. Maniacs, perverts, who have no notion of reality, constantly offering solutions, measures to be taken, and never leaving you in peace."

Saint-Denis' nose whistled sadly in the darkness. The Jesuit gravely bowed his head, and Saint-Denis observed him distrustfully, wondering if it was to Morel that he was thus giving his approval. "And yet I didn't say anything to him. I wanted to spare him, almost to protect him, even to justify his confidence in us. That was the contradiction: I wanted both to tell him the truth about us, and to help him deny it. He had taken paper and tobacco from his pocket and was rolling himself a cigarette, as he stood there in front of me, his legs firmly planted, his hair tousled, and his gaze frank and straightforward without a trace of cynicism; and he went on without a sign of embarrassment or shame.

" 'What happens is that people don't know, and so they can't help me,' he was saying calmly. 'But when they open their morning newspapers and see that thirty thousand elephants are being killed every year to make paper knives and billiard balls, and that there's a man who's doing his damnedest to stop this mass murder, they'll raise hell. When they hear that out of a hundred baby elephants captured for the zoos eighty die in the first days, you'll see what public opinion will say. There's such a thing as popular feeling, you know. That's the kind of thing that makes a government fall, I tell you. All that's needed is for the people to know.'

"It was intolerable. I listened gaping, absolutely struck dumb. The man had faith in us, totally and unshakably, and that was something, a faith in us that looked as strong, as natural, as irrational as the elements, as the sea or the wind—something, by God, that looked in the end like the force of truth itself. I had to make an effort to defend myself—not to succumb to that amazing naïveté. He really believed that people still had the generosity, the heart, in the ugly times we live in, to worry not only about themselves, but about elephants as well. It was enough to make you weep. I stood there in silence, staring at him—admiring him, I should say—with that gloomy, obstinate expression of his, and that damned briefcase. Ridiculous, if you like, yet also disarming, because I felt he was completely convinced by all the beautiful things man has sung about himself in his moments of inspiration. And with it all, a pigheaded obstinacy—the revolting thoroughness of a schoolmaster who's got it into his head that he'll make humanity do its homework and would not hesitate to punish it if it misbehaved. You can see from what I say that he was a highly contagious man."

The Jesuit smiled in the shadow.

"I now understood just how far wrong my first impression had been. I had come to meet him expecting to find a man worthy of his legend, and I had been disappointed by his simplicity, his small stature, his rather rough appearance. But that simplicity was the very sort possessed by all the heroes of popular tales whose victories and naïvetés will never cease to be told and retold. Yes, I now looked at him quite differently. I was learning by heart that blunt expression of his, that resolute and angry face under the tangled hair, and I thought I could already hear a voice saying: 'Once upon a time there was a rather simple fellow who loved elephants so much that he decided to go and live among them and defend them against the hunters, and give his life for them if necessary . . .' He was now speaking to me again. He had adopted a sly expression and an almost confidential tone, and at first I thought I was dreaming, and then I wanted to grab my hat, smash it on the ground and do a year's worth of swearing then and there.

" 'Dogs aren't enough any more,' he was saying, with satisfaction. 'You see, up to now, dogs were enough for a good many people. They consoled themselves in their company. But the way things have been going, people have been seized by such a need for friendship and company that the dogs can't manage it. We've been asking too much of them. The job has broken them down—they've had it. Just think how long they've been doing their damnedest for us, wagging their tails and holding out their paws—they've had enough . . .'

"He laughed, but I swear to you it wasn't amusing. He'd finished licking his cigarette, and he put it into his mouth but did not light it.

" 'They've had enough, I tell you. It's natural: they've seen too much. And the people feel lonely and deserted, and they need something bigger that can really take the strain. Dogs aren't enough any more; men need elephants. That's the way I see it.'

"Again, I took a good look at him. As you know, it's often been said that he was a particularly passionate and cunning anarchist, a sort of extremist of hidden humor and irony. I myself had a moment of doubt. I took a good look at him: but no, nothing, not a trace of irony, not the tiniest wink—perfectly serious and a little sad. He lit his cigarette and glanced at me, to see if I agreed. I tried to laugh encouragingly, but he only seemed surprised. Then something turned over in my stomach, and I think I must have gone a bit green. I even believe I had tears in my eyes. I suddenly felt as if he had just been speaking about me. It was true, what he'd said: dogs aren't enough any more . . . We need a greater company. He stood in the gently swaying grass under the moving clouds, and he looked at me in an almost friendly, almost kindly way. I no longer knew what to think. I still don't know, for that matter. All I can tell you is that when I described to Minna that amazing outburst of his, she raised her head, her eyes gleamed in triumph, she clasped her hands violently as if struggling against an irresistible impulse, and again I saw upon her lips a smile of perfect understanding. 'And then? And then?' she hurled at me. 'And then,' I said to her, rather dryly, 'I swore into my beard and gave up.'

"I assumed a vaguely protective tone. I told Morel that I would be at Fort Lamy in a few days' time, and that I would give the authorities an account of our interview. I asked him to keep quiet and give me time to plead his case. I added that his activity had so exasperated some of the hunters, among them Orsini, that the elephants were in great danger of paying for it all. I asked him, finally, if he hadn't a personal message for someone at Fort Lamy, in which case I would gladly deliver it. He hesitated.

"'We've practically no ammunition left,' he said. 'You can let them know.'

"I couldn't see very clearly what that had to do with my offer to carry a message to Fort Lamy; he didn't, after all, imagine they'd send him some, did he? But yes, I thought all of a sudden, that's exactly what he did imagine; and once more I realized with consternation that he did not feel isolated at all, lost in the jungle, surrounded by hatred and spite, but on the contrary, at the heart of a universal sympathy; he was sincerely convinced that at the mere news that he was short of ammunition, the whole world would rush up hill and down dale to bring him some. I believe I burst out laughing. In any case I threw him all the ammunition I had, except a few loose cartridges for the road. You'll tell me I had no right to supply an outlaw—that's exactly what I did, all the same. No wonder everything's going to pot with administrators like me. No wonder the government can no longer rely on anything." Saint-Denis puffed mockingly into his beard.

"Then I glanced toward the group of armed men under the rock. He noticed my glance and nodded. 'That's right,' he said. 'Go and talk to them. Then you'll be able to explain back in Fort Lamy that you've really tried everything. Go by yourself: so they'll be able to tell you what they think of me without embarrassment.'

"For the first time his face wore an expression of open gaiety. He took the bridle of his pony out of the hand of the tall black horseman in the blue burnous who was waiting for him, jumped into the saddle, and moved off through the elephant grass. I spurred my horse toward the waterfall."

## XIX

"I HAD KNOWN that I would not find Morel alone. I knew that Africa still had plenty of those adventurers always ready to jump at a chance to break the law—to rob, pillage, and in general 'live a life of freedom.' Our continent has not yet lost all its attraction for men who feel free only with a gun in their hand. So I fully expected to find Morel surrounded by some of the outlaws who had long been eluding us. I was not disappointed. The first man I recognized as I approached from the heath was Korotoro, the almost legendary robber of Indian and Syrian shops whose exploits were recited in all the marketplaces, and who had escaped from the prison at Bangui a short while before. He was squatting on the ground with a sub-machine gun on his knees, laughing and gesticulating with

another Negro. He did not glance at me. But I soon forgot Korotoro. You know, I'm sure, that when, on my return to Fort Lamy, I
reported what I had seen at Morel's camp, I was practically called
a liar and accused at first of wanting to inflate the affair beyond all
proportion and probability, so as to make a legend of it, a projec-
tion of my own misanthropy. It is, of course, possible, and even
probable, that one or two of Morel's companions whom I met then
gave me false identities, for the simple reason that all the police
forces in the world must have been dreaming of them tenderly. But
as for claiming, as people did, that no one had seen them except me
and they were therefore the product of my imagination, the imagination of a misanthrope who lived too much alone and was trying to
supply himself with a mythical company after his own heart—well,
Father, that was really doing me too much honor, and I won't be
the one to protest. I accept gratefully this tribute to my imagination.
Anyhow, you should have seen my face when I first recognized in
the group a man I knew very well, the Danish naturalist Peer Qvist,
who was supposed to be on a scientific mission in Central Africa
for the Danish Museum of Natural History in Copenhagen and
whom no doubt you've met yourself. He was an ancient man—old
isn't the word—thin as a lath, with his immobile, lined face set always in the same severe expression, and hiding under his patriarchal
beard an exasperated sensibility and a proverbial bad temper. He
was exactly the kind of person whose frustrated humanitarian senti-
ments end by becoming indistinguishable from a simple hatred of
humanity. I don't know his age, but I'm sure he looked at least fifty
years older than he was, and he stared at me in silence out of his
little eyes, which were blue and cold, like ice-floes. At his side, leaning on a rifle, was a man with a sarcastic face whose identity I never
learned, and who is one of Morel's companions that no one ever saw
again—one of those said to be the product of my imagination. It has
since been asserted that he managed to get across into Kenya and
that he was one of the two white men who were supposed to be
fighting side by side with the Mau-Mau in the Kenya forest. Certainly you know the legend according to which there were several
white men with the Mau-Mau, and that one of them went by the
name of General France. Nothing's known about it for certain—

merely a few rumors from captured Kikiyus—and nothing will be known until they're duly killed—and even then it'll be necessary to look sharp and get there before the ants. All I was able to find out about him, in a conversation lasting two minutes, was that he claimed to be a Parisian; when I tried to convince him of the folly of their enterprise, he cut me short with a laugh:

" 'Look here, my friend, for three years I was a bus conductor in Paris. I recommend it during rush hours: it gave me what you might call a knowledge of human nature—a good, solid knowledge which prompted me to change sides and go over to the elephants. I hope that'll do for you, as an explanation.'

"His companion was a strange person, with a flushed face, blue, bulging eyes starting from their sockets and a small grizzling mustache between inflated cheeks that seemed to be holding something in—a sigh, a peal of laughter, or some ultimate vomit. He sat there on a rock, shaking a little, seemingly in the last stages of alcoholic stupor; he was dressed in remnants of an elegance made for quite other climes; his tweed suit and his small Tyrolean hat with a feather were torn in several places; he held a sporting gun on his knees; it was clear that his clothes and their owner had seen better days. When I tried to exchange a few words with him, his companion, to whom I had just spoken, interposed; he told me that 'the baron, though he comes of a very noble family, has decided to break completely with the human species: his disgust is such that he refuses even to have recourse to human language.' Thereupon the so-called baron, as if to confirm this, broke wind in a series of most amazing volleys. 'You see,' said his acolyte, 'you see, he expresses himself only in Morse. Hates the very sound of human speech.' It was perfectly clear that these anarchists had no intention of revealing their true identity, and that they were trying to make a fool of me, and although I made a vague effort to remember the last index cards of wanted criminals, which reached me in my wilderness every three months, I had only to glance at the last man in the troop to lose interest immediately in such small fry.

"He was standing somewhat apart, at the foot of the rock, and I was surprised that I had not recognized from afar his giant silhou-ette: but it was the first time I had seen the former deputy for the

Oulé to the French Parliament not wearing a well-cut European suit. He was bare-chested, with only a military tunic thrown over his shoulders, and he was holding a tommy gun in his clenched fist— yes, Waïtari. . . ." Saint-Denis pronounced the name with an edge of bitterness. "As I say, I knew him well: it was I who, twenty years before, had got him his first scholarship in Paris. I had several times, in those distant days, sent him money taken from my own meager pay, in response to pressing letters, and of course he had never forgiven me for that. I did not blame him: I preferred ingratitude to servility. Later—much later—he had toured my territory as a member of Parliament and, on his return to Brazzaville, had had a great deal to say about me: apparently, I wasn't doing anything to 'free the backward tribes from the servitude of the past.' In that, too, he was right: I am in no hurry to do so. On the contrary, I have a more and more irresistible longing not only to preserve intact the customs and rites of the African forest, but sometimes even to share in them myself. But enough of that. I need only tell you that when I saw there, in the elephant grass, a tall, proud figure holding one of our modern weapons in his fist, I knew, at once and fully, what was really at the bottom of this business, much more clearly than if he had made me one of those fine speeches in the French he spoke with so much eloquence. And, as always, I was affected by the beauty of the African sky above him. I went up to him. We stared at each other. He was standing a few feet from the waterfall, in a swirling mist which fell on our faces and danced around us, in an attitude of hostility and disdain, and although I knew that he was first and last a politician merely posing for a poster on African revolt, there was around him an air of authenticity impossible to disregard: the authenticity of sheer physical nobility and beauty. He was a magnificent product of a selection which it would be difficult to call 'natural': for centuries, his forefathers had rid themselves of the weaker products of their race into the hands of Arab or Portuguese slave drivers. The Oulés had long been the greatest tribe of slave owners in the heart of Africa. I stood there, humbled by his glamour, waiting for him to speak, with a piece of tobacco between my clenched teeth. He did not offer me his hand.

"'I'm glad you came here,' he said, and his voice seemed to bor-

row some of its accents from the basalt rocks that surrounded us
—but perhaps he was merely trying to cut through the thunder of
the waterfall. 'Your duty is to tell the world the truth about us. The
colonialist press is trying to throw a smoke screen of cheap humani-
tarianism over the African revolt.'

"I felt the spray mixing with my sweat and cooling my face and
I thought of all the strange things I had seen in my time in Africa
and I chewed my tobacco and looked at him and waited for more.
Above the waterfall, in the eddies of spray, the sun was throwing
a rainbow bridge between the towering rocks.

"'Morel is an eccentric. But he is useful to us. He helps us to stir
the world, to put across our image of African revolt. There's at least
one belief we share with him: it's time to stop the shameful exploitation of African natural resources. As for the rest . . .' He
shrugged. 'Morel is a pathetic idealist of the outmoded humanitarian type.'

"'Well, I think you should let him know,' I said.

"Waïtari was not listening: he had ten generations of Oulé absolute rulers among his ancestors, and his years of speech-making in
the French Parliament didn't help things. Suddenly, I remembered
a photograph of another tragic figure, Kenyatta, the spiritual leader
of the Mau-Mau revolt, who was then rotting in some jail in Tanganyika; in that photograph Kenyatta stood in his same nudity, covered only by a leopard-skin, and with the same air of authenticity
—except that the photograph was the frontispiece of an anthropology
text he had published at Oxford.

"'How many supporters do you have among the Oulés?' I asked.
'Four, five, a dozen? The whole tribe is against you . . .'

"Again he shrugged his magnificent shoulders. 'They are too backward to know better. People like you took good care to keep them
that way. But the Oulés aren't all that matters. It's high time to end
the great black silence. I want our voice to be heard in Asia, in
Soviet Russia, in America, even in France . . . I am not speaking
to the Oulés.'

"He hesitated. Then it came: 'You know how I lost my parliamentary seat in the last election. The government threw all its
weight against me . . .'

"I knew. But he shouldn't have brought that in. This was an error. He felt it himself: 'Not that it would have changed anything.'

" 'You'll end up in jail,' I said.

"He smiled. 'Your jails are merely waiting rooms where all the heads of new independent nations have sat. . . . I am quite willing to take my turn. As for the elephants, they'll survive at least as emblems on our flag. They are only an instrument of propaganda, an image of our liberty on the march, of an irresistible force that nothing can stop . . .'

" 'Yes,' I said.

"For there he was right. There was still in Africa a marvelous, irresistible freedom. Only it belonged to the past, not to the future. Soon it will go. There'll no longer be herds swirling against the forests and crushing them in their passage. The elephants were the last individuals. They belonged to the past, not to the future.

" 'How's your wife?'

" 'She's in France, living with her mother. She's French, you know.'

" 'Yes, I know. So are your children.'

" 'My two sons are in school in Paris,' he said calmly. 'I want them to have a good education.'

"I nodded. He was not being cynical. He knew us, that was all. He knew he could trust us with his sons. I was clenching my teeth, looking at this black man who was really a French politician and who had but one dream: deliver Africa to the West. It would be an independent Africa, of course, a new nation, and a totalitarian one, but a dutiful image of the West, of our poisoned minds. I looked at this black traitor who was trying to surrender my lovely land, my magic continent to everything I hated most, that is, the materialistic West, and I thought: for this you deserve to be burned alive by your people. There is no greater crime you can commit against them. I thought all this, but I didn't say it. I merely spat my tobacco on the ground. That was the best use I could make of my spittle. He wasn't interested in what I might think or feel. I didn't matter. What mattered was what I would say back at Fort Lamy, what story the newspapers would carry. And as for me, my only concern, and more than ever, was whether my old friend Dwala would keep his

promise. I knew that he had the power to change a man into a tree
after his death, and I had his solemn promise to liberate me, once
and for all, from a disgusting species I couldn't bear belonging to. At
my age, what frightened me more and more was the idea that I
might be born once again in the skin of a man. It was a fear that
would sometimes wake me up in the night and throw me into a cold
sweat. In the end I made a deal with Dwala, who promised to
change me into a tree after my death, making of me in my next life
a strong tree, with a thick bark, with taproots reaching deep into
African earth—all this in exchange for a few small administrative
favors, like giving up the idea of a road through the Oulé hills. I
remembered my old friend's promise and felt much better. I wiped
my face and my beard and I said nothing of my thoughts. Not that
I didn't feel like giving him a piece of my mind. I felt like telling
him: '*Monsieur le député,* I've always yearned to be a black man, to
have a black man's soul, a black man's laughter. You know why?
Because I thought you were different from us. Yes, I thought you
were something special, something different on this sad earth of
ours. I wanted to escape with you from the white man's hollow
materialism, from his lack of faith, his humble and frustrated sexuality, from his lack of joy, of laughter, of magic, of faith in the rich-
ness of after-life. In fact, I wanted to escape from everything you're
learning from us so quickly, from all the things people like you,
*Monsieur le député,* are daily injecting in the black man's soul. Soon
there'll be no Africa left: people like you, *Monsieur le député,* for
all their talk of national independence, will deliver Africa to the
West forever. You'll accomplish that final conquest for us. Of course,
to achieve that, people like you will have to exercise a tyranny and
a cruelty compared to which colonialism will soon appear as child's
play—and in the name of Marx and Stalin, you'll accomplish that
conquest for us. For it is our fetishes, our pagan gods, our preju-
dices, our racism, our nationalism, our poisons that you dream of
injecting into the African blood. . . . We've never yet dared to do
it, but under the name of progress and nationalism, you'll do the
job for us. You're our most rewarding fifth column. Naturally, we
don't understand this: we're too stupid. We're trying to fight you, to
destroy you, to prevent you from delivering Africa to us forever.

Maybe that's the only chance Africa's got; maybe it'll manage to
evade both you and us; maybe it'll find and follow its own way. But
that's a very small chance indeed. Racists have long proclaimed that
Negroes aren't really men like us, but maybe it's only another false
hope they're dangling under the eyes of our black brothers.' That's
what I felt like telling him, but of course I didn't. I didn't particularly want to see on his face that expression of scorn and superiority
I always find on the faces of my colleagues in the service when I
tell them those things. I know exactly what they think of me. 'Poor
Saint-Denis, not a bad chap really, but he's gone completely native.
Backward, lonely, and misanthropic, like a rogue elephant. It's high
time to get rid of people like him.' So I took good care to say nothing
and merely stuck a new piece of tobacco between my teeth. Even
so, I could see the glint of irony in his eyes.

" 'Stop trying, Saint-Denis. For years, you've been one of us. Your
place is among us. You've given the best of yourself to Africa and
you would save the honor of France and of the service to which
you belong, if you came to fight and perhaps to die for African
independence on our side. This would be the crowning achievement
of your life—of all the years you've devoted to our land.'

"I confess I felt tears coming to my eyes. You see, Father, I
haven't been spoiled during my days: encouragement and signs of
gratitude or recognition have been very few, if any, along my road.
A lonely eccentric, that's all I was for them. And yet, to take only the
struggle against the tsetse fly, I had opened whole new regions to
farming and saved I don't know how many human lives. The only
indication that these efforts did not pass entirely unnoticed was the
nickname 'Tsetse' which stuck to me, and even there I'm not sure
whether the young colleagues who gave it to me meant it as a
compliment. And there at last was Waïtari himself recognizing the
historic services I had rendered to my people, to Africa, which was
my land and from which no force could tear me away. Here was a
nationalist leader accepting me as one of his people, and offering me
a brotherhood that no one, man, woman or dog had ever offered me.
There was nothing in the world I desired more than to be accepted
by the Negroes as one of them, to help them to protect themselves
against the ambushes civilization was laying along their track. For

twenty years I had had one aim only, you could almost say one obsession: to save my blacks, to protect them against the invasion of new ideas, against the materialist contagion, against political infection, to help them to save their tribal traditions and their marvelous beliefs from the West, to prevent them from going our way. Nothing enchanted me more than to see my black people practicing their rites, and whenever, in one of my tribes, I saw one of the young men suddenly replace his ancestral nakedness with a pair of trousers and a felt hat, I personally took the trouble to go over and kick his ass. Penicillin and D.D.T. were as far as I was prepared to go by way of concession, and I assure you that the man is not born who would get more out of me. My old friend Dwala and I had always been in the front rank of those who defended Africa against penetration by that odious armored beast known as the West, and had striven bravely to preserve our Negroes from its materialistic claws. I made it my business personally to see that certain government instructions about the 'political education of African masses' should meet with the only fate they deserved, in the communal latrines. I had made it my chief aim in Africa to hinder the spreading of our poisons—of our absurd political notions of democracy, self-government, parliamentary institutions, political parties, and all that threatened the African way of life and the traditions of the African tribes. I was here to watch over a pastoral civilization, to prevent it from going our way, and I was ready to do anything to carry out my self-appointed task. That is why, when I heard Waïtari express his recognition of the work I had accomplished, I couldn't help feeling deeply moved and grateful for this brotherhood he was offering me. All the more so since, on this earth, I've nowhere to go. I'm no longer a white man, and not quite yet a black man, either. If humanity can be compared to a tribe, then you may say I'm completely detribalized. So you see, Father, the temptation was great. But I didn't give in and stood my ground firmly. I had only to remember who Waïtari really was, in spite of his black skin: a ruthless Western politician, a carrier of all our ills, a speaker for Western values; I had only to listen to his deep voice, speaking French better than I've ever heard it spoken in my life. He was singing me a song of treason—of treason not to France, but to Africa, a betrayal of its customs, its magic, its spirits, and of its very soul. I was not going over to the side of a man whose only purpose was to throw that soul to the political bulldozers and party machines, so that African tribes could become that unrecognizable pulp, the masses. I felt anger in my clenched fists and I tried to keep my voice calm.

" 'As long as I'm here,' I told him, 'no one is going to replace our magical rites by party meetings.'

"He looked at me scornfully. 'You're a reactionary and a racist, Saint-Denis . . . a typical product of colonialism. You love Negroes out of sheer misanthropy, because you think they aren't really men. We'll no longer accept that sort of love . . .'

"I felt weary and lost. Perhaps he was right. Perhaps black men were really men like ourselves, in which case there was nowhere to go, nowhere to lay my head. Perhaps the only thing left to me was to strike up a friendship with a jumping bean, like Colonel Babcock. I felt myself lost at the very heart of an immense and cynical beastliness, from which there was no way out. And as if to confirm me in this agreeable impression, I suddenly saw appear between the trees a dirty yachting cap and a stocky figure overflowing with strength and vitality, which seemed to me vaguely familiar, although I didn't recognize the worthy gentleman immediately."

～ XX ～

"THE MAN, carrying over his shoulder three huge fishes threaded by their eyesockets on a stick, stopped for an instant when he saw me, then came up to me with open arms, while an enormous laugh shook his jet black beard.

" 'Saint-Denis, may the high seas rock me! What are you doing here, you old hermit? Come to join us? A need for company? Or perhaps gone off with the government cash, nobly sought refuge in the *maquis* with the money-bags? *Inch'Allah!* May the deep swallow me up if it isn't our most misanthropic, our most ancient, worst-tempered and most solitary colonial administrator!'

"I tried hard to recall who the scoundrel was, for I could already tell, from the disgust he inspired in me, that we must have been previously acquainted.

" 'Well, precious—don't we recognize our pals any more? That's what comes from spending one's life alone in the depths of the bush: in the end all human faces look alike. Habib, skipper of the high seas, the one and only ship's master after God, and his presence here proves to you that the old hand hasn't yet given up the voyage!'

"I was surprised that I hadn't immediately recognized that brute by his air of happiness and his healthy, earthy look. He had flung his arm round my shoulders, not paying the slightest attention to my forbidding expression, which I made even more grim and disapproving than usual. Waïtari, Korotoro and Habib, I said to myself: so that was the kind of company Morel had surrounded himself with. He was obviously only an instrument in their hands, a stray idealist, the only one among them who really had the fate of the elephants at heart. I felt much better immediately—I took, as they say, a hair of the dog that bit me. I could now go back to my hole, keep away from yet another squalid human machination, and wait for it all to pass, my arms folded, with nothing bright or hopeful around me, except those distant stars—and even there, let's be frank: it's only their distance that gives them that purity and beauty. In short, things were returning to normal. It was obviously a typical human enterprise, very much of this earth, with nothing true or sincere about it, and doomed irremediably to the usual exploitations and treachery; the elephants were merely another device to deceive us. I inquired, with all the irony I could put into my voice, after the fate of that other worthy pilgrim whom I had known as associated with Habib on his earthly voyage.

" 'Won over by a noble cause, old man, won over by the beauty of a certain ideal. Rushed over to the rescue of the elephants, to the defense of natural splendor, has sacrificed all for the survival of that powerful image of African freedom. Ready to die for the noble cause of people's right to self-determination, anxious to carve his name upon history side by side with those of Byron, General

China and General Russia of Mau-Mau fame, and the great Law-
rence of Arabia! Therefore added his own feeble breath to the
blowing wind of revolt! Present, as always, behind all great causes,
irrevocably committed to them! Came and woke me up in the middle
of the night, spoke to me nobly, took his Männlicher and his cya-
nide, left all his other worldly goods and made off, barely an hour
or two in advance of the police—an old habit of ours—to the side of
the elephants. Accused immediately of all sorts of common crimes
—and yet there's nothing common about his character: friend of the
arts, great educator, lover of youth, Oxford and Cambridge, man of
the world in every sense of the term. So here we are once more,
mixed up with a noble cause, always ready to serve, ideals don't
die—obliged to live on shit sometimes, but don't die! Unfortunately,
the boy's got a very sensitive soul: lying flat in his tent just now,
with hell's own attack of dysentery, begs me to let him go, but shall
keep him alive till he bursts; have caught him some fish, we must
try and save our elite; however, all is well, life's worth living, let an
old sea-dog tell you—and God knows the bastard knows what he's
talking about!'

"He gave me another pat on the shoulder, and walked away on
those bow legs of his, with their amazingly solid, muscular, truly
earthly calves below the rolled-up trousers, and disappeared with
his fish and that grin of happiness which said so much about it all.

"I felt, all of a sudden, strangely relieved.

"However lonely I might be, I wasn't yet ripe for that sort of
company. For now I saw very clearly what was lurking behind this
campaign for the protection of elephants and to what purpose
Morel's generosity and folly were being exploited.

"True enough, a man like Peer Qvist had joined the fight as a
great naturalist, a lifelong and passionate defender of natural
splendor every day more and more threatened by ruthless men trying to tear the roots of liberty from the human soul and poisoning
the earth, the air, the oceans and the very sources of life with their
'ultimate weapons,' to the point where not only man's freedom but
man himself was perhaps on the edge of extinction. This was
enough to explain the old Dane's presence here, his anger, his misanthropic fury.

"Behind him stood Waïtari, who believed that a new world war was imminent and who expected to appear after the fall of Europe, as the first hero of Pan-African nationalism. Behind them stood, as in the shadow of all great causes, mere bandits and murderers, as a pledge of earthly triumph. Behind them again, the silent awakening mass of the black peoples whose hour was striking, whatever happened. Behind them again, very far behind, and perhaps only in Morel's heart, came the elephants.

"It was in fact a great cause, with the company a great cause always keeps: men of good will and those who exploit them, generous endeavor and sordid calculations, an ideal over the horizon, but also the treachery of ends justifying means. Man's oldest company, I tell you, a noble cause and a pack of scoundrels behind it, a generous dream and all the purity that's needed to cause great massacres . . ." Saint-Denis fell silent for a moment. Perhaps because of his high, almost Mongolian cheekbones, his naked skull and his light body, Father Tassin thought that he looked like one more rider-toward-the-horizon thrown by his noble stallion.

"I said goodbye to them and went straight to my pony, which N'Gola was holding ready. For a while Peer Qvist rode by my side. He held himself very straight in the saddle, with a severe expression, one stirrup longer than the other to support his stiff leg—he had smashed the joints of his right knee in some Arctic crevasse. I asked myself why, when he hadn't said a word to me, he chose to accompany me during those few minutes. Perhaps because he had suddenly felt closer to me than to the others.

"Our horses advanced along the stony track between the rocks. The sun had just gone down into the forest, and every bush, every tree, seemed to be sharing in its scarlet spoils. As we moved slowly forward, a sound like thunder rose toward us from the banks of the Galangalé, the whole forest seemed to shake and yield under some furious assault, and the air, the sky itself, swelled with the trumpetings of the herd as it blazed its way toward water. In a few moments the cracking of uprooted trees, the trembling of the earth and rocks and the calls of the elephants took on the proportions of some natural cataclysm. I listened. I was used to it, and yet, every time, that living thunder made my heart beat faster, and it wasn't fear, but a strange contagion. I listened. The forest seemed to be opening on all sides, and the din was such now that it was impossible to make

out its direction. I felt surrounded, lost in the middle of some total
upheaval. But from the height where we were I could see, on the
other side of the ravine that hid the stream, a whole part of the forest quivering as though shaken by a cruel fear, and the tops of the
trees suddenly tilting, and falling like feathers; and then I saw them,
packed closely against one another, the great gray shapes I knew so
well. I thought: Soon there will be no more room in the modern
world for such need of space, for such royal clumsiness, such magnificent freedom. And I could not help smiling, as I did each time I
saw them, with relief, as though the sight of them reassured me
about an essential presence. In this age of impotence, this age of
taboos, of slavery, inhibitions, and almost physiological submission,
when man is triumphing over his most ancient truths and renouncing
his deepest needs, it always seemed to me, as I listened to the earth's
most ancient thunder, that we had not yet been finally cut off from
our sources, that we had not yet lost ourselves forever, that we had
not yet been once for all castrated and enslaved, that we were not
yet altogether subdued. And yet it was enough to listen to that noble
fury, it was enough to witness just once the passage of that living
landslide, to understand that soon there would no longer be room
among us for such liberty. But it was hard, very hard, to bow one's
head in acceptance, and not to take one's place at Morel's side.

"At the end of the path down, Peer Qvist reined in his horse. I
thought that ever since I had known him I had seen but one expression on that face. It was an expression of extreme severity among
wrinkles so deep as to make it almost august, and his small blue eyes
seemed to retain something of the eternal Arctic ice-fields which
they had long ago contemplated in the company of Fridtjof Nansen.
Above the gray, round beard the lips were hard and straight, without a trace of forgiveness.

" 'Listen to that,' he said. 'That's the finest sound in the world, the
sound of freedom.'

" 'We've heard that sound ever since we've been in Africa.'

" 'But today you aren't the same, Saint-Denis. Formerly that sound
reached only your ears. Today it reaches your heart, and you can no
longer resist it. Once upon a time, when the din wouldn't let you
sleep, you took a gun, and that settled it. Nowadays your guns disgust you even more than that sound alarms you. I suppose that's

what's called coming of age. What will you tell them at Fort Lamy?'

" 'What I haven't stopped repeating to them for years,' I answered gruffly. 'That it's time to do all we can for the African elephants. That protection of nature is man's most urgent task on earth.'

"His face made no movement. I said to myself: When people get very old, their faces tend to jell once for all into a single expression; they aren't easily stirred.

" 'Do you think they'll send troops against us?'

" 'There are hardly any in French Equatorial Africa. But the hunters will do their best . . .'

"His face remained as severe as before, but he said with a trace of humor: 'It must be amusing to be killed at my age.'

" 'Hilarious,' I assured him. 'How old are you?'

" 'I am very old,' he said gravely. He added, as a matter of course: 'I'm glad to die in Africa.'

" 'And why?'

" 'Because this is where mankind began. The cradle of humanity is in Nyasaland. It's been pretty well proved.'

" 'Odd reason.'

" 'One dies better at home.'

"Yet another one, I thought, who's trying to find a home on earth. I asked: 'And Morel?'

" 'We are all in search of another company . . .' There was sadness in his voice. 'Poor Morel,' he said. 'He's put himself in an impossible situation. No one has ever managed to resolve the contradiction there is in wanting to defend something human in the company of men. Goodbye.' "

## XXI

"THAT NIGHT I hardly slept a wink, but turned over and over in my tent; never until then had I felt so alone or so deserted. Perhaps even the elephants are too small, I thought, as I stared into the darkness, and we need a far bigger and more affectionate presence at our side.

"I returned to Fort Lamy and had a stormy interview with the Governor: I showed him on the map where I had met Morel but he said he had known me for a long time and had no confidence whatsoever in my information—and there he was not altogether wrong. I tried to tell him that he was doing everything the hard way, and that it was much simpler to get the governments concerned to sign a new international agreement on the protection of nature and put an end to the big game hunting as a sport. He lost his temper completely, spoke of *l'apaisement,* shouted at me that he was not yet ready to bow down before the black flag of misanthropy raised by Morel and his kind, and that his confidence in humanity's bright and noble future remained unshaken. He assured me that as an old humanist and democrat, he would not tolerate such a manifestation of hatred, spite and irony against the human species on the territory for which he was responsible to the Republic. He left his desk, bore down on me on tiptoe and, bending toward me, whispered in tones full of hatred that the elephants were a mere political diversion and that of course he knew what the real issue was, but if communism triumphed in Africa the elephants would be the first to die. He went back behind his desk, sat down and asked me ironically if I knew that the elephants really represented the last great Rights of Man, clumsy, embarrassing and menaced from all sides, yet indispensable to our survival—he pounded violently at the pile of newspapers on his desk—that was what certain French newspapers were making of it; as for him, his only answer to all those muddled intellectuals, to all those crackpot eggheads and ink-spatterers would be a laugh, the big, hearty, healthy laugh of a good republican, fully confident of man's achievement and future. Thereupon he opened his eyes to their widest, showed his teeth and began to shake with absolutely ghastly laughter—aha-ha-ha-ha!—so that we had to make him lie down on the sofa while we ran to fetch his wife."

Saint-Denis chuckled for a while into his beard. "Perhaps I'm exaggerating a little, Father, but it's difficult to imagine the exasperation all the headlines then being printed about Morel had thrown them into at Fort Lamy. I came out of Government House extremely satisfied with myself, accompanied by Foissard, who explained to me that the Governor was now getting no sleep, that back in Paris they were unable to convince the Americans that the whole business really had anything to do with the preservation of the African fauna, that the French press was accusing the government of having invented Morel, lock, stock and barrel, to cover up grave political disorders, and that everyone was laughing at the naïveté of France who thought the world still capable, at its age, of believing in elephants."

⚊ XXII ⚊

"THAT'S WHAT I told Minna, as I'm telling it to you today, and I believe I've never in my life had the honor to be listened to by a woman with such intensity. She sat there on the arm of a chair, her hands clasped, in that attitude of total stillness which betrays a passion barely contained, and I confess I even forgot that this almost violent interest she accorded me had nothing to do with me. It was impossible not to feel moved, and even a little disturbed, by that flood of passionate generosity, by all the kindness and sympathy and desire to help and to protect one could sense in her. Yes, she was a woman who had much to give."

The Jesuit looked at his companion with some surprise.

"When I reached that Homeric message to humanity with which Morel had so candidly entrusted me, and when I repeated to her his last words, 'Tell 'em I've practically no ammunition left,' her lips trembled, she stood abruptly and went to the other end of the room to make some quite useless gesture—move a vase or a cushion—and remained there, with her face turned to the wall, silent, while her shoulders shook visibly. I felt rather lost. I knew she had had many misfortunes in her young life, and I had at first believed that, to use Morel's famous expression, a dog's company was not enough for her, that she too needed a greater friendship, something on the scale of her loneliness on earth, which was why she was so concerned about the elephants. I told her that she mustn't take things tragically, that Morel would probably be declared insane by the doctors or at least

not entirely responsible for his actions, and would get off with a year
or two behind bars.

"She turned toward me with a violence, an indignation, that left
me speechless. I often dream about her, and that's how I see her,
standing up, her hands on her hips, with her wrap open, her hair in
battle disarray, shouting like a fishwife in that dreadful German accent of hers which immediately, by some miracle, made her appear
less beautiful.

"'So, Monsieur Saint-Denis,' she flung at me, 'you think that because a man has had enough of you, enough of your cruelties and
atrocities, enough of your faces and your voices and your hands—
you think that he's mad? That he must be locked up because he no
longer wants to have anything in common with you, with your scientists, your police, your bombs, your labor camps, your machine guns
—with all that shame and horror? Believe me, there are plenty of
people like him in the world. No doubt they haven't the courage to
do what he is doing, because they're too defeated, and too—too
tired, or cynical, but they understand him, they know exactly what
he's trying to say. They go to their offices, or to their camps, or to
their barracks, or to their factories—all the places where people obey
and are sick of it—and those who can, smile when they think of him,
and of his free elephants, and they do this . . .'

"She grabbed her glass.

"'They drink his health . . . *Prosit! Prosit!*' she repeated, gazing
at a point in space over my shoulder. I never could bear that German word, and there was something particularly painful about it in
the mouth of a woman. There was also a certain coarseness about
her, which suddenly revealed itself in her voice and gestures, in that
wrap left open with complete indifference—I felt she had known
many men . . . many.

"'My dear child . . .' I began.

"She cut me short. 'And let me tell you something else, Monsieur
Saint-Denis; your skin, you know, is worth no more than the elephants' hide. In Germany, at Belsen, during the war, it seems we
used to make lampshades out of human skin—for your information.
And don't forget, Monsieur Saint-Denis, that we Germans have always been forerunners in everything . . .'

"She laughed. 'After all, it was even we who invented the alphabet.'

"No doubt she meant printing.

" 'And don't look at me like that. I don't need your damned pity. It's true that I've known men, too many of them, but one gets used to it. And you can't judge men by what they do when they take off their pants. For their really filthy tricks they dress up—they even put on uniforms, flags and decorations.'

"She lit a cigarette and poured herself a little more brandy. I felt completely out of my depth. I couldn't understand how that girl who was so gentle, who always seemed so subdued, so frightened, was capable of such an outburst. I tried to explain that she had mistaken the meaning of my words about Morel. I merely meant that he had fallen into the hands of a band of political agitators and bandits who were exploiting his good faith, and that we could do nothing for him. She cut me short. She explained to me impetuously that I was wrong, that there was still time if only I would agree to help her. All she asked of me was a message for my friend Dwala, so that she could get in touch with Morel. Of course I tried to make her see reason, I reminded her that it had taken me twenty years of devotion to win the confidence of the Oulé tribes, and that what old Dwala had done for me was not transferable. He and I were old allies, attached to a code of honor which it was not possible for me to break without completely undermining my position in the region I administered. The few villages in which Waïtari had sympathizers were strictly watched, and she would walk straight into the arms of the first commander of a military outpost who came along. I doubted, besides, if Waïtari had more than a dozen friends, and they were mostly in the towns: the tribes didn't trust him. He was one of us, his head was stuffed with our notions, and he despised their rites. I reminded her, lastly, that Morel was, after all, accused of subversive activity, and that the best thing she could do was keep clear of all that—she, a foreigner . . . to be frank, a German.

" 'So,' she shouted at me, 'you want him to go on until he kills someone, so nobody will be able to do anything for him? You talk about your duties as administrator; don't they consist in making the attacks cease, and in bringing Morel back alive? You'll even get congratulations from the government,' she flung at me, in a tone I didn't like at all. 'If only I could speak to him—I'm sure he'd listen to me.'

"I too was sure. Clearly she had certain means at her command.

"'And don't you feel, Monsieur Saint-Denis, that he's a man who trusts you, who relies on you, who's asking to be helped? A man who has . . . who has need . . . who has need of protection, of friendship?'

"Her voice broke, her eyes filled with tears: it was an argument not easy to resist. I considered rapidly. After all, her idea was not so mad, provided certain precautions were taken. I don't know how to explain it to you, but I was convinced that Morel would yield to her entreaties and would follow her: probably I was putting myself in his place. . . . It even seemed to me that here was a chance which I had no right to miss. I suppose I saw myself as a sort of Machiavelli, full of cunning, making use of a woman in love to get hold of a dangerous enemy. After all, one could always rely on love for this sort of job. All police specialists knew that. She would serve us as bait; he must be skillfully played, that was all. You see, Father, that I not only gave in to her, but even gave myself clever airs. The truth was that it wasn't possible to say no to her youth, to her beauty, to that disabled, pathetic expression of hers as she stood there before me. I therefore offered to send N'Gola to see Morel, to find out if he would agree to meet her. Meanwhile, the best thing would be for her to leave Fort Lamy and wait for his answer at Ogo, my district center, where she would be my guest, and from which she was not to budge on any account. If Morel accepted the interview, a place outside the Oulé country, somewhere in Ubangi or in the Cameroon, would have to be agreed on. If it was a success, so much the better. If not, she would return quietly to Fort Lamy, explaining that she had spent a few days in the bush.

"She showed an impulsive gratitude toward me which irritated me, perhaps because it had chiefly to do with someone else.

"'Come, come,' I said to her, 'don't thank me; we'll see if you succeed. We'll see if it's really a case of solitude—I mean, if he's run amok for lack of somebody at his side. That's how I understand it, although I've nothing in common with your Morel.'

"She lit a cigarette and smoked nervously. We would have to be careful in any case, she said to me: a battalion of Senegalese was expected at Bangui and would be sent immediately into the Oulé country. It would be much better to settle the whole thing before the arrival of the troops. I was rather taken aback. I did not know that the government took so serious a view of the matter as to move troops which were so much needed elsewhere—and how had she found it out? No doubt by listening to the conversation of those gentlemen on the terrace of the Tchadien, I thought. I promised to give N'Gola the necessary orders immediately; as for her, I was leaving Fort Lamy in a few days' time, and she could go with me. She was put out at this delay. Couldn't she leave for Ogo tomorrow? It would be better not to be seen traveling together; she didn't want to cause me trouble. I remember that, as she said that, she looked at me for the first time with real kindness. 'Very good,' I said to her, 'as you wish.' And indeed I didn't mean to stay long at Fort Lamy. N'Gola would leave at dawn, with the convoy of Portuguese lorries which started every morning for Bangui. After which, we should simply have to wait for his return.

"She was now shivering in the cold air and had drawn the wrap over her bare knees again. It was two in the morning. But I could not bring myself to leave. I went on talking to her about all sorts of things: the forest, the climate, my black people . . . She looked exhausted and was obviously not listening to a word I said. I can't even remember at what moment I caught myself explaining to her all I had done in my district against the tsetse fly. It's odd: ever since I exterminated that damned fly, I've thought of it all the time— you'd say I missed it. After all, it kept me company. In the end she held out her hand to me and accompanied me to the door—dismissed me, in fact. As I went out, as I passed under the triumphal arch of the hotel entrance, I saw, leaning against one of the pillars, a pale panama hat, and by the red glow of a cigar, the face of Orsini. He was standing there in the attitude of a pimp counting the customers, and stared at me with an astonishing expression of cynicism and hatred. I went home, woke up N'Gola and entrusted him with his message, and he went off in the darkness toward his destination with all the suitable impassiveness he so well knew how to display."

~~~~ XXIII ~~~~

"I HEARD NO MORE of Minna for some time. That night I began a violent bout of malaria; I lay shivering under my mosquito-net for two weeks, and when I did manage to open an eye, I usually saw the anxious face of Dr. Terrot.

"At the first step I took on getting up, I stumbled on Schölscher's assistant, comfortably installed on my terrace, reading one of my books. He looked slightly embarrassed and explained to me that Schölscher had tried to see me himself before leaving for the south, but that the doctor had forbidden anyone to disturb me; he had therefore ordered his assistant to ask me certain questions about Morel. For three days he had practically not moved from that chair. I told him with some asperity that it would have been simpler to post a sentry in front of my door. I added that I had told them all I knew, and what was more, they were attaching an absurd importance to the whole damned thing. He listened politely. He kept one hand in his jacket pocket and displayed the meticulous, strait-laced, cavalry-officer elegance that went well with the stick he carried under the arm, the white *seroual* and his shapely chin. I didn't like him. I longed to say disagreeable, unjust things to him, merely to counterbalance all the sweet things he must hear from the lips of women.

"The lieutenant gave my ill-humor a chance to blow over with a patience which only irritated me more, because it clearly proceeded from what he no doubt imagined to be the indulgence due to old-timers whom age and solitude had rendered rather eccentric. He told me that the French Union was passing through difficult times, that terrorism was taking hold in the north, and that it was essential that French Equatorial Africa should give an example of steadiness. The territory was completely denuded of troops: you could travel through it as far as the Belgian Congo without meeting a gendarme. In these circumstances any outbreak of banditry might have incalculable consequences. He had himself a certain sympathy for Morel; unfortunately, the man had not understood that the world of today was no longer capable of concerning itself with elephants. People had other preoccupations. They were no longer interested in anything except their own skins. The lieutenant made a gesture of helplessness. 'We also must take into account the international situation. The United Nations are convinced that the French government has invented Morel in order to cover up the true cause of the disorders, which is to be found in the national aspirations of the African populations. Indeed, the very mention of the elephants is causing tremendous irritation there—they say that the French, instead of facing their problems realistically, are still busying themselves with frivolities.'

"I told him, with biting irony, that his lecture on high politics had been extremely brilliant and that it was amusing to watch eggs giving lessons to the hen, but that I was fully aware of the dangers of Morel and of his mythical beasts, and had nothing to learn from him about them.

"'What you are doubtless also fully aware of,' he said dryly, 'is that the girl, you know, that . . . singer at the Tchadien, has disappeared, and we have every reason to believe she has joined Morel. . . . Schölscher thinks you might be able to give some extremely interesting information on the subject, Monsieur Saint-Denis, and explain to us, in particular, what the girl was doing at your place, at Ogo, ten days ago . . .'

"He explained to me that Minna had been seen leaving one morning in a small lorry, with the American major, ostensibly for a hunting expedition which was to last several days. At first nobody had paid any attention, but the couple had vanished and the lorry had just been found abandoned at the end of a track, in the heart of the Oulé country. . . . He watched me closely, leaning his chin on his stick.

"I raised my eyes. 'Go on.'

"Well, he had to remind me that I had been the last person to see Minna before her departure, if Orsini was to be believed. He appeared to be taking a great interest in the affair, Orsini did—he considered Morel a foreign agent sent into French Equatorial Africa to foment disorders and that Minna served him as informer, picking up bits of information from her . . . customers, and as a go-between. The lieutenant appeared embarrassed. Orsini must have other reasons also for taking an interest in the girl: she was rather pretty—perhaps I too had noticed that detail. I didn't bat an eye. I told him somewhat haughtily that I did not deny having played some part in the business, but that the girl had gone to see Morel simply and solely to persuade him to give himself up, to try to save him. In my opinion our best chance was to give her her head. She would bring him back to us as docile as a sheep. 'Women,' I concluded rather bitterly, 'have at their command certain means of persuasion which the best-organized police forces do not possess.'

"The lieutenant listened politely and indulgently. 'You will no doubt be surprised to learn,' he said, 'that according to the first reports the girl took a regular arsenal with her in the lorry—arms and cases of ammunition—enough to sustain a siege. They've just made use of them to attack and partly burn the premises of Wagemann Company, east of Batanga-Fo. Our troops are busy cleaning up the region and we hope to finish before the rains—with a little luck.' It was therefore perfectly clear that, far from going to Morel in order to persuade him to give himself up, she had gone there to help him hold out, to supply him with arms and ammunition which she must have had ready for a long time—her sudden departure seemed to indicate that he needed them urgently—perhaps a message to this effect had been brought to her by someone . . . The lieutenant pressed his chin upon his stick and gazed at me pensively."

## XXIV

"I WAS NO LONGER listening. I was thinking of my friend Dwala, and of the promise he had made me, or rather of the bargain we had struck. It had happened several years before, and I had since continued faithfully to pay the agreed price—a cow and a goat, every

spring. I remembered his forbidding expression when I had first
spoken to him about it, and how much persuading he had needed,
and how finally I had had to lose my temper and threaten to thrash
him—which was merely a way of bargaining, and he knew it perfectly well, especially as I was dependent on his good will. He was
sitting on a mat in the corner of his hut, a short, naked, shriveled
crosspatch with only the short white hair on his cheeks and chin and
skull visible in the shadow. He told me he had a bellyache and I
had better come back another day and anyhow he didn't know at
all whether he could do that for me; I was a white man and a Christian, I wasn't from his tribe, or from his land, and he hadn't the
necessary power to undertake the business for a nonbeliever in true
spirits. I reminded him of all the services I had done him since we
had known each other, and as for being a Christian and a nonbeliever, I had more faith in him and his spirits than certain young
puppies of his own tribe, and he knew it. He went on saying to me
'maganja ouana,' go away to your own people, but I knew it was
merely to raise the price, and he knew I knew. In the end I began to
yell, promising him that, if he refused, I would have a road driven
through the Oulé country, and right through his village, and he
knew I never would, but that counted in the bargaining all the
same. He groaned, raised his fists, swore to me that he had never
done this for a white man and that it was a thing no one had done
before him, and I knew he was accepting. We agreed on the price,
and he told me he would give me a good place. But I had known
my place for a long time, I had spent months looking for it, compar-
ing, wandering over the hills and through the woods. I needed a
wide view and, at the same time, I did not want to be alone, I must
have other trees about me. In the end I had chosen a beautiful hill
with a view over the great Oulé plain which I loved so much, and
which was full of Africa, with its herds of elephants that were not
in danger of becoming mythical beasts for a long time to come.

"It took us a day and a half to get there, and when we had made
the journey Dwala again began to make difficulties and become suspicious, telling me that it was too far from where he lived—he wasn't
sure if his powers extended so far. He suggested another spot,
nearer his village and belonging to his tribe, and he half closed that

damned eye of his, and I knew he wanted me to buy a piece of land from him, while this one I could have for nothing. I swore at him and told him what I thought of his suggestion, and Dwala looked at me rather reproachfully: 'Why get angry?' he seemed to be asking me, 'I have to try.' I showed him exactly the place I had chosen. He suggested another hill, entirely bare, where I would have more room. But I needed that view, and the morning sun in my eyes, and I didn't want to be alone again, this time I must have some other trees about me. There were some fine cedars there and I pointed out one of them to him, to give him an idea of what I wanted. He shook his head, grumbled, needed more persuasion, and told me that he would try, but that I must ask the missionaries, and especially Father Fargue, to make their visits to his village a little less frequent—they disturbed him, they hadn't a good influence on the spirits, and he wasn't sure to succeed if they came too often. I promised.

"That's what I was thinking about, sitting on my terrace, while the lieutenant talked to me. I knew that Dwala had the power to make of you, in your next life, a tree, and I had seen with my own eyes trees, pointed out to me by N'Gola, which had once been members of his tribe. He knew their names and stories, and he told me: 'That one was eaten by a lion,' or: 'that one was a great Oulé chieftain.' These trees are still there and I can show them to you; you'll see for yourself that there's no doubt about that power of Dwala's. But it was the first time he was doing this for a white man, and he was so worried about possible consequences that on the way back, in a village where he stopped, he got drunk on palm wine, and in spite of this he groaned all night and stared about him in terror, and I knew he often did get drunk, but I think he had really taken great risks with his spirits to oblige me.

"That's what I was thinking about, more and more tranquilly, while the lieutenant continued to talk to me of the absurd and already remote affairs of a species which was practically no longer my own."

# ∼ PART THREE ∼

## ∼ XXV ∼

THEY CAME IN SIGHT at the top of the hill, in the tall grass through which the horses moved forward slowly, their muzzles raised; Morel was leading, with the eternal briefcase attached to his saddle; Idriss came next, in the rustle of bamboos and grass, with his aquiline profile and alert nostrils, with his eyebrowless yellowish eyes, both lively and steady under the white turban, that did not miss the slightest quiver of the savanna, the eyes of a man long used to the jungle and who had seen beasts of every coat cross his path: there were moments when Habib himself laughed uneasily beneath that steady and experienced stare. For three hours now they had been coming down the hills toward the rendezvous, and the captain of the high seas, with his yachting cap over his ear, a dead cigar butt between his lips, and his feet in dirty white shoes stuck high into the Arab stirrups, had some difficulty in keeping in the saddle: he was not altogether in his element on horseback. But he had his orders from Waïtari: he was not to lose sight of that madman Morel.

"He's capable of any folly. He's so convinced the world's public opinion is on his side that he would think nothing of giving himself up to the French in the belief that he'll be not only acquitted but acclaimed, and carried out of court on the shoulders of a triumphant crowd. The moment he's captured and questioned, his eccentricity will become so apparent that he'll lose all value for us. Morel is useful to us only as long as he remains a legend: at this very moment the Arab radio is presenting him to the world as a hero of the

African fight for independence. What I'm saying is that it's essential to stop Morel from getting caught . . . from getting caught alive, that is. I have nothing against inspired idealists, as long as they are useful—but if we are faced with the choice, it is better for him to disappear with his legend at its peak, and go down to posterity as the first white man to give his life for African freedom . . . than to expose himself as a mere crank."

He raised his hand: "Needless to say, I'm not suggesting anything . . ."

Habib nodded approvingly. He had taken good care to banish from his face all trace of mirth. He had a true professional's passion for all manifestations of human nature, and he had acquired a very intimate knowledge of it which most frequently revealed itself in one way. He would throw his head backward, his eyes would become narrow clefts of darkness, his beard would quiver, and he would place one hand on his chest as though to repress the delight which inflated it. But as an arms salesman to any worthy cause willing to pay him, he took good care not to show openly the hilarity caused in him by all the "legitimate aspirations of the people," "liberators," "revolutionary tribunals," and other defenders of elephants of Morel's type: they were his bread and butter. He listened to them dead-pan and he waited till he was alone. And now, as he followed Morel toward the rendezvous through the rustling of the yellow grass in which the horses plunged, neighing uneasily, he allowed his hilarity to break out freely behind the backs of his companions, and shook with silent laughter at the remembrance of that Negro liberator, that commander without troops, standing all alone in his cave in the heart of wilderness—his HQ, as he called it—his military tunic thrown over his shoulders, his powerful hands resting on a map of "operations," conjuring up in his thunderous voice the picture of an African Federation from Suez to the Cape, of which he already saw himself as the uncontested head. That was undoubtedly a dream of greatness and power destined to follow into the dust all the other dreams of human greatness and power, under the eyes of the truly Great and the truly Powerful One.

He had tried to get his young friend De Vries to share the comic side of the business, but De Vries, stretched out on a mat with his eyes full of resentment, tortured by his bowels, never unclenched his teeth except to hurl vehement reproaches at him, making him responsible for the desperate situation in which they were—as if, exclaimed Habib, marveling at the naïveté of youth, as if there were anyone on earth who could be considered responsible for the desperate situation in which he found himself. De Vries listened with exasperation to the flowery language of the Lebanese, whose resistance to every trial he did not possess; exhausted by colic and fever, by the flies and the mosquitoes and the hours on horseback, he really seemed on the point of depriving Habib of his earthly company. In the end Habib had grown worried. He tried to persuade Waïtari that it was in their interest to move to the Sudan: there was talk of a great conference at Bandung, at which all the colonial peoples would be represented, especially those of black Africa, which had been somewhat neglected up to now. It was essential that he withdraw for some time from direct action, in order to present himself before the international tribunals and make his voice heard. After all, they already had something to show. Farms set on fire, an elusive *maquis* defending the natural resources of Africa against colonial exploitation—the moment had come to appear to the world as the true leader of the African revolt. Otherwise, the floor would be left free to N'Krumah of Gold Coast, to Tserape of Nigeria, and to others, who were already claiming the leadership of the awakening continent.

Waïtari was all the more easily convinced, since he had long been of the same opinion. He stood there in the cave with his fists clenched, pressed against a map, his high-precision watch glittering on his wrist, with his French army bush-shirt, and the French military tunic thrown over his shoulders, very much the "leader of the African Army of Independence at his HQ": he remembered a similar photograph of Tito during the war. Sometimes he felt crushed by loneliness. He practically never left the cave—one of the four or five "bases" which he had managed to organize secretly during his last official tours as a member of the French Parliament, with a view to the world conflict he had at that time believed to be imminent. But his timing had been off. The conflict had not taken place. He had found himself alone, without troops, cut off from both the French

and the Africans; and three of the five "bases" at which he had accumulated arms were pillaged by the villagers or discovered by the
authorities. He had to take refuge in Cairo where he had vegetated
miserably on a meager pittance from the Arab League, until the
news of the "campaign for the protection of the African fauna" had
reached him. He had immediately seized the chance which thus offered itself. Here was an instrument of propaganda such as he had
never dreamed of: it was easy to show that elephants were a living
symbol of African power and freedom. But he had come up against
an almost incredible wall of incomprehension. In spite of all the
efforts of the Arab radio, world public opinion continued to believe
in Morel and his elephants.

The world took them seriously and literally.

People quite genuinely and sincerely believed that somewhere in
the depths of Africa there was a Frenchman who was standing up
alone for the splendors of nature.

Leaning heavily on the map, listening to the arguments of Habib,
whose astuteness annoyed him, he felt more lonely and more remote
from his goal than ever.

The cave smelled of earth and decay, it was airless in spite of the
two openings through which the light fell with a dazzling and painful brightness upon their faces in the gray gloom. Against the wall
there lay an air mattress, a pile of clothes, an oil lamp and a loaded
Sten gun. Farther in, there was a crate of automatic rifles, but most
of the ammunition was of a different caliber from the weapons.

"In Cairo they are ready to listen to you as never before . . . The
press is full of stories on African revolt. But if you stay here any
longer without giving your version of the real issue at stake, the
attractive legend of Morel and his elephants will become too well
anchored in popular imagination for you to be able to give it any
other meaning . . ."

Waïtari nodded bitterly.

"I see your point. I must say it would be rather upsetting if the
French got out of it with a few fine new laws on the protection of
African fauna . . . They're quite capable of that. Indeed I admit
that if I didn't know Morel as I do, I'd believe he was an agent of
the Deuxième Bureau sent out to lay a nice smoke screen over the

African revolt . . . The number of people in France and elsewhere who are suddenly taking the fate of elephants to heart is very suspect, to say the least . . ."

Habib lowered his eyes, to hide his amusement. That Negro Napoleon with the military tunic flung over his shoulders, standing proudly in front of his wretched map of "operations" in a remote cave in the Oulé country, without weapons, without support, without partisans, with nothing behind him but wilderness, with his orator's voice which only the French masses could appreciate at its true value, with his need for greatness, his dream of History with a capital *H*, and his clenched fists, suggesting so well the power to which he aspired—that was a spectacle of human pretension at which his heart rejoiced.

Even now, as he made his way down the hills in the wake of Idriss, he shook his head in wonder at the idea of the lonely Negro waiting tensely in the recesses of a dark cave for the world to take notice of him. Probably they would all end up in prison, but that merely awakened in him memories that were by no means disagreeable; he had spent some of his best moments in prison—sexually speaking, that is. He enjoyed a perfect physical and moral balance, and sometimes he even felt an astonishing certitude of immortality pervading his body, coursing in his blood; he would then press his hand to his chest and free himself of this excess of plenitude by throwing his head back in one of his silent laughs, mouth open, eyes shut, till his whole face became a mask of oriental mirth, the motives of which nobody could ever understand, but which was a simple manifestation of his love of life, of his certainty of being at home on this earth.

Now he followed his instructions, keeping an eye on Morel, true to his promise to make sure that the eccentric did not fall alive into the hands of the police, for it was more than likely that the rendezvous was a carefully laid trap. But Habib had no intention of doing any harm to the man who was so defending bravely the splendors of nature. On the contrary, he was enjoying himself thoroughly in his company. He merely wanted to be on the spot at the right moment, the inevitable moment when another believer in man's greatness would learn his lesson. That's what the idealists were for: to

have their noses rubbed into the earthly truth. Fundamentally he
thought of himself as a teacher, a moralist—he liked to see the futility and insignificance of human pretensions properly understood
and humbly acknowledged. If need be, he was ready to give events
a push—just the little push needed sometimes for the lesson to
sink in.

His eye once more caught Idriss' steady, attentive glance and he
prudently replied with a friendly wink. The old man was undoubtedly one of the best trackers in French Equatorial Africa, and what
he did not know of the splendors of nature was not worth knowing.
Prudence was advisable. For a long time he had been thought dead,
and the news that Idriss had emerged, so to speak, from the beyond,
and was now at the side of Morel, had caused furious discussions and
cries of disbelief on the terrace of the Tchadien, among other places.
Orsini himself, Orsini the old-timer, had sworn that the thing was
impossible, out of the question, unthinkable; Idriss was dead; he
had known him in his time and had seen him age and wilt away,
harassed by some deep-seated sickness—"they're all riddled with
pox, you know"—and in the end go back to the forest like all lonely
aging beasts at the approach of death.

"And suppose," someone had said, "that the sickness you've just
mentioned was . . . a kind of remorse, a feeling of guilt awakened
in the great tracker by the sight of the emptying earth, barren of
the huge herds with which he was so familiar?"

Faced by such naïveté, such utter ignorance of the natives, Orsini's voice found some of its most sarcastic accents. Yes—he expected something like that would turn up. This was the way to build
legends in Africa. That was all we needed: the ghost of Idriss coming back to earth to defend the African herds against the ever-
improving weapons of the white hunters. He emitted a short laugh
that was half a cry, half a hymn of hate, paused for a moment and
then began again, with the implacable calm of a man who has never
missed his target. What struck him most in the nincompoops who
had only just arrived in Africa was both their impudent self-assurance and their complete ignorance of the native soul—the words
"native soul" in Orsini's mouth caused in those present an utter
stupefaction and an almost passionate curiosity to see what Orsini

THE ROOTS OF HEAVEN [133]

might have to say about it. Any man, he went on, who had been
studying the native soul daily for some . . . let us say, forty years,
could tell them that, to the blacks, the elephants were nothing but
meat on the hoof, grub, something to fill your stomach with, if you
could, when you could, as much as you could, period. The idea that
a professional tracker like Idriss could suddenly start suffering from
a sort of poetic remorse, soulfulness, regret at the memory of the
animals he had tracked down—such an idea could only come to
birth in decadent brains and exquisite sensitivities freshly arrived
from Europe—which were the beginning of all our troubles in
Africa and elsewhere, be it said in passing. To Idriss, as to all the
other blacks he had known—and he had known a certain number
of them, all alike—an elephant was first and foremost five tons of
meat, plus the ivory into the bargain, if they could steal it or
smuggle it away. The idea that Idriss might, so to speak, come back
to haunt the scenes of his crime, outraged by the disappearance of
the big elephant herds which were so close to his soul—such an
idiotic idea only revealed the kind of men they were sending us
nowadays in Africa, and the reasons for our decline—and he was
referring particularly to a certain officer of the Camel Corps whose
job was to look after the security of the country.

"But after all," said someone, much less from conviction than in
order to drive Orsini into his last ditch, where he always emitted his
finest cries, and sang his most perfect hymns of spite and resentment,
adding new sounds to the African night, "but after all, if Idriss was
really an exceptional man, why couldn't we attribute exceptional
feelings to him? Then there'd be nothing extraordinary in his appearing at Morel's side to defend what he probably had most at heart.
Besides, some Oulé villagers swear they saw him at the Frenchman's side, with his white headdress and his blue burnous, and the
elders recognized him, talked to him, and they were even saying
that he hadn't changed, that he still had the same ageless face with
its mark of Arab blood—in a word, that it was Idriss all right, they
were quite definite on the point."

But Orsini took care not to react as expected—he never did—he
had too much sense of drama. All right, he said, he would not insist. Idriss was back from the shadows. But since the point was

obviously to give this affair the proportions of a legend, why not say clearly that the specter of Idriss had returned from the beyond to spread the sacred fire of African independence, to brandish the torch of holy war—and that he was sent to Morel's assistance by Mahomet himself, which would naturally confer upon the scoundrel an irresistible glamour, a supernatural character, to the great advantage of the political agitators whom he was serving—and this whole legend of the return of Idriss had, precisely, no other purpose. As for him, d'Orsini d'Acquaviva, an old African hand—a type of man apparently no longer needed, be it said in passing—who knew the elephants and the Negroes—five hundred to his credit and he was only counting the finest specimens—he was going to bed—he was sure they would excuse him—he made bold to wish the legend-lovers good night—warning them, however, charitably, that they would have a rude awakening, and sooner than they thought. He threw a note down on the table—there were people from whom he would accept nothing, not even a drink—and merged with the shadows, and the African night suddenly lost one of its strangest voices.

But it was no phantom that was now following Morel down the hills through the bamboo and grass; it was the man whom the Huette brothers themselves acknowledged as "the greatest tracker of all time," and in their mouths, that meant thousands of elephants killed in forty years of hunting. With his blue burnous, his white turban high over the forehead, his face free from wrinkles except the two harsh furrows running from the nostrils to the corner of the lips, and his yellowish eyes, Idriss followed the Frenchman wherever he went and helped him in his movements through the bush— which explained the ease with which he escaped pursuit. His gaze kept watch over the jungle, and Habib felt himself included in that attention. And yet, for once, his conscience was almost clear. He had no intention of killing Morel to prevent him from giving himself up or falling into a trap, and revealing to the whole world his naïveté and his lack of political purpose. He cared nothing for Waïtari's plans and political ambitions. He was merely a free-roving buccaneer whom the hazards of a difficult voyage had thrown into these agitated waters. He had come into touch with Waïtari when the latter was quietly gathering arms for his future *maquis*—and he had supplied him with weapons—at a price. He was no more concerned with "people's right to self-determination" than with this Morel's boundless love of elephants. He sold arms, that was all, and to any side which cared to buy them. On the point of being arrested in Fort Lamy, after the explosion of the lorry carrying grenades to the tribes, he joined Morel simply because he had no other way out at that time. He had had a stretch of bad luck. De Vries' sickness was the worst of it: the Lebanese was seriously worried—he felt that his young protégé was, so to speak, about to slip through his fingers, thus depriving him of one of his greatest sources of earthly pleasure. A doctor was needed, and hospital care, and he was not sure that his friend would hold out as far as Khartoum, even if carried on a stretcher—and this would not make the journey any easier. If there was one thing that Habib could not understand, it was that a man could fall ill, lack physical or moral health, in fact, that a man could have difficulties with life. He clucked incredulously, then straightened his dirty yachting cap and dug his heels into his pony so as not to fall too far behind his humanitarian and presumptuous friend, who thought man was big enough to take the protection of nature into his own hands.

## XXVI

IT WAS NOON, and the light was so strong that everything it touched —the grass, the bush, the ant-hills, the rocks, the bamboos and, further off, right at the bottom of the slope, a herd of motionless elephants drowsing in the heat of the day—lost its color and retained no more than a gray or black silhouette in the trembling heat.

Morel reined in his horse, and for a moment they paused on top of the hill in the midst of that world of hot ash. From the east, the weak puffs of wind carried a smell of burning bush—fire was always present around you in Africa, living the royal yet nomadic life of a solar horde, raiding the bush and the villages at every dry season, and it seemed comic, in the face of its sudden eruptions, that man should ever have dared to boast of having invented it.

A furrow ran across the hillside, hissed through the grass like a rip through fabric: wart hogs. A white marabou came in sight above them and wheeled slowly as if to signal their presence; then gradually, on all sides, every living thing that became aware of the presence of man took to flight—and Morel knew that the panic extended each time for many miles, emptying a whole corner of Africa of all that had learned to know man for what he was. For a moment, as usual, Morel felt a violent disappointment at that flight; then he smiled ironically at his old dream of being admitted, accepted, his dream of birds that would not fly away at his approach, of gazelles that would continue to browse calmly as he passed, and herds of elephants quietly allowing him to come near enough to touch them. Habib, just behind him, said in that deep voice made deeper still by a restrained mirth:

"Yes, you're one of us, and every beast knows it: try hard as you may, there's no other company for you, brother. Rub, brush, spit, wash; you'll always smell of man: a mighty smell, Your Human Highness, and nothing you can do about it!"

Morel was almost getting to like this scoundrel, for his frankness and cynicism had a ring of deep conviction which seemed to have its roots in a sort of professional intimacy with life, in some absolute experience, so that when, sometimes, the man threw his head back, narrowed his eyes, and let out a roar of laughter to high heaven, it seemed to convey a final knowledge which nothing could contradict or undo. He gave him a glance that was almost friendly, and moved forward again through the high grass, so thick now that the horses raised their heads to protect their nostrils and stepped high, sniffing uneasily at some wild beast or its lair.

They skirted the bamboo forest and came out upon the bed of a dried-up marsh: the rains were late and already the waterholes and springs of the Oulé hills offered nothing more than a cracked crust of rapidly hardening mud.

On their left, about three hundred meters ahead, they saw the

motionless herd of elephants like granite idols abandoned there by
the adepts of some vanished cult. Only two or three males, with
gigantic tusks, were wandering slowly over the cracked bed in
stubborn search of water, sometimes raising their trunks and sniffing
the air for some trace of humidity which would announce the coming of the rains. Morel knew that the marsh was but a stage in the
seasonal migration of the herds to Lake Mamoun, on their circuit,
usual at this time of year, from Mamoun to Southern Birao, the Yata,
the Nguessi and the Wagaga, where they were normally sure to find
water even during the worst drought. During the drought of 1947
the whole of this region had been proclaimed a game sanctuary by
the government: and for several weeks at that time there was to be
seen the greatest concentration of herds the human eye had ever
perceived—the newspapers of the time had called it "a vision of Para-
dise Lost"—and one had only to wait quietly at the edge of the forbidden zone to be sure of a choice trophy. Lovers of a nice shot
had flocked there from all over the world, certain of getting their
money's worth: over fifty safaris in one month, a fine congregation
of impotents, alcoholics and those females whose sexuality is so
pleasantly tickled by bullfights and who reach their climax with a
finger on the trigger and an eye fixed on the horn of a rhino, or the
tusk of a fine male—with a professional hunter at their side, just in
case. Instinctively Morel clenched his fists, anger rising to his nostrils, pinching them and making them turn white; and yet, this time,
there was nothing to fear and no risk of safaris: the Ornando incident had had a salutary effect and the lovers of virility looked elsewhere for satisfaction.

But it was easy to see, from the state of the marsh and the nervousness of the herd, that the drought was going to be severe and perhaps disastrous: rising out of the bed of dry mud, the naked burnt
reeds showed, by the extra eighteen inches of their still green stalks,
the normal depth of the water now vanished. For the last few days
he had noticed that the elephants were no longer sending their
scouts on in advance, to check the ways through or the state of the
fields they meant to visit. Instead they seemed to be moving in
compact, bewildered bands. Yet there was still water waiting for
them at several points along their route, where they would be able

to give themselves over to those aquatic displays he had so often watched: rolling in the mud and squirting one another, or lying in the water for hours, writhing their trunks luxuriously and heaving deep sighs of delight.

He took cigarette paper and tobacco from his pocket and began to roll a cigarette while he observed the herd with an affectionate smile. This was what he stood for: a world where there would be room enough even for such a mass of clumsy and cumbersome freedom. A margin of humanity, of tolerance, where some of life's beauty could take refuge. His eyes narrowed a little, and an ironic, bitter smile came to his lips. I know you all, he thought. Today you say that elephants are archaic and cumbersome, that they interfere with roads and telegraph poles, and tomorrow you'll begin to say that human rights too are obsolete and cumbersome, that they interfere with progress, and the temptation will be so great to let them fall by the road and not to burden ourselves with that extra load. And in the end man himself will become in your eyes a clumsy luxury, an archaic survival from the past, and you'll dispense with him too, and the only thing left will be total efficiency and universal slavery and man himself will disappear under the weight of his material achievement. He had learned that much behind the barbed wire of the forced labor camp: it was our education, a lesson he was not prepared to forget.

He smoked his cigarette, motionless in his saddle and watching the herd with a smile, as if he had no other care. There were about sixty animals there and farther on, on a hillside beyond the yellow bamboo forest, he could see the first silhouettes of another herd. Peer Qvist estimated the number of elephants in French Equatorial Africa and the Cameroons at less than sixty thousand, and the approximate total for the African continent at a hundred and fifty thousand—and there were few of these that died of old age or that had not been, or were not destined to be, a hunter's target three, four or five times. The protection of fields and harvests against the herds was an absurd excuse, since a few firecrackers would be enough to scare the animals away. As for the permit system, there was not a game warden who did not agree that, to every permit granted, fifteen or twenty animals were killed illegally.

The fight to the death between men frustrated by a more and more enslaved or acquiescent existence, and the last and greatest living image of liberty that still existed on earth, was being played out continuously day by day in the African forest.

But whatever the difficulties he was facing, he refused to compromise: it was essential that man should shoulder on his difficult road a supplementary burden, encumber himself with the ancient giants. The first results of his campaign were encouraging: it was being discussed everywhere, the press had hold of it; he had become a popular figure, he had stirred public opinion, and he felt confident that gradually everyone was beginning to see what was at stake.

He went on smoking quietly, watching his dazed and harassed herd. He was sure now of reaching his goal, but patience was needed, and it was difficult to be patient. The number of animals who lived in cruel suffering, sometimes for years, with bullets in their bodies, wounds growing deeper and deeper, gangrenous and swarming with ticks and flies, could not be estimated, but one had only to talk to the Huette brothers, or to Rémy, or to Vasselard, to know what they thought about it. Three days ago he had himself killed an elephant which had had its left eye torn out by a bullet and showed a wound that laid bare the skull: he had found it on the Yalé river bed staggering in circles, trying to relieve its sufferings by plastering wet mud on its forehead. He knew that the last of the great hunters devoted a great deal of their time to tracking down wounded animals to finish them off—and this not simply because they were becoming dangerous. He was sure these men felt a secret friendship for him and would, if need be, come to his assistance and help him to carry on.

The passion of the collectors of African "curios" and souvenirs was a complete and disgusting mystery to him. A few days before, he had attacked and razed a tannery belonging to one of French Equatorial Africa's "experts" in the treatment of skins; the man's name was Herr Wagemann and his tannery was situated a few miles north of Gola. There was one thing that distinguished his enterprise from that of every trader, Indian, Portuguese and others, in lion

skins, leopard skins and zebra skins, whom Morel tracked down
with equal tenacity: Herr Wagemann had had an idea which even
the manufacturers of Belsen lamp shades of human skin might have
envied him.

It was indeed quite simple, but you had to think of it. You cut
off the legs of elephants about eight inches above the knee.

Out of these stumps, suitably worked, cleaned out and tanned,
you made waste-paper baskets, vases, or even champagne buckets
and umbrella stands.

The tribes of the district had nicknamed Morel Ubaba-Giva,
which meant "father of the elephants," and he would not have asked
to be known by a finer name. He must go on standing up for the
African elephants, and it must be left to the people, especially to
the French, to grasp the full meaning of his campaign. He trusted
them to do that—it was something that concerned them directly: it
was part of their tradition.

He remained there a little while longer, then stubbed out his
cigarette against his saddle, and suddenly, to the surprise of Habib,
who shook his head and clicked his tongue at the sight of the wild
hope shining in the eyes of that crazy Frenchman, he began to
hum a tune and, picking up the reins, spurred his horse eastward
through the rushes onto the dried earth which leaped under the
hooves. When he reached the top of the hill on the other side he
turned once more to smile at the elephants with such an expression
of pleasure that the Lebanese scratched his ear and swore, with a
grudging admiration, at the magnificent madness that dwelt in the
man and which had all the air, fallacious of course, of human in-
vincibility; then followed the die-hard who—to use once more an
expression he had used before De Vries without further comment—
"still believed in it all."

They arrived at the village two hours later and moved forward
among the huts. A few children ran to meet them, but the inhabitants avoided looking at them with a settled determination not
to get mixed up in what they evidently regarded as a quarrel of
white men among themselves. This put Morel in a bad temper, and
he was hurt in spite of everything by their indifference and lack of

understanding; he would have liked the Africans on his side. The villages generally emptied at the approach of his group, and all he found in them was some old women, and alarmed mothers clinging to their children. He was unable to understand the reasons for this hostility or fear. After all, he always paid for his supplies and, after the first few excesses, he had imposed on his men, especially on Korotoro and his friends, an iron discipline. Was he not defending the very soul of Africa, its future and its integrity? And yet he could not help thinking once more of the answer given him by the old black schoolteacher at Fort Archambault who had pushed away his petition with a gesture of contempt:

"Your elephants are the idea of a well-fed European. To us elephants are meat on the hoof: when you give us enough cows and oxen, we'll think again . . ."

## ～ XXVII ～

THEY HAD WITH THEM four ponies and a load of three crates of arms and ammunition and one of whisky, and Johnny Forsythe had no idea what would happen when they reached the last cartridge and the last bottle. The great unknown, as they say. He scratched his cheek and marveled at this astonishing absence of future and from time to time glanced at the girl who was following him through an incandescent landscape in which the very shadows seemed to be fleeing from pursuit. He did not know what was waiting for them at the end, but no hopes were barred. He grinned and shook his head. Perhaps he would end like so many others, begging heaven for help no one, to his best knowledge, had ever yet received—at any rate, not in the form of quality whisky. The future was a shadowy zone, which might perfectly well be hiding a French prison, a bullet, or the pained, so pained, face of the American consul at Brazzaville, who had told him after one of his drunken fights: "You must understand that each of us here is responsible for our country's prestige."

What that distinguished person would say now awoke the greatest curiosity in Johnny Forsythe. The consul had undoubtedly been the finest example of a mammal walking on its hind legs that he had ever had the good fortune to encounter. "Man: a mammal walking on its hind legs"—this was the admirable definition he had found one day as he turned over the pages of a French encyclopedia which lay about in the house of his friend, the black teacher at Abéché. The French had the gift of reducing all things to their true proportions. He grinned again and shook his head.

"You ought to stop drinking for a while, Major Forsythe, you can't go on like this."

"I'll stop drinking soon enough. As soon as I'm among the elephants. What makes me get drunk is the company of men. I don't like it."

Since the start of their journey he had absorbed a quantity of alcohol enough to kill a man of lesser stamina—or perhaps simply less intoxicated. Minna had had to drive the jeep during the last stage because he was incapable of steering. They were to leave the jeep at Niamey and wait for the guide Morel had sent them, whose name was Youssef—a boy who had twice come to make contact with them at Ogo. But when the jeep drew up at the agreed-upon place no one was there. During this part of the journey they had taken no precautions: they were hardly more than twenty miles from the road between Fort Archambault and Fort Lamy, but nobody suspected them yet, nobody knew what they were transporting, and their presence there, while noteworthy, was not suspicious.

Night had fallen suddenly, like a heavy veil, as they drew near the spot where Youssef was to meet them.

She stopped the jeep, left Forsythe sprawled on the seat, and got down. A thousand sounds and voices were beginning to be heard and among them the sonorous pulsation of insects was the only familiar and reassuring note. At night Africa recovered all its mystery and strangeness, its innumerable discordant accents, its cries, appeals and laughs; and sometimes the earth trembled at the passing of a herd. The lonely track stretched ahead in the glare of the headlights. The air, still touched by a trace of desert coolness, was puls-

ing with a quick, rhythmic beat that seemed to provide the sky itself
with a voice and a breath.

Suddenly, as though irritated by the noise of insects, by that choir
of the minuscule, a roar which no distance ever seemed to diminish
arose, and it seemed to her that the very clouds around the moon
began to flee more swiftly into the distance. Her heart leaped; she
swallowed her fear convulsively and listened for a while, trembling
and yet happy and gazing at the sky, to the only voice that could
rise into the starry vastness without ridicule. The roar appeared to
her to be coming nearer, and she recoiled, retreated from the night,
returned, sat down on the running board, and picked up her bag.
Cut off from the darkness by the headlights, uneasy, almost scared,
she found courage in familiar reflexes: she crossed her legs, pulled
her skirt down over her knees, took out her lipstick and a mirror
and made up her lips with a defiant air. And suddenly she began to
laugh: every roar from the lion was answered by a deep snore from
Forsythe in the jeep.

Then there was silence, and the insects returned; she took her
shawl, put it round her shoulders and sat there shivering, happy, far
from everything, lulled by the blue and phosphorescent waves of the
night. The sky was so bright that the millions of white butterflies
fluttering over the road seemed to join the Milky Way, and so bring
it within reach. She wondered if Morel would let her remain with
him, if he would let her do all she could to defend the elephants.
No doubt he would ask her for her reasons, and she would not be
able to give them. She had acted instinctively, first because she had
a great love for animals and then—even though she herself could not
see the connection very clearly—because she had often felt lonely
and abandoned, and also because of her parents killed in the ruins
of Berlin, because of her "uncle," of the war, of poverty, of her
executed lover, of all the men whose weight she had borne. . . .

"Oh, anyhow, I didn't know why I did it," she told Schölscher
later, with a shrug, picking a cigarette from the pack of *Gauloises*
he had brought her and leaning toward the lighter he was holding
out. "They've all asked me why, and they've never believed me
when I told them that I too wanted to do something for the protec-

tion of nature . . . And besides, after all, there had to be someone from Berlin with him—*es war doch aber ganz natürlich dass ein
Mensch aus Berlin bei ihm würde, nicht?* . . ."

She looked Schölscher in the eyes, to see if he understood, as she
sat there quietly with her glass of brandy and her cigarette, and
there was an almost bewildering simplicity about her: all the newspaper publicity seemed to have had little effect on her. She told
Schölscher that they had waited on the track for what seemed to
her hours, and that she had begun to doze off, sitting there between
the two glaring headlights, when a hand touched her shoulder and
she saw a pale figure in front of her: Youssef. She returned to the
steering wheel and the boy got in behind. They drove till dawn,
then abandoned the jeep in a thicket at the end of the track, where
Youssef had left the horses. They slept there, then started again,
this time on horseback, in the direction of the hills, and at the end
of the afternoon there came into sight in the elephant grass an extremely stout form installed upon a pony. Under a white pith helmet
a familiar face and a red beard caught the sunshine as in a net.

Father Fargue did not seem particularly pleased to see them: he
was grumpy and monosyllabic and asked them without any curiosity what they were doing in this forsaken region . . . He had
evidently just avoided saying "God-forsaken," and he shook his
head at the thought of the blasphemy. Forsythe gave him a few
confused explanations, the gist of which was that they were on their
way to Duparc's plantation, having been invited to spend a week
with him.

"Well, you've come too late," growled the missionary. "He burned
the plantation three days ago . . ."

"He? Who?"

"Morel, who do you think? They gave Duparc a good thrashing
and set fire to the house. . . . It seems the poor man made the
mistake of killing some twenty elephants this year—animals that
were trampling his harvest."

"So that's still going on?" Forsythe asked with a laugh.

Fargue gave him a furious glance. "Is it still going on? I should
think so . . ." He muttered something which he cleverly smothered

in his beard. "I've just done four days on horseback over the hills to try and lay my hands on that son-of-a—, but the blacks are in such a funk when you mention his name, that you can't get a word out of them. . . . I'm sorry, mademoiselle, for your ruined weekend. You'd better come and spend the night at Ada, there's a White Fathers' mission there. It's on your way, and they've got fresh vegetables and wild strawberries."

It was not on their way, but they could not admit this. That evening, after one or two bottles of red wine, Fargue gave free rein to his bitterness.

"I should like to explain to that fellow," he thundered, banging the table with his fist as if he were trying to convert it too, "I should like to explain to that chicken-hearted fellow that it's not good enough to stop halfway, that the elephants are all very nice but there is, after all, something more, there's something bigger, something more important to us and more beautiful—and he doesn't seem to have any suspicion of it! For after all, let me put it to you, what's become of God in all this?"

He banged the table so hard that it was difficult to remember that it was not a human being, difficult to believe that it had not done him any harm.

"Let that table alone," Forsythe advised him. "It will never understand."

"Oh, I don't know," said the Franciscan gloomily; "when I bang, I bang. After all, there's something to be disgusted at, you must admit. When a man has that in him, such a love, I mean, he should let it grow, not let it miscarry. He shouldn't stop at the elephants, big as they are!" He spat so hard that a cloud of dust flew up from the ground. "And I'll tell you something else: sometimes I feel as though he's attacking me personally . . ."

"How do you make that out?"

Fargue was silent for a moment, then opened his arms wide and shouted, almost plaintively: "How do I know? Perhaps he's right? Perhaps I'm not doing enough? Perhaps the lepers and the people with sleeping sickness aren't the whole story? Perhaps I ought to go among the elephants as well?"

Johnny Forsythe was beginning to enjoy himself. "Fargue, how long is it since you had a wink of sleep?"

"Eight nights," shouted the missionary, giving the table a bang with his fist that would certainly have done more for religion aimed at some infidel. "I have elephants swimming before my eyes from nightfall to dawn! You won't believe me, but some of them even make signs to me with their trunks."

"What sort of signs?"

"How do I know what sort of signs? They say, 'Come, come, come,' with their trunks, that's all!" He imitated the gesture with his curved forefinger, taking on as he did so a particularly satanic, roguish expression, with one eye half-closed. "If only I knew where those elephants came from!" He groaned despairingly. "As if one could know! Anyone may be letting them loose on me, and when I say anyone, I mean anyone!"

"Oh," said Forsythe, "as long as it's only elephants, as long as it's not some pretty Foulbé girls . . ."

"Ah, you think so, do you?" said Fargue. "Well, with Foulbé girls you at least know where they come from, and when you see them suddenly in front of you at night waving their breasts and bottoms . . ."

He broke off. Forsythe was listening to him with obvious interest. Fargue reddened, and banged the table again. "But before I embark on anything," he shouted, "I want to know where those elephants come from. I want to know what's behind all this, before I help him. If this is all that fellow's got left, if elephants are the only thing he believes in, because they've not enough faith in them, not enough heart, if it's just another trick to act as if God didn't exist and something else had to be put in His place—well then, by . . ."

He clenched his teeth and began banging the table so hard that suddenly, out of the depths of the night, a noise of African drums arose somewhere from the depth of the forest.

Fargue seemed rather surprised. "What's that?"

"Nothing," said Forsythe calmly. "They're answering you. Without knowing it you have summoned them to the Holy War with your tomtom, and tomorrow we shall all be exterminated."

Fargue gave them a dark look, stood up and went out rather unsteadily, after wishing them good night. Forsythe laughed, stretched, then stood up in turn without a trace of drunkenness. If there was one thing he could still do, it was hold his liquor.

"Good night, Father," he shouted into the darkness. "I'll be very sorry when you go to Heaven with the last elephants, and I never see you again!"

At dawn they took to the track again, and after two hours on horseback along a path through head-high yellow grass springing out of gray rocks, a path among euphorbias that looked like men in ambush, they saw a blue figure on the hilltop, waiting for them. They were in a place called Geiger Hills in honor of all the make-shift prospectors who had come and wandered about there with geiger counters in their hands. No uranium had been found, but the dreamers of the deep remained convinced that somewhere be-neath that pile of rocks there lay fabulous veins which they would one day discover.

As they reached the hilltop, they saw Habib among the first huts of the village. On horseback, with the dirty yachting cap over his beaming face and unkempt black beard, he looked like a sailor who had come ashore on a terrific spree—and with him was Morel, wear-ing a scorched felt hat, a khaki bush-shirt and shorts, and smiling, with the old briefcase attached to his saddle. She recognized him immediately. He came toward her quickly with hand outstretched and with a light of pleasure in his dark eyes to which it was hard not to respond.

"How did it go?"

"Oh, it went all right."

Forsythe turned toward the hills and made them a sweeping, somewhat theatrical gesture of ironical greeting—he had been drink-ing since dawn: "And now we say goodbye to the world of progress and moral achievement; we say goodbye to the blessed fathers of the atom, of brain washing, of peoples' democracy and massive re-taliation; we say goodbye to the dust of two hundred scientists and spiritual leaders . . . It's time to say goodbye to all that, to change species, to come over to the elephants and live in the wilds among honest animals . . ."

Morel was not listening to him. He had taken Minna by the

shoulders and was looking at her with those dark, gentle and now humorous eyes of his.

"Thank you. What you have done for us is very brave, and very useful. Two of our hiding places for arms have been found, we've practically no ammunition left, and . . ."

He smiled at her.

"And besides, the intention matters even more than the rest. But it's not going to be easy."

"I know."

"It will take quite a while yet . . ." He laughed. "The protection of species isn't exactly what the politicians are interested in right now. But the people are. What we're trying to say has brought out an extraordinary response, and it seems all the newspapers are taking it seriously. So sooner or later we'll reach our goal. The new conference on the protection of African fauna meets two weeks from now in the Congo, and we'll make it our business to attract the world's attention to its labors in a . . . striking way. But it's hard going and it requires a lot of patience."

"I'm in no hurry."

"You can go back to Lamy whenever you wish. Idriss will take care of that. They'll ask you questions, but they won't do anything to you. They won't dare. They know quite well we have public opinion on our side . . ."

He was completely serious now, as if he really believed what he was saying. If there was irony in him, a desperate or sardonic humor, he had buried it deep, like an ultimate weapon kept in reserve.

She smiled at the memory of it, and, looking at Schölscher as if in answer to a silent question, she said, "Sometimes he seemed desperately serious and at other times there was a great gaiety in his eyes . . ."

And Schölscher remembered the voice of some journalist on the terrace of the Tchadien, a voice remarkable for its ill-concealed bitterness: "You must understand that for anarchists like Morel, to attack society was no longer enough. They had to attack our whole species, humanity itself . . . That was the real purpose of his campaign: he hated us."

And now again this girl, who spoke of these first moments of their meeting in the Oulé hills with a pleasure and animation that conveyed better than her words what she had felt. She broke off for an instant, brought the cigarette to her lips and said with a rather mysterious and at the same time triumphant smile: "He knew that I understood him perhaps better than anybody else . . . I, *ein Mädchen aus Berlin.*"

At the end of the village there was a hut larger than the others, with steps of beaten earth and some outbuildings. At the door stood a Negro in shorts and a khaki shirt, wearing a felt hat and carrying a submachine gun. He grinned at them. She was slightly alarmed, and Morel must have noticed; he said, "He's never killed anybody. We're good friends."

Inside the hut in the windowless half-light she saw a fat man with graying hair, his fly half unbuttoned, fanning himself nervously with a Japanese fan, evidently not so much to fight off the heat or the flies as to calm the terror that could be read in his olive-colored face and imploring eyes. When he saw Morel come in, he set his fan moving at almost a machine-like speed, stood, and, as he did up two buttons out of respect for the young lady, in whom he recognized without the slightest surprise the tart from the Tchadien—he was evidently long past any surprise—said:

"Monsieur Morel, you cannot treat us like this. For four days now you have held me prisoner in my own house, and I must ask you to leave. I don't want to have trouble with the authorities. I can't allow my depot to become the headquarters of a terrorist organization. The black man who is guarding my door is one of the most notorious bandits in French Equatorial Africa and has behaved toward me in a manner which I cannot tolerate. I have a good reputation and during the war I contributed both financially and morally to the Allied cause. I don't want it to be said that I have been helping terrorists, that I have been encouraging sedition and foreign agents, especially as I am an Arab and we are always being accused of everything in Africa. I must ask you to leave my house at once."

Morel picked up the jug of water from the table and drank. "If you were with the Allies during the war, you must be with us today, my friend," he said. "It's the same thing. It's the same fight. You must help us to do something for the protection of species, that's what you and I were defending during the war, isn't it?"

The fan fluttered frenziedly in the stubby hand. "Monsieur Morel, I don't wish to contradict you, I don't understand your intentions, I haven't any idea what your real purpose is, but you're insulting me greatly if you think me simple enough to believe that all this is really about elephants. I tell you, Monsieur Morel, I'm not a fool, far from it, and I have three sons who at this very moment are receiving the best possible education, in Paris."

"And what is it all about, then?"

"I don't want to know, Monsieur Morel, what it's about, I'm not interested. I don't meddle in politics."

"Of course you don't meddle in politics," said Morel. "But all the same we've found over fifty tons of ivory under your roof, ready for packing, sawn up into little pieces in the usual way, so they can be put into pots and sent across the frontier and loaded on board ship near Zanzibar."

"That ivory was delivered to me by the natives. It was gathered legally from animals that had fallen in the forest. I have men who search the forest to find the dead animals. It doesn't come from hunting. Besides, Monsieur Morel, I must beg you . . ."

"Shut up, you scum," shouted Morel. "Seventy miles from here the bush has been literally ravaged by fire on a front of over twenty-five miles—I'm sure you have nothing to do with that. A few nights ago I couldn't sleep, because, in the Yala river bed, animals covered with burns were making a noise like the damned before they managed to die. If you examine the river bed, as I did, you'll see that it's been ploughed up by elephants rolling in it to soothe their wounds . . . But that's not all . . ."

"Monsieur Morel, I beg you once more not to insult me . . . You have no right . . ."

". . . that's not all. No one has ever seen your porters return to the villages from which they were recruited . . ."

The fan fluttered jerkily.

"I see you have understood. It appears that a man under forty

fetches 1,500 riyals in the oases—in the market at Litz, to be precise—and that a well set-up lad of fifteen with his anus intact will
fetch 4,000 . . . I have it all in my briefcase: official figures supplied by the United Nations Anti-Slavery Commission . . . No
wonder your chaps never come back. You shove them on board the
*sambouks* along with the ivory. The ones that are Moslems are promised a pilgrimage to Mecca . . . This gives me the full right to
call you a son-of-a-bitch, doesn't it?"

At that point she first saw in the half light, upright against the
mud wall, a white figure with his aba edged in gold and one hand
resting on a hip, and when the man began to speak in a jerky, guttural voice, she saw also his almost-yellow face with two lines of
black beard running from the chin to the lips. What he said must
have been insulting, for his companion looked embarrassed and the
fan fluttered rapidly in his hand.

"What has *he* got to say?" asked Morel.

"What he said doesn't matter, Monsieur Morel."

"What did he say, since he's a man with courage?"

"He consigned you to the dogs."

Morel smiled. "Nice of him. I'm sure that, coming from him, it's a
recommendation that will come in useful one day. What's his name?"

"Isr Eddine."

"Tell him that every time I see a mangy dog I will say I have come
with an introduction from Isr Eddine, elder of their tribe."

"Monsieur Morel," said the trafficker, with a pained expression
as he fanned himself, "we have a saying that words fly out easily but
come back slowly . . ."

Morel gave them a glance that was almost friendly.

"I've long known that man has honor. You will pay off your
porters and send them home. Meanwhile, you will tell your wife to
get us a meal. And another thing: you will tell this gentleman of
the sands that if I once more hear a boy yelling in his hut at night,
I shall do him such an injury to his dignity, in the place where he
carries it, that he'll return home lightened of a great burden. The
women of the village have been talking to me. Every night you can
hear distinctly that he is busy breaking some mother's heart."

"Dried and salted meat inflames the blood," said the trafficker sententiously. He got up and went into the yard, where an opulent Negress in an indigo calico dress was bending over a stone hearth. His companion followed him with that noble gait which is conferred by draperies floating above sandals and a fine head carried with all the dignity one could demand.

They were alone. It was the first time she had been alone with him since their meeting on the terrace of the Tchadien. But she told Schölscher that she had thought about him so often that in the end—after all, she had hardly seen him—she had completely transformed him. To begin with, he had nothing of the heroic stature with which she had invested him in her memory, and his face had none of the extraordinary nobility with which she had clothed it. It was a simple, square face, rather ordinary except for the eyes, which were very fine, very French—at least as far as she could remember from the soldiers she had met in Berlin. As soon as the two men had gone out, he had turned to her with a laugh.

"As you see, they dress me up in all sorts of ways . . . Some attribute deep political aims to me: it seems I'm a French agent trying to create confusion and cover up the revolt seething in Africa. But to others I'm a Communist. And to others, again, I'm paid by Cairo to stoke up the fires of nationalism . . ." He shrugged. "And yet the reality is so much simpler. Luckily, after all, there's something called popular feeling. Contrary to what people believe, it's no legend—it isn't just something that is good for making songs about . . . Our job is to touch popular feeling, and that's what we're busy doing. We've got to hold out for a few weeks longer, until the rainy season if possible, when they won't be able to do anything about us. We need a little more publicity, to reach the largest possible number of people who will understand what we're trying to say. The protection of nature concerns them directly . . ."

That was why he stood so confidently upon the hills, as she so often saw him at dawn, with bare chest, a rifle in his hand, and a slightly mocking smile on his lips, mounting his vigilant guard over the threatened giants.

## ⚊⚊ XXVIII ⚊⚊

AT THIS POINT of the twentieth century the task was more than ever urgent and difficult, and in those who had almost lost hope, who had long been awaiting some encouraging sign, Morel's campaign was awakening a tremendous sympathy. In the phrase used on the terrace of the Tchadien by a journalist who was trying to explain "the man who went over to the elephants," when one has said that "not all Germans are like that, not all Russians are like that, not all Arabs are like that, not all nationalists are like that, not all Communists are like that, not all Chinese are like that, not all men are like that," one has said all there is to be said about mankind. It's no use, after that, yelling, defiantly and proudly, "Johann Sebastian Bach! Einstein! Schweitzer!" to the skies; the skies have long known everything about it.

It suddenly seemed as though all the disappointed idealists who could afford an airplane ticket were trying to get to French Equatorial Africa in order to rally to the man who had become the spokesman of a hope that refused to die, and at Duala, Brazzaville, Bangui and Fort Lamy the controls had to be multiplied in order to detect among the tourists the "volunteers" who had come to join up with Morel.

Among them there were naturally cranks of the classic type, impatient to set sail for the moon, but there was also at least one really significant addition which created a tremendous sensation and helped to attract the eyes of the world to the Morel campaign.

On March 15 the American newspapers had announced in enormous headlines that Professor Ostrach, one of the most eminent scientists of our time, and one of the fathers of the hydrogen bomb, had disappeared without trace. Ostrach not only knew the details of the H-bomb, but was fully familiar with the potentialities of the new basalt bomb, on which the greatest minds of the century in the U.S.S.R. as well as in America were working day and night with the typical devotion of scientists to a sacred cause—an especially decisive and ultimate weapon since it destroyed not only the fauna but also the flora of the earth, and might even, after some additional study and testing, be capable of totally disintegrating all the liquid on the surface of the globe from the great oceans to the smallest of springs.

It was recalled that during the Spanish Civil War Ostrach had given money to help the orphans of the Republicans and that he had several times tried to persuade his fellow-scientists to reduce the power of the basalt bomb so as to conserve some elementary form of life on earth, in particular plankton, and, generally speaking, the marine environment in which the human adventure had once begun and in which—who knows?—it might perhaps one day begin again under better conditions. An investigating committee pronounced him, however, free of all suspicion as a security risk; as for his efforts to reduce the destructive power of the bomb, they were described by members of the commission and by an indulgent press as examples of "an idealism and a naïveté frequently found in great scientists." This then was the man of whose disappearance the whole world learned one fine morning.

In due course it was discovered that he had flown to Europe, under an assumed name. For a fortnight there was no news of him, and it was generally thought that he had joined the team of Soviet scientists whose work on the basalt bomb was progressing rapidly. But at the beginning of May the native chief in one of the Baga villages to the northeast of Laï informed the district administrator of the presence, in the resthouse at kilometer 40, of a white stranger who seemed to be waiting for someone—and Morel had just been reported in the vicinity. The stranger, in spite of his protests, was transferred under escort to Fort Lamy, and there he readily admitted that he was of course Professor Ostrach.

The sensation was so great that the number of journalists already present at Fort Lamy trebled in twenty-four hours. Ostrach was a young man with a long neck, a huge Adam's apple, short graying hair and ironical eyes, who pretended to be very much surprised by the storm he had aroused. After a courteous interrogation by the police, in the course of which nothing could be got out of him except that he had not sought to communicate any atomic secrets to the elephants, he held a press conference on the terrace of the Tchadien. No, he had not been trying to join Morel. All he had wanted to do was to take a few photographs of elephants at liberty; he had a profound love of nature, and hunting with the camera was one of his favorite sports. So he was trying to photograph elephants? Yes, of course, he did not see what harm there could be in that. Didn't he know that the African Communist party had adopted the word *"komoun"*—elephant—as a watchword for the whole of Africa, and as a symbol of the party's struggle against the West? No, he did not know that. Otherwise he would certainly not have tried to photograph elephants. He was completely unaware that they were subversive. In his own country they were a political symbol of irreproachable patriotism. Henceforth he would have no truck with them. He wished to state this unambiguously and categorically. He wiped the sweat from his forehead. "Jesus Christ!" he said. "Make it quite clear that I'm not politically conscious and that I just wanted to photograph these elephants without any evil intent and perhaps without realizing the consequences it might have. I haven't been a man in the public eye all my life, and I'm not accustomed to weigh carefully everything I do or say. Jesus Christ, now that I think of it, I remember that I took my children to the Bronx Zoo two or three times, to show them the elephants, and that I forgot to tell that to the Senate Committee when they were checking up on me. But as I've just told you, I haven't a very highly developed political sense, and I didn't realize that, in view of my work on nuclear problems, it wasn't the thing to do. I am profoundly sorry. But after all, it wasn't I that put those elephants in the Zoo, and I do think the government ought not to leave them there if there is something subversive about them. Jesus Christ, I can't think of *everything*, can I?"

"Professor Ostrach," asked a journalist, "are you a Catholic?"

"No, I'm a Jew."

"Then why do you invoke the name of Our Lord all the time?"

Ostrach looked alarmed. "What, is He mixed up in it too? I mean to say, along with the elephants—has He become subversive? It's just a phrase, you know, and you can perfectly well know somebody's name without thinking like him . . ."

The little man seemed very alarmed, but there was a touch of the ham in him; he was moved by a violent, almost desperate humor which, in truth, was itself not far from being a form of subversion.

So he had not been trying to go over to the elephants like Morel, under the spell of some sort of neurotic disgust at humanity? No, certainly not—it was absurd to think that humanity disgusted him to that extent. His smile became even thinner than before. No, humanity did not disgust him to that extent. Otherwise would he have devoted the best years of his life to providing it first with a hydrogen bomb and then with a basalt bomb?

One of the journalists gave a short, desperate laugh, and once more Schölscher saw in the American scientist's eyes a gleam of that ancient, imperishable human gaiety, like a guarantee of survival.

Did he consider that the elephants were the only species threatened with extinction?

"Excuse me," said Ostrach, "but I can't discuss atomic secrets that may have something to do with national defense."

"Is it true that the cumulative effect of atomic experiments and the radiation they generate may in the end cause grave suffering to the whole of mankind and that the consequences may be tragic for future generations?"

Once again he felt unable to discuss questions relating to national defense. And, anyway, scientists must be left to continue their work calmly in the quiet and serenity of their laboratories.

"Yes, but what work?" shouted someone at the other end of the terrace, in a voice full of hatred. "What work exactly? Isn't it going to end in the destruction of our whole species?"

"No hope is forbidden to us," said Ostrach with a radiant smile. "Obstacles must not be placed in the way of pure and scientific research, whatever the consequences may be. The practical results do not matter. What counts is the free and disinterested manifestation of the genius of man."

"In other words, if a scientist blew up the whole earth or poisoned it to the core, this would be a free and disinterested manifestation of the genius of man?"

He refused to join his questioner in taking such a pessimistic view. Scientific research must remain completely free from any consideration of possible practical consequences.

He remained several days longer at Fort Lamy, taking numerous outings in the district, followed every time by a regular caravan of journalists who had no doubt about his intentions—neither indeed had Police Commissioner Kotowski, who saw to it that the scientist was provided with an escort that never left him for a moment. Thus every morning for eight days a motorized caravan left Fort Lamy, following the scornful, mocking little man at the wheel of his station wagon, who chose the roughest tracks in the district and every now and then turned about, waving friendly greetings to the journalists and policemen who followed him, cursing. If an emissary from Morel was waiting for him somewhere along his route, no one ever knew.

But no doubt Ostrach's aim was not so much to throw off the journalists and join the man who had come to the defense of nature, as to give the campaign its full news impact and its full meaning, a task in which he succeeded admirably; and he then took the return plane, with friendly greetings to the exhausted representatives of the press who hardly dared believe their luck as a small, sad and yet sardonic face gazed at them with irony through one of the port windows.

Yes, Schölscher knew that Morel was no longer alone, that everywhere eccentrics—or simply men of good will and understanding—were attempting to come to his side. At Fort Lamy, at Bangui, the post offices were flooded with letters and telegrams addressed to him, and from every corner of the globe, and in every language, the Governor received letters, the beauty of which was equaled only by that of the violent language he himself growled into his beard. In all those who followed current history closely and with growing misgivings and who had had enough of being made ridiculous by the political, military, scientific and other aberrations committed in their name, Morel's campaign seemed to strike a sensitive string and to correspond to some secret rage, fear, shame or expectation which, as they read about his exploits, found at least a momentary satisfaction.

To a large part of the public, Morel had become a hero. But it would have been difficult to find anyone who admired him as much as that girl who had for some weeks shared his adventure and so didn't even have the excuse of distance and imagination which is almost always indispensable to the birth of legends. During the whole of the trial, whenever Morel's name was mentioned, she raised her head, came to life, and listened with a smile, forgetting the public, the judge and the police sitting beside her. When a witness called Duparc told how he had been dragged out of bed by Morel and a group of black men, thrashed and tied to a tree while his property was set on fire, she had suddenly sat up straight on her bench with her eyes sparkling in anger, and had cried out in her extremely German accent and in that voice which was almost vulgar when she raised it too much:

"And why don't you tell the whole truth, Monsieur Duparc, and if you're ashamed to tell it, well, I can do it, and so can Monsieur Peer Qvist and Monsieur Forsythe, and others too who are here . . ."

Duparc seemed deeply moved and turned toward her.

"I didn't ask to give evidence," he said tersely, "but I was going to tell all the truth anyway, and I don't need a German to remind me . . ."

She had heard talk of "the Duparc business" as soon as she had joined the "*maquis*"—Habib had alluded to it several times in front of her, with a jolly and silent laugh, and a wink of complicity, as if to show that his good friend life had taken a hand in it, and in the end she had asked Morel, with some apprehension: "What is this Duparc incident that makes him laugh so much?"

He was sitting close to her, with his bare chest shining in the light of the oil lamp, and on his shoulders she could see the scars of the lash from the camp in Germany; she caressed them with her fingertips and then kept her hand resting on them for a long while, the second German hand to touch his shoulders.

"There's nothing really tragic about it," he said slowly and quietly, "and I suppose Habib is right to laugh at my anger and shock . . . At the camp in Germany, I had a comrade who used the name Robert in the Resistance and was the most courageous man I've ever met; ginger-haired, sturdy, with powerful fists and steady eyes, he was one of those who never gave up hope. He was the irreducible core of our block; all the political prisoners grouped instinctively around him. Always cheerful, with the cheerfulness of a man who has gone deep down into things and come back reassured. When our courage got low, when we were ready to despair and to give up, he always found something to put new life into us. One day, for instance, early on, he came into the block walking like a man with a girl on his arm. We were crumpled up in our corners, dirty, disgusted, sick, despairing, vanquished, in fact, and those who had some strength left were groaning, complaining and blaspheming aloud. Robert walked right across the hut, still offering his arm to an imaginary girl, while we watched him in some astonishment; then he made a polite gesture as if to invite her to sit down on his bed. Even in the midst of the general depression, some signs of interest showed themselves. The men propped themselves up on their elbows and stared in stupefaction at Robert courting his invisible girl. Now he stroked her chin, now he kissed her hand, now he whispered something in her ear and every now and then he bowed to her with the courtesy of a bear. At one moment, noticing Janin, who had his trousers down and was scratching himself, he got up and threw a blanket over him.

" 'What?' squeaked Janin. 'What's got into you? Haven't I a right to scratch?'

" 'Behave yourself, damn you,' thundered Robert. 'There's a lady present.'

" 'What?'

" 'You mad, or something?'

" 'What lady?'

" 'Of course, it's easier not to see her,' said Robert between his teeth. 'I'm not surprised . . . There are some of you who pretend not to see her, don't you? So you can stay dirty . . .'

"Nobody said a word. Perhaps he had gone mad, but he still had strong fists, in front of which even the common criminals kept a respectful silence. He returned to his imaginary lady and kissed her hand tenderly. Then he turned to the gaping prisoners.

" 'Let's make it quite clear: as of today, there's going to be a change. To begin with, you'll stop whining. You'll try and behave in front of her as if you were men. I say "as if"—it's the only thing that matters. You'll make, for her sake, one hell of an effort to keep clean and to behave—otherwise you'll have me to reckon with. She won't be able to stand this stinking atmosphere for a day—besides, we're Frenchmen, it's for us to be gallant and polite with a lady present. And the first man who shows disrespect—who breaks wind, for instance, in her presence—will get a thrashing . . .'

"We stared at him, gaping, in silence. Then some of us began to understand. There were a few hoarse laughs but we all felt confusedly that, at the low ebb we had reached, if there wasn't some convention of dignity left to sustain us, if we didn't cling to some fiction, to some myth, there would be nothing left but to let ourselves go, submit to anything, including the Nazis, to give in and to betray. From that moment a quite extraordinary thing happened: the morale of Block K rose suddenly by several points. There were unheard-of efforts at cleanliness. One day Chatel, who was certainly at the end of his tether, on the point of giving in, threw himself on one of the convicts—probably to boost his own courage—on the pretext that he had 'failed to treat Mademoiselle with proper respect.' The explanation that followed before the stupefied camp authorities was our delight for several days. Every morning two of us unfolded a blanket and held it up in a corner 'while Mademoiselle dressed,' in order to protect her from indecent glances. Rotstein, the pianist, although he was the most exhausted of us, spent the twenty minutes' break at noon gathering flowers for her. The intellectuals in the group made witticisms and speeches in order to shine in front of her, and everyone called upon what manhood was left in him to show himself unbeaten.

"Of course, the camp commander was soon informed of it. That very day, during break, he went over to Robert and with one of those smooth blue-cheeked smiles of his, said, 'Robert, I'm told you have brought a woman into Block K.'

" 'You can search the hut, can't you?'

"The Nazi sighed and shook his head. 'I understand these things, Robert,' he said gently. 'I understand them very well. I was born to understand them. It's my job. That's how I rose so high in the party. I understand them, and I don't like them. I can even say that I hate them. They are what made me a National Socialist. I don't believe,

Robert, in the omnipotence of the human spirit. I don't believe in the
noble conventions or in the myth of dignity. I don't believe in the
primacy of the spiritual. That kind of Jewish idealism is what I find
most intolerable. I give you till tomorrow to get rid of that woman
from Block K, Robert. What's more . . .'

"His eyes smiled behind his eyeglass.

" 'I know all about idealists, Robert, and about humanists. Ever
since we came into power, I have specialized in idealists and humanists. I've got spiritual values just where I want them. Don't forget that, essentially, we are, like the Communists, a materialistic
revolution. Therefore . . . tomorrow morning I shall come to Block
K with two soldiers. You will hand over to me the invisible woman
who does so much for your morale, and I shall explain to your comrades that she will be taken to the nearest military brothel to satisfy
not the spiritual but the *physical* needs of our soldiers . . .'

"That evening consternation reigned in Block K. A considerable
number of its inmates were ready to give in and hand the woman
over—the realists, the reasonable ones, the smart ones, the prudent
ones—the ones who were adaptable, who had their feet firmly
planted on the ground—but they knew that nobody would ask their
opinion, that the question would be put to Robert. And that he
would not give in. One had only to look at him: he was jubilant. He
sat there thoroughly happy, with sparkling eyes, and it wasn't even
worth while trying: he would not give in. For if we had no longer
enough strength or faith to believe in our own inventions, in our
myth, in all those noble stories we'd told ourselves in our books and
in our schools, he at least was refusing to give up, and observed us
with those small, stubborn, mocking eyes of his, prisoner to a power
far more formidable than that of Nazi Germany. And he was obviously delighted at the idea that the thing depended entirely on him,
that the S.S. were unable to take away from him by force that invisible creation of his mind, that it rested with him alone to consent
to hand it over or to recognize that it did not exist. We gazed at him
with mute supplication. In a certain sense, if he consented to give
in, if he set an example of submission, everything would become
easier, much easier, for if we were able at least to rid ourselves of
our convention of dignity, then no hope would be forbidden to us.

But one had only to see his grinning face to realize that he wouldn't fall in, that he was not going to swallow the bait. I think, that evening, the common criminals in Block K must have thought we had really gone mad. Those of them who understood gave us cynical grins and amused, indulgent glances of men of sense, men full of experience, hard-boiled realists who had learned to adapt themselves and live on good terms with life, glances like Habib's . . .

" 'What are we going to do?'

" 'Listen, suppose we let her go tomorrow and then bring her back in the evening?'

" 'She wouldn't come back,' said Rotstein softly.

"Robert said nothing. He was listening with interest.

" 'What I hate is that they plan to throw her into a brothel . . .'

"Emile, the little Communist railwayman from Bellevue, who had followed all this with a profoundly disapproving expression, at last exploded, 'But you're absolutely mad, Robert, absolutely mad! You can't mean to cling to a fiction, a joke, a myth! You'll be put in solitary confinement or tortured, or be shot, and for what? for a crazy thing like that! Our job here is to survive, get out alive and tell other people what it's been like, to make this sort of crime impossible in the future and to build a new world—not cling to myths, to idiotic conventions, to fairy tales!'

"But Robert was quietly enjoying himself, and Emile buried himself in his corner, turning his back to us to make it clear that he wasn't going to have any part of it. Next morning, Robert made us all stand to attention. The camp commander arrived with his two S.S. men and examined us through his eyeglass. His smile looked even bluer and more twisted than usual, and even his eyeglass seemed amused.

" 'Well, Monsieur Robert,' he said. 'How about that virtuous young lady?'

" 'She will stay here,' said Robert.

"The officer grew slightly pale. His eyeglass began to quiver. He knew that he had put himself in an awkward spot. His two S.S. men merely bore witness to his impotence. He had placed himself at Robert's mercy. He was dependent on Robert's pleasure. There

was no force, there were no soldiers, there were no weapons capable
of making that fiction leave the block. Nothing could happen to it
without our consent. He had just broken his teeth against man's
loyalty to his own convention, and whether it was true or false
mattered little provided our human face caught the light of its dignity . . . He paused for a bare second—so as not to accentuate and
prolong his defeat.

" Right,' he said. 'I see. In that case, follow me . . .'

"Before going out, Robert smiled at us. 'Take good care of her,
fellows,' he said gently.

"We thought we would never see him again. But he was returned to us a month later, somewhat thinner, with his nose rather
flattened and with some of his nails missing, but with no trace of
defeat in his eyes. He came into the block one morning, about thirty-
five pounds less of him, lost somewhere in the mysteries of solitary
confinement. His face was the color of clay, but he had not changed.

" 'A nice little cell,' he told us. 'Three and a half feet by five, so
not a hope of lying down—there were moments when I felt like
banging my head against the wall to try and get out into the fresh
air. Talk about claustrophobia! . . . So in the end I had an idea.
When I couldn't stand it any longer, I would close my eyes and
think of the herds of elephants at liberty, running freely across
Africa, hundreds and hundreds of magnificent animals that nothing
can resist—no cement wall, no barbed wire, nothing: they rush forward over the great open spaces and smash everything in their way,
and nothing can stop them. That's liberty, I tell you! So when you
begin to suffer from claustrophobia, or the barbed wire fences, the
reinforced concrete, the absolute materialism, just imagine this:
herds of elephants charging across the wide open spaces of Africa.
Follow them with your eyes closed, keep their image inside you,
and you'll see, you'll feel better and happier, and stronger . . .'

"And it worked. We did feel better, and we found a strange secret
exaltation in living with this image of all-powerful liberty before
our eyes. And we came in the end to look at the S.S. men with
smiles, as we thought how, from one moment to the next, this magnificent charge would pass over them and there'd be nothing left

. . . We could almost feel the earth tremble at the approach of that power coming to our rescue from the very heart of nature and which nothing could stop . . ."

Morel fell silent for a moment and appeared to be listening, as though he were still waiting to hear that reassuring tremor in the African night.

"After the Liberation I lost sight of Robert. One day . . ."

There was a trace of bitterness in his voice and a shadow came suddenly over his face, and the voice itself grew deeper and growled with suppressed anger, and he began to look as the public imagined him to be—the man who had "run amok."

"There's a law which allows you to kill as many elephants as you like when they're trampling down your fields and threatening the crops. It's a wonderful excuse for the good shots among us. All you have to prove is that an elephant has crossed your plantation and has trampled a field of squash, and there you are, free to decimate a herd, to indulge in reprisals, with the government's blessing. There isn't an administrator who doesn't know what excesses this 'law' has led to for years. There isn't a game warden who hasn't demanded stricter control over these punitive expeditions. And so I took the matter in hand a bit. I wanted to show them that the elephants had at last found a helping hand, and to draw attention to man's crime on the eve of the conference about the protection of the African fauna, which was to be held in the Congo. Some time ago I heard that a certain Duparc, owner of the only cotton plantation within a radius of a hundred and fifty miles, had killed nearly twenty elephants in the course of these 'punitive' roundups. It appeared that his plantation lay across the seasonal migration route of the herds which go up north in the dry season and always follow more or less the same course—it passes by the waterholes which their scouts identify for them beforehand. Duparc complained that the herds on their way north seemed to have chosen his plantation as their rendezvous, as if they were certain of safety there. They would meet there by the hundreds and hold long discussions before starting on their way. To cut a long story short, I had Duparc seized when he was in bed one moonlight night—he slept with his doors and windows open—and when I arrived Habib and Waïtari had already set fire to his house. Still in pajamas, he was tied to an acacia tree and was watching his property burn. I went up to him to read him the sentence, as I do usually, in the name of the world committee for the defense of elephants. We saw each other face to face for the first time: I recognized Robert . . ."

Morel fell silent for a good while, and she did not know whether he was remembering something or trying to forget. She now understood Habib's joy and the tremendous good-natured laugh which silently shook his chest when he alluded to this incident; and Schölscher too remembered the Lebanese—how, standing between two policemen in the dock and leaning forward, he had given, with obvious delight, his evidence on this happy reunion of two idealists, as if inviting the public and the judges to share in its truly earthly taste.

"Never have I seen two men stare at each other with such bewilderment. They had both of them been in the fight against the Nazis and they had made friends in a German concentration camp. Their faces were superbly lit by the flames leaping from one window to another, and their expressions were really worth watching. Morel was the first to recover speech. 'You!' he stuttered. 'You! If there's any man who ought to be on our side, defending the elephants, it's you! And you're the first to kill them just because they trample your field!' Duparc stared at him dully, and his jaw dropped. 'They were ruining my plantation,' he shouted. 'They cost me three million francs last year; and they destroy my natives' gardens regularly. After all, I've the right to defend myself! And if you want to try and make me believe that elephants are the real issue . . . take a good look at your lieutenants!'

"That," laughed Habib, "was meant for me. Then he started struggling so hard against the cord binding him that the acacia trembled as if it were being torn up by the roots. Probably he wanted to run to his house with buckets of water, unless perhaps it was to throw himself into the flames—a fine end, my word, for an idealist. Morel too waved his hand in the direction of his colleague's house —a gesture of impotence. Then he bent his head. 'You had no right to hunt elephants,' he repeated. 'Not you. Not you. Untie him . . .' Then he moved away in defeat."

Morel had told her the story calmly, in an even voice, like someone who is used to it, and then added: "Well, men forget easily. But
it proves nothing. On the whole, people are beginning to understand. Any fellow who's known war, fear, who thinks of his children
and of the hydrogen tests, and of political oppression, is beginning
to understand that the protection of nature concerns him directly. . ."

She could see his shoulders and the deep white scars on them,
and she stroked them with her fingertips. A lizard ran over the mud
wall in the light of the oil lamp, and he suddenly smiled and pointed
at the little creature.

"Anyway, there's a forestry inspector at Laï who summed the
whole thing up very well when I went to see him with my petition.
He told me that for years he'd been making report after report to
get more effective protection for the African fauna . . . he's a black
man himself, which perhaps makes him better able to understand.
Anyhow, he told me: 'At the point we've reached, with all the things
we've already destroyed or are about to destroy, we need all the
company we can find . . . man needs friendship.'"

She repeated his words with a kind of triumphal solemnity, as if
they had an almost historical importance, then looked the officer in
the eye and said, with suppressed violence: "And people have
tried to represent him as a misanthrope full of hate, detesting people, when he only wanted to defend us, to protect all the living and
all the hunted . . ."

No one knew the desert better than Schölscher, who had spent so
many nights alone there on the starlit dunes, and no one understood better than he did that need for protection which sometimes
grips men's hearts and drives them to give a dog the affection they
dream so desperately of receiving themselves. And certainly this
deep feeling of helplessness had never been more agonizing than
now. The ironical and at the same time angry cry which had suddenly arisen from the depths of Africa was listened to everywhere
with the deepest sympathy, and that was enough to explain why
Morel seemed informed in advance of every effort made by the
authorities to get hold of him. Schölscher remembered an expression of barely disguised satisfaction which he had caught even in

the Governor's eyes when he had come to report to him the arrest of all the "terrorists" with the exception of their almost mythical leader.

"So our friend has slipped through our fingers once more? Everybody's there except him? It looks as if he had friends in high places . . ."

"Yes, the papers say it often. Personally, I think, if Morel remains impossible to catch, it's because he's no longer there . . ."

"Meaning?"

"That he's fallen victim of nationalists who were using him. A bullet in the back in some thicket."

"I don't believe a word of it," said the Governor.

He looked hard at the officer across his desk, with a damp, dead cigarette butt stuck in his beard, and with his flat eyes and that inveterate smoker's cough. He was a pretty typical product of the Republic, a liberal, skeptical, disillusioned man, and yet deeply attached to those old principles which the French still inscribe upon their flags—"*Liberté, Egalité, Fraternité*"—and which are as outmoded and out of place in the modern world as the elephants themselves.

"You're a bit too much in a hurry to bury him, my friend. Perhaps you think we shall be rid of him that way, but you're wrong. If Morel has got himself killed by the nationalists, then he's really going to become troublesome. The legend of a man who isn't any longer there to speak himself can be made to say absolutely anything . . ."

"That, I think, is the reason why we shan't see him again alive . . ."

The Governor stared at him almost with spite.

"I don't know which religious order you are thinking of joining, Schölscher, but I think I can guess . . . You don't seem to be overflowing with trust and admiration for human nature. For my part, I'm convinced that our friend is still on his feet and will still cause us plenty of trouble . . ."

This was said hopefully and almost with satisfaction.

Such was also the opinion of the journalists, who were flooding their papers with highly colored cables, quoting "reliable" witnesses who had recognized Morel in disguise in ten different places

at once. Peer Qvist himself, after his capture, sitting in front of a
thermos of steaming tea and with a fat cigar in his mouth, thoroughly at ease and ironical before the audience of officers which
had crowded into the C.O.'s office at Laï, where he had been
brought under heavy escort, had given his deep voice an indulgent,
almost kindly tone as he remarked, "You are wrong, gentlemen, if
you think you're rid of him. He's an obstinate chap who knows
what he wants; he'll still pose you plenty of problems, believe me."

Forsythe had been no less confident. As he lowered the volume
on the gramophone which someone had lent him, continuing to beat
time with his foot, he dismissed with a shrug any idea that something might have happened to Morel. "I don't know where he is.
But I'm sure of one thing: he's all right. And as long as the necessary measures aren't taken for the protection of nature, he'll go on
fighting and making his voice heard."

But there was one ominous note that confirmed Schölscher in his
misgivings: from Cairo, the Arab radio announced that Morel had
been killed by the French "colonialists" in a skirmish among the
Oulé hills. Schölscher had gone to see Waïtari several times in his
room in the military hospital to which he had been transferred. The
former deputy for Sionville was in excellent health, but the instructions from Paris were imperative: he was to be treated with
every possible consideration. Waïtari received him each time with
the cold courtesy appropriate between civilized opponents.

"I've already told you all I know. I parted from Morel about a
week before what you call his disappearance. There's an American
journalist who followed him, it appears, to the end: you'd better ask
him. But since you seem to want to know my personal impression,
I can let you have it: Morel will not be seen again alive."

"You seem to be more than convinced, you seem . . . informed."

"The colonialists can't allow a Frenchman to take part in the
struggle against them for African independence. Everyone admits
that Morel was a character, an eccentric even, but his sympathy for
our cause was equally certain. The elephants, to him, were merely
a symbol of African freedom . . . You can do what you like, you'll
never manage to obscure this obvious truth. That's what he meant,
in that vocabulary of his—which was perhaps absurd, but sincere—

by 'defending the splendors of nature . . .' He meant liberty."

Somewhere, thought Schölscher, in some remote thicket, the corpse of a man was probably rotting away so that his legend might be useful to a cause, an ideology. He looked at the African who stood before him in his gray flannel suit: one of us, he thought suddenly.

"There seems to have been a violent quarrel between you . . ."

"There were differences. We weren't always in agreement about methods . . . about the means. You had the same conflicts in the French *maquis* under the Occupation, and they occurred among the North African fellahin . . . but he was on our side."

"Even after what happened at Lake Kuru? I went there after you'd left, you know. I saw . . ."

"I've already told you, Morel was an eccentric. That in no way diminished the sincerity of his attachment to the cause of African independence, but it didn't make relations with him any easier. We collided several times, and quite violently. But I can assure you there was no difference between us when our freedom was concerned . . ."

And Habib, walking handcuffed between two soldiers to face all the demands for his extradition that were now beginning to pour in —one of them for trafficking in drugs—but still as solid as ever, as sure of his time-honored complicity with life, which would once more get him out of the mess somehow or other, saying good-humoredly, "I can't help it, I've always been a philanthropist. For the legitimate aspirations of the peoples, arms and explosives were necessary, and for the legitimate aspirations of the human soul, drugs were necessary. Always in the front rank of the benefactors of humanity, you see."

And here, now, was this girl repeating through her tears, "I tell you, his was the greatest love on earth, but at the trial they called him a misanthrope, someone who loathes mankind."

"Did he ever explain to you exactly how he got the idea of his campaign for the protection of species?"

Yes, of course he had explained it to her. After the arrival of the American troops, he had left the prison camp rather bewildered and even a bit discouraged—he had confessed this to her with a slightly embarrassed shrug, as if he wanted to excuse himself for having felt discouraged even for a moment. He hadn't known very clearly what to do, how to begin—at what point to attack the job, how to set about it, to prevent the thing from ever happening again: he was in pretty poor shape and the task sometimes seemed to him crushing. He wandered about Germany like a vagabond, sharing the life of millions of displaced persons and refugees who were straying along the roads. One evening, in some German town, he noticed a little girl on the pavement. She had no coat and was crying. The passers-by gave the little girl disapproving glances: it was a shame to let a child out in the streets without a coat in such cold weather.

"Don't cry. Can't you see you're upsetting everybody?"

The girl stopped crying and examined him attentively. She was obviously trying to decide what sort of person she was dealing with.

"You don't need a dog, mister?"

The puppy was a white one, sitting dejectedly in a puddle, and it too seemed to have no coat.

"We can't keep it. Mummie's got to go to work, we haven't any money. Before the war she didn't go to work, and we even had a car."

The dog had one black ear. Vaguely a fox terrier, and God knew what besides. A dog can be useful, he thought gravely. It can guard the house, guard the orchard, sleep at your feet by the large fireplace in the living room after a hard day's work . . . It was not very convincing. It can keep you warm by sleeping huddled against you, wag its tail when you come home and shove its muzzle into your hand. In fact, it can keep you company. He took the puppy by its scruff, lifted it and placed its wet behind in the hollow of his hand.

"Is it a boy?"

"You can see for yourself it's a girl."

He gave the child a disapproving glance. This detail made the thing impossible. In the life he was leading a bitch might easily become an encumbrance. She would certainly have a litter every six months. It was always like that after a war. Nature tried to recoup in one direction what she had lost in another. No, decidedly, a bitch would not do.

"Right, I'll take her," he heard himself saying. "As for you, run

along home. You can tell your mother this is no time to let you go
out without a coat."

"It isn't her fault. She's out at work. She can't look after me."

"Get along!"

The child hugged the dog, then ran off crying. Morel felt profoundly depressed. He ought not to have yielded to the temptation.
He felt the puppy shivering in his hand. He put it into the pocket
of his duffel coat and kept his hand on it—a cold damp ball which
gradually grew warm and ceased to shiver. That was how he acquired company. They traveled the roads together, meeting other
men and other dogs—people from the Baltic states, Poles, Czechs,
Germans and Ukrainians, a whole lost humanity wandering in search
of a roof, of a bit of bread, of some corner where they might at last
lay their heads. He looked at them all attentively and asked himself
what on earth he could do for them. The puppy was in his pocket
and he could feel its affectionate muzzle in his hand. But to help
and to protect, he needed a far bigger pocket and a far more powerful hand than his. It did not seem to him enough to work for the
refugees or to go into politics, to struggle against poverty and oppression—that wasn't enough; he would have to go further, as far
as he could, explain what it was all about, what was at the bottom
of it all; but he did not know how to begin.

He spent days sitting by the roadside, with the puppy beside him,
wondering where to begin. He would really have to raise some re-
sounding and angry protest, a call to help that would touch human
beings in the most distant parts of the world. He would have to get
straight down to essentials, not disperse his efforts, really touch the
heart of the matter. He remained sitting on a bench, stroking the
animal and thinking, as he sucked a stalk of grass.

One morning the bitch had gone off for a run in the fields, and
that evening she had not come back. Not the next morning either.
He never saw her again. He wandered all over looking for her, questioning people, but it was not a time when people were interested in
lost dogs. Finally, someone advised him to go to the pound. He
went. The man led him in. It was a place about fifty yards by ten,
surrounded with barbed wire. Inside it were about a hundred dogs,
mostly mongrels, the kind one saw on every road of Europe or Asia,

animals with no pedigree . . . They gazed at him intensely, hopefully, all except the most discouraged ones, who seemed to know
their fate and who did not even raise their heads to look at you.
But the others—they had to be seen to be believed, the ones who
still hoped to be rescued, and who pricked up their ears and looked
at you as if they knew how you felt . . .

"What do you do with them if nobody comes to claim them?"

"We leave them there for a week and afterward put them into the
gas chamber. We recover the skins, and make gelatine and soap
out of the bones . . ."

For a moment Morel was silent. She could not see his face, only
his gleaming shoulders with their traces of the lash.

"I think that's where it got hold of me. At first I nearly knocked
the man out—and then I said to myself: No, not immediately, not
like that. I took a good look at those dogs, out of whom gelatine
and soap would be made, and I said to myself: You wait a little,
you human master race, I'll teach you, I'll teach you to respect
life. I'm going to have it out with you, and with your gas chambers,
your atomic bombs and your need for soap . . . That evening I got
together two or three lads off the roads—two from the Baltic states
and a Polish Jew—and we carried out a little commando raid on the
pound—gave the keepers a good thrashing, set the dogs free and the
hut on fire. That's how I began. I was sure I'd made a good start.
From then on, there was only one thing to be done: to continue. It
wasn't worth while to stand up for this or that separately, men or
dogs—it was essential to attack the root of the problem, the protection of nature."

. . . And Peer Qvist turning his eyes in the direction of the open
window and saying with a sudden flash in those pale eyes of his:

"Islam calls that 'the roots of heaven,' and to the Mexican Indians
it is the 'tree of life'—the thing that makes both of them fall on their
knees and raise their eyes and beat their tormented breasts. A need
for protection and company, from which obstinate people like
Morel try to escape by means of petitions, fighting committees, by
trying to take the protection of species in their own hands. Our needs
—for justice, for freedom and dignity—are roots of heaven that are

deeply imbedded in our hearts, but of heaven itself men know nothing but the gripping roots . . ."

. . . And that girl sitting there in front of him with her legs crossed, with her nylon stockings and cigarette and that silent gaze, in which could be read that stubborn need, not so different from what Morel had seen in the eyes of the stray dogs at the pound.

. . . And Father Fargue, sitting red-faced at the steering wheel of his jeep, setting off in search of the man he called "the biggest pagan we've seen in French Equatorial Africa since Governor Condé"— Governor-General Condé had reduced the subsidies to the Christian missions in his territory and had required the Sisters of Charity to have medical diplomas. With his red beard kindled by the sun, his singing Marseilles accent, his cassock hitched up above the thick thighs exposed by his shorts, watched admiringly by the boys and the sisters of the mission, he really looked as if he were setting out on a crusade—but not even all that was comic and childish about him could deprive him of the dignity conferred upon him by his love for his Maker. Schölscher often wondered how it was that the church authorities put up with his language, or with his way of doing good as you force a purge through the teeth of a resisting child —but the answer lay in a faith so evident that his very physical strength seemed to have its roots in this living splendor.

"I'm going to find him and give him a piece of my mind," yelled Father Fargue, addressing the audience. "When I think that right now he may be sitting on some hill, watching those pagan herds of his with a happy grin and getting all excited about the elephants, when he's only got to raise his eyes to find something much bigger and more wonderful, I'd like to kick his ——! Protection of nature! I've been busy on that for a long time, I do what I can, I know as well as he does that we all need protection, but it isn't enough to sign petitions and organize meetings; you've also got to ask for help in the right place . . ."

A sister ran out from the mission, her skirts bunched in her hand, carrying the breviary which he had forgotten. He stuffed it into his pocket, leaned his full weight on the accelerator and was away in a jet of dust, while Schölscher, who had come to question him about Minna and Forsythe, whom he was the last man to have seen, followed with friendly eyes that human mass whose physical strength was nothing compared to the faith and spirit that dwelt in him.

On his return to Fort Lamy, Schölscher had found the Governor in a particularly murderous mood, gazing with no pleasure at a sheet of typescript. "Marching orders," he said. "The Oulé country to be combed with troops, helicopters and what not . . ."

"How long can you delay the expedition?"

The Governor gave him a sidelong glance.

"Let me tell you, Schölscher, without wishing to be disagreeable, that your request has not yet been granted: you are still among us, not in a Trappist cell. You must put off for some weeks yet the moment when you'll at last be able to turn your back on our poor little human affairs and go wandering among the stars. For the time being you are still in uniform, at the service of law and order, not of divine pity or of Christian charity. Really I'm beginning to feel that the Republic created the Desert Camel Corps only to make it possible for our officers to get their initiation into mysticism at government expense . . . In the long run Père de Foucauld is costing us dear in terms of our best officers. It's a regular recruiting campaign that Heaven's carrying out on the Sahara borders . . . If I understand rightly, you still cherish the hope that our lonely friend'll raise his lovelorn eyes much higher than the elephants . . ."

"You could at least tell them that to start operations in the Oulé country a fortnight before the rains doesn't make much sense . . ."

"In Paris they don't seem very disturbed by tropical rains. It appears they don't make you wet—in the ministries. I've just seen a messenger who came all the way specially to tell me precisely that. Borrut is engaged in doing all he can . . ."

"You can also make it clear that the use of troops in the most peaceful region of Africa would immediately give the affair a character which it doesn't have . . ."

"That is . . .?"

"A political character," said Schölscher.

The Governor began to lose patience.

"Listen to me, my friend. I know that in the extremely . . . private world in which you live, people haven't much belief or interest in human affairs, but I should like to point out that this century has seen the triumph of a doctrine which already holds sway over half the population of the globe and which states, precisely, that all human affairs are nothing *but* political affairs . . ."

"That's no reason for encouraging them in that opinion," said Schölscher.

"Up to now we've had a great deal of luck. Popular imagination has taken to the elephant story, and the newspapers have helped us a lot: in fact, people believe it. But if you read certain other newspapers, you'll find that there is talk of a secret training camp organized by the 'Army of African Independence,' and that that camp is said to be in the Oulé country—and they add that Morel is merely a Communist agent and that the elephants are a mere propaganda trick, a symbol of African freedom. You and I know it isn't true, or in any case not as simple as that, but you and I think in terms of Africa, and back there they are thinking in terms of Europe. . . . And besides, after all, Waïtari exists. By the way, it's very nice of Herbier to explain to me how Waïtari and company crossed the frontier into the Sudan with the help of the Arab slave-traders, but it would have been much nicer if he had picked them up on their way, since he's so well-informed . . ."

"Herbier has three district guards to cover a territory of 100,000 square miles," said Schölscher.

"All right. Everybody's doing his job admirably, isn't he? It's quite moving. I'm surprised Paris doesn't congratulate us every day . . ."

He picked up a pencil.

"There's another thing. As though by chance, everywhere Waïtari has passed, the Oulé tribes have begun to make trouble. I know: it's much the same every year at the time of the initiation rites . . . but it's never gone so far before."

Schölscher said nothing.

The Governor knew as well as he did why the Oulé tribes began to make trouble, as he put it, at the same time every year.

Toward the middle of the dry season the herds started on their seasonal migration toward the waterholes. Then the elephants brushed past the villages and tormented the eyes and hearts of the most hunt-loving of all the hunting tribes of Central Africa. Three quarters of the Oulé traditions and magic rites had to do with war or hunting: both had become impossible, or hemmed about by severe official regulations. Every time he went on tour the Governor received petitions drawn up in solemn and touching language, asking for powder and hunting weapons, and vehement protests against the confiscations of the ivory and meat taken from animals killed because they were trampling the squash fields. Without such confiscations, elephant hunting by every means, including fire—already practiced on a considerable scale—would soon have ended in the extinction of the herds. When the abundance of elephants at the time of seasonal migration became particularly provoking, the Oulé people lost their heads and turned against the administrators or hurled themselves, lances in hand, against the great beasts in the manner of their ancestors. The attraction of the meat went to their heads and they were incapable of resisting the call of their blood.

But most important of all was the fact that, in all their magical rites, elephants' testicles played a major part, and the young people who were able to bring back these trophies were permitted to sit in the council of the tribe as men. And so every year, at the time of the initiations, they suffered from an intense feeling of lost virility, which was sometimes so strong that it caused real crises of despair and even suicide. It was true that this year such aberrations had been particularly serious.

"I know," said the Governor wearily, although Schölscher had said nothing. "I know all that . . ."

He waved his hand in the direction of the door.

"But just you try explaining it to them. Try explaining that the Oulé tribes aren't out to win political or national independence, but elephants' balls. Just you try . . ."

The door opened and Colonel Borrut came in with the visitor, a young man who was very sure of himself and who wore a flannel suit as though to indicate that he was in too much of a hurry to bother about dressing for the tropics. The Governor stood up and introduced them.

"I was saying to the Colonel that if the rains are going to begin in six weeks' time that's all the more reason for starting the police operations immediately. It's essential to prevent the fire from spreading and perhaps gaining a hold over the neighboring tribes . . ."

"There's no fire," said the Governor. "As for the tribes, perfect calm prevails in the whole district. To them it's a business between white men. If Morel hasn't been caught yet, it's not because he is helped by the tribes—on the contrary it's because the tribes are keeping clear of this. I was the first to ask for police reinforcement. But not for armored cars, helicopters and flame throwers . . ."

"Remember Indochina, sir. The policy of too little and too late led to disaster."

The Governor tried to look amiable.

"Monsieur," he said, "believe it or not—and I admit it's very difficult to believe—there is, in the Oulé hills, a man who really has got it into his head that he will stand up for the African elephant against the hunters. He has with him a Danish naturalist who, forty years ago, had already been thrown in jail in his own country after he had led his students in an attack on the whalers' offices, in protest against the extermination of whales in the North Sea. For forty years now this old man has been mixed up in struggles of this kind. When there's any question of standing up for nature, you'll always find Peer Qvist in the first rank. Between the two of them, with the help of a few other enraged humanitarians, they've wounded three or four hunters and set fire to several ivory stores and two or three plantations. There are, of course, political agitators among them. Waïtari has been with this man, and I am convinced he will do everything he can to pull the political chestnuts out of the fire . . . I'm not belittling their criminal actions. But we are a long way from Indochina."

The young man crossed his legs. *"Monsieur le gouverneur,* you have contrived to present this business to the press from the very start with great skill . . . We have all admired it. But the idea that this man Morel might really be interested in the splendors of nature, that he might be anything other than a professional political agitator appears to us absolutely absurd. Let's not deceive ourselves . . . What we are up against is a new nationalism, the right of peoples to self-determination . . ."

The Governor looked completely disgusted. He gave Schölscher a black look, as if to say: "You see, I told you so: they all come here with their own obsessions." Even when the Kikiyus in Kenya, robbed of their African gods, consoled themselves with rites into which human semen and children's brains entered as essential ingredients, back in Europe they saw in it merely the political frustration of a people laying claim to the sacred traditions of the West. The young man went on talking politely, but with an insistence that showed clearly that he was not speaking only in his own name.

"Before I left Paris we received your dispatch about the rebellion of the Oulé tribes . . ."

"There's no question of rebellion," said the Governor. "If you had also read the dispatch I sent last year at the same period—people never look at the whole of a file—you'd have seen an account of exactly the same happenings, also announced in advance. The Oulé villages are situated on the path of the seasonal migrations of the herds toward the waterholes. In the dry season in those hills you can watch the greatest concentration of elephants still to be seen in Africa. A few years ago I saw elephants surge for hours about a village in which we sat powerless, expecting to be crushed together with the huts from one moment to the next. That was during the drought of '47. This year we have a drought which promises to be at least as bad: in the Gornon villages they've begun to find gazelles with broken backs at the bottom of the wells . . . This is the season when, before our time, the young people of the Oulé tribes used to set out into the hills after a ritual initiation ceremony, and those of them who came back with elephants' testicles were consecrated as men and had the right to sit in the tribe's councils. We've suppressed all that to protect the elephants—and also to protect the Oulé people: one boy out of every three was killed in those jousts. The result is that the young people of the Oulé tribes are suffering from a feeling of lost virility. They marry, of course, but they feel there is something lacking, and while it's easy to suppress a magic tradition it's difficult to fill up the strange voids which it leaves in what you call the primitive psychology and what I call the human soul. The result is that every season, when the herds go by, the Oulé people lose their heads and demonstrate their frustration as best they can; and this year it has been more violent than in previous years."

"It might be simpler to authorize them to hunt elephants for one or two months every year. I will mention this in Paris."

"We are bound by international agreements in this matter," said the Governor rather dryly.

"That can be arranged. It would be better to relax the regulations a bit than to see, every year, disorders which are naturally exploited abroad for political propaganda against us . . ."

Schölscher was unable to suppress a quiver of ironic anticipation. That Morel's desperate campaign should result in a still greater relaxing of the notoriously insufficient laws for the protection of the African fauna, and of the elephants in particular, would really be a perfect parable of all human endeavor.

Even now, after the last word had been said or printed—if there was such a thing as the last word on this affair—facing again this big German girl who believed so wholeheartedly that man was strong and generous enough to take the protection of nature into his own hands, even now, months after the trial, Schölscher could not help smiling at the memory.

He had come to see her for the last time in the Fort Lamy jail, still wearing his white Camel Corps uniform, with his blue kepi and his stick, and the golden stripes of rank still on his shoulders—but already he was beginning to feel ill-at-ease in this disguise: he was leaving next morning for France and the Trappist monastery of Chauvigny.

He didn't quite know why he had come to see her once more. His faith did not need reassurance about the utter futility of man's effort to become his own master and protector. But somehow he felt irresistibly drawn toward those two. And their pathetic adventure reminded him forever of Peer Qvist's fervent words: "The roots of heaven are forever planted in their hearts, yet of heaven itself they seem to know nothing but the gripping roots . . ."

But he hadn't come to proselytize or to preach.

He took a miniature bottle of brandy from his pocket and put it on the table.

"I've almost forgotten. I bought this for you."

She laughed. "Thanks."

"You know, there's one thing I never quite understood. It never came up at the trial. Herbier ran into you some twenty miles south of Gola, in the middle of a band of Oulé tribesmen who had just set fire to the Mobile Medical Unit. They were yelling, demanding the right to hunt elephants freely, as much as they liked. And yet Herbier said in his report that Morel was certainly at their head, that they were acclaiming him and that he seemed to be in agreement with them . . ."

Yes, she remembered that perfectly, because it was the first time she had seen him completely bewildered. Waïtari and Habib had left them a fortnight before, to go off to the Sudan in company with two traffickers who knew the way across the frontier, and with the porters who were carrying De Vries, apparently dying, on a stretcher. On his way, in the villages where they stopped to rest, Waïtari had held regular public meetings, explaining to the tribes that they should rise in order to get satisfaction for their legitimate demands. He spoke to them of Morel, who was going to give them "liberty"—which consisted, for them, of the right to kill as many elephants as they liked and to help themselves to all the meat they desired. The result was that every time Morel appeared in an Oulé village the young people began to follow him, dancing and acclaiming him, in spite of the counsels of prudence from the elders, who were much more skeptical about promises, whatever they might be and whatever their source. It was impossible to calm them. It was the initiation season, and they were drunk with palm wine, and perhaps still more drunk with the crackling that resounded from the bush around them and the sight of the herds fleeing the drought toward Lake Kuru. Morel had not realized the contradiction at first —he looked pleased and at one point he had turned to Peer Qvist and said, "I think they're beginning to understand."

They had just left the village of Ldini, because a helicopter had flown obstinately over the village several times, and they were climbing in the direction of one of the two caves they had prepared in the hills, from which Morel intended to make his famous "commando" raid on Sionville—the operation that was destined to create such a sensation. The Dane, for his part, did not seem convinced; he was listening attentively to the clamor of the young people who surrounded them dancing. His small eyes, pale as ice, which reflected a total absence of illusion, observed the scene intently. By his side Johnny Forsythe, with a red spotted silk scarf about his neck, his bare chest showing under his airman's jacket, was laughing and raising his joined hands like a triumphant boxer, while their scared horses jostled one another in the dust and shook their bits.

"Well," said Johnny Forsythe, "I've become popular at last, and it was none too soon. I haven't caused such interest since I came back from Korea . . . Either I'm very mistaken, or I'm the first Southern gentleman to be acclaimed like this by Africans. What are they singing?"

Peer Qvist said nothing and, after giving Morel a strange sharp glance, urged his horse forward. She noticed that Morel had at first listened with satisfaction but, after a few seconds, suddenly looked bewildered, gazing fixedly straight ahead with an inscrutable expression. It was only when they had left the village that the Dane at length translated for him what the young people were singing:

> We shall kill the great elephant
> We shall eat the great elephant
> We shall enter into his belly
> Eat his heart and his liver
> We shall never again be hungry
> As long as there are Oulé hills
> And elephants to kill.

Johnny Forsythe shook with a laughter that nearly threw him off his horse. "That's a hymn to liberty for you," he said.

She thought Morel was going to kill him. For a moment she saw him as people had tried to represent him to her—the man who had run amok, with his jaws clenched, his eyes full of hate, and every muscle of his face stretched so tight that the whole face seemed to close like a fist.

"Shut up, Johnny. It must be very consoling to take refuge in cynicism and to try and drown your own remorse in a consoling vision of universal swinishness, and you can always try whisky, when that fails. For centuries those people were hunters, and now hunting has been taken away from them, without anything taking its place. When you separate people from their past without giving them anything in its place, they live with their eyes on that past . . . They're not the ones to blame."

Forsythe looked at him for a second almost tenderly. Then he bent down, grabbed the bottle of whisky from the pouch attached to his saddle and threw it to Morel.

"Here," he shouted genially. "You need it more than I do."

Morel caught the bottle, then smashed it against a rock.

"Hell," said Johnny Forsythe sadly. "It was the last one."

All the way from Mato to Valé they were received with enthusiasm in the Oulé villages through which they passed. At Valé they were surrounded by a dancing, yelling crowd, from which the cry of *"komoun"*—elephant—resounded in particularly triumphant tones. Some of the young tribesmen in the group had just come from a neighboring village where they had taken part in the pillaging of the Mobile Medical Unit, and had beaten up the staff and set fire to the medical stores. They ran after Morel along the track, sometimes getting ahead of the horses, in a state of extreme excitement, singing and pushing one another.

But at the next village they were met by silence.

The place looked completely empty and deserted.

There were only some yellow dogs barking and some children with swollen bellies who watched them pass, standing at the thresholds of the conical mud huts.

Hardly had their horses entered the village when they saw coming toward them a man who seemed to have been waiting for them in the deserted square.

He was a white man.

He gripped a rifle firmly in his hand, and was followed by two armed black soldiers. It was Herbier, who was on a tour of inspection in the district.

He had long been familiar with the mood of the Oulé tribes at the height of the initiation season, but the burning of the Mobile Medical Unit was the gravest outbreak of violence he had had in some years. Herbier had immediately rushed to Gola with his "troops"—two Massa guards who had been with him for the last three years. When he saw the group of horsemen moving into the village, followed by the young tribesmen exhausted after a fifteen-mile run but still strong enough to brandish lances and give a few menacing yells, he picked up his weapon and marched to meet them through the empty village. The two Massa guards followed him with completely expressionless faces, guns in hand.

Korotoro, with a grin of extreme delight, had taken aim at the administrator as soon as he had started to march toward them, and remained in this position during the whole time they remained there. With his bristling mustache and small round belly, Herbier had neither the physique nor the style for this role, but it was hard not to admire his courage. A few menacing cries rang out from among the young tribesmen, but they quickly fell silent and took refuge behind the horses.

"I hope you've no illusions about what's waiting for you, Morel," said the administrator. "I also suppose you don't care a damn. When you play the crazy fool for so long, you're certain to win. You will win. You'll get a bullet through your head all right, take it from me."

"Well," said Morel, "that's what the head seems made for, doesn't it?"

"If I hadn't a wife and four children," said Herbier, "I'd have pressed the trigger and it would be done by now. Then I'd have died happy, knowing I'd really done something for Africa. But I've got kids. So I have to restrain myself."

"We're all in the same boat," said Morel with a smile. "You shouldn't take it so hard. I too have to restrain myself. I stick to protecting elephants . . . You see, I don't ask too much."

"You're a coward," said Herbier. "You take advantage of circumstances like a coward. You know we don't want to use force and thus give the whole world the idea that there's political rebellion in the Oulé country, and that we're stamping it out . . . I suppose you're paid to create such an impression. At the beginning I thought you were sincere. Now I think you're a puppet of Cairo, or somewhere still farther off."

"You don't need to use force," said Morel genially. "I'm ready to give myself up. You know my terms. All you have to do is to ban

elephant hunting in all its forms and to take all the measures required for the protection of the African fauna. Then I'm ready to
stand my trial. And I defy you to find a French court that would
condemn me . . ."

Herbier laughed. It was not perhaps a very successful laugh, but
he did his best to show he was laughing. Then, all at once, his face
became as angry as before. He pointed in the direction of the young
tribesmen from Gola.

"Do you know what they're demanding? You ask them. Make
them talk. Go on, I tell you, just ask them!"

He shouted a few words in Oulé to the young men. For a moment
they stayed there, behind the horses; then they could be heard talking among themselves. Finally one of them stepped out in front of
Morel. He must have been slightly under twenty. With his shaved
head and his body streaming with sweat and gray with dust, he
placed himself in front of Morel and began speaking rapidly, striking the ground with his assagai. As he spoke and felt that he had an
audience, the attention centered on him began to go to his head, and
at one moment he sent a cloud of dust flying toward the administrator with his naked foot.

Herbier listened gloomily, rifle in hand, without moving. Sometimes he gave Morel a quick glance, as if to make sure that he
understood.

The young man said that for years he and his people had been
trying to obtain justice, but that now, thanks to Ubaba-Giva, thanks
to Waïtari, they were going to get their rights. The French prevented them from hunting freely and imposed severe fines on those
who attacked the herds. The administration did not give them
enough powder, they were obliged to cast their own bullets, the
tusks were confiscated from them. It was unjust. He and his people
were great hunters—no other tribe, not even the Wango, not even
the Sara, could compare with them—but the government forced
them to languish in their villages like women and they were forbidden to match themselves against the elephants. They were supposed
to stay there with folded arms while the plunderers of the Kreich
tribes came calmly over from the Sudan, killed as many elephants
as they liked and set off home with the tusks and the meat, laughing

at the Oulés, and no one said a word to them. The young people of the Oulé tribes no longer had a chance to prove that they were men. At the initiation ceremony, they were obliged to make do with buffalo testicles, to the great shame of their dead ancestors, and this was why there were so few births in the tribes and why among the newborn there were more girls than boys. And soon there would not even be an Oulé country any more, for everyone knows that the Oulé hills are herds of elephants killed by Oulé hunters on which the grass has grown.

He spoke in a jerky, rhythmic voice, and at the end it was a real hymn that rose to his lips, and even his anger at length died down as if he had at last expressed it fully; it gave place to gravity when he came to explain how the Oulé hills had been born. Soon, he concluded, pointing at Morel once more, they would be able to rejoice the spirits of their ancestors by adding to the Oulé hills many fresh hills, which would grow in the tracks of the slaughtered elephants as far as the eye can see. He had forgotten his anger completely and raised his voice in a sort of solemn declaration. His face was grave, and it was hard not to believe that that was really how the Oulé hills had been born, and Morel had to shake himself so as not to fall under the spell. Here was yet another popular leader in the making.

"There," said Herbier with satisfaction, "now do you know?"

"I've known all this for years," said Morel. "I'm not a racist, and so I've never believed that there was any difference between black men and white. But that's no reason to get discouraged . . . And now, old man, get out of the way, or we'll ride over you."

They set their horses in motion and left the administrator alone with his two Massa guards in the village that looked dead. But that evening Morel had recovered his cheerfulness and confidence, and when they at last halted at the entrance to the bamboo forest, with the gray hills of the Oulé country stretching to infinity below them, and as they watched that vast petrified herd, which from time to time came alive and moved, he had come over to her and, sitting by the fire, with his eyes fixed on the cigarette he was rolling, he had talked to her about all this with obvious serenity. There was a trace of self-satisfaction, almost of conceit, in his voice, and one could feel he was really relying on his tactics to attain his aims.

"You see, if I simply told them that they're disgusting, that it's time to change, to respect nature at long last, to leave a margin of humanity in which there would be room even for all the elephants in Africa, that wouldn't worry them much. They'd shrug their shoulders and say that I'm a visionary, a fanatic, just about fit to be locked up. So one's got to outwit them. That's why I'm quite willing to let them think that the elephants are only a pretext, a symbol, and that what's underneath it is a terroristic movement for African independence, and that the defense of the elephants is merely a method of protest against the exploitation of Africa's natural wealth by white men. That—there's no doubt about it—has a good chance of waking them up, alarming them, making them do something, making them take me seriously; and the cleverest, most astute thing to do is obviously to deprive us of the pretext—that is to say, to ban elephant hunting completely. That's what they will do, at the coming Congo conference for the protection of African fauna. And it's all I ask for. The rest . . ."

He waved his hand.

"Everything has to begin somewhere . . ."

. . . And Father Fargue, who had spent so many weeks wandering about the Oulé hills, in search of the miscreant who wanted to make man his own protector and believed himself big and strong enough to cope with this task: "Just you let me find him, my friend, that's all, and I'll make him see so many stars that he may in the end see clearly by the light of them. I'll teach him to address his appeals and petitions to the right quarter . . ."

. . . And Peer Qvist, sitting there with a very straight back in front of his piping hot tea, after his arrest, with that face of his in which the very wrinkles suggested by their hardness strength much more than age: "I'm an old naturalist. I defend all the roots that God has planted deep in the earth—and also the ones He has planted forever in the human soul—call it a need for justice, for freedom, for dignity . . ."

. . . And Colonel Babcock, lying in his room in the Military Hospital at Fort Lamy, with a Senegalese sentry on the veranda guarding his door—as if one armed man could stop the escape which was in the making. Schölscher had been struck, as he came in, by the

impeccable orderliness of the sheets and pillow, an indication of
the patient's exhaustion much more than of the nurse's care. Colonel
Babcock, who no longer tried to conceal his sense of humor—the
only attempt at insubordination allowed to an officer of Her Britan-
nic Majesty: "Decency, that's what he was standing up for. He
wanted human beings to be treated decently, a thing that had practically never happened to them up to now—except in England, of
course. His was a magnificent protest, and an officer and a gentleman could not remain indifferent to it . . ."

He stopped to recover his breath. In the pause a small dry sound
made itself heard in the room, proceeding from a cardboard box by
the Colonel's bedside. The box was open. Inside it there was a jumping bean, which sometimes gave a little leap. When it did, the
Colonel sent it a friendly glance. Everybody at Fort Lamy now
knew of his little hobby: for months now he had been carrying
about with him everywhere one of those Mexican jumping beans—
beans inhabited by a tiny worm. The little worm tries to rid itself
of the carcass encasing it, the only result being to make the bean
leap slightly. For some time past, the first thing Colonel Babcock
did, whenever he went to sit on the terrace of the Tchadien, had
been to open the box and lay it on the table in front of him. Sometimes he would effect a formal introduction.

"Meet my friend Toto," he would say, and usually the bean would
choose that moment to give one of its little leaps. The Colonel would
then order a glass of whisky for the creature whom he had once
called his "companion in misfortune." No one at the Tchadien paid
much attention to this innocent fad: they had seen others.

"Of course loneliness has something to do with his case. I know
what I'm talking about: it wasn't till quite recently that I had the
luck to meet with a real, a great friendship . . ."

In its box the bean gave a little jump and the Colonel smiled at
it; with his emaciated face of a Spanish grandee, his pointed gray
beard and mustache, and his fine motionless hands, he did not look
like a terrorist, and yet that was exactly what he was. Humor is a
silent and polite dynamite which enables you to blow your own way
of life sky-high every time you have had enough of it, yet with the
maximum discretion and without making a mess.

"Poor Toto," said the Colonel. "He gets quite upset about me. He's worried about my heart. It's nice to know that someone will miss you. If what he's afraid of happens, can I ask you to adopt him? Oh, of course. You're already fixed up with company. People keep saying that you're going to retire into a monastery . . ."

There was much kindness in those dark eyes.

"I believe Morel was defending a certain idea of decency—the way we are treated on this earth filled him with indignation. At bottom, he was an Englishman without knowing it. To cut a long story short—I suppose you came here to ask me for an explanation—it seemed to me quite natural that a British officer should be associated with that business. After all, my country is well known for its love of animals."

Toto gave a little leap; he semed to be enjoying himself thoroughly.

"And so one morning I took my jeep, and of course I took Toto whom you see there—he too has a very kindly nature—and I took arms and ammunition as well, and made off toward the Oulé hills, where this Frenchman was said to be, along with a few other rebels . . . As you know, I didn't get very far. I don't know whether it was the excitement, or merely the approach of that physiological misunderstanding which is called death—but I had a tiresome heart attack shortly before reaching Gola, and here I am with a sentry at my door to stop me escaping. The clerk of the court has told me that I shall be charged with attempting to aid and abet the rebels . . ."

But after the conversation he had had with the doctor, Schölscher did not think the Colonel would have to face that. And indeed he died a few days later, and his last wishes were scrupulously respected, in spite of the obvious disapproval of the British Consul who had come specially from Brazzaville to be present at the ceremony. The latter saw nothing unnatural in the Colonel's coffin being covered with the Union Jack, but that they should place upon this flag a jumping bean, which kept giving little leaps during the whole ceremony, seemed to the distinguished Civil Servant the height of bad taste and a proof of just how far the influence of life among the French, when not properly withstood, could undermine the character of people who fail to keep a hold on the healthy discipline of the Old Country.

. . . And finally Haas, who had emerged from the reed beds of Lake Chad at the news that at last they were preparing an expedition against Morel, in which he wished to take part at all costs. "If this so-and-so is really defending the elephants, I'll take off my hat to him and join him. But if he's using them to play politics, or just as a trick, if it's another ideological dodge, propaganda—well then, I'd like to teach him not to foul the last clean thing men still have about them . . ."

But while people all over the world were giving their own interpretation of the adventure, those who were living it in Morel's company were unanimous in what they said: he had one idea, and one only—to defend the elephants.

He was capable of spending hours hidden behind bushes, watching the giants at liberty with his eyes smiling and happy, and often Idriss was obliged to lay a hand on his shoulder to prevent him from going too close. In the evening, when he returned, he would sit down near the fire with his gun between his knees and his little felt hat on the back of his head, saying in that common accent of his which was always more noticeable when he was happy or deeply moved:

"One day, they'll teach the black children in the schools: it's Morel, a Frenchman, who saved the elephants in Africa. They'll say that just as they say that it's Fleming who discovered penicillin. Perhaps one day I shall even get the Nobel Prize—if, one day, they have a Nobel Prize for humaneness . . ."

He imagined himself surrounded by universal sympathy, and he always talked as if there were millions of poor devils in the world who had nothing to bother about but the splendors of nature. Every time he saw a herd of antelope blast suddenly through the yellow grasses, his eyes shone with pleasure, and a grin of happiness came to his lips. Minna smiled herself, recalling those moment of total freedom when she was still at his side among the Oulé hills. Then sadness came over her face, and she gave Schölscher one of her long, insistent glances. He must have suffered a great deal in captivity, that's what it was—those two years he had spent in "the pound," as he used to say, had marked him forever. He couldn't bear the sight of cruelty, and when he became angry, that was always the reason. One evening they had seen the horizon covered with smoke and they had caught the men from one of the villages returning from a fire hunt. The fire spread for several days, devastating the whole district, and for weeks they stumbled over dead or dying animals. Morel had fallen into a terrible rage and had had the huts of all the village notables burned. At the trial, this was quoted as an example of his "madness," as they called it . . .

She shook her head. "I tried to explain to them, but they didn't even listen. They were all solid people who haven't suffered enough, so they just couldn't understand . . . All they wanted to prove was that we were anarchists or nihilists, as they kept repeating all the time . . . All those questions they asked me were meant to prove that I was a sort of outcast with a grudge against the whole world, and that was all. I was supposed to answer *yes* or *no* to their questions, and they didn't give me a chance to explain anything, so in the end I shrugged and let them have their way—you can imagine how little I cared . . ." She shrugged, repeating her gesture, and Schölscher saw once again the tall German girl standing at the bar, the judges in their crimson robes, the faces of the public sweating in the heat, and even the hum of the electric fans which seemed to give heat a voice.

"And so your only motive for joining Morel was your love for nature?"

"Yes."

"To help him carry on his campaign for the protection of nature?"

"Yes."

"You had no other motive?"

"None."

"Had you had sexual relations with Morel?"

"Yes."

"After or before you went to join him?"

"After."

"Were you in love with him?"

"I . . ."

"We are listening."

"I don't know. It wasn't that . . ."

"It was your love of nature?"

"Yes."

"Is it true, as the German police reports indicate, that after the Liberation you worked in—if I may use the expression—a house of prostitution?"

"I . . ."

"Answer *yes* or *no*."

"Yes."

"For how long?"

"When Berlin was taken, the Russian soldiers had shut us up in a villa at Ostersee. They had raped us. We remained there for several days. Afterward, when the military police found us there, we were labeled 'prostitutes' to make things simpler."

"After leaving the . . . villa, as you call it, did you go back to live with your uncle?"

"No. I stayed in the hospital for some time."

"Were you ill?"

"I had venereal disease and was pregnant."

"Did you have a child?"

"The hospital doctors prevented that."

"At your request?"

"Yes."

"How old were you then?"

"Seventeen."

"You must have had a feeling of resentment against men, hadn't you?"

"I was very unhappy . . . but I didn't feel resentment against anyone."

"You had no grudge against anyone?"

"No one."

"So little that, after you left the hospital, you became the mistress of a Russian officer, didn't you?"

"Yes."

"Did you live with him for long?"

"Six months."

"And after that?"

"He was posted somewhere else. He deserted to stay with me. My uncle denounced him and I never saw him again."

"Did you encourage him to desert?"

"No."

"Were you in love with him?"

"Yes."

"And your uncle denounced him?"

"Yes."

"The officer was arrested and probably shot?"

"Yes."

"It was your uncle's fault?"

"Yes."

"And after that you were all alone?"

"Yes."

"And where did you go then?"

"I went back to live with my uncle."

There was no movement in the room. The President paused, to give the effect of this admission time to sink in.

"Didn't it matter to you then that he had denounced the man you loved?"

"It mattered."

"And yet you went back to live with him?"

"It was very difficult to find a place to live in Berlin at that time."

"Have you ever heard talk of the Russian Nihilists?"

"No."

"And so you went back to live with your uncle?"

"Yes."

"Did you have sexual relations with him?"

The defense counsel leaped to his feet. "*Monsieur le président,* these questions are a disgrace to French justice . . ."

"I must request the accused to answer my question. We have before us the complete report of an inquiry by the Berlin police, together with certified testimonies from the Allied Control Commission. Did you have sexual relations with your uncle?"

"He wasn't my real uncle," said Minna, in a voice that trembled slightly. "He was my uncle by marriage . . ."

"You had sexual relations with him?"

"My parents were killed in a bombardment when I was fifteen, and he adopted me immediately afterward. He forced me immediately to have sexual relations with him . . ."

"Didn't you complain to the police?"

"No."

"Why not?"

"I was ashamed."

"You preferred to go on having sexual relations with your uncle, rather than complain to the police?"

"Yes. And besides . . ."

"And besides?"

"It wasn't very important. Millions of men were being killed. The whole town was in ruins, and children were dying in the streets. That wasn't what mattered."

"The sexual behavior of human beings has no importance, is that not so?"

"It isn't what matters," she repeated obstinately.

"After that, you performed as a . . . naked dancer in a Berlin night club, did you not?"

"Yes."

"You sometimes had sexual relations with clients?"

"Yes."

"For money?"

"Yes."

"That was something to which you attached no importance, was it? It didn't matter?"

She looked desperately right and left, as if in search of someone who would understand and defend her. In the courtroom Schölscher sat with his kepi on his knees, fixing her with friendly eyes. Saint-Denis, seated between two Dominican fathers, had risen, then sat down again, his face pale, and his fists clenched. On the bench where the accused sat, Peer Qvist folded his arms on his chest with a serene yet severe expression, and Habib seemed to be enjoying himself enormously. Forsythe bent his head. Only Waïtari and his young companions seemed untouched and looked as if they were not even listening. She searched for a moment more, then tears began to roll down her cheeks.

"But all the same, you say when you joined Morel with arms and ammunition, you felt no special resentment against men?"

"I wanted to get away from that. I wanted to help him."

"Is that why you joined Morel? To help him?"

"Yes."

"And you claimed that you acted without any resentment?"

"I wanted to help him defend nature."

"You were in love with him?"

"I don't know."

"Did you know him well?"

"No. I'd only seen him once."

"And that was enough to launch you on an adventure whose consequences you were surely not unaware of?"

She remained for a while without saying a word, keeping her hands on the bar and shaking her head violently as though to rid herself of their questions. It was she, all the same, who had the last word. She looked at them all stubbornly and, with that obstinate expression already familiar to the public, said: "He was a man who believed in something different."

In the cell, with the small square of white sky against the window, the young officer with his crew-cut hair and the German girl, her nylon-clad legs crossed, a cigarette in her hand, faced each other helplessly.

"He was a man who believed in something different." Schölscher stared at her in silent wonder, remembering that vibrant, vehement cry of longing, trying once again to understand how it was possible to come so close to the truth and yet be unable to see it.

Around them, around the jail, in those desert wastes he knew so well, along the caravan's tracks and in the oasis' shade, in the cool of the mosque and in the heat of the sands, even the humblest bedouin was finding the answer and the company for which those two longed in vain.

He smiled to their invisible yet reassuring presence:

Less than two hundred yards away Araf Irnit, a merchant from Kano, who had successfully sold his load of myrrh, now sat down under an acacia tree beside his donkey. He put on his glasses and indulged in a moment's rest, the Book in hand, his lips moving silently as they repeated the verses: "I have placed my trust in the Living One, who dies not. Praise be to God, Who hath no children, Who hath no partners in His realm, and Who needeth no helpers. Let us proclaim His greatness. Thou art here but for a moment. Glory to Him Who was a hidden treasure, Who let Himself be known and fashioned His creature." His lips continued to move, while his eyes explored the empty square, rested upon his donkey, followed three black-veiled women with jars of oil on their shoulders—then his lips moved more quickly and he closed his eyes and pressed his chest heavily. "There is no other Roof, there is no other Door, there is no other Beauty, there is no other Tenderness. Welcome to my heart, to my eyes, and upon my lips, Thou Who liftest up the stones." For a moment he wondered if he had not sold his merchandise rather too cheaply—immediately he beat his breast, swaying, then took off his glasses and wiped his eyes. "I thank Thee that Thou art Thou, Thou art rich, Thy creature is poor. Thou art glorious and Thy creature is vile. Thou art measureless and Thy creature is contemptible. Thou art great and Thy creature is small. Thou art strong and Thy creature is weak. I thank Thee that Thou art Thou . . ."

He repeated the verses softly, glancing occasionally at the shadow of the acacia tree gradually gaining upon the square, or at a Gola horseman passing by with his blue veil over his face, or at a group of children playing in the evening dust; and when his attention began to wander he struck his breast, raised his eyes and voice, and swayed; then, when he felt thoroughly rested, he slipped the Book into its case under his burnous, mounted his donkey, dug in his heels and moved off along the road, wondering if he was not unwise to set out at evening with so much money on him, since all the Gola people were notorious robbers.

At the same moment, a little farther south, Fatima, a Foulbé tribeswoman, whose husband was a soldier of fortune in the Fezzan, was sitting in the doorway of her *hadja*, receiving the gifts and congratulations of her neighbors. Inside lay the body of her dead child and Fatima smiled as she touched the hands of all those who brought provisions for his journey who had already been chosen though so young.

A camel caravan on its way back from Murzuk to the Fezzan, loaded with salt in leather bags, was just halting, a hundred kilometers to the west of the first waterhole, the well at Sara; and in the nakedness of the desert fifty men—among them the notorious Kamzin, who had guided to safety on the Algerian borders more than fifty caravans loaded with automatic weapons—knelt in their white burnous and bowed their foreheads to the sand as Kamzin, one eye barred with a white streak and part of his nose eaten away by lupus, muttered at each dive: "*Baraka-toum il Khadhizi, Ia Ilahi, M'ana Tadhour Ilahi . . . del Kahdhir,* Oh my God! be present among us, Oh my God! May the *Baraka of Ouwaïs,* the *Baraka* of the great on earth, be present in our midst."

Schölscher could see them all, all those who had made it possible for him to temper his Christian faith afresh in Islam. But he knew that it was useless to extend a hand to one too far from you, and with an irony that was slightly cruel he pushed the pack of cigarettes toward her.

She inhaled the smoke, pulled her skirt down over her knees again and shook out her hair cheerfully. Oh, she bore them no grudge. One must try to understand them too. Morel had slipped through their fingers yet again, so they were getting their own back on those who were caught. They were furious and probably scared: it was said that Morel was planning an attack while the court was actually in session, that he had been recognized in disguise in the Arab market, that he was going to carry out a commando raid to set free the accused and beat up the judges—and anything might be expected from the adventurer who had brought off the Sionville coup.

That Sionville business—they simply could not swallow it: for a whole week the papers talked of nothing else, and that of course was precisely the aim of the expedition. The new conference on the protection of the African fauna was about to be held in the Congo, and Morel had decided to strike what he called "a direct blow" in order to influence the delegates and rivet the attention of the world on them. At that time they were living in a cave on the outskirts of the equatorial forest, which began there, on the Oulé escarpments, in a tangle of bamboos, rocks and thorns. A truck was to wait for the

"commando" on the first Tuesday of June, on the south side of the
Oulé range, along the track leading from Lati to Sionville; after the
raid, if all went well, the group was to make for the Sudanese frontier and Khartoum, where Waïtari was then meeting representatives
of Cairo. Idriss was to guide them through the forest to the truck,
return to the cave, and then proceed with Youssef and Minna to
Lake Kuru, where Waïtari had set up what certain newspapers were
already describing as a "training center of the African Army of Independence," located by the journalists, each exercising his own
imagination, at twenty different places in French Equatorial Africa.
The two parts of the group were to join up at Lake Kuru and cross
the thirty miles separating them from the Sudanese frontier by truck.
In Forsythe's words—his military instincts were excited by the boldness of the plan—the scheme had "about as much chance of success
as I have of beating Ike for the Presidency." There were two garri-
sons on the only road to Sionville, seven hours' journey away; and
even if they managed to carry out the raids they were certain to be
intercepted on the return trip.

He expounded all this to Morel, who told him calmly, "The
trouble with you, Jack, is that you have no trust in people. Of
course they can stop us on our return trip. So what? They'll look
the other way, that's all. The people are fed up, they read the
papers, they see what happens, they're angry and ready to give us
a hand. Perhaps they aren't prepared to stick their necks out themselves, but they're glad that somebody's doing something to defend
their good name. It's as simple as that."

Johnny Forsythe shook his head, and searched for a trace of irony
in Morel's eyes. The Frenchman seemed absolutely serious.

The only thing that worried him was the coming of the rains.

The "waterless track," as the desert region between them and the
Sudan was called, extended eastward from the Oulé country all the
way to Lake Kuru: more than a hundred miles of red dust, stones,
euphorbia and rocks without a single waterhole; but a few hours'
rain would make it impassable from Gola onward. This was the beginning of June and not a drop had fallen yet on the exhausted land.
The whole of Africa was crushed by drought. The decision to risk
the crossing in a week's time, after Sionville, was difficult to take.

Idriss, called to give his opinion, hesitated for several hours, staring at the sky, his eyes reduced to slits and his nostrils quivering, sniffing out any trace of humidity, and then at last made his pronouncement: the drought was not near its end. The forest seemed empty of life; the animals had fled in search of water. The slender thread of the Galangalé stream had long ago disappeared among the stones. They themselves had to go down to a village well three miles away for water. The elephant herds were abandoning their usual seasonal track and were making for Lake Kuru, which never dried up; but to get there meant crossing over a hundred miles of desert waste, and only the fully grown animals could undertake the venture. Idriss gesticulated, looking at the sky; his arm emerged from the large blue sleeve as he talked with an animation no one had ever seen him display before. Such a thing had never been seen in living memory, he told them, and, coming from him, the statement had an authority no one dreamed of questioning. Over his pocked face fleeted an expression of superstitious fear, which took the form of religious fervor. He prayed, suddenly, and knelt for hours, it seemed, with his forehead bowed to the ground: it was quite moving to see the most famous tracker in French Equatorial Africa imploring heaven to protect the herds he had helped to decimate. They could see he was both stunned and fearful, stricken with a feeling of awe at the extent and imminence of the disaster; crouching there in his burnous, every now and then he picked up a handful of earth, which ran off like sand between his fingers, then silently shook his head.

The voices of the forest had fallen silent; the whirring of the insects had gone; at dawn there was not a trace of dew on the ground. The branches seemed to have lost their sap and broke under the slightest pressure. The absence of herds was almost total: not a buffalo in a district where they had been seen by the thousands; not a kudu on the hills; not a wart hog or a porcupine in the undergrowth; they began to find baboons dead at the foot of the trees. On one occasion they saw an old elephant coming down the bed of the Galangalé alone, and that same evening they found the animal dead among the pebbles, abandoned by its herd, being too old to attempt the crossing.

That was the year when, on the shores of Mozambique, maddened elephants, who had come down to the sea after weeks of thirst, died in a few hours after gulping salt water; when bands of baboons threw themselves into the village wells and drowned there in yelping clusters; when almost the whole of the harvest was lost; when in all of Central Africa, as far as the Indian Ocean, the word "water" became a universal prayer, an anguished chorus of men, earth, and beasts.

Morel had lost some of his assurance and spent hours gazing at the sky as though in search of some sign of mercy. Forsythe observed him with a certain irony, but he liked him too much to show openly what he thought; once only he had laid his hand on the old brief-case in Morel's clenched fist, and said, "You really don't know whom to apply to, in a case like this, do you?"

Morel nodded calmly. "True enough. But we have an old saying —popular wisdom, they call it. Not to be dismissed lightly. We say, 'Do your damnedest, and let the chips fall where they may.'"

Next day at dawn the small "commando" of four men plunged into the forest to carry out what was destined to become Morel's most sensational exploit, and to give his campaign a new and world-wide renown.

## XXIX

FORSYTHE WAS TO SAY later that their three days and two nights across the Oulé range where horses were useless remained to him a nightmare of thorns, rocks, heat and almost unbearable physical effort. After his capture he told Schölscher that Morel seemed driven by some implacable inner force. "Even now I have only to close my eyes to see him marching forward forever—out of time and out of space—eternal in his endeavor, with that magnificent obsession in his heart. Believe it or not, somehow I kept up with him." He grinned. "During those last few years I had soaked in a fantastic quantity of alcohol—and I sometimes felt as if each red cell of my blood was howling for its usual ration. I remember once, when I just couldn't get up at the end of a few minutes' rest, Morel came up to me with a flask of brandy. But to my own surprise I refused. I swore at him, let my blood cells howl, and set off marching again, under the approving eye of Peer Qvist, who was watching me sternly.

"The Dane was ancient and had a stiff knee, but the old battler showed no sign of fatigue. He was a huge figure, climbing tirelessly through the shafts of sunlight and the shadows, along the rocky path, through the galleries of the forest, between the crags and the bamboos, across dried-up marshes and over hills, invincible and as if immortal, followed by Korotoro, who was treading the ground lightly, his felt hat over one ear, showing his small white teeth now and then in a smirk of encouragement.

"Idriss was showing the way and his white burnous kept appearing and disappearing among the trees.

"Last came Morel, clutching that briefcase which by now had become for me something like the very symbol of his madness . . ."

They reached the rendezvous at five in the morning and saw the truck. Idriss left them without a word and plunged back into the forest. Three young Negroes in khaki were sitting close to a fire. They leaped up, machine guns in hand. Morel walked toward them.

"Put away those guns," he said angrily. "No one knows who you are, no one suspects you of anything, so of course you have to attract attention."

The three young men glanced around as in search of someone, and one of them uttered the name of Waïtari. Morel told them Waïtari was already in the Sudan and they looked grim and disappointed. They were devoted to their leader and were longing to fight, perhaps to die by his side, and his absence made them feel uneasy, unsure of themselves and lost.

One of them was called Madjumba. He was an Oulé tribesman with the powerful shoulders of his race; he hid his nervousness under a perpetual scowl; his very voice, which transposed into French the rapid, jerky, guttural rhythm of his native speech, seemed to possess only one tone—that of diffidence.

The second of them, Inguélé, had a gentle face whose fine features and timid expression reflected a delicacy of feeling which he did his best to hide. Politics had little attraction for him, he was embarrassed when the subject came up, and he seemed to have joined them out of some almost poetical inspiration and longing; perhaps also his almost feminine grace made him want to prove his virility by taking part in the expedition. Though he was the most pleasant of the three, the most cultivated, and probably the most naturally courageous, he was entirely dominated by his companions, especially by Madjumba, following him even more blindly than he followed their legendary leader—it soon became apparent that he knew Waïtari mainly from his friends' exalted descriptions. He radiated that pure light which sometimes makes youth a rare, flashing symbol of man's mastery over his human condition, and he was the one whom Morel respected spontaneously, perhaps because he had recognized in him that natural quality of dignity.

The third, N'Dolo, was the son of one of the most prosperous merchants in Sionville, whose lorry, without his knowledge, had been pressed into the service of the expedition. He was the intellectual of the group, with an expressive mobile face that disciplined itself to show detachment and coolness, no doubt because he knew how often his race was reproached for being too emotional. He was the typical young scholar who decides to become a man of action and put his theories into practice. He told Morel that he and his comrades had had part of their education in France "because we are the sons of parents who belong to the privileged class."

After a few minutes' talk with them, Morel looked worried and disgusted, and said, in reply to a look from Forsythe, "We've poisoned them already."

Then he climbed up beside N'Dolo, who was at the wheel. During the whole of the drive the student questioned him insistently, with a volubility that gave no time for reply and was merely an attempt to cover the lack of assurance felt by a boy trying to deal on equal terms with a man of forty. He betrayed also a certain animosity and irritation, caused no doubt by Waïtari's absence and by the uneasiness he felt at finding himself in the company of a man whom he obviously considered to be a crackpot, and whose aims must have appeared to him incredibly naïve and quite unre-

lated to his own. With his eyes fixed on the narrow track between
the interminable walls of trees, and his hand sometimes leaving the
steering wheel to steady his glasses on his nose, he kept repeating
that for him and his friends, the elephants were only a pretext, a
useful means of propaganda, the symbol of the exploitation of African natural resources by foreign capitalism. They knew of course
that colonialism had implanted itself in Africa because of ivory,
before turning to more lucrative sports. The elephants were also a
convenient image of African power on the march—a power that
nothing could stop. Personally, elephants as such left him unmoved—one way or the other. If anything, indeed, they were an
anachronism, a weight tied to the legs of a new, modern, industrialized and electrified Africa. They were a survival from the tribal
darkness. He turned toward Morel, who said nothing and sat looking quietly ahead.

N'Dolo crammed his glasses closer to his eyes and just avoided
a rut. The truck scraped against the bushes. A leopard slowly
crossed the track without turning its head; sometimes baboons fell
from the branches in front of them and set off running, with the
male covering the rear, uttering cries and threats; then the female
would seize hold of the babies, who would cling to her fur, and the
whole yelping family would disappear among the trees.

"We don't want any of that," said N'Dolo, jerking his head in their
direction. "We don't want to go on being the world's zoo, we want
factories and tractors instead of lions and elephants. We must first
get rid of colonialism, which delights in this exotic stagnation, the
principal advantage of which is that it produces cheap labor. We
must get rid of that at all costs, and then, with the same energy and
freedom from sentimentality, get down to indoctrinating the masses:
crush out the tribal past, hammer the new political ideas, by every
means, into brains darkened by primitive traditions." A period of
dictatorship was of course indispensable, for the masses were not
ready to take control; Ataturk's experiment in Turkey and Stalin's
in Russia were historically justified.

Morel listened calmly; he had long ceased to have any illusions
about what was in store for Africa.

And no doubt one had to make allowances for youth in this boy, unsure of himself and trying to hide his nervousness. His arrogance and cockiness were merely a whistling in the dark. A pity, all the same, Morel thought, that a kid of that age should pitch his demands so low. When a man is young he should have large ideas, be more generous, more intransigent, refuse compromises, refuse to admit limits . . . But just try explaining to these young yet stunted hearts that we had not only to move forward but to encumber ourselves with the elephants as well, take a weight of that size along on the journey. They would call you crackpot—which was what you were, in any case. They would shrug and call you a maniac—or even a humanitarian, a thing even more outmoded, backward, outdated, done with and anachronistic than the elephants. They would not understand. They had spent a few years in Paris, but they had still to undergo a real education—one which no school, lycée or university could supply: they had still to undergo their education in suffering. Then they'd be ready to understand what this was all about. For the time being he must be content to take advantage of their truck. The next conference on the protection of the African fauna would be meeting in a week's time at Bukavu. Usually its decisions attracted no attention in the newspapers, but this time he was going to see that they did . . .

He sighed with satisfaction, dug his fingers into his tobacco pouch and began to roll a cigarette. Suddenly the truck stopped short; he was thrown against the windshield. A flutter of red partridges, the rapid trotting of a porcupine, and then the trees shook and bent with the advancing din, and fell uprooted by the deafening avalanche as about twenty elephants marched out of the forest, blocking the track in front of them.

They were on the edge of the Bioundi national reserve, and the animals evidently felt safe—or perhaps the drought made them indifferent to all but their deepest preoccupation: water. They paid no attention to the truck.

One baby elephant alone, the only one in the group, turned hopefully in their direction as if to play, but its mother recalled it to order.

The giants moved along the road for a moment, then turned to the right, leaving the bank strewn with branches and the track blocked with leaning or fallen trees.

N'Dolo exclaimed, with a gesture of impatience: "Now you see! How can one be expected to build a modern country with that around?"

He turned to Morel. But the Frenchman, who had been kneading the tobacco with his fingers when the lorry stopped, was sitting there motionless with a leaf of cigarette paper stuck to his lower lip, and his dark eyes were laughing with such pleasure that the student, with a gesture of irritation, fell silent: the man was really a crackpot who had never recovered from his years of captivity. Waïtari was right to try and take advantage of his mania, but it was waste of time to discuss serious matters with him.

Inside the truck, Johnny Forsythe, seated between Inguélé and Korotoro, who had fallen asleep on his shoulder, was enduring a long diatribe from Madjumba on the Negro problem in the United States. The student had an impressive knowledge of the facts and statistics and quoted them profusely—lynching, segregation, the economic condition of the Negroes in the South and in the big cities. As the truck trundled through the Oulé forest, the young man recited all these things to him with mounting indignation, treating him almost as personally responsible for them. Forsythe listened with a bitter smile; this was almost word for word what he had heard from his Chinese Communist captors in the prison camp.

"Yes," he said, "there's a lot of truth in that. But we've made some progress, you know."

The gentle Inguélé seemed relieved by this conciliatory tone. Forsythe could not understand what that timid boy was doing among them, with his graceful movements, his long eyelashes, and that fine face with features of a nobility which was perhaps only another name for beauty. He was not effeminate, but like many youngsters in whom virility did not exclude gentleness, he must often have had to endure wounding jokes. Perhaps in his decisions, ideas played a smaller part than did a boy's ardent desire to assert his virility even at the cost of his life.

"In any case you're remarkably well informed," said Forsythe. "I suppose you were educated in France?"

"I did in fact receive a good political education in Paris," said Madjumba. "Here in Africa I went to school with the fathers, but with them one learns nothing. They are survivals of another epoch, they belong to the past, they are fossils."

He fell silent, and threw a quick glance in the direction of Peer Qvist, and then lowered his eyes sullenly to the small Bible which the Dane was holding.

But the ancient adventurer had not been listening. With the Book on his knees he was dozing. For some time now he had only had an hour or two of real sleep each night, and he recognized in this a sign of old age, which had no other grip either on his will or on his heart. And so it happened that more and more frequently he sank into this state of reverie, between sleeping and waking, somewhere between the present and a distant past: memories of acreage, animals, forests, whole species, whole regions made safe for life; and sometimes too of men long gone, faces stamped with hate, cynicism, stupidity, faces met by the way, and of which nothing now remained. His delicate lids were half open, motionless, as he watched the pale sun rise on herds of reindeer in Lapland, in the taiga of the Far North where the cold itself was blue-gray; and then the terrified faces of the children who had scuttled away from the tree when, at the age of nine and with a club in his hand, he had given the first sign of that bad character which would later make him a celebrity, by defending his first nest against marauding urchins; or the Finnish forests, slowly, inexorably sacrificed to newsprint. He had first pleaded for them before the officials of the Czar, and when his objurgations had left them unmoved, he and a few of his students had formed a flying squad which attacked the woodcutters' camps. Of course people had said he had political aims, that the forests were only a pretext for trying to rescue Finland from the hands of the Czars—in the end, indeed, he had fought for the liberty of Finland also: nature and liberty, these two things went together. Yes, he had never compromised over his duty as a naturalist and a preserver of wild life—the only official title he would not have disdained—and it had involved him in more fights, controversies, cam-

paigns and polemics, it had caused him to be thrown in more jails
in more different lands than he could remember. Leaning against the
canvas of the truck, his huge calloused hands closed like taproots
about the Bible, his sparse gray hairs sticking to his temples under
his large South African felt hat, his rifle at his feet and his eyelids
still around those two slits of blue light paled by old age, he
watched the North Sea, and the whales which had perhaps been
saved because he had one day sacked and burned down the headquarters of the Whalers' Union; the expression of a small Koala bear
which used to come and sleep with him, clinging to his arm as
though it were a branch, and the face of Fridtjof Nansen, who was
not only a great Polar explorer but a man driven by a profound love
for all the living roots planted in the earth by the omnipotent force,
some of which were forever embedded in the heart of man. He had
once come to see Qvist in prison, had put a hand on his shoulder
and had told him sadly: "Peer, they say you are a misanthrope, but
you are younger than I am, and I can see you living long enough
to be forced one day to rise up in defense of the very species they
say you hate so much, one that is every day more threatened—our
own . . ." Nansen, who had devoted his last years to this task and
had brought into existence the first passport for refugees, for the
hunted, the homeless—Nansen had been clear-sighted once more: a
time came when Peer Qvist had to call upon the world to fight
against the death camps and the forced labor camps, against the
merciless uprooting of man's freedom, against the hydrogen bomb,
against the more subtle but already foreseeable menace of the waste
from atomic piles slowly accumulating on land, in the air, in the
depths of the seas—a time came when he rose to the defense of our
own species with the same anger and fury with which he had once
defended birds. His was a stubborn, desperate and yet triumphant
reverie. He saw the face of his friend Kaj Munk, the pastor whom
the Nazis had shot because he defended one of the most tenacious
roots heaven had ever planted in the hearts of men—the root they
called liberty. He saw himself fighting against soil erosion, against
land killed by intensive exploitation—expelled from one place, un-
desirable in another, blackballed from this institute and that acad-
emy—then invited to return ten years later when facts had proved

him right. But it was already too late; as though an official recom-
pense could make up for the crime which had been committed, and
bring back the vanished and the destroyed. In the end, his great age
and his eccentric character brought him a sort of indulgent, con-
descending immunity and even popularity—that old pigheaded Peer
Qvist, he's still around, still trying, he's even got himself involved in
that business in Africa. Every official Organization for the Defense
of Fauna and Flora had blacklisted him: his "methods" were de-
plored and he was reproached also with having often been mixed up
in political struggles. And that was true. The roots were innumerable,
infinite in their variety and beauty, and some of them were deeply
implanted in the human soul—a ceaseless tormented aspiration, a
need for infinity, a thirst, a presentiment, a limitless expectation:
liberty, equality, fraternity, dignity . . . There were no roots more
deep and, at the same time, more threatened. He had never compromised in his task as a naturalist, and the enemies of all the living
splendor had always found him in their path. And still everything remained to be done, and yet he was so old . . . Well, anyhow, he
thought, the French say that bad temper and stubbornness make
one live longer, so I may still be around for a while . . . He felt a
hand on his shoulder, Forsythe's.

"Yes?"

"I'm just explaining to this young man why we're here. He doesn't
believe in the elephants. He doesn't believe that we're really interested in them. He says that that may be true for Morel, who is
mad, but that after all there are more important things to defend,
tasks more urgent, as for example, people's right to self-determination. I've explained to him that I joined the elephants simply because
I don't know where else to go. I didn't feel like bearing the name of
man any longer because it stank to heaven, so I did my damnedest
to change species. Elephants or rats, anything goes, anything better
than man. What about you?"

"Oh, me," said Peer Qvist in that deep severe voice of his which
it was so difficult to suspect of humor, "I've been sent here on an
official mission by the Copenhagen Natural History Museum, that's
all."

Shortly before sunset they saw a truck coming toward them, and

Morel got down to help N'Dolo steer past it on the narrow track. He had no fear of being recognized: the old passport photographs which had been published in the papers had too little resemblance to his present appearance. The driver of the lorry turned out to be a Portuguese named Sanchili. He had ventured out on the road—which would become impassable within two hours if the rains began—because his wife was about to have a child at Nguélé, where he had his stores. It was his ninth child. They chatted for a while in the middle of the road, smoking, and the Portuguese complained that business was bad.

"I'm an ivory exporter," he said. "And with all these plastics—"

Morel looked at him, scratching his cheek pensively. He hesitated for a second. "Well," he said, at length, "I hope for the sake of your children yet to come that you won't meet Morel on your way. He'd have removed what makes a father of you."

The little Portuguese shook with laughter. "That's a good one, that is. I'll tell my wife. I admit I wouldn't like meeting him. Just imagine: I'm the biggest ivory trader in the district. Well, we must be on our way. Here's my card. Come and see me at Nguélé."

"It's a deal," said Morel. "I'll be seeing you."

"My store is on the outskirts, by the road. You can't miss it. You'll be welcome. Well, good luck, and see you soon."

Morel watched him move off, then climbed back into the truck.

XXX

TOWARD 10 P.M. they drove through Sionville, along the river, then took a road among the mango trees, stopping at last on an eminence in front of the gate. Morel jumped down. The night had a presence, a body, a rustling life; you could feel its sweating, its intimacy; the choir of insects was a single intense pulsation that gave the darkness an agitated breath, heaving flanks. Now that the truck was silent, Morel could hear the night's presence all about him: they were far from the desert and its emptiness. A hand touched his shoulder; it was N'Dolo.

"I'm coming with you."

"You will stay at the wheel, as planned. If you're too scared to face the waiting, well, that's just too bad."

The student went back to the truck. Morel walked slowly toward the gate. The others were already waiting for him, Sten guns under their elbows. He was carrying only his briefcase. Drawn up inside the garden were half a dozen American cars. That was not in the plan.

"Do we fix the tires?"

"Not now. Later. If any want to leave, let them. If they find all their tires punctured while we're inside, that would only give the alarm."

As they drew near the villa belonging to Challut, who was the owner of the only newspaper in Sionville and of some of the biggest independent mines in the district, they saw lights through the big French windows and heard music. A branching stairway went up to the terrace; the windows were open and they could see couples dancing. Korotoro stood still for a second, his machine gun raised.

"Ain't that lovely," he said, shaking his head with a wide smile.

The old Dane nodded gravely. "It reminds me of my first ball," he said in his sepulchral voice.

They left Peer Qvist and Inguélé in the bushes in front of the villa and followed a path among the bougainvillaea as far as the printing house. It was in a shed at the end of the garden. Morel went in first. An old Negro with gray hair and a green eyeshade above his glasses was bending over the rotary press. In a corner two other Negroes in shorts were playing checkers at a table.

"Hello, there."

The two checker players raised their heads. Their faces remained expressionless, but they swallowed hard. The typesetter looked at them calmly over his glasses.

"Hello," he said.

The other two remained stiff, their mouths gaping, their eyes rolling in silent terror. One of them still held the piece he had been about to move. Forsythe leaned over the game, grinning amiably. "Who's winning?"

There was the distant sound of an approaching car, of brakes, and of voices. Madjumba wheeled instantly toward the garden, his Sten gun ready.

"It's only the guests arriving, boy," said the old man. "They never come here."

Morel fumbled in his briefcase. He took out a sheet of paper, looked at it with a satisfied air, and laid it on the table.

"Put this on the front page. Smack in the middle, in a box."

The typesetter bent over the text, pencil in hand.

Communiqué of the World Committee for the Defense of Elephants: The following sanctions have been taken against hunters and ivory merchants who have failed to obey the Committee injunctions. Haas, the elephant trapper, and Longevielle and Ornando, hunters, caught redhanded, have received corporal punishment. The properties of Sarkis, Duparc and Banerjee and the tannery belonging to Wagemann, who manufactures vases, waste paper baskets, champagne buckets and various other exquisite ornaments from the severed feet of elephants and hippos, have been razed. Next on the list, Madame Challut, the woman champion of big game hunting in French Equatorial Africa, is sentenced to a public flogging. The Committee recalls once more that it has no political character and that considerations of ideology, doctrine, party, race, class and nationality are completely foreign to it. It appeals solely to the feelings of dignity in every human being without discrimination and with no other thought than to call for a new international agreement on the protection of nature, beginning with the elephants, the biggest and the most cumbersome of man's company on earth; and it is confident that, whatever their race or creed, all men will unite behind the Committee in this urgent humanitarian task. We have no other aim than to stop the murder of animals that goes on in the African jungle and elsewhere. At the moment when, at Bukavu, a new conference for the protection of the African fauna and flora is meeting, the

Committee deems it necessary to attract the attention of world public opinion to the work of the conference, which too frequently in the past has taken place amid general indifference. The Committee solemnly undertakes to call an end to its activity as soon as the indispensable guarantees for the protection of elephants have been given by the governments concerned. Signed, on behalf of the Committee: MOREL.

The typesetter showed no sign of surprise. While he was reading, Morel observed him, with a trace of anxiety.

"Well, what do you think of it? How do you like it?"

"I like it," the old Negro said.

Morel looked pleased. "Well then, get busy with it."

The typesetter set to work. The two checker-players had not moved. Korotoro went up to them and with a laugh swept the pieces with his gun barrel. They rolled their terrified eyes, their Adam's apples jumped spasmodically and they sweated silently and profusely. After a while Forsythe, who was sitting on a stool and sucking a flower he had torn from a bougainvillaea, became restless.

"What about a drink?"

The old man put his pencil behind his ear. "If you like I can bring you a bottle of beer from the kitchen."

"And give the alarm?" said Madjumba sharply. "Who's going to fall for that?"

The old man paid no attention to him and turned toward Morel, who was busy rolling a cigarette.

"Go ahead," the Frenchman told him calmly.

"Are you mad?" cried Madjumba. "Suppose they have a telephone?"

"They have a telephone," said the typesetter.

"Go ahead," Morel repeated without raising his eyes. "Bring us some sandwiches, too."

The old man left the shed. Forsythe shook his head ironically, looking at Morel. "That's grand," he said. "It does me good to see a man who really believes in human nature. All the same, my friend, there are moments when I don't understand you."

"That won't kill me," said Morel, with a grin.

The time passed slowly. Madjumba's face was shut in fierce hostility. Motionless, with his Sten gun resting on his forearm, his
head raised high, he looked both contemptuous and watchful. He
had never understood very clearly what Waïtari's motives were in
supporting this French madman, who now stood there licking his
cigarette as calmly as if he were at some Red Cross meeting in
Geneva. But he had, as always, obeyed his leader without hesitation, and he was now ready to die under the bullets of the colonialists. N'Dolo's long explanation, a few weeks earlier, when Youssef
had arrived with the orders for the expedition, had only half convinced him. "The thing is to lay claim to every disorder, and make
political capital of it," N'Dolo had explained volubly. "To every
public brawl, even a husband beating his wife, to every fight in the
street. People must be made to see that the party is behind it. People must be made to think that we're strong, and then they'll add to
our strength. That's why Morel is so important to us. Before he
started his idiotic campaign the country was too calm, too peaceful.
The tribes don't give a damn for independence, they don't know
what it means, the very word doesn't yet exist in our speech. It's
impossible to rouse masses that aren't yet masses but only a primitive pulp. We've got to speak over their heads to those who are
capable of understanding us, to the outside world, to the U.S.S.R.,
to the United Nations, to the Arab League. We must make it clear
that elephants are nothing but a flag, a symbol of African freedom
and of its irresistible strength. That's why it's so essential to make
use of Morel and to capitalize on his publicity. Waïtari knows what
he's doing . . ."

Madjumba had obeyed, and now he was trapped here at the side
of this happy idiot who believed that nothing could happen to him
and who imagined himself surrounded by a sort of universal sympathy. He was standing there, with his idiotic briefcase, a cigarette
dangling from his mouth. The student would have liked to kill him
for leading them into this trap—anything to free himself from his
nervous tension, his impatience, and his need to rush forward shouting his name at the top of his voice—after all, his blood was that
of the warriors who had dominated this part of Africa for centuries. The old typesetter was a slave of the colonialists and he

would of course betray them to his masters. They would be finished off like rats. He held his weapon ready, turned toward the door and the night full of pulsating insects, determined not to let himself be taken alive.

He heard steps on the gravel. The old man was coming back with a plate of sandwiches and two bottles of beer. He gave Madjumba a crushing glance and set to work again.

In a corner there was a pile of newspapers and Morel began looking through them. Whenever he found an article about himself, he carefully tore the page out, folded it, and put it into his brief-case. He also glanced through several American magazines, and held them out to Forsythe. "Look, Jack, they're talking a lot about you, back home."

Forsythe shrugged cynically. "Sure, and I can imagine what they've got to say."

He had to read the article twice before he could believe what he read, and even then he sat there helplessly with the magazine in his hand, looking at Morel, and it was only something warm and kind in the Frenchman's eyes that made him at last believe that it was true, that they had really understood, back home.

"I can tell you exactly how it felt," he was to say later to Schöl-scher, after his arrest, during his first interrogation at Lamy, gulp-ing a burning drink of tea, exhausted, his eyes still swollen and red with the glare of the sun and sand, but obviously at peace with himself and with the world. "I can tell you exactly how it felt to be suddenly understood and forgiven, or at least discussed with a cer-tain amount of sympathy and—the hell I'm ashamed to say it—with pity. I remember that my first thoughts were for the elephants: an almost superstitious impulse of gratitude. 'The elephants have done that for me,' was my first thought, and I could almost see their at-tentive little eyes watching me with irony—but of course those were only Morel's eyes. What had happened was exactly what I've been secretly hoping for, a dim, confused hope which I never really ad-mitted even to myself. It seems that after the sensation caused back home by the news that Major Forsythe, the 'turncoat,' as they called me, had joined up with Morel, some journalists took a second look at my case. And by God! they were getting my message all right.

They were suddenly beginning to understand the despair and the shame—not the shame for having done what I did—but the shame of belonging to the species capable of such ruthless cheating and dishonor, the species of merciless lies and distorted thoughts, of total dishonesty and betrayal of any shred of basic decency that is supposed to make a man a man and differentiate him from animals. I really have become a 'turncoat,' but this time totally and truly: I've walked out on the very species to which I had the misfortune to belong through no fault of mine, but through what was after all only an accident of birth. They were now saying that when I had accepted the so-called 'proofs' and had rushed to the radio to shout out my indignation and shame, I had merely been guilty of excessive belief in human decency and honesty: the idea had simply not occurred to me that some of the most distinguished people in the world, Nobel Prize winners, great moral, scientific and even religious leaders, could have taken a hand in a base and dishonorable fabrication. Reading the signatures, looking at the evidence, it never occurred to me that humanity had sunk so deeply into dishonor as to be capable of such total betrayal of every elementary shred of dignity it had left. But of course that was exactly what had happened. In spite of our beautiful and noble tales about ourselves we were still crawling on our bellies in the mud; but when you're twenty-five, it takes some convincing before you can believe it. We all know now that the plague-infected American flies were a fabrication, a propaganda trick, a political expediency. But I had already been kicked out of the Air Force when I found out that little truth about ourselves. I say about ourselves: the fact that a lie was a Communist one doesn't make a damned bit of difference; we all belong to the human species and no other beast could have thought that one out. Of course, all the writers underlined the naïveté, the childishness of my demonstration when I sided with Morel and his elephants, animals which at least ignore the human subtlety of ends justifying the means. But somehow, even that seemed to work in my favor, and they were adopting a somewhat paternal, protective attitude toward me. There was even some talk of rehabilitation . . . And as I've told you, I had the feeling that the elephants had done all that for me. Morel was watching me with considerable interest, and his eyes were full of their dark, ironic kindness. 'Well, your shares seem to be going up back home,' he said. And all I was able to answer was: 'Yes, they do.'"

Toward midnight the three thousand copies of the newspaper were ready. As they left the shed the old typesetter went up to Morel and held out his hand.

"Good luck," he said. "I'm sorry I'm an old man and can't do much to help you. But I'll tell my grandchildren about you. I've read a good deal and I can understand what it's all about."

They carried the piles of newspapers to the truck. The garden was ringing with a triumphal chorus of cicadas. N'Dolo was sitting tense at the wheel. He looked as if he was driving the motionless truck through a nightmare of fear. Without a word he turned on Morel a glistening face, whose panic seemed suddenly to communicate itself to the booming violent pulsation of the insects.

"It won't take long now," said Morel. "It's all right. Go and puncture their tires. We're almost through."

"A car arrived. They didn't ask me any questions, but—"

"I know, I know. Get going with the tires."

They went back into the garden and were joined by Peer Qvist and Inguélé in front of the villa.

"Come on, let's go," said Morel, pushing his little felt hat back on his head.

They moved toward the two wings of stairs leading to the terrace, the gravel creaking under their boots, holding their Sten guns tight, in their tattered clothes, unshaven, covered with dust and sweat, and Forsythe, who was advancing by the side of Morel, grinned at the idea that they probably looked like one more revolutionary mob marching to assault the palace.

But this time, he thought happily, remembering all the small bands of men who had walked through centuries, weapons in hand in defense of a cause, against overwhelming odds—this time, it was not like all the other times; this time, he thought, marching on, a stalk of grass between his grinning lips, this time it was for something really worth while: not for an idea, not for another noble lie, not for men, but for animals.

They heard the music and saw the couples whirling past the open windows.

" 'The Blue Danube,' " said Forsythe. "I think this is going to be my favorite waltz."

They went up the stairs and onto the terrace and walked in all together through the French windows. They heard a woman's gasp, the sound of a breaking glass, then a stunned silence through which "The Blue Danube" went on until Madjumba struck the needle aside with the butt of his Sten gun.

Two dozen people in evening dress and white dinner jackets backed away and stood petrified, glasses in hand, among the *petits fours* and champagne buckets.

Morel stopped under the bright chandelier, looking around, a cigarette in the corner of his mouth.

The armchairs, the sofas were upholstered in zebra skins. There were animal skins everywhere—leopard skins, lion and antelope skins—and some magnificent elephant tusks along the walls—horns of kudu and okapi, truly choice pieces.

There was not a sound now, except the comic tinkling of glasses on a tray held by the white-gloved and shaking hands of a colored waiter. Forsythe went up to him and put his arm round his shoulder.

"You know what? Let's go and cut the telephone wires. It's good fun."

And this is how Dr. Gambier—one of the guests—later described the scene, reclining in a comfortable chair, with a somewhat retrospective amusement.

"Morel was a little in front of the others, with a cigarette butt sticking to his lower lip. He stood there with his legs wide apart, unarmed, and he was holding a crammed briefcase in his hand. By his side there were two young Negroes who looked to me really dangerous—they had their fingers on the trigger. A third had taken up his position behind us—he had an old city slicker's felt hat on his head and was busy cramming *petits fours* into his mouth by the handful. There was Peer Qvist, the bad-tempered old eccentric whom most of us knew well. And then there was that American adventurer of sad repute. He was said to have been chucked out of his country's army, washing up first in Cairo and then in the Chad, probably in the pay of the Egyptians—at any rate that's what people said—like some of our deserters from the Foreign Legion. He seemed to be taking the whole thing as a huge joke: he had a mocking grin on what was a rather handsome freckled face, a handkerchief knotted round his neck, a leather jacket wide open showing a bare chest, and powerful hands grasping his weapon.

"But the main thing was Morel. He had hardly any resemblance to the published photographs of him, but there was no mistaking who it was, and I heard a pair of extremely pretty lips whisper—as though with their last breath, but not without excitement: 'It's Morel.' He looked about him, over the armchairs upholstered in skins and the walls covered with tusks, and as he did so his face darkened and there was a sudden fire in his black eyes. He suddenly looked dangerous, his jaw showed its line, he threw his cigarette butt on the ground, stamped on it violently, and moved a step closer to us.

"So there he was, in front of us, over seven hundred miles from the Oulé hills in which he was supposed to be hiding. Not one of us stirred; we remembered only too well what had happened to Haas, Ornando and a few others. I was not the least worried, but I couldn't help looking at Morel with immense curiosity. For months we had been talking of him and him alone, and yet it was difficult to believe in his existence—he was more like a legend to us—and quite a few of us were convinced that the authorities had invented him, him and his elephants, to distract attention from the political unrest that was the real cause of trouble in the Oulé country. I say 'quite a few of us,' but I was never one of them. I believe in the wonders in Africa: it's a land where anything may still happen and its adventurers have not yet said their last word—and by adventurers I don't necessarily mean those who prowl about its gold, its diamonds and its uranium. I've always believed that Africa was still the land of incredible wonder and now here she was doing her very best before my eyes.

"Challut was of course the first person to recover his wits—which is not surprising in a man who can't be said to lose them easily. 'What the hell is this?' he shouted. Morel looked at him sideways.

'We've nothing against you,' he said. 'But we've a word to say to your wife. The Committee for the Defense of Elephants can't forget that she holds the women's record for elephant hunting in French Equatorial Africa. A hundred animals killed, to my knowledge.' His voice shook with restrained anger. Then he slowly opened his briefcase, pulled out a sheet and read that incredible document to us—you know, the one we were to find next morning printed in Challut's own newspaper.

"I must say the effect was sensational. When he reached the passage that says 'Madame Challut, the woman champion of big game hunting in French Equatorial Africa, is sentenced to a public flogging,' there was a gasp and all eyes turned to our hostess. She had gone very pale. You know her: a small woman, energetic, fortyish, rather pretty in spite of that slight mannishness in her voice and movements. She was certainly the last person to whom such a thing could happen. She had seized her husband's arm. 'You're not going to let him?' she cried. To my knowledge, that was the first time she had ever asked him for aid and protection."

Challut took a step forward. He was a strong man, rough-looking in spite of his white dinner jacket, a former miner in the north of France and then a gold prospector, a man who loved to repeat "I'm a self-made man" in a tone of deep conviction. He lowered his head, and his voice too deepened, coming from the very recesses of his wounded dignity. "If you do that, Morel," he said slowly, "I'll have your skin, even if it costs me all I've got. I know who's behind you. I know the tune. The elephants, you say. But it's only Europeans who have hunting weapons and who can afford permits, and what you mean is that we are the only people who are exploiting and exhausting Africa's natural wealth. That's a tune I've heard ever since I've been here, but the truth is that African wealth isn't exploited enough, and that without us it wouldn't be exploited at all, and its very existence would be unknown. Without us, the so-called 'colonists'—and I'm not ashamed of that name—not a single vein of ore would be discovered, and the population wouldn't have doubled in twenty years. When I arrived here I found only syphilis, leprosy and sleeping sickness: I cured my people, fed them, clothed them, gave them work, houses and ambition—the desire to do what we do. It's men like me who have been, and still are, the leaven of Africa. You and your lot call that 'shameless exploitation of Africa's natural wealth'; I call it building up a new Africa for all, and first of all for the Africans. But because ivory was the first thing we were after when we came here at the turn of the century and because we're the only ones to hunt with modern weapons, you've thought it smart to make elephant hunting the symbol of capitalist exploitation. Yes, I've read all this in the Communist press. But I didn't need their help. I'd understood already."

"Um," muttered Morel.

From his satisfied air it was obvious that he was finding this interpretation attractive. He was to say, later, to Peer Qvist: "That was a good one, I hadn't ever thought of that. He thought it all out by himself, Challut did, just like that, quite naturally, as easy as belching. Well, if the shoe fits. The obstinacy of those people is funny. That someone may simply be fed up with them and their ways and may want to look for another company, that just cannot enter their heads. They can't believe it. There must be a trick behind it, a dishonest trick, something crooked, something political, something they can understand. They're so used to sniffing at their own behinds that when someone wants to get a breath of fresh air, to turn at last to something different, and more important, and threatened, something that's got to be saved at all costs, it's quite beyond them." He said this quietly, and with an air of complete sincerity, sitting by the fire, and Peer Qvist almost lost patience and was already opening his mouth to tell him that he was wasting his time with his pretense at misanthropy, and that he knew very well what Morel really stood for—he was just opening his mouth to say this when he met Morel's attentive, barely ironical gaze and, with a good Scandinavian oath between his teeth, the old sentry of the earth and of its living beauty curled up under his blanket and turned his back on the grinning Frenchman.

"I'm right about all this, am I not?" shouted Challut. "Good. You can now get out of here, till we meet again. But if you dare touch a hair of my wife's head . . ."

An expression of rather coarse amusement appeared on Morel's face. He seemed to be slowly savoring an excellent joke.

"It isn't a hair of her head that's going to be touched," he said. "But she's going to learn her lesson. The oldest among us will be the one to do the job, so that there may be no misunderstanding."

He nodded to the Dane. Peer Qvist advanced imperturbably toward Madame Challut, who began yelling: "Don't touch me!"

"It was hard not to smile," Dr. Gambier was to say later, "in spite of Challut's silent fury—three Sten guns were pointed at him—and his wife's cries. Peer Qvist did not go at it half-heartedly, and since he is one of the oldest men I know—though some of that too is a carefully put on act—his gray beard and severe expression deprived the scene of any scandalous flavor, and to see little Annette Challut wagging her naked bottom in the air under that patriarch's blows was a quite unforgettable sight, I can tell you. And after all, between ourselves, it was not altogether undeserved. Little Madame Challut was overdoing things a bit. Think what you like, but there's something wrong with a woman whose greatest pleasure is to kill elephants. When all's said and done, there are other ways of getting satisfaction . . . or consoling yourself. As a doctor I don't go much for this kind of psychology, but she did, after all, seem to be a bit too obviously taking some sort of revenge on those huge males. Anyhow, I wasn't the only one who felt that it wasn't entirely undeserved, and the gravity with which the old Scandinavian acquitted himself of his task reinforced still more the impression that she was merely receiving a salutary lesson. Yes, in spite of all that's been said about him, I believe Morel was entirely sincere; and, as you know, even the professional hunters no longer conceal their disgust for the safaris."

As they left the villa, Challut appeared on the terrace, clearly silhouetted against the light of the window with a rifle in his hand. Madjumba had already raised his Sten gun when Morel knocked its butt from his shoulder.

"On whose side are you, Monsieur Morel?" shouted the boy. "Ours or theirs?"

"There are still other sides, my friend," said Morel almost gaily.

"I'm on the side of the elephants, as you may know. You must learn to control your nerves. You'll be able to kill as many people as you like, your own and others, when you're the boss. For the moment, I am in charge here."

They heard the snick of a rifle and jumped into the truck and N'Dolo drove off at full speed.

"Slower. There's no need to hurry . . . We've got a good start. You fixed the tires?"

"Yes."

They threw piles of newspapers at the door of the hotel where the houseboys would come and collect them at five in the morning on their way to the market. They were driving through the shanty town of planks, corrugated iron and tarred cardboard, which stretched for nearly a mile along the riverside to the east of Sionville, when in the light of the headlamps they saw an astonishing figure standing in the middle of the road with one arm raised.

It was an Oulé tribesman who must have been nearly seven feet tall. He was leaning on a stick and was dressed in a black suit, a stiff collar, a white topee and white sand shoes. Behind him, half-hidden by the dust which the wind was carrying in their direction, there were two or three other motionless silhouettes. N'Dolo applied the brakes violently. The man stepped forward.

"Greetings, comrades," he said. "We were beginning to get worried. We haven't much time left for distributing the stuff among the workers, but you can be sure it will be done. Comrades, allow me to congratulate you. It's a fine idea. Even our illiterate comrades who haven't had a Marxist education all understood when we explained to them what the elephants meant. And the warmongering monopolists, the colonialists and their political lackeys—they too understood, when they began to find the word *komoun* chalked up on the walls of their homes. The proof that they understood is that their police have already begun rubbing it out. The party will support you to the utmost. It's a fine political slogan, comrades, and we shall know how to make good use of it."

He suddenly raised his fist. *"Komoun!"*

*"Komoun!"* said Morel, raising his fist obligingly.

Korotoro threw out the last packet of newspapers at the man's feet, and they left him like that—an eternal figure standing there with clenched fist, leaning on his stick in the African night.

Morel was not displeased at this misunderstanding.

As long as the protection of the elephants was only a humanitarian idea, only a question of decency, of generosity, a margin of freedom to be preserved at all costs, his campaign had no chance of going very far with the governments concerned. But as soon as it threatened to turn into a political movement, it became explosive, and the authorities had to do something about it, take a real and active interest in the protection of the African fauna, forbid elephant hunting in all its ugly forms, ensure the threatened giants with all the protection and friendship they needed so much. He was convinced that some clever strategists among the governments concerned would do precisely this—and it was all he asked. He pulled out his tobacco pouch and cigarette paper and gropingly, in spite of the jolting of the truck and the darkness, rolled a cigarette and lit it.

"Why are you laughing?" asked Forsythe.

The match went out.

## XXXI

DAY WAS DAWNING, and the hills were beginning to come toward them from the east; it seemed to Saint-Denis as if they had been traveling all night from very far to listen. Father Tassin's face was also emerging from the shadow, a face on which the marks of a sleepless night were invisible, as though hidden among those of old age.

"Night is over, and we've spent much more time in silent remembrance and wonder than in talking. But you seem to know all I know and more about this tragic adventure, and as you plan to start back to your excavations this morning, no doubt I shall never find out what brought you into these hills. I can't tell you anything about Morel and Minna that you haven't already learned in the forty years you've spent poring over the rocks to pick up traces and fragments of what human beings were a million years ago: their most primitive weapons already speak of their courage and of the struggle they have waged since the beginnings of prehistory to overcome their fate. Courage: that, no doubt, is the last word on it all—a rebellion against the harsh law which was imposed on us from the beginning. It's enough to pore over the pathetic fragment of some stone weapon fashioned by the first human hand, to hear rising toward us, from the depths of geological past, a heroic hymn, a triumphant epic of human endeavor and courage, a dream of dignity to which Morel and his companions have merely added one more page, another episode.

"Ever since the government appointed me to watch over these hills, over the last great herds in Africa, they have kept me company, and I feel rather as if I too had joined Morel. It's often been said that he is no longer alive, that he was killed by one of his companions for political reasons. I don't believe a word of it. No one's been able to prove anything one way or the other, and personally I feel sure he's still among these hills. I often see him among the moving shadows, rising above the earth with his eternal briefcase, still convinced that man is capable of taking the protection of nature into his own hands. To me he's only gone into hiding, to rest and be ready to start on his campaign once more. In short, he hasn't yet said his last word.

"And Schölscher, walking forever under the curious stare of the merchants in the bazaar, an elegant figure with his white *seroual*, his stick under his elbow and his sky-blue kepi: his face has the calm expression of a man whose heart is at peace because he has found all the friendship of which he has need. He's now in a Trappist monastery at Chauvigny, and on the terrace of the Tchadien many explanations of his decision have been given—all except the most obvious one. As with many officers of our Camel Desert Corps, his close touch with Islam, during the many years he spent in those parts, played some part in his sudden resurgence of faith. I think his decision was made through contact with the desert wastes and with those who inhabit it—with the burning sands and the burning faith of Africa. It's a land to which fallen branches and ambitious men return more quickly than elsewhere. More than any other, it's a land of transition, of ephemeral encampment, a halt in a journey, and the very villages seem barely settled on it and as though always ready to move on. Every one of us here has been taught his lesson in human insignificance, and Schölscher was no doubt more sensitive to it than other people, and that's all.

"Yes, sometimes the merest trifle—an exceptionally bright night, a particularly sharp moment of solitude—is enough to make me see them all and hear their voices. Minna, shaking her head obstinately with that stubborn expression, just as I saw her do at the trial when she was asked if she had joined Morel because she was in love with him, repeating again and again, as often as was necessary, to try to convince them: 'I went on my own account. I wanted to help him to defend the animals. And I wanted someone from Berlin to be with him.'" Saint-Denis smiled bitterly. "After all, Father, to understand their demonstration one doesn't have to be very intelligent: it's enough to have suffered. She wasn't very intelligent, and she certainly wasn't educated—and yet her face had its share of mystery; there was a sort of humor in it sometimes, and a kind of desperate irony, when, sitting there between two policemen, with her legs crossed, her skirt well above her knees, and sometimes giving her fair hair a shake, she looked at her judges, who were unable to understand; but she had suffered enough and so she knew without hesitation what it was all about. At the beginning the judges had tried to help her. They had tried coaxing her, especially after my evidence. I had said that she had gone with my agreement, and that if she had taken him arms and ammunition it was simply in order to win his confidence, but that her principal aim was to make him give up his mad struggle and persuade him to surrender. But she had brushed aside this proffered hand indignantly. 'I wanted to do something to help him defend animals,' was all they could get out of her: the result being the six months' imprisonment to which she was sentenced. Right to the end she refused to admit that she was in love with him—sometimes angrily, as though they were trying to rob her of something, to diminish the significance of what she had accomplished. Even the evidence which seemed to prove clearly that she had—to use the language of the court—'sexual relations' with Morel aroused in her merely a shrug of the shoulders, together with that calm statement, repeated once again, 'I told you: I wanted to help him.'

"Peer Qvist, that old sentry, the 'night watchman of the House of the Lord,' as he liked to call himself, Peer Qvist, grasping the Bible in his hands and reaffirming to the Court his determination to carry on his defense of the whole infinite variety of roots which Heaven had planted in the earth and also in the depths of the human soul—roots which gripped them like a premonition and a longing, a tortured aspiration, a craving for justice, for dignity, freedom and love.

"He appears often to me among those hills, stone-faced and yet fierce, his pale eyes almost closing under the sheer weight of the heavy lids, a lonely sentry under the stars.

"And Forsythe, too, who had come to understand that human nature was not something to be rejected with disgust, but simply to be protected: I read in the papers that, when he left prison and returned to America, he was forgiven and accepted—and that he's carrying on a passionate campaign for the defense of nature in his own land.

"And Habib, led handcuffed to the lorry after the trial, but still good-humored, his captain's cap worn cockily over one ear, glancing from time to time at one of the policemen—a noticeably strong and well-built young man; during the trial he had amused himself enormously, never missing a word of what was said, and obviously enchanted by the efforts made by the human insects to alter conditions which suited him so perfectly. As he went by he called to me, with a reassuring laugh: 'My voyage's not over yet!' He was right: he made good his escape while being transported to Douala, with the aid of a guard whom he took with him. He's said to be busily engaged now in the smuggling of arms in the Eastern Mediterranean, ever ready no doubt to serve the 'legitimate aspirations of peoples, and those of the human soul in general,' as he used to put it. I've never been able to help feeling rather drawn toward him— he was so much at home in all that!

"And don't let's forget Orsini . . ."

Saint-Denis stopped for a moment and turned to look at the hills, which now stood close, youthful and attentive to each fresh gleam of dawn. It was now light enough for him to see in the Jesuit's hand a rosary, its beads running slowly through the long white fingers. He fell silent, in order not to disturb what he believed to be a morning prayer, but the Jesuit noticed his look and with a smile encouraged him to go on: he had long ago given up the small routines of his calling but the rosary kept his fingers busy and helped him to smoke less.

"And don't let's forget Orsini: he would never forgive us if we did. The whole of his life was only one long protest against his lack of importance: that, I'm sure, was what drove him to kill so many magnificent animals—some of the finest and most powerful in creation. One day, I won the confidence of a writer who comes regularly to Africa to kill his ration of elephants, lions and rhinos. I had asked him where he got this need and he had had enough to drink to make him sincere: 'All my life I've been half-dead with fear. Fear of living, fear of dying, fear of illness, fear of becoming impotent, fear of the inevitable physical decline. When it becomes intolerable, I come to Africa, and all my dread, all my fear, is concentrated on the charging rhino, on the lion rising slowly in front of me out of the grass, on the elephant that swerves in my direction. Then at last my dread becomes something tangible, something I can kill. I shoot, and for a while I'm delivered, I have complete peace, the animal has taken away with him in his sudden death all my accumulated terrors—for a few hours I'm rid of them. At the end of six weeks it amounts to a real cure.' I'm sure there was something of that in Orsini—but above all, there was a violent protest against the smallness and impotence of being a man, the smallness and impotence of being Orsini. He had to kill a lot of elephants and lions to compensate for that.

"So don't let's forget Orsini: it would be a grave error. I am conscious of him on the prowl around the entrance to this story, like a soul in agony, protesting against the lack of attention, trying to get in. After the Sionville raid, all those who saw him on the terrace of the Tchadien could feel that he did not mean to take it lying down, that he intended to take up the challenge. His whole attitude changed. His voice was no longer heard, and he sat there, at his table, in his white clothes, holding his head high, like some monument of silent outrage and scorn. No one now dared question him or give him a tap on the shoulder: one would have felt as if one were interrupting a cult, the cult of silent hatred which he was celebrating.

"What was going on in his head, beneath that impeccable Panama hat, we found out only later—after he had issued his summons 'to a strictly confidential meeting to discuss certain necessary measures.'

"He had sent out this rather mysterious invitation to the greatest hunters in French Equatorial Africa—and some of them came. They came chiefly because they distrusted Orsini, and because they did not mean to let him act in their name without knowing exactly what he had in mind. And so they met in his bungalow, from which every trace of Africa was carefully excluded—only good European furniture, and not a single trophy—he was not one of those who decorated their walls with 'vermin.' He received his visitors in silence, shaking hands with them in a confidential, mysterious way, without looking them in the eyes, then he sent the boys away and shut the doors: a real conspirators' meeting, as everyone distinctly felt.

"Some of our greatest professional hunters were there. The brothers Huette, although they rarely came to Fort Lamy and lived with their wives and three black children in North Cameroons; Bonnet, who had lost an arm in the First World War, but who gave all those who had two arms the impression that they were crippled —a ruddy man with close-cropped gray hair, gold teeth, and one sleeve in his pocket; Ganders, for whom big game hunting had been only one chapter in a tumultuous life which had led him from the Rue Fontaine world of pimps and gangsters to Popski's famous 'private army' which operated against Rommel in the Libyan desert; Goyé, a tall, wiry man with hollow cheeks who, along with the oldest Huette brother, was the only one who could still remember the time when professional ivory hunting was free, and whose reputation was second only to South Africa's Pretorius.

"Orsini went from one to the other, filling their glasses; then he stood up, looked at them silently for a moment, and began to speak.

In certain circumstances the usual legal methods became insufficient, and one had to be capable of taking justice into one's own
hands. He didn't need to go into the situation: they were sufficiently
informed. For the last six months not a single foreign tourist had
come on safari to French Equatorial Africa. No one could blame
them: they were not going to risk their lives for the mere pleasure
of hunting. Morel's activity had been shamefully exploited by the
press, and this campaign was reaching a point at which the very
principle of big game hunting was threatened and their good name
was at stake. In short, their profession—one of the finest and the
noblest—was in danger of being discredited once for all. And this
because some politicians were in secret agreement with Morel and
with Waïtari and were, like them, in the pay of the Arab League,
which had made the killing of elephants a symbol of the so-called
exploitation of Africa by white men. It was essential to put a stop to
this once for all, and there was only one way to do so: to force
Morel out of his hole. This therefore was his proposal . . .

"The others listened in silence. Bonnet was the first to speak:

" 'No. Count me out,' he said briefly.

"The others stared at Orsini in disgusted silence.

" 'Listen,' growled Goyé. 'If I could lay my hands on Morel, I'd
rough him up. But I don't see why elephants should pay the price.
On the main point that fellow's right: there've been enough of them
slaughtered. The tourists can be told to hunt with cameras.'

"Ganders sucked at his cigar and looked cynically at Orsini out
of his puckered eyes. The three brothers Huette stood there heavily
and showed not the slightest trace of interest. Orsini had gone pale.

" 'You won't be able to lay hands on him in any other way,' he said
in a voice trembling with exasperation. 'There's only one way to
make him come out of his hole and that's to go through the bush
killing elephants until he goes mad and comes after us. I know
perfectly well it's against the law, but there are times when the law
is helpless, and then one has to take justice into one's own hands.'

"Ganders took the cigar out of his mouth: 'In short, what you propose is to send him your visiting card?'

" 'If you like to put it that way.'

" 'A fine way of writing one's name.'

"Bonnet was the first to leave, followed by the brothers Huette who had not opened their mouths all evening. Ganders and Goyé stood up in turn.

" 'All right, if that's how you feel, I'll go it alone,' Orsini burst out. 'Are you afraid of a fine? Challut would pay it for you with pleasure.'

" 'Listen, brother,' said Ganders. 'I've killed a lot of animals in this life of mine, and some men too, if I remember right. I haven't much of a memory. If you've accounts to settle with Morel, go ahead and kill him, but don't try to hit below the belt. There are rules to every game. But if you want my advice, drop it. You'll do us more harm than good. Morel will soon be forgotten. He'll pass quickly. Men pass quickly.'

" 'I'll go it alone,' Orsini repeated. 'I'll do it my way.'

"And so he did.

"The news of Orsini's triumphal march through the bush reached us at Fort Lamy ten days later, and as the thing was happening in my territory I was immediately requested to put an end to his exploits. It wasn't difficult to find him: he was doing all he could to let everyone know where he was. The drums in every village announced his progress through the bush, and the lovers of meat gave him a triumphal welcome at each stage. Orsini was moving down the Yatta, killing every elephant he could find without discrimination—males, females and their young. He was sure word of his exploits would reach Morel. In short, as Ganders had put it, he was sending him his visiting card. He did not avoid the natural reserves, and had recruited two or three good shots in the villages he went through: in the whole land they talked of him and him only. He had become a popular hero, the provider of meat, the Father, the Good and the Generous, the Providential One—in a few days his extremely earthly glory rose to the sky. Those who had caught sight of him in the course of this triumphal march—Rodriguez at Oussa had tried to argue with him—have told me he seemed in a state of trance, almost visionary, drunk with triumph, his hollow cheeks darkened by a dirty stubble, that he spent sleepless nights sitting with a superior smile on his lips in the villages where they danced till dawn in his honor, leaving in the small hours in pursuit

of the elephants which the drought had chased toward the few remaining waterholes. It really seemed as if between him and those
ancient giants there was some deep personal account to be settled,
and he was challenging Morel at the top of his voice.

"Four days after his departure from Fort Lamy, at seven in the
morning, when I was expecting to reach Orsini's last encampment in
the early afternoon—the rains came at last that evening, making up
for their belated appearance by an unequaled violence—I saw a
strange procession moving through the yellow grass. I recognized
first of all a familiar figure—the white topee and rusty cassock of
Father Fargue; behind him two porters with a stretcher and a group
of black men with still-bleeding gobbets of meat stuck on branches.
Fargue shook hands with me without a word and gestured toward
the stretcher. It took me a second to recognize Orsini's face under
the stubble which had climbed right up to his scraggy cheekbones:
the terrible suffering in the eyes was the only familiar clue. I lifted
up the blanket, but at once let it drop.

"Fargue asked me if I had any morphine, but I'd left my medicine
chest in the jeep fifteen miles away. 'There's hardly enough of him
left to suffer anyway,' Fargue growled. 'It's almost twenty hours
since the elephants crushed him. I've never seen anyone cling to
life like that.'

" 'How did it happen?' I asked, much more to say something than
otherwise: the glance under the blanket had been enough.

" 'They just went over him,' said Fargue. 'From what the boys
have told me, they'd got within a hundred yards of a herd and
Orsini left two guns at that point and went to take up his position
a bit farther forward, in order to shoot one or two more at the moment of the stampede. The rest of the story I have from him—and
perhaps he's just delirious, because he'd been in this state for hours
by the time he was brought to me, and he no longer knew what he
was saying. In any case he claims that when he had reached the
clearing beyond the bushes he suddenly had a feeling of danger and,
turning his head, saw Morel standing there, about fifty yards away
from him. He swears it was Morel all right—alone, holding his
briefcase, and completely motionless, as if he had always been
there, as if he had always been waiting for him. Orsini took aim

and fired. He missed—at fifty yards, mind you, which is already surprising enough in one of our best big game hunters and confirms
my opinion that he was the victim of a hallucination due to nervous
fatigue and to his obsession with Morel. He told me he fired again
and again, and missed every time. It was then that the elephants,
terrified by the shots or, if you prefer, to use the expression this un-
fortunate man stammered out to me: "to come to Morel's rescue,"
rushed upon him and trampled over him—and there you see the
result, which isn't exactly the prettiest sight I've ever seen . . .'

"I went up to Orsini again; after all, I had my report to make, and
there were fierce discussions going on at Fort Lamy as to whether
Morel was still alive or had just been killed, as some claimed, by
one of his companions, for political ends. I bent over him. 'Orsini,' I
asked, 'are you really sure it was Morel?' His lips, which were
covered with blackened cuts, moved slightly: 'Certain,' he muttered. 'But . . .' It was a 'but' that put everything in question once
again. 'Try and answer.' He made a desperate effort to speak once
more. 'But I've thought so much about him . . . even in my sleep
. . . I saw him all the time . . .'

"The evidence was not conclusive. Suddenly I smelled the bleeding elephant meat which the villagers were taking home. Orsini's
eyes turned in the direction of Father Fargue, his black lips moved,
and his last words were the most terrible, the most outrageous and
frightening ever heard. 'I want to live!' muttered those remains of
a man.

"Even Father Fargue seemed shattered. 'Pig!' he muttered. But
it was he who closed Orsini's eyes.

"So much for Orsini. But as I've said already, his evidence doesn't
seem conclusive to me—Morel occupied his thoughts too completely.
Which doesn't mean that I take any more seriously people who say
our stubborn Frenchman is dead simply because, for some time now,
he hasn't been seen. He had too many friends—there was a tremendous sympathy for him—I believe he simply went into hiding. It has
even been claimed that you yourself, Father, gave him refuge at one
of your excavation sites—but I see from your smile that the accusation is quite unfounded, and that you did not come this far to ask me
for the latest news in order to take it back to him. The connivances

with which he was surrounded were real. They extended from the wireless operator who held up the message reporting his presence, to the now celebrated gesture of my friend and colleague Cérisot, a gesture bound to reinforce the opinion, widely held abroad, that our officials in Africa do not obey their orders and that they carry out policies of their own. But it was a thoroughly French and thoroughly understandable gesture; my friend Cérisot wasn't caught unprepared; he didn't miss the opportunity so dear to the heart of every Frenchman to speak his own mind . . ."

From Sionville to Yango is only six hours by road. The radiogram informing him of the "terrorist raid" on the presses at Sionville and ordering him to arrest the "bandits" on their return journey reached administrator Cérisot at five in the morning.

It barely left him time to organize what he called "a reception committee."

Cérisot was a plump, energetic man, always rushing about the bush gallantly doing his best against the oldest companions of man on earth, which still looked over his shoulder in Africa: drought, plague, resignation and superstition. But more and more often it seemed to administrator Cérisot that those four dark companions were no longer his worst enemies, and that now it was himself that man had to fear most.

Carefully and even solemnly the administrator folded the radiogram.

He suddenly felt that this was an occasion he had awaited for a long, long time, perhaps all his life; it was not often that a little man doing his best somewhere in the jungle could speak his mind to the rest of the world.

He was by no means sure that the crazy Frenchman would extend his optimism so far as to pass through Yango—he had no doubt abandoned the truck after leaving Sionville, taking to the forest; but if he showed himself confident enough to come by, he would get the reception he deserved.

Cérisot hurried.

First he put on his old lieutenant's uniform—he hadn't worn it for fifteen years, and had a great deal of trouble getting into it; he managed to do so only by sacrificing at least half his respiratory capacity. He then mobilized his full military forces, numbering three guards, plus the radio operator, plus eight villagers who had seen service in the army; he issued them rifles and posted them along the road. He placed himself at their head, wearing his kepi boldly over one ear.

Then he waited, looking frequently and impatiently toward the road that extended almost to infinity between the tall equatorial trees.

He was in exactly the right mood. That very morning he had heard, on the radio, yet another tale of human freedom uprooted and pulverized, yet another tale of barricades, of brave men left to fight and die alone under an iron fist, for their deep, torturing, immortal longing to be free, to keep that small root of heaven alive in their hearts.

He had stood there with his head bowed in distress and shame as the announcer recited what he called the "world news," a daily and brutal denial of all those noble verses that man sang about himself in his schools and universities, in his churches and in his books.

It seemed to him that the human mind itself was striving more and more to deprive the species of what little dignity it still claimed, and he sometimes felt almost consolation in the galloping progress of cancer, which at least proved that man was not the only one to treat nature with cruelty and contempt.

He was an indignant and determined little man.

Twice he inspected his "troops," fiddled severely with details of their dress and put them through a brief drill to check their reflexes. So, when he finally saw the approaching truck, far down the road, administrator Cérisot was ready.

He turned to his men: "Attention!"

In the truck they must have seen them; it accelerated in a cloud of dust and Cérisot could now see a machine gun taking aim at him through an opening torn in the canvas.

"Present . . . arms!"

The truck passed at full speed in front of the French officer saluting, and the soldiers, at rigid attention, presenting arms.

From the driver's cabin Morel looked at them without a trace of surprise, simply lifting his hand in a friendly gesture; then he leaned back tranquilly in his seat, his arms crossed, looking again at the long road stretching ahead of him under the tall trees; and then he said, as if speaking to himself, in a quiet voice:

"Yes, people everywhere are beginning to understand. I've always known they would."

At Banki the corporal received the same radiogram at the same time as his colleague at Yango. He stared at it for a while, pencil in hand, without a trace of expression. He was a Negro from the Ubangi who had seen ten years' service in the army and had learned a great deal of what the French taught about their own history and their own long struggles for the protection of nature. The road passed in front of his office. He read the message several times, then hid it under some papers and sat there looking from time to time at the road. He had to wait nearly two hours. When the truck had finally gone past, he followed it with his eyes, gave it time, then bent over his radio set. "Repeat your last message. Reception bad." He transcribed the message a second time, acknowledged receipt and then took the telegram to the C.O.

They drove on without a break, stopping only to fuel up from the cans they carried. At each halt, the three young men consulted in low voices, now and then glancing indignantly at Morel. Madjumba was the one who seemed most hostile; he exerted an almost physical ascendancy over the other two. He was not as articulate as N'Dolo, nor as sensitive as Inguélé, but he exuded a fierce, almost muscular determination, and it was not hard to see that his voice was the source of the others' fierce passion. Morel did not pay much attention, but Peer Qvist watched them out of the corner of his eye. When, having driven through the forest since dawn, they stopped for a second time to fill up from the cans and warm up some coffee, N'Dolo walked up to Morel who, pale, disheveled and panting, was leaning above the overheated engine.

The student steadied his glasses on his nose, and said, "You owe us an explanation. By what right did you state, in the published manifesto, that our activity had no political character? Who authorized you to do that? Why didn't you submit the text to us before publication? Our help was given you unconditionally, but you've no right to belittle the aims of our movement before public opinion."

Morel gave him a tired glance. "Well?" he said.

"That declaration was plainly directed against us. You had no need to do that. You have betrayed us. We are a political move-ment. We are a commando of the Army of African Independence. You have sabotaged our action at its crucial moment. You have de-prived it of any political significance."

Morel stood up, pushed his hat back and wiped his forehead; he was depressed and exhausted and there was a trace of exasperation in his voice.

"Listen, my friend," he said. "You are young, and what I have to say should be said to Waïtari, but since you are so eager—the only thing that interests me is the protection of the elephants. I know you don't like that: but I don't care—take it or leave it. I've said what I was after plainly from the beginning. You came along with me of your own free will. All right. You've said that you too had the protection of the elephants at heart. That you too were interested in natural splendor. All right. Fine. You proposed to help me, un-conditionally, with no strings attached. I accepted your help: it came in handy, and I don't turn anyone down. Of course you had your reasons—I'm well aware of them: I'm not as much of a fool as I seem. I had my own. But that didn't prevent us from going along together, because we were in agreement about the basic purpose, the elephants, about the defense of a margin within our civiliza-tion in which our basic right to live and roam freely could be pre-served. But you mustn't forget that you came with me, that I never asked you for anything, that I didn't come looking for you, that Waïtari has always said that he wanted to give me a hand because the elephants were very dear to him as well, because they were Africa. He told me that when you become the masters, you will make the protection of the elephants a sacred matter and will put it in your constitutions. I accepted this in good faith. But if nature doesn't interest you as much as all that and nationalism is enough for you, if collective independence is all you want and the elephants can go to hell provided you get it, you should have said so before.

You shouldn't have said they were the one thing dear to your heart. I'm not playing politics. I'm standing up for a margin, a refuge for something I care about. What has that got to do with politics? But to console you, I'll tell you one other thing. They'll make a political movement of it all right. You can rely on them. They'll never agree to its being anything but a political movement. So you've no need to worry."

"Are you—yes or no—for the right of peoples to self-determination?" shouted N'Dolo.

Morel looked sincerely upset. He turned to Peer Qvist: "Nothing to be done, he just won't understand."

"You are against African independence," said the student. "That's the truth."

"Do I make myself clear or don't I?" yelled Morel. "Nations—I don't give a damn about them. The old ones, the new ones, mine, yours, the lot of them. I don't play marbles. I've outgrown that. Is that plain? Right. The one thing I am interested in is the protection of the elephants. I want them to be there, alive, healthy, fat and visible. I want you to burden yourself with them, whatever the urgency and the difficulties of your own tasks. No nation alone can guarantee that margin; they all have to get together for that, accept the principle, insure respect for it. I've sent my petition to every country in the world, and to the United Nations as well—everywhere where there are post offices. I'm appealing to them—I'm saying to them: You must come to an agreement about my animals; it's important. Perhaps they will. If not, there will have to be new states, new nations created, African or others, new nations who will agree to burden themselves with elephants, who will take the protection of this cumbersome freedom in their hands. But I want to be sure that this time those new nations will keep their promises. I've been cheated too many times. As for ideologies, I distrust them on principle: they usually take up all the room, and elephants seem useless when one's in a hurry. As for nationalism, limited to just that—the sort you can see all over the place at present, and a hell of a lot it cares about the protection of natural splendors—that sort of nationalism's just one more foulness invented by man in this world, and he's invented a fair number. And now that I've made an excellent speech, and your doubts have been set at rest, you might help me with the cans."

When N'Dolo had moved away Morel turned to Peer Qvist and asked him: "That's plain enough, isn't it?"

"Yes," said the Dane, rather sadly. "It's plain enough. But he'll never be convinced. I've had long experience of this. They'll explain to you that national independence is much more important than individual rights. In Finland, when I was defending the forests, the Russian officials kept explaining to me patiently that pulp for making paper is after all more important than the trees. They understood only when there were almost no forests left. And the whalers kept explaining to me that whale oil was needed on the market and was much more important than whales. It goes on and on."

From that moment on the three young men would not speak to Morel and did not conceal their hostility. As N'Dolo drove, his face was full of hatred, and when their eyes met, Morel saw in his an arrogant contempt. Once, after two or three such glances and a silence of two hours, the student jerked out:

"I'll tell you what your elephants are. They're just a dodge, a camouflage, they give you a clear conscience, a protective smoke screen, understand? Behind which you can calmly get on with the dirty work of colonialism."

Morel nodded quietly.

"Well, I'm damned," cried the student in exasperation. "Do for once answer me directly, instead of sliding out of everything! Are you for the liberty of the people, yes or no?"

Morel had instinctively opened his mouth to reply but stopped in time. It wasn't worth it. If they still hadn't understood, it was because they hadn't got it in them. You either have or haven't. They weren't the only ones who had not. Obviously, humanity was not capable of respecting that elbow room, that margin, if civilization was not willing to burden itself with the elephants among other difficulties. If society insisted on considering this margin a luxury— well! Man himself would in the end become a useless luxury. Personally, of course, he didn't care. His misanthropy was indeed notorious, officially recognized and proclaimed. He sat up straight and wiped his forehead, and the gleam of gaiety in his eyes that was

never completely hidden appeared on the surface, and he knew that
neither Peer Qvist nor Forsythe were surprised at his smile. As for
the others, as for the world in general, it had long been saying that
he was mad.

At the next stop, the three young men still kept apart, taking their
meal alone. They never put down their weapons: it was as if they
expected to be attacked when their backs were turned. Peer Qvist
observed them indulgently. He was used to young people and he
understood their ill temper. But the one who really never took his
eyes off them was Korotoro. Sullen, and with his greasy felt hat
crammed down over his eyes, he kept his Sten gun always ready on
his bare knees, and said to Forsythe, with a sign in the direction of
the students: "They're cooking up something dirty."

It was during this last halt that Forsythe got to know Korotoro a
bit better. Between the young American officer, a scion of one of the
oldest families of the South, and the Negro vagabond who had
dragged his felt hat and his insolent smile through all the prisons of
Africa, there was an instinctive sympathy, simply because a certain
shared experience of persecution had in the end given them something in common. They often slept next to one another; and to a
friendly blow on the shoulder from Forsythe, Korotoro would reply
with his rather cruel but dazzling display of white teeth. That evening, as they halted among the euphorbia bushes and the darkness
of the desert around them resounded with the calls of the herds in
their exodus toward water, Forsythe saw Korotoro squatting on the
ground in the moonlight, holding his machine gun on his knees like
a bassoonist waiting for his cue. For the first time, Johnny Forsythe
asked himself what had driven this bad actor into Morel's wake, and
why he was following him so loyally.

"Tell me, Koro . . ."

Even in the darkness Korotoro's smile was visible.

"It's a year now, you've been going everywhere with him. Do you
love elephants as much as that?"

The big smile became bigger. "I don't give a damn about elephants."

"Then what? Are you with the others? For African independence?
Are you a partisan like those three?"

He spat and said proudly: "I was a deserter from the French Army, so . . ."

The meaning of that was not very clear, but it was said in a tone of superiority, and with a gesture of contempt aimed at the three students who were standing near the truck.

"All right. Well, why are you with him?"

Korotoro spat again. "I have no one," he explained shortly.

That was obviously the closest he could come to a declaration of friendship for Morel; there was not, and never would be, a better reason for being there.

It was to Korotoro that they owed their escape from certain death. The attentiveness with which this plunderer of Syrian shops and markets followed the slightest gesture of the three conspirators had certainly prevented them from carrying out their plan earlier. Forsythe was to reproach himself bitterly for not having paid them the attention they deserved—although their whole attitude was a demand, almost a claim, for attention: they could not endure not being taken seriously. Their conviction that they had been betrayed, and the slightly paternal indifference with which they were treated, and which they interpreted as a sign of contempt, drove them in the end to the final break—and indeed probably further than they had at first thought of going. Forsythe was to admit later, to Schölscher, that he had never for a moment foreseen what they were planning.

"I wasn't watching them. I could see, of course, that they weren't pleased, but, if anything, that made me smile. And besides, after all, I had something else to think of. At Sionville I had drunk, if I may use the expression, from a poisoned spring—the spring of hope. The idea that I could at last go back home holding my head high, as they say, that my compatriots had understood that the guilt had never been mine, that my only fault had been honesty, an excessive faith in human beings, in their decency, that they had heard what I was trying to shout at them from the depths of Africa, had completely unsettled me. I felt drunk with hope. After what I had been through, you must admit that this was something to think about. I was lying on the sand, staring at the stars, and I swear to you that I could see more than there were. Never had a night seemed to me more beautiful. I even believe I started singing at one moment—anyhow, I was a thousand miles from worrying about our three young men.

"I was dozing off, when suddenly I heard the sound of an engine. Raising my head I saw the truck moving off into the night at full speed. I saw Korotoro run several steps forward, then take aim with his machine gun and fire. A burst of fire came from the truck and I saw Koro leap in the air. I saw him fire again and yet again in the direction of the receding truck, then fall, never letting go of his weapon, till the last bullet had skipped along the sand. I remember his felt hat rolling along the ground; and the first thing Morel did, when he saw he was dead, was to pick up his hat and clap it on his head. It was a brown felt hat, a symbol of European civilization. He was very attached to it; there must have been a sort of friendship between the two of them. You can get attached to anything.

"We buried him like that with his felt hat on his head, after digging him a grave with our hands. Then we looked at one another. It was still fifteen miles to the lake, but we knew that Koro's vigilance had probably saved us. He had watched the three fanatics so attentively that they had not been able to carry out their plan earlier. If they had done it at the previous halt, forty miles back, we'd have been done for—without water, without food and without arms. During practically the whole of the drive Koro had kept his finger on the trigger, but in the end he had dozed off for a couple of minutes and that was all they had needed. We had betrayed them, you understand. We had dared to proclaim to the world that our struggle had no political character. That it was much more important. They had therefore broken with us and made off straight toward the Sudanese frontier to lay their complaints before their beloved chief. They wanted to create a new nation, and what Morel was trying to preserve no doubt seemed to them ridiculous, laughable, worthy only of a decadent sensibility.

"I must say Morel took it badly. It wasn't, of course, the idea of doing fifteen miles on foot across the waterless track that worried him. I swear to you he never gave a thought to exertions, difficulties or dangers. But he was very fond of Koro, they had been together a long time, and although the bastard had one day stolen his watch

—he had searched him and found it on him—there was a sort of friendship between them. But there was also something else: the three students. I believe he imagined that because they had been brought up at French schools and universities and had studied the 'humanities,' as you say in your country, they ought to have understood what was really at stake. But those are things you don't learn in schools. You have to have been really desperate to know what respect for nature means. And those fellows, for all their education, had a long way to go. Korotoro couldn't even read, but he must have felt all this instinctively. He attached more importance to friendship than to anything else. He had been desperate, and what you learn from that is an instinct for self-preservation, a need for protection.

"Morel realized at least this, and expressed it rather clearly, just as we were picking up our things to try and cover as much ground as possible before the real heat of the day, and were setting out on foot among the elephants, buffaloes and big brown herds of antelope which began to be visible as the sun rose against the high red cliffs on the horizon. 'If those three idiots haven't yet reached the stage of being willing to give their lives, if necessary, in defense of elephants, it's because they haven't yet suffered enough themselves. I'm coming round to the belief that colonialism hasn't been a harsh enough school for them, that it hasn't taught them enough about things—that French colonialism has, in spite of everything, treated nature with a certain respect. They've still got a lot to learn, and French people don't give that kind of lesson. The men of their own race will take care of that. One day they'll have their Stalins, their Hitlers, and their Napoleons, their Führers and their Duces, and then their very blood will cry out to demand respect for nature. That day they will understand.' "

# PART FOUR

~~~ XXXII ~~~

THE CLICKING of the amber beads in the man's hand irritated Waïtari even more than the unconcern with which the Egyptian listened to his pleading as he lay—sat was not the word—in the armchair opposite. The amber *masbaha* dangled languorously from his hand over his crossed knees, and for an hour the sharp click of the beads had punctuated all that Waïtari was saying. The Egyptian's face had a tired and intelligent look, with features that were scored and yet delicate and with lips that almost vanished when he smiled. He wore a tarboosh on his graying hair, but his European clothes were of Italian silk, well cut.

The sun weighed heavily on the awning spread over the inner garden of the Hotel Nile at Khartoum, where the meeting was taking place. In the center a fountain splashed languidly on the green-and-blue marble mosaic. On each side of the staircase, motionless and absent, stood a houseboy in a white robe and turban, with a silver salver under his arm. Waïtari could feel exasperation rising within him. He could no longer bear this atmosphere of oriental torpor in which any idea of action appeared absurd.

"I suppose that's your last word?" he asked abruptly.

The man raised his hand. "My friend, there's no such thing as a last word in politics. Let's say that for the moment it's very difficult for us to give you active support. We are too busy in Tunisia, Algeria and Morocco, where we are just obtaining the positive results you know about. I've spoken to you very frankly. To diversify our efforts at this moment would be pure folly. Your merits, in our eyes, are great, all the more so since you are—let's admit it frankly— practically alone. But we have no interest in creating sporadic and insignificant disturbances in French Equatorial Africa. That would merely emphasize our lack of preparation. We can't be everywhere at once. Those are the reasons for our refusal—for the time being. The day will come, I assure you."

His voice and face underwent a slight tremor. Waïtari knew these faces in which the skin remains impassible while the blood itself is laden with passion: the Egyptian was a fanatic, and, what was more, a religious one.

"If I understand you rightly, you are serving first and foremost your religious beliefs. In Cairo I heard a great deal about the people's right to self-determination."

The other nodded slowly. "Our first duty lies with those who are closest to us. We must first defend our faith against the materialist barbarism which is flooding over us from the West."

He fixed his eyes on the amber *masbaha,* but the line of his lips grew more slender: a shadow of a smile. "Besides, for us, as you are certainly aware, Marxism is a Western doctrine."

Waïtari knew that his contacts with the French Communist party were well publicized. "I see no connection," he said coldly. "I don't see why I should have refused Communist support in my fight for independence. You yourself don't mind accepting arms from Czecho-slovakia and Russia."

A tired gesture; the hand that made it was the very opposite of Waïtari's—weak, long, narrow, all delicacy, slenderness and tremors.

"Let's not get involved in this sort of discussion. All I mean to say is that you must have patience. At the moment every cartridge and every dollar we have at our disposal is needed elsewhere."

For a second, Waïtari looked silently at the Egyptian. Then he began to speak. He was glad the conversation had been in French; it was the only language in which he could give his best. He spoke at some length, and when he had finished he had obtained neither the arms nor the money nor the "volunteers," but he had no doubt about at least one result he had achieved: his host was left with the conviction that this powerful Negro with the voice of bronze and the gift to dress African passion in the well-cut clothes of French logic was a new star rising in the political firmament of Africa.

Unfortunately, important as he was, this man was only the smallest, almost insignificant, fraction of the world audience he had to reach. The first conference of the representatives of the colonial peoples was to meet soon at Bandung, and its organizers had not thought fit to invite him. He was determined to make sure that such an omission—such an affront—would not occur again. He must at all costs acquire the necessary stature; and terrorism, even if ephemeral, even if without any practical effect, was still the only line of action. There could be no question of provoking a revolt of the tribes, for their chiefs and witch doctors were hostile to him, and the tribes themselves were cut off from him by an impassable barrier of ignorance, superstition and primitive practices. But it would be enough to supply the newspapers with the few indispensable headlines to gain admittance to the international circles where decisions were made.

He went back to his room, stretched himself out on the bed and stared angrily at the equestrian engravings hung on the walls: they would soon be the only trace of the British left in the Sudan. So nothing more was to be hoped from Cairo. He was back once more to the starting point: he must find money. Arms traffickers didn't give their wares for nothing and "volunteers" did not join up on the strength of promissory notes. He had no doubt about his ability to find a solution—perhaps because he had no doubt about his own destiny. He could feel his destiny in the strength of his own voice, in that of his hands and in the very dimension of his solitude, to which absolute power alone could provide a sufficient answer. The boundless aspiration which sometimes kept him awake all night was in itself like a promise of victory, a sort of haunting memory of the ten generations of Oulé chieftains who were his forebears.

There was a knock at the door, and he was not sorry to admit Habib, who carried with him that robust if cynical conviction of the infinity of resources offered by the earth to those who knew how to inhabit it. His cocky self-confidence was based on a certain intimate knowledge of human nature, and when he looked at you you felt that for him you were an old habit, that he knew all about you long before meeting you. Yes, he was already aware of the negative result of the interview with the representative of the Arab League. This failure must not be taken too seriously. There might be a way, *inch' Allah.* He was here with a little scheme which had germinated in the inspired brain of his friend De Vries as he lay, bored stiff, in the hospital—yes, he was now fully recovered, thanks be to the Almighty —a stroke of luck which had literally been steered in their direction by a favorable wind. A real intervention of Heaven in their favor— and that wasn't a mere phrase, for it had to do with the appalling drought all over East Africa. It might, with a little luck, bring in some ten thousand pounds.

Habib pulled a map from his pocket and unfolded it on the bed. "There," he said, cutting short his flowery rhetorics and placing an enormous finger on a blue patch. "That's the Kuru. A lake. The only place in the whole region where there's still water."

〜〜 XXXIII 〜〜

On June 22, toward noon, the aircraft from which American camera-man Abe Fields was photographing the extraordinary concentration of elephants on the banks of Kuru flew low over the lake: a hundred square miles of dunes, water, birds, rocks and reeds. The aircraft had been circling about that region all morning; it had landed once at the El Garani airfield south of the Bahr el Gazal to fuel up, and had then taken off again.

Lying on his stomach in the nose of the plane, Fields snapped shot after shot of one of the most dramatic stories of his career.

The vast desert to the east of the lake was covered with animals dying in an agony of thirst or still struggling to reach the waters of Kuru. The hundred fifty miles of the "waterless track" were strewn with carcasses, and when the aircraft came low over the ground thousands of birds of prey rose up in its wake, then fell back again, softly and heavily. Compact masses of buffalo stood motionless in

the red dust, scarcely raising their heads at the passage of the aircraft, then moved off once more, each time leaving behind them
hundreds of animals who could no longer follow the herd but still
tried to get to their feet with a spasmodic jerk of their hooves; the
"track" was covered with moving brown and gray spots; and dispersed over the whole of the region from the desiccated marshes of
Bahr Salaman, their usual place of retreat in the dry season, the
elephants were stubbornly making their way toward the waters of
Kuru, hundreds of them stopping abruptly in a sudden abandon-
ment of strength which left them motionless, trunks inert. Raised by
the herds still on the march, the famous red dust of the Bahr el
Gazal, sometimes so thick that the sun was reflected in it, made
the camera work particularly difficult.

Fields knew nothing about African fauna and was almost incapable of distinguishing a buffalo from a tapir, but he did know
that the public was always particularly touched by the suffering of
animals and he was sure he had stumbled onto a fine subject. To
make this tragic exodus of the herds more clear to the public, he
had photographed one after another the dried-up beds of the principal *bahrs* and lakes of the region, the cracked bottom of the
Mamoun, that of the Yro, and the marshes of Bahr Salaman now
displaying, mile after mile, their geological nakedness. His pilot
had come down so low over the bed of the Bahr el Din that he had
been able to photograph about a hundred crocodiles, some of them
on their backs: the bed of the watercourse was furrowed by their
dying convulsions. Lake Kuru itself was baked dry in its outer
creeks: only at the center did some ten or fifteen square miles still
gleam among the islands of red rock, earth and reeds. Several hundred elephants stood motionless in the water and among the reeds,
while the still damp mud of the outer marsh to the north was animated by a prodigious stir of birds; but this was a sight impossible
to photograph—when the aircraft came lower it was immediately
caught in a heavy cloud of living bodies, and the pilot had to turn
away quickly to save his propellers. Fields had to content himself
with one picture from a height of 600 feet; the birds looked like a
vast, colorful plantation.

Abe Fields had photographed many things in his life, from the machine-gun swept roads of France to the devastation of hurricane Hazel in the Caribbean, including the Normandy beaches and French soldiers being blown up by mines in Indochina, but he had never yet seen a sight like this. Not that he had any illusions about the emotion he was feeling: it was strictly professional, inspired by the unique and exclusive character of the story he was handling, far from any competitor. He had long ceased to harbor any illusions about the quality of his emotions; he had seen too much, and if, in his career as a hunter of pictures, he had allowed himself to participate otherwise than through the eyes in all the scenes he had photographed, he would long ago have been a hopeless drunkard. (Fields was the first to admit that he drank too much as it was.) But the hard carapace with which he successfully protected himself now guaranteed him a position at the top of a profession in which there was no lack of coldly expert hands and hardened eyes.

Fields was a short, agile man who had had a difficult start and had gone to Spain during the Civil War with a fierce determination either to leave his carcass there or to come back with a really sensational story. At a few yards' range he had taken a couple of shots, which had remained famous, of Republicans being mown down by a machine gun during the first attack at Guadalajara: that made him. (He was wounded himself while taking the pictures, but in his enthusiasm had felt nothing.) Since then, the only major event he had not succeeded in photographing was the extermination of his family in Poland, and even that—so his enemies said—wasn't his fault: he just wasn't there.

For some time he had been out of luck: he had missed the first massacres in North Africa, and he had come to the Chad to do a story on Morel, but had had no more success than the twenty other journalists who relieved one another at Fort Lamy. He had then gone to Khartoum, on a tip about a rising of the army there, in the conflict between the supporters and opponents of union with Egypt, but the troops who had mutinied briefly had already been brought under control again by the time he arrived. He had of course heard talk about the lack of rain and about the drought, but this had not suggested any definite picture to his mind, and it was only when he heard about the mass migration of the herds, and of the elephants driven mad by thirst throwing themselves into the sea on the Mozambique coast, that he suddenly scented a story and decided to take a look. He hired a plane, and on the first flight realized what a break he had. Now he was in action and thanking God for his windfall.

The only plane he had managed to find in Khartoum was an old Blenheim left there by the British, which its owner, Flight-lieutenant Davis, formerly of the R.A.F., used for training "volunteers" for all the sensitive centers of the Middle East. Fields hired them both. The crate did not seem worse than many other machines that he had flown in, when it was essential to get there first. (Fields was not afraid of accidents: they had often made it possible for him to get his best pictures. Besides, he had the firm and curious conviction that he was not destined to die in an accident but of cancer of the prostate or of the anus. He was quite unable to say where this certainty came from, but perhaps it merely reflected his general view of life.) He took a few more shots, then came back to the seat beside the pilot. He closed the shield of the intercom.

"What I don't understand," he said, "is what they eat. There's water, I know. But the soil is absolutely bare."

"The reeds," said Davis. "There's plenty of them. Elephants love a nice tasty reed."

Davis had a brilliant war record. Afterward, being too old to fly in the R.A.F. and totally unable to live on the ground, he had become one of those flying hobos in the Middle East and Africa, ready to do anything to remain in their element, which was anywhere upward of a thousand feet above the ground. Since 1945 he had been exhibiting, in all the bars from Alexandria down to Khartoum, his blotched cheeks, his well-bred voice, his outmoded Air Force slang and his blond handlebar mustache—but also and chiefly, his profound love of flying. Until the arrival of the Germans he had been an instructor in the Egyptian Air Force; then he transported arms to Tripolitania and the Sudan; and at last he found himself with a Blenheim and a Beechcraft ready for odd jobs at an airfield not far from Gordon's Tree airdrome, where he had known better days.

"They feed on rushes. It seems rushes are very good when you eat them by the roots."

The left-hand engine began to spit, the plane trembled, and the right-hand engine stopped dead. Fields clutched his bag of negatives and quickly secured it and the two cameras round his neck. (Fields was used to plane failures and forced landings and was always ready for them.) They were then about fifteen feet above the herds. Davis looked for an empty sandbank and saw one right in front of him, from which a cloud of birds had just risen; he thought happily that with the insurance money he would be able to buy two crates in reasonable condition. The aircraft glided over a group of elephants standing in the water, but just as it touched down two of them, lying on their sides and half-submerged, suddenly got up under the left wing; the plane swung around, hit the ground with its tail and split in two.

Fields was flung out of the cockpit and found himself sitting on the sand with the bag of negatives and the cameras miraculously intact. He got up at once, put on his glasses, adjusted the lens, took a photograph of the machine with the elephants in the background, and one or two close-ups of Davis sprawled over the controls with his chest smashed in. Then he looked around.

Seen from ground level, the lake looked much bigger and the herds even more numerous: the elephants surrounded him almost on all sides. For a moment Fields felt apprehensive, but the animals were in such a state of exhaustion that the crash of the plane among them had not produced any reaction, apart from a general scattering of the birds. (The only birds Fields recognized were a large number of marabous and giant juburus, which he knew from having seen them every morning from his hotel window at Fort Lamy.) The birds were already coming to rest again, among them some small white waders which were landing on the backs or flanks of the elephants. Eastward, toward the distant towering cliff, there was a compact, tawny, living mass of what Fields thought were antelopes, completely motionless in the sparkling and glimmering of the air, the water and the red rock. Fields decided that he could safely strike out into the water: the lake came to an end some hundred yards or so in front of him in sand dunes on which he could see native huts, some of them half in ruins and apparently abandoned. They were scattered the length of the dune for about

a mile and a half. At the northern end of the dune was a figure
running in his direction. He waddled cautiously toward it, holding
the bag of films and cameras well above his head, but discovered
at once that the water was nowhere more than three feet deep. He
reached the dune without difficulty and was quickly joined by the
man, who turned out to be a tall fellow with ginger hair and naked
torso, a red-and-white bandanna knotted around his neck with the
knot at one side. The face, liberally freckled, seemed to him vaguely
familiar.

"Was there anyone else on board?"

"Yes, he's dead," said Fields in bad French. He tried to remember
where he had seen that face before. He took his cigarettes from the
pocket of his shirt and automatically extended the pack. The
freckles suddenly showed a joy out of proportion to anything Fields
knew about the desire to smoke.

"Holy Moses! American cigarettes! They're the first I've seen
since . . ."

Fields was no longer listening. He had recognized the freckles.
They had figured in what might be described as a prominent manner in the American press during the Korean war, spread out on the
front page as a mark of ignominy, over the word "turncoat." After a
total eclipse of long duration the freckles had reappeared on the
front page but their character had slightly changed: when Fields
left Paris for the Chad they had become almost popular. It was only
now that Fields understood where his luck had brought him. What
twenty journalists had sought vainly for months, a providential
plane crash had obligingly thrown before his camera.

"Keep the pack. I hope they don't bring back unpleasant memories."

Forsythe laughed to hide his embarrassment at being recognized.
They exchanged a few words about the accident, standing there on
the dune among thousands of birds, buffalo, antelopes and elephants
motionless in the heat, bogged down in a quivering atmosphere in
which the mirages amplified the herds to infinity. (The estimates
which Fields gave of the number of elephants in the Kuru varied
between one and two thousand. When the films he had taken before
the crash were developed, the number of elephants there that morn-

ing was estimated at about seven hundred.) He stepped back a bit
and took a photograph of Forsythe. Then they walked along the
dune toward the huts. Field said later that from that moment he
had only one idea in his head: to photograph Morel. He held his
camera ready and was so overcome by emotion that his knees began
to shake. (The idea that the shaking might be due to the crash never
occurred to him.) At the same time he was struggling against another feeling, much deeper and more obscure, whose exact nature
he was not too anxious to examine closely. Morel's stand had struck
a muted chord within him: a man does not spend over twenty years
in the front row of world news, as a professional observer of humanity's behavior, without an indignation like Morel's rousing a
poignant, if obscure, sympathy. He also felt a little uncertain: it
was not impossible that Morel was merely a particularly clever political agitator in the service of Cairo or even of Moscow, or both.
Fields was thus divided between skepticism and hope, and this revealed itself in a certain nervousness. He kept steadying his glasses
on his nose and looking around in search of a figure which he
imagined in advance as gigantic, legendary, suddenly appearing
against the sky with a rifle under its arm—but all he saw was a large
number of elephants, which interested him much less.

He answered Forsythe's questions absent-mindedly. From the professional point of view this in itself was a strange remissness on his
part: Forsythe excited immense curiosity in the United States. But
with Forsythe, Fields knew where he was, whereas Morel opened
before him horizons where everything remained to be explored, and
where perhaps something very near his heart was involved. He did
however confirm what Forsythe had known since the Sionville expedition: the American public was beginning to show a certain sympathy for him, and the indignation, remorse and fist-shaking of that
new kind of "turncoat," the heartbreak and disgust behind the gesture of the exploited and betrayed American who was siding with
animals, were fully understood. The press was going into the whole
business of "proofs" again, and there was criticism of his "dishonorable discharge" from the Air Force.

"Anyway, 'they' are now passionately interested in your adventure." Fields did not say who "they" were: he never referred to the

public otherwise. His own words reminded him of the story he was handling and all his professionalism returned to him. He took one or two more photographs of Forsythe and began to ask questions. Johnny Forsythe answered with bitterness, nervously smoking one cigarette after another.

"Well, as you know, I was turned out of the Air Force, and I went and buried myself in the Chad, to get myself forgotten—and try to forget. I spent most of my time getting drunk. The classic way of going downhill, you know, with all the usual stages. I won't go into that. My family offered me a small allowance on condition nothing more should be heard of me: in the South we have a highly developed sense of honor. At Fort Lamy things didn't go very well either: once I had to sock a guy who offered me a drink 'to help me forget.' Then the day came when the same fellow offered me a round again—without saying anything, it's true, just with a smile, and I accepted: I hadn't enough money to buy myself all the stuff I needed. Only the blacks were decent: they used to laugh, but not at me, it's the way they see things. In short, things were going badly. Then Morel came to see me with his petition. Of course I signed it! No one in the world was better placed than me to understand what he was talking about. It's a bit too easy to say that it was the Communists who led me astray, and that it's enough to get rid of Communists in order to . . . you know the theory. Whether the Americans were or were not guilty, whether the Communists were or were not guilty, it was all the same. Mankind—the best of it and the worst of it—was completely caught in its own refined deceit, its own sanctified hypocrisy, covered with dirt from head to foot. Well, they had called me a 'turncoat' and I was going to justify that name. I was going to walk out on them all, on all the dirt, on the whole damned species. Nobody could understand better than I what Morel was trying to shout in their ears. He's a man defending a certain idea of dignity, below which no one should be allowed to sink. When it became clear what the result of his petition was, that is, nothing, just general ridicule, I helped him: we built up a stock of arms. You know what happened after that. Here we are."

Fields nodded. He searched for his cigarettes and remembered that he had given them to Forsythe. He asked him for one. He made

no comment and Forsythe wondered if he had been listening. Instinctively he felt esteem for Fields. The little man had just been
through a dreadful plane crash and he had seen him calmly wading
among the elephants with his glasses and his camera as if he were
crossing a street. True, his profession had probably hardened him.
He was obviously a man who had seen a great deal. A Jew, he decided, looking stealthily at his face, at that something in the eyes.
He thought suddenly that there should have been a Jew with Morel
since the beginning—preferably a survivor of the German gas
chambers.

He told him that they had been at Lake Kuru for the last ten days,
ever since their raid on Sionville—purpose of the raid had been to
attract world attention to the Bukavu Conference for the Protection
of the African Fauna; that they were living in abandoned huts of a
village of Kaï fishermen who had been driven away by the 1947
floods and who had been resettled on the heights at the western end
of the lake. Morel had left two days ago for Gfat, which was a
junction of camel tracks between the Chad and the Sudan on the
other side of the frontier. The one and only merchant in that part
of the world apparently had a radio set, and he was hoping to learn
something of decisions taken at the conference which had just
ended.

"He's convinced that they're going to take *some* steps, and if they
do so he means to give himself up. He's sure he'll be acquitted by
the French courts. Probably he's wrong, overoptimistic as usual. I
don't know."

He fell silent and then added with a trace of embarrassment in his
voice that he was planning to go back to the United States as soon
as possible. Here again Fields made no comment. They had reached
the other side of the dune, and from a long way off Fields recognized the young woman who was waiting for them beyond the huts,
beside some horses. He stopped and took a photograph before drawing near. He had often heard Minna spoken of at the Tchadien and
had looked with curiosity at the snapshots taken of her by various
people and always willingly displayed: in fact, she had set his
imagination going, and now he felt disappointed. She was pretty
but in a rather ordinary way—only her mouth had something touch-

ing, almost pathetic about its flat yet full lips; it was impossible, though, to imagine that girl having the strength of resentment, of bitterness, to make her take arms and ammunition to the man known currently as "an enemy of the human race." There was a certain sweetness about her, too, something quiet and forlorn at the same time, which made it difficult to imagine her in such a role.

She told Fields that she had seen his accident from the dune, but had not had the courage to come near. She had thought all those in the plane had keen killed instantly, and she shook her head incredulously, staring at Fields from head to foot as though to make sure that he was really all in one piece. Fields told her that his pilot had been killed but that he himself was unhurt. (An X-ray photograph taken at Fort Lamy Hospital later showed that he had three broken ribs.) He spoke to her in bad German, looking all the while for the best angles. He asked her to take off her big felt hat with its chin-strap, and took a picture of her against a background of elephants motionless in the vast vertical mirror of the mirage, of rocks bristling with rushes and of white waterbirds. While he worked, she talked to him about the misery of the herds with an animation and sympathy that made Fields wonder if this girl was the least bit conscious of what she had done, of the strangeness of their meeting in this landscape from the earliest ages of the world, and of the curiosity which her adventure was exciting almost everywhere; he was to say later that he had never had the impression that he was among terrorists, but rather among members of some peaceful scientific expedition who paid no attention to anything but their job.

"I'd better do something about your dead pilot," said Forsythe. "In this heat . . ."

Fields offered to give him a hand when he had taken a few more pictures. He was longing to lay hands on Morel himself, but he had to resign himself to patience, and he accepted eagerly when Minna asked him if he would like to see Peer Qvist; he tried to remember all he had been told about the Danish naturalist, whose famous eccentricity and bad temper had this time made the elephants their excuse for expressing themselves. Opinions about him were somewhat divided: some claimed that under that patriarch's head of his he concealed an exhibitionist's thirst for publicity, others believed him to be sincere but mad, others again would recall that he had been one of the signatories of the Stockholm appeal for the banning of atomic weapons and that he had been mixed up in the Spanish war, and saw in him merely an agent of the Communists. (Fields later had the opportunity of asking Peer Qvist about his signature to the Stockholm appeal. The naturalist told him that his only reason for signing had been the appalling consequences to fauna and flora of atomic radiation. It was not merely a matter of danger to man himself, but what was much more important, he said, a danger to marine fauna and birds.) While they were walking along the dune toward the Dane's hut—Fields noted that they had apparently chosen to live fairly far from one another, and this seemed to him rather odd—Minna told him the drought was so bad that the evaporation was like a tide. Every morning the reeds, dunes and rocks seemed to have grown during the night. It was enough to see the state of exhaustion in which the herds were reaching the Kuru, and how they then remained prostrate for several days without eating, to imagine what was going on elsewhere . . .

"*Schrecklich!*" she said. "*So schrecklich!*"

Fields said a few suitable words. He could not say that he had any particular love for animals. He had once wanted to buy a dog, but it was impossible in his vagabond profession, and once in Mexico, during a bullfight, he had ardently wished for the death of the matador, disgusted by the sight of the wounded bull. He had rarely in his life taken sides for anyone or anything from the bottom of his heart, but that time he had done so: he was for the bull. That was not a professional desire for a sensational shot: he had his camera with him all right but he had shut his eyes. "Look at that fellow shutting his eyes!" said a man next to him, in English. "You know, a bull's only meat on the hoof!"

Fields observed him coldly: Bronx, he decided, in spite of the flamboyant shirt and the cowboy hat. "It's hard to know where meat on the hoof begins and where it ends," he said to him in a tone of voice that left no doubt of the unfriendly insinuation.

So Abe Fields had no special tenderness for animals, and he felt slightly shocked hearing the girl talk about the African herds as though they were the only things that counted. It hurt his moral sense: sixty per cent of the world was starving, so that the word *liberty* could have no meaning for it; there were, after all, causes more urgent than a campaign for the protection of nature.

But this last thought suddenly aroused so unexpected a response in his heart that he wondered if there were not in this girl and in Morel a somewhat astonishing ulterior motive, and if this protection of nature, which they advocated with such emphasis and such tenacity, did not conceal a kind of enormous spirit of tolerance and of respect for human life also, a need for tolerance and dignity that went far beyond the apparent simplicity of the aims they were pursuing. He felt the shudder of anticipation that meant he was on the track of some exceptional story. He tried to restrain his professional excitement: even if he had scented the truth it was not of much concern to him, because it was something he could not photograph. And it was difficult to imagine that poor girl—probably quite uneducated, a typical product of the Berlin night clubs—concealing beneath her commonplace and even slightly vulgar beauty, beneath that blue-gray, insistent gaze which always seemed a little injured, so deep an understanding of the oldest, yet most urgent, of the problems encountered by man in his uncertain progress on earth; she must have a naïve belief that the Frenchman was really only defending the elephants, or perhaps she had just fallen in love with him without trying to understand all the implications of the desperate campaign he had undertaken. But then she stopped for a moment to look at the thousands of birds standing on the sandbanks and on the palm trees in the now deepening evening light, and he read in her face such an expression of happiness that instinctively he grabbed his camera.

"What brought you to do this?" he asked abruptly and almost rudely; he always preferred snapshots.

She turned her head away and Fields suddenly had the impression that it was to hide an ironic smile.

"What's so surprising?" she asked, with a shrug. "During the war and—since, I've learned a lot."

"I don't see the connection."

"I am sure you don't. Well, at Fort Lamy I read the petitions which Monsieur Morel was passing round and I wanted to do something myself. That must surprise you, because I'm German and you think . . ."

Fields felt irritated. "I don't think anything. I don't know what your being German has to do with this. It doesn't explain why you've risked bringing arms and ammunition to an outlaw."

"I come from Berlin," she said obstinately. "We saw a lot in Berlin. Oh, I don't know how to explain to you. You either feel it or you don't. I suppose a time came when I had had enough. I suddenly needed—something else."

She shrugged. Of course, thought Fields. He knew that. Something else. Something different. That was what his editors were constantly asking him for. They were right of course, but it would be a damned difficult story to do in photographs. "Something different!" It had never been photographed before and probably never would be. They had arrived at the end of the dune and Minna pointed out to him the last hut in the village, which stood slightly apart from the others. "There it is."

They found the Dane lying motionless on his back with his eyes half open. Fields had never met him but had read many articles about him, and the magazines published his photograph as often as they could: he was good copy. His was an infinitely ancient face, with a certain ascetic hardness rare among Europeans. (Fields had seen as good or better among the Chinese and the Indians. The only white men's faces that could stand comparison were those of some missionaries in Asia: often they lost all European character and ended with slit eyes.) Fields bent for a look at the book in the hands of the sleeping man: the Bible. With a face like that, he thought, there's really no need for a visiting card. He took a picture, with the Book well in evidence.

The Dane opened his eyes and stared at them fixedly; but Fields felt that he was still a long way off, and was still seeing what he had just left. Fields explained about the crash and told him who he was and what he was doing in that part of the world. They began to talk and Minna left them alone. Peer Qvist told him that there was no precedent, to his knowledge, for the rains being so late, and that the consequences for Africa would be terrible. He spoke of this with such emotion and with such an expression—it was almost fanatical

—in his eyes, that Fields sensed more than a mere naturalist's compassion.

"Yes," said the Dane after a silence, "there are moments when it seems a blasphemy for man to try to take the protection of nature into his own hands, when it looks as if heaven itself had decided to tear its living roots out of the earth."

Fields muttered something indistinct. He was not a believer. He asked the Dane if he would let him take a few pictures and this led to a curious misunderstanding. Fields was thinking naturally of permission to photograph the aged adventurer himself, but the latter understood him differently.

"Of course," he said, with a proprietor's sweeping gesture. "Take all the photographs you wish. This is one of the biggest concentrations of birds the human eye has observed for a long time. If you can send me your pictures later in Denmark for my collection, I shall be grateful."

Fields gladly promised. Before going out, the Dane picked up the Bible and slipped it into his pocket. While they were walking along the dune Fields asked him in what circumstances he had come in contact with Morel.

"You can say I've been attached to him by the Copenhagen Museum of Natural History," said the Dane with a trace of mischievous humor in his eyes.

He seemed to have no great love for officialdom. Fields pressed the question and Peer Qvist in the end explained to him that he had been one of the first recipients of Morel's petition. Morel had asked him to mobilize public opinion in Scandinavia on the side of Africa's elephants. In the letter accompanying the petition Morel spoke of Denmark, Sweden, Norway and Finland. "Countries which have partly solved their own problem of protecting nature and should now help in solving it all over the world." Peer Qvist fell silent for a moment.

"To a certain degree he may be right. I should not dream of saying so to my compatriots, who are far too pleased with themselves as it is, but there's no doubt that Scandinavians have an instinctive respect for all forms of life."

When he had received Morel's petition, he began by addressing

himself to the Geneva Committee—with no result other than prudent reserve. Indeed he had had a fight with them. Quite recently
again they had refused to support him, when he had spoken against
the establishment of guided missile bases on two small islands in
the South Pacific which were a way station for thousands of rare
birds in their migration to the Arctic.

They were afraid they'd be accused of meddling in politics.

In the end, he had become so interested that he had taken a plane
to Chad. Morel was then still at Fort Lamy, walking about from
door to door with his briefcase.

"He confided his plans to me. I can't say that I discouraged him.
I had a lifetime of similar struggles behind me, and I knew that
he could get results by awakening the curiosity and interest of the
masses. Besides, Morel isn't a man who is easily discouraged. All
the same, I stressed the difficulties. He told me: 'Oh, you know I'm
used to that. I've already done something of the kind once before.
The hardest fight I have ever had to put up was in defense of may-
beetles . . .'"

Peer Qvist was obviously about to digress to may-beetles, but
Fields politely brought him back to the subject of their conversation. May-beetles and Pacific islands interested him only moderately.
The old man evidently had a tendency to ramble. (A few years later,
when he met Peer Qvist in Sweden at Upsala, shortly before the
naturalist died, the latter, obsessed by his memories, did at last succeed in telling him the story of the may-beetles, and Fields only
then discovered that in spite of the fine pictures he had taken, he
had missed the essential clue about Morel.) When Fields interrupted him as tactfully as possible, Peer Qvist fell silent and gazed
at him ironically.

"Well," he said, "I see I am wasting your time. You've come here
to take photographs, not to listen to my explanations. Besides you'll
be able to question Morel himself. He's bound to be back shortly."

Beyond the reeds Fields saw a long line of Kaï fishermen, completely naked, each with a basket on his back, moving forward in
the water, their assagais in front of them, every few steps. They
shouted in a gasping monotone, their voices culminating in a short,
sharp cry whenever they struck the water with their assagais. Peer

Qvist told him that they sometimes killed as many as three sheatfish with a single blow. At one time, they would also have cut the tendons of exhausted elephants, a form of hunting practiced with more courage by the Kreichs of the Sudan, who attacked on horseback with their sabers the herds in the Bongo hills. But Morel had attended to that as soon as he appeared on the scene and now, reluctantly, they left the elephants alone.

Just as they rounded the barrier of reeds, Fields saw a compact mass of birds lifting and settling again like many-colored clods sent flying by some prodigious gallop; then a group of five elephants appeared in a cloud of red dust which the reeds brushed from their flanks. As soon as they reached the water they dispersed, the two animals in the middle collapsing, and then lying on their sides without a sign of life, without a stir of the trunk, while the others waded forward into deeper water.

"They were holding up the two in the middle," said Peer Qvist. "God only knows how long they had been marching like that."

Fields had missed their arrival and let the camera fall to his chest. (Three months earlier Fields had terminated the exclusive contract which tied him to an American magazine. He had formed his own agency in Paris. His story on Lake Kuru was to bring him in more than $100,000—the highest price ever paid for a single picture story to a member of his profession.)

He spent the next two hours taking color photographs of the birds which in tens of thousands covered the whole surface of the marsh, a slow movement of white, black, gray and pink, sometimes striped, sometimes divided into great uniform patches of birds of one feather that had remained together; a living plantation, an aquatic fauna that seemed to come from the depths of the earth rather than to fall from the sky. (Fields had always felt a certain hostility toward beauty. In its presence he felt even more isolated. He was by nature rather sensitive and had a great need of harmony and concord, and in the presence of beauty he always felt like a false note. He had once had to do a story on Carpaccio and the hours he had spent in front of the frescoes had made him sick. He had the same reaction in front of magnificent landscapes; he invariably preferred a small smoky bar where one felt at home.) While he worked, Peer Qvist gave him the names of the species, with an owner's pride, but Fields made no attempt to remember them; he concentrated on his work; it was much simpler to submit the photographs to a specialist later for identification. (An expert from the New York Museum of Natural History recognized in them twenty-seven species of birds, a good half of which came from Europe.) He also surreptitiously took several more photographs of the Dane. The picture of this ancient sentry with the keen eyes under his wide South African hat, standing guard with his rifle on the shore of a sea of birds, was one of the most strangely moving things he had ever seen.

Peer Qvist seemed to be favorably impressed by the feverish rapidity with which the reporter went on with his task. On the way back he was in a more affable mood and Fields sensed that he had gone up a little in the old man's opinion. He took advantage of this to question him about some of the famous campaigns of the past, and was rather surprised when the Dane, after a long enumeration of the species he had defended—they seemed to include the whole of creation—finished rather abruptly by saying: "And liberty, everywhere!" shutting himself up immediately in a morose silence as if in memory of all the earth's living beauty that had been uprooted and had vanished.

Fields was beginning to understand his companion's ways, and took care not to interrupt his reverie. They walked in silence toward the other end of the dune, where Minna was busy preparing a meal; Forsythe was standing there, joking with her, with an open can in his hand, which he was emptying straight into his mouth with the help of a knife. (Fields felt then that Morel must have prepared his campaign with care and well in advance. Apart from a great variety of canned food, cases of ammunition, first aid and camping stores, a lot of equipment had been buried in the sand, showing all the signs of careful planning. It came out at the trial that this preparation had been the work of Waïtari who, long before he had joined up with Morel, had been planning to set up in the Kuru a training camp for the leaders of the future African Independence Army. The existence of such a camp in French Equatorial Africa had at that time been duly reported in the newspapers and denied by the authorities. Waïtari had begun establishing those bases as early as 1948, at a time when the third world war appeared to him a certainty, and while carrying out his last official tour of French Equatorial Africa as a member of Parliament, before taking refuge in Cairo and making his famous broadcast against the French. Since then, almost all those who had bowed and scraped while he was officially in power had reported these concealed stores to the authorities, with the exception of old Ghaliti, the chieftain of a Kuru village and one of the most highly respected gunrunners of the Sudanese border regions.)

The lake was now beginning to vanish in gray mist; the trumpeting of elephants, to whom the first cool of the evening was restoring a little animation, was beginning to be heard; and Fields shivered suddenly under a touch of fever; his side was hurting him and he was beginning to feel all the accumulated exhaustion and strain. He scarcely managed to touch his food; he excused himself and, almost fainting, went to lie down on the sand. One idea alone kept him going: to be ready to photograph if Morel arrived before dark. After a while he asked Peer Qvist if he expected much from the Bukavu Conference.

"I think they will do something this time," said the naturalist. "The whole world is challenging them to stop at least the hunting of elephants . . . but that'll be only the first step. As you know, we've attracted world attention to their discussions—in a striking way."

A little later Forsythe spoke to him about the pilot. "I thought the best thing to do was to lay him in the water for the time being. . ." He held out to Fields the pack of cigarettes he had given him. "I've rescued his cigarettes."

Fields felt embarrassed. He had completely forgotten Davis.

"I've wedged him between two rocks in six feet of water, so he won't be trampled by the elephants. We can bury him later. I've put his personal belongings in your hut—that one over there—in case you'd like to send them to his family."

"I hardly knew him," said Fields.

He had scarcely finished speaking when he saw three men on horseback come in sight over the top of the dune.

One of them was a white man.

Fields jumped up and grabbed his camera. Every trace of fatigue had left him, and he took his first picture of Morel less than thirty seconds after having caught sight of him. He estimated at that moment that he had no more than five or ten minutes of decent light ahead of him, and he made full use of it. It was a long time since he had felt such excitement, professionally speaking—more exactly, not since the first hours of the liberation of Paris (Fields had not much love for the French, but he adored Paris). He used half a roll of film before establishing the slightest personal contact with Morel. The two Africans accompanying him stared at Fields mistrustfully, but Morel appeared pleased as Forsythe explained the journalist briefly. Morel passed the bridle of his horse to a young boy in a white robe, sat down on the sand and began to eat with appetite and rather noisily, letting himself be photographed with a certain satisfaction.

The taller and older of the two Africans was of a clearly marked Arab type with a snub nose and tufts of gray hair above and below his lips. He was wearing a blue burnous and a white turban round his head, and Fields remembered that the ease with which Morel had always escaped from the police had been attributed at Fort Lamy to the presence at his side of one of the most famous trackers in Equatorial Africa, a man whom everybody had long thought to be dead. Probably this was the man.

The other was a youngster with a thoughtful and attentive face. There was something both intense and secretive in his expression, a contained violence beneath the immobility of his features, and this intrigued Fields from the moment he saw him. But the dramatic hours which followed his arrival on the Kuru made him forget the youth, and it was only much later, during the trial, that he got to know what a decisive part he had played in Morel's adventure. But even then no one could say with certainty whether the Frenchman had come victorious out of the tragic and silent conflict, or if that slightly ironic but calm confidence which he had shown in human dignity had led him to his end in some hole in the bush, where the ants have the last word.

As he ate, Morel told them about his expedition to Gfat. The local merchant, a curious fellow, who obviously did not subsist only by his trade, let him listen to his radio all right, but the two broadcasts from Brazzaville had made no mention of the Bukavu Conference. The best thing to do was to follow Waïtari to Khartoum as planned: if the nations represented at the Conference had made the necessary commitments, so much the better; if not, he would have to carry on the fight. In any case, there was no point in remaining on the Kuru. That fellow at Gfat was probably an informer—paying thus for the free passage of hashish caravans. It was essential to discover the results of the Conference and how public opinion had reacted to the campaign. Then only would it be possible to decide what ought to be done.

Fields, who was listening attentively, felt rather at sea. There was in Morel a simplicity, a directness, a lack of all complication, something that suggested a great deal of common sense and practicality. This was only a quick first impression, but Fields was used to snapshots. Morel had the assured manner of a man who is getting on quietly with a job that has to be done. With his emphatic, slightly vulgar way of speaking, and his straight features, he made Fields think of the working-class *bistros* of Paris, and it was odd to see him and hear him talking there among the elephants of Africa. The chief characteristic of his face was obstinacy, in the straight, short forehead, in the strong line of mouth, but there also was a trace of a very French irony deep in the eyes.

Fields finally made up his mind to ask the one or two questions he had prepared in his head during the day. (Fields was not used to interviews. When the story required a text—and this was rarely the case with him—someone else provided one. It was a job no one liked; he had the reputation of bringing back photographs that crushed any text.) He began by talking to Morel about the curiosity he was exciting everywhere—the petition now boasted hundreds of thousands of signatures.

"People say you have ulterior political motives. They say that for you the elephants are the symbol of African liberty and independence. The nationalists proclaim this openly and give you their support."

Morel nodded. "I know. Everyone thinks it very clever to ride the elephants. But nobody does anything for them. But I don't mind

that: I don't mind if everyone associates the elephants with whatever there is left in him that's clean. I don't give a damn whether
they're Communists, Titoists, Nationalists, Arabs or Czechoslovaks.
That's of no interest to me. If they all agree sincerely on the protection of my elephants, that suits me fine. And I know there are
some really clever fellows who say my elephants are symbolic, alle-
goric, or whatever they call it. But that's not true at all. My elephants are a living thing—they breathe, they suffer, and they die,
like you and me. We're doing a well-defined job here—the protection
of a certain natural splendor, beginning with the elephants . . . No
need to look further."

"You've been in the maquis for several months now. How do you
explain the ease with which you've always escaped from the authorities?"

Morel laughed. "I suppose everyone wishes me well."

"You've wounded hunters and burned farms. But you've never
killed anyone. Is it accident?"

"I aimed as well as I could."

"So as not to kill?"

"You never teach a man anything by killing him. On the contrary,
you make him forget everything."

He appeared very proud of his phrase.

"The authorities—and some of the hunters—state that contrary
to your declarations, the elephants are not in any way threatened
with extinction. That in fact they are given all the protection necessary."

"And so it's all right to go on killing them?"

Fields did not know what to say.

The Frenchman looked at him mockingly. "There are whole regions in the world where they have already disappeared," he said
slowly. "Everyone knows which regions those are: they're on the
map. Indeed, they take up most of it. There are other parts where
they are gravely threatened. I know, there are the reserves, but
when people start boasting about the reserves they say a lot about
what's going on elsewhere. I can show you parts of the world five or
six times as big as France where the elephants haven't been seen for
two generations, yet the local government will calmly tell you that

they're to be found everywhere, that they're living freely and un-
molested, and that it's you who are deliberately refusing to see
them."

For the first time there was a note of anger in his voice. Fields
began to have palpitations. He did not feel up to all this. He felt
also that the heart of the matter was there within his grasp, that he
needed only to ask the right question. But all he found to say was,
"I'd be grateful if you'd explain to me once more the nature of your
relations with the nationalists. We in America are very interested in
this problem."

"All who come to me with help are welcome. Nationalism, you
know—whether it's white hunters or black hunters, the old ones or
the new ones—I'm against 'em all. I'm on the side of anyone who
will take the necessary steps. Races, classes, or nations—that's only
another name for hunting. If France, when she leaves Africa, could
make sure that the elephants will be respected, that would mean
that France would remain in Africa forever. I'd be a bit surprised,
but who knows."

He added as if incidentally, "I was in the Resistance, during the
Occupation. I fought not so much to defend France against Germany, but to defend elephants against hunters."

Fields clutched his camera tightly. It was a nervous reaction.
He had no intention of taking a photograph. It was indeed too dark.
He could hardly see Morel: just a shadow, sitting on the sand. He
tried to adjust his shortsighted eyes to the stars. He too was sitting
on the sand, with his legs apart. He had put his handkerchief,
knotted at the four corners, over his head to protect himself from
the sun, and had forgotten to take it off. He could hardly see Morel
now, but he listened to him attentively. He was also beginning to
see the stars.

"I was never exactly crazy about politics. I was even against
political strikes. When a worker in the Renault factories goes on
strike, it isn't for political reasons, it's to be able to live like a human being. He too is really defending nature."

Morel was silent for a moment.

"As for nationalism, it has no right to exist except in football
matches. What I am doing here I could do just as well in any
country." He burst out laughing. "Perhaps not in the Scandinavian

countries. And even there—I shall have to go there one day to see for myself."

Fields was still looking for the question he ought to put. The right words, and everything would be said. He had them practically on the tip of his tongue.

"Well," concluded Morel. "I think that's clear enough? Good night."

He got up and moved away. Fields now had a fairly precise idea of it all, but he wondered if he was capable of getting it down in writing. He was conscious of the pain in his side as he moved: the tension had fallen. He also began worrying about the quickest and safest way to get his pictures and interview through to his Paris agency. He was very conscious of the commercial value of the story and was beginning, as was usual with him, to be obsessed by the fear that something might happen to the films. The best solution would be, of course, to go back to Khartoum. Morel himself intended to go there, but he did not yet know when, and Fields felt it would be better to leave at once. According to Forsythe, he might hope to meet with a caravan at a point known as Gfat Well and get a lift at least as far as the El Fasher road. But the forty miles of desert between here and Gfat required a physical effort which he would do well to make at once, without waiting for the pain to get worse—it was clearly tending to do so and might become unbearable. (Fields had never before traveled on horseback for any important distance.) Nevertheless he decided to stay. He was well aware that this decision was not at all a professional one: he was finding it hard to part from Morel.

## XXXIV

THE LORRIES WERE MOVING along the track in single file at a crawling pace that seemed to underline the difficulties of the enterprise—the heat, and the limitless wastes of this Bahr el Gazal landscape with thorn bushes hugging the stony ground and tufts of dry grass in which a cloud of dust set up by a hyena was something of an event. The track itself seemed to Waïtari largely an illusion: a few tufts of grass less, that was all.

"It will be a mess if it starts to rain," he said.

"The weather forecasts said nothing of rain, *inch Allah!*" said Habib.

De Vries had been driving for fourteen hours. Waïtari could see his profile with its small, round, brutal features below his plastered fair hair, and steady pale blue eyes that never left the track. Habib was sitting next to him, a dead cheroot between his teeth.

The driver's cabin was so overheated that even the rivulets of sweat came as a relief. Waïtari felt worried, exhausted by the slow jolting of the lorry and dazzled by the desert light which he was no longer used to, furious with himself for not having thought to bring dark glasses. Every time he looked at De Vries he wondered how he managed to keep on staring at the almost invisible track among the stones, for hours on end, with those eyes of his so pale that they seemed almost transparent.

The nearer they drew to their destination, the more doubtful seemed to him the chance of success. The only guarantee he had was the assurances of De Vries, and also Habib's optimism—but then, in him, optimism was second nature. It was rather late in the day to think of that now. Anyway it was his only chance to get hold of at least some funds. And as for the risk of running into a French patrol, that was the best thing that could happen. They had forty armed and uniformed men in the lorries, and a communiqué of the "our troops attacked a group of rebels" kind would be most welcome. The Cairo radio would do the rest.

Unfortunately he was no longer used to such physical exertions. For twenty years now, he had lived in comfort—and he felt the lack of it cruelly now. What he loved more than anything else was a good debate, public meetings at which he could make heard from the dais, that throne of democracy, that voice of bronze whose power over the masses he knew. He longed for Paris, for the meals prepared by his wife, for the atmosphere of political excitement at public meetings where his black face had once commanded attention. Perhaps he had made a mistake. But the die was cast. All that was left now was that international no man's land where future leaders

of future nations were trying to hold out—and even there the essential thing was to have a name, to stake his claim to leadership in
Africa. If he were to wait for the national aspirations of the Oulé
tribes, he might just as well address himself to posterity, that is to
say give up any idea of a personal career. In the Oulé, Massa and
Go dialects there was no such word as "nation," and the tribes were
still interested only in their witch doctors, in magic ceremonies and,
of course, in meat. Up to now the only Oulé aspiration he had
been able to exploit with any success had been their need for meat—
the old need of men in Africa, and indeed of all men. It was a
deeper and much more urgent need than the one for new political
institutions. In his youth he had often seen an animal shot down and
eaten where it lay by villagers, the greediest of whom absorbed as
much as ten pounds of meat at a sitting. From the Chad to the
Cape the Africans' craving for meat, eternally stimulated by in-
adequate or ill-balanced diet, was the strongest and most fraternal
bond the continent had in common. It was a dream, a longing, that
never diminished, a physiological cry of the body, stronger and
more torturing than the sexual instinct. Meat! It was the oldest, the
most truly real and sincere, and the most unanimous aspiration of
humanity. He thought of Morel and his elephants, and smiled bitterly. To the white man the elephant had long meant merely ivory,
and to the black man it always meant merely meat—the most
abundant quantity of meat that a lucky hit with the assagai could
procure for him. The idea of the "beauty" of the elephant, of the
"nobility" of the elephant, was the idea of a man who had had
enough to eat, a man of restaurants and of two meals a day and of
museums of abstract art—an idea typical of a decadent society that
takes refuge in abstractions from the ugly social realities it is incapable of facing, and makes itself drunk on vague and twilight
notions of the beautiful, of the noble, of the fraternal, simply because the purely poetic attitude is the only one which history allows
it to adopt. Bourgeois intellectuals insisted that a society on the
march and in full spate should encumber itself with elephants
simply because in that way they themselves hoped to escape destruction. They knew that they were just as anachronistic and cumbersome as these prehistoric animals; it was just a way of claiming

mercy for themselves, of asking to be spared. Morel was typical of them.

But to human beings in Africa, the elephant's only beauty was the weight of his meat, and as for human dignity, that was first and foremost a full belly. Perhaps, when the African does have his belly full, perhaps then he too will take an interest in the beauty of the elephant and will in general give himself up to agreeable meditations on the splendors of nature. For the moment, nature spoke to him of splitting the elephant's belly open and plunging his teeth into it and eating, eating till he dropped, because he did not know where the next morsel would come from. He was now going to make it all quite clear, by putting an end to the sentimental myth of Morel and his "noble" giants, by lifting the idealistic smoke screen thrown over the true aims of the African revolt. And it was essential to get hold of some money. He had forty men in the three lorries, all armed and equipped; none of them had been paid. If the expedition ended in failure, the only hope left would be a French political jail—they had learned to treat their political opponents well. For the time being, he was entirely in the hands of MM. Habib and De Vries. Odd how all great chapters in human endeavor depended at certain moments on vulgar scum. Arms traffickers, spies, *agents provocateurs,* shady money-lenders—they were intimately bound up with some of mankind's noblest achievements. Which did not, unfortunately, mean that having them with you was enough to guarantee success.

He turned toward Habib and caught him staring mockingly at the kepi which Waïtari was holding on his knee. It was an old sky-blue kepi of a lieutenant in the French Army, which he had always kept for sentimental reasons. He had merely taken off the lieutenant's pips and replaced them with a general's five stars. Not the gold stars of a French general, but black stars which he had had embroidered on the blue ground. A general without troops of course, he thought under that mocking gaze, but his troops were in India, in Asia, in America, even in France. His troops were international public opinion, not the primitive African tribes, but the conscience of the civilized world.

"Yes, I know, a general without an army," he said haughtily.

"But ideas don't need troops; they make their way by themselves. And if anything goes wrong, it's essential to be in uniform if we don't want to be treated as bandits."

Habib nodded approvingly, but Waïtari had entirely misunderstood the meaning of his wondering glances. He continued to look sideways with astonished fascination at the sky-blue kepi with the black stars. Once again he felt an infinite gratitude to life for all the precious jewels it had sown so abundantly in his path. It was a profoundly French kepi, and five little black stars sewn on in place of a lieutenant's pips said quite clearly what they had to say —chiefly the lengths to which men would go in their loneliness. He looked ahead of him, whistling softly. Men were unique, incredible, admirable, pure gems thrown on earth for the delight of the amateur. For his part, he had strenuously refused to put on a uniform and had merely kept his yachting cap. He had always been a freebooter, navigating the high seas, perhaps not under his own flag but always on his own business, and he intended to remain so. He was just an adventurer, a lover of life, not in the service of any cause, and if there was an ideal that inspired him it was simply and solely that of being always up to the marvelous possibilities offered by life. And also, circumstances permitting, to procure for his interesting young friend various distractions, sporting and otherwise, the need for which was understandable at his age, and at the same time to enable him to settle a certain personal account with this Human Highness, the protector of elephants.

"Nothing will go wrong," said De Vries curtly. "I know this bit of country. The only military outpost is on the frontier, 150 miles to the north, and they have six men there."

"And it isn't going to rain," Habib added. "You can rely on my luck, on my *baraka*: the old bitch never lets me down . . ."

Forsythe was beginning to lose patience. He could not understand Morel's obvious reluctance to leave the Kuru. He could not see what they stood to gain by remaining near the lake. Morel could say as often as he liked that the district was bare of troops: it had been imprudent of him to go to Gfat. This would have had no importance if they had left the lake immediately afterward, but he was ready to bet that the news of their presence here had been duly conveyed to all concerned. The Well of Gfat was where every intelligence agent from the Sudan to Egypt and from the Chad to Omdoram came to refresh his gullet: with its three shops and about twenty houses of mud and stone, it was a point very difficult for the caravans to avoid as they crossed the border, and they were always ready to do services in exchange for a little leniency in regard to their cargo. In short, there was a danger of being stupidly caught, just at the moment when he had a faint hope of starting life again. The results of the Congo conference were no doubt known at Khartoum, and Morel himself admitted that they should go there before deciding what to do next.

But now Forsythe was convinced that even if the delegates at Bukavu took the necessary measures, Morel would continue to hang around the herds for the rest of his life. He hadn't a penny, and as soon as the last gleam of his ephemeral fame had passed, he would become one more of those African derelicts whose history people mutter with a pitying smile, not even bothering to lower their voices: "Ah, here's Morel. I thought he was dead long ago. And yet, God knows, he has had his moment of fame . . . His hour of glory, as they say." And then a long story, awakening only a few vague memories among those who listened— "Ah yes, of course, I remember . . . the man who defended the elephants . . ." accompanied by another amused glance at the bum in question, together with a trace of compassion—what a good thing the rest of us had always stuck to business.

Forsythe smiled bitterly: he knew all that by heart—and he had no intention of going through it again. He could of course leave Morel there and go to Khartoum on his own, but his Korean experience had left him with an almost morbid need for loyalty. And there was Minna. He tried vainly to understand her attitude, her complete indifference to Forsythe's argument. She would smile and that was all. Besides, they hardly saw each other. That also was extraordinary: they lived all four of them in separate huts, each by himself, and hardly spoke to one another except at the meals which she cooked. Forsythe, in whom his compatriots' gregarious instinct was strongly developed, and who needed company, became indignant sometimes:

four monstrous solitudes, refusing to join forces. Even Idriss and
Youssef kept away from each other: they lived apart and practically
never conversed. Morel spent his days by the lake among his elephants. Peer Qvist would disappear into the marshes, busy, no doubt,
counting the thousands of birds to see that none was missing. Minna
alone remained on the dune, sitting on the shore, staring for hours
on end at the birds and the herds with an expression of pleasure,
almost of happiness, which seemed to exclude him, his apprehen-
sions, and indeed everything that was not before her eyes.

Once again Forsythe felt rejected. Formerly he would have found
this perfectly natural. He too was not particularly attracted by human faces or the company of men. But now the psychological bond
with the three others had snapped. He knew now that there was a
certain sympathy, a friendliness, awaiting him back home, that he
was no longer an outcast, that there was a way back. And it seemed
to him more urgent now to go back and carry on the campaign
there, make their voices heard, than to remain with their backs
turned on the rest of the world. It seemed to him that Morel's, Peer
Qvist's, and Minna's obstinacy broke human bounds, that their in-
transigence and insistence were becoming impossibly pure, and that
they would soon be lost completely in regions which had nothing
earthly about them, beyond the point of no return.

One morning he tried to convince Minna that it was impossible
for them to go on wandering in this no man's land. He found her
engaged in conversation with the two Kaïs who came every morning
and brought her fish cakes, the mere sight of which raised her spirits.
He had no idea what they were talking about: each spoke in a language the other did not understand—Minna talked to them in German and they answered in Kaï with expressive nods and gestures.
Somehow, they made sense to each other. This went on for a quarter of an hour every day, after which, apparently well satisfied, they
went off with huge grins. He told her that they had no reason now
to remain here, that it was becoming dangerous, that they had done
all that was possible for Morel and his elephants, and that he was
proposing to go to Khartoum. To his surprise she immediately
nodded approval.

"Perhaps you will find a lorry at Gfat," she said. "Apparently they pass through there sometimes."

"And what about you?" he said indignantly.

"What do you mean, me?"

"Aren't you coming?"

"Where should I go?"

"With me."

"And where should I go with you, Monsieur Forsythe? Perhaps you will ask me to marry you?"

"Of course," he said, with a not very convincing effort to recover his cynical tone. He added immediately: "I'm serious, you know."

She smiled at him. "Thank you," she said. "But I shan't marry you simply because I don't know where to go. You know, Monsieur Forsythe, there's such a thing as love."

"Morel?" he asked simply.

She shook her head. "No, not Morel. Perhaps Morel is something more, but he isn't that. No, it isn't Morel. It isn't anyone—now."

She suddenly turned away her head and moved off. Forsythe watched her walking over the dune toward the low line of the sky above the reeds; he thought of what people used to murmur at Fort Lamy, those stories they told about her tragic adventure with a Russian officer who was shot. That must be it, he thought as he watched her move away over the dune, and wished bitterly and with all his heart that he were an executed Russian officer.

"On Lake Kuru?" repeated the Governor. "That's hardly in my territory . . ."

But it *was* in his territory. Everything happened always in his territory. He was always entitled to whatever trouble was around.

When a tribe decided suddenly that it could not do without elephants' testicles for its ceremonies and in consequence ran amok because it was not allowed to cut off enough of them, it was bound to be one of the Oulé tribes in his district, and not in the Chad, although there were just as many of them there.

When the leopard men took it into their heads that they had not been heard of for too long, and so clawed to pieces five villagers in one month, it was bound to be one of *his* tribes.

When a dead man disappeared mysteriously from the family table just before he could be painted green, blue and yellow—the original purpose of the rite was to render the body untouchable and reserve it for the spirits—and all that was found of him later was well-gnawed bones, it was bound to be in the Oulé hills, and a passing journalist was bound to stick his nose into the business, even though it was the first time in fifteen years that cannibalism had occurred.

And when some mad dog of a misanthrope decided to go over to the animals, it was in his territory, under his nose, in his capital, that the man's most sensational exploit took place.

And indeed he had been expecting it from the beginning.

As soon as he had heard about Morel's first exploits in the Chad, he had felt uneasy, a little worried. "Come," he had said to himself. "What's wrong? Why is it that it isn't happening in my territory?" It was obviously a mistake and Morel must have realized that, so when he felt the need to administer a thrashing to someone to relieve his feelings, he chose Sionville and the Challut woman, whose husband had political influence in Paris. The consequences made themselves felt at once. The Governor's successor was said to be practically on his way.

And yet the Governor of the Oulés felt strangely happy, even elated. That was the Africa he loved: something new and unexpected always came out of it. You could talk of progress, try to lead it in a new direction: it always had a surprise in store for you, something extraordinary, unpredictable, and utterly senseless. If there was still a country capable of living legend, that country was Africa, all right.

He turned toward Borrut. The Colonel, who had been concerned with the capture of Morel from the beginning, had been lent to him by the Governor of the Chad. Which proves, thought the Governor, what we knew already: soldiers find more indulgence from their superiors than civil servants do.

"Well?"

Borrut ran his finger rapidly over the map. "This little blue point here—as you say, it isn't in your territory but in the Sudan—the well at Gfat . . . It's a caravan rendezvous and was rather important in the time of the slave trade. It still is, although the type of goods has changed. The El Fasher route passes much farther to the north, but for those who think it preferable to avoid it this crossroads is invaluable. We've got a man there. It's a dangerous spot for an informer, what with the British leaving and all that. That makes him very exigent, but he's worth the price. Morel turned up at his shop four days ago. He just walked in, out of the desert, with two Africans—one of them, they say, is Idriss, but I'd like to see for myself: Idriss must have died long ago, unless he's a hundred—and went straight to the radio set and listened to the news for five hours on end. Like all megalomaniacs, I suppose he couldn't resist the desire to know what was being said about him."

The Governor was thoughtful. He had just come back from the bi-annual meeting at Brazzaville, where he had met with nothing but ironical or pitying glances. Little Santex, that fat humbug with the name like a sanitary towel, had even tapped him on the shoulder and asked him, "Well, my dear fellow, how is your protégé?" His colleagues had treated him like some important invalid or fragile object. Some of them still maintained that the elephants were a myth, a smoke screen, and that Morel was a nationalist agent, and when he had said no, he had had the majority against him. They all agreed though that care must be taken not to destroy this fiction, since the whole world had fallen for it, which was much better than to admit the existence of a nationalist movement in Equatorial Africa. And it was true that public opinion had "fallen for it" as they put it—that the public believed in Morel and his elephants. Telegrams and petitions in his favor were arriving by thousands from every part of the globe. To the people, Morel was the hero of a cause that had nothing to do with nations and political ideologies, a cause that had nothing to do with Africa and touched what was deepest in them—a secret rancor—a confused dream of being able one day to emerge victorious from the difficulty of being a man. They were staking a claim to respectful and decent treatment. They believed in this campaign for the defense and protection of nature. And the Governor too believed in it. It was in Africa that man had first appeared, millions of years ago—this too was altogether typical of Africa and its fantastic ways—so it was natural that he should come to Africa to protest as violently as possible against himself.

"Go on, Colonel. What happened then?"

"He bought some matches and a hundred packs of *Gauloises*. Then he went off again—in the direction of Lake Kuru. Our friend followed him as far as the track. There isn't the slightest doubt."

"Has the Chad done anything?"

"They've sent a Camel Corps Company from Afna. Schölscher is with them."

"Sending camels to the Kuru?"

"Yes, I know. But there weren't any other troops within four hundred miles. It comes at a bad moment. The Sudan frontier is bare. Wide open. For forty years there were the British and us. That made two police forces instead of one, and we only had to reckon with Kreish bandits after ivory making raids to the south of the Bongas. Now . . . the British are gone and our troops are busy elsewhere. Something like a thousand miles of fresh frontier to be watched."

And the Colonel swept his hand across the map.

"The essential thing is to stop him from taking refuge in the Sudan. After that, it will just be a matter of picking him up. In forty-eight hours it will be done."

"Ye-es," said the Governor.

The Colonel looked hurt.

"Well, anyway, I don't mind telling you that I shall be relieved when this is over," said the Governor in a more friendly tone. "He's become much too popular. When he's in prison he'll be able to spend his time reading his mail. I suppose they'll say he's unbalanced and not responsible for his actions. By the way, you know that my successor has practically been announced."

Borrut put on the usual polite expression of sympathy.

"It's Sayag. I wonder what attracts him to this place."

"He's a great hunter," said Borrut. "He comes to Africa at least once a year to hunt."

The Governor looked keenly interested. "A good shot?"

"Oh, world-famous. He was one of the great professional ivory hunters twenty or thirty years ago."

The Governor's face cleared perceptibly. He accompanied Borrut as far as the door with every courtesy. The Colonel had never seen a doomed man take it better. When he had gone, the Governor went into the next office and asked his private secretary to join him.

"Tell me, there are still a few journalists left here, I believe? Or have they all gone?"

"There are still two or three. We're lunching together in a few minutes."

"Good. Do you know Sayag?"

"I met him at your place last year. He'd come out here to hunt."

"Yes, of course, I remember. Well now, look, apparently he's coming to replace me. You can tell the journalists: there's no secrecy about it any more. Tell them he's a very capable man who knows Africa marvelously well. He comes here regularly every year to hunt. *To hunt:* insist on that. Apparently he's the greatest elephant hunter we have in France. At least five hundred elephants to his credit. Well, make it as big as you wish. Tell 'em that by taking up the post of Governor, he will give a fresh impulse to big game hunting by tourists. Tell them that under that impulse we shall be able to oust Kenya as the great safari country. That's all; I see you've understood. Wipe that dirty smile off your face and go ahead."

He went back to his desk, sat down and thought for a moment. Then he grinned.

Seated at a folding table in front of his mobile surgical unit, Ceccaldi was listening absently as Father Fargue poured out the indignation accumulated during the weeks he had spent on horseback wandering over the Oulé hills in search of Morel, with no one to listen to his oaths except his horse, Butor. It was with some apprehension that the doctor had seen that barrel of a man come down the slope toward him—the mount that carried him must have been the largest, strongest and most determined horse on earth—and now he was exposed to the sound and the fury.

Squatting on the ground in their white *boubous*, hundreds of sick awaited their turn with a patience that might come either from hope or from resignation.

An epidemic of onchocerciasis had thrown French Equatorial Africa into one of the great humanitarian battles of its history. The scourge had driven whole populations from their homes, and in some villages half the inhabitants had already gone blind.

Major Ceccaldi had been operating on the cysts almost without a break; he had had three hours' sleep since the beginning of the campaign. So he had only very little interest to spare for Morel and his elephants. But Father Fargue was an old fighter against evil in all its forms, and it was difficult for the doctor to refuse his attention to a man who had always been at his side in the thick of the battle.

"So they say it's in the concentration camp that he got that dream of elephants in him," roared Fargue. "So what? Does he think he is the only one to have that thirst for liberty in his soul? We all suffer from claustrophobia; we're all fed up with our prison— with this carcass!" He hit himself a violent blow on the chest.

"There isn't a real Christian in the world who doesn't dream of being set free. But that's not in our hands and all we can do is to raise our eyes to Him Who created the soul and its prison and shut one up in the other! Eh?"

"Obviously, obviously," said Ceccaldi with much courtesy. He was watching the long file of stricken natives walking toward the tent. He wondered why the blind always look up to the sky. He stood up.

"Excuse me, but the patients are waiting."

Visibly satisfied with his great theological effort, Fargue also stood up. "All right," he said. "I came to give you a hand."

It was the best time of the day. It was not hot yet, and the birds flying above the herds had the colors of the dawn. Thousands of waders, marabous and jabirus were wandering among the elephants, or still sleeping with their heads under their wings on the dunes and rocks, and the pelicans had hardly room to take off. As on every morning, a little more of the red earth had emerged from the water; in normal times the rocks with their tufts of grass, birds and rushes were no more than islands of vegetation scarcely showing above the surface; now as much as fifteen feet of naked rock and earth were visible, running from one cliff to the other, from sand dune to sand dune: one could walk across the lake without getting wet.

The herds had become still larger during the night.

It was difficult not to be gripped by a feeling of awe at the sight of hundreds of petrified gray giants emerging from the pale rose-colored mist, of waterbucks, their motionless antlers rising above the water like the masts of some scuttled fleet, of gazelles, oryx and buffalo packed so close together that sometimes they looked like solid land; and twice during the night he had heard the roar of a lion.

The eastern approaches to the lake were covered with dead animals and among them, the morning before, Morel had come across the improbable body of a lonely giraffe grotesquely spread out less than a hundred yards from the water. He had stared at it a long time in wonder: it was hard to imagine how this fragile animal had managed to cross some hundred miles of rocks and sand.

But the elephants were the most tragic sight, perhaps because their very bulk underlined their exhaustion and helplessness. They stood in the water without moving, heads lowered, trunks inert, and the only trace of life about them were the white herons walking on their backs. This was not only physical prostration but also a nervous reaction after the weeks of terror they had been through before reaching water.

Morel knew that elephants were slower than other animals at recovering from alarm. In his articles, Haas, who had lived among the Chad elephants for twenty-five years, used to say that often a female whom he had robbed of her young, after hunting for them in a mad rage for some hours, would suddenly lose all trace of energy and stand inertly while the other members of the herd tried in vain to make her move up by butting her with their foreheads. Sometimes she would collapse on her side and lie so for hours, her eyes closed. He claimed that he had been able to approach one of these poor animals and stroke its trunk without producing the slightest reaction. "Stroke the trunk of the poor animal," this was the literal expression used by that remarkable man. His sympathy did not prevent him from continuing to take their young and send them into captivity. Into captivity. Elephants in captivity . . . Morel could feel the blood rush to his face and he clutched his rifle fiercely with a total hatred for all the world's captors. When he had at last succeeded in lodging a bullet in Haas's buttocks, he felt he had not lived in vain. He had then gone up to the swearing Dutchman, to make sure he knew from whose hand it came. Under the acacias, the boys kept a respectful distance. "I read your article about your captures," he said. "I said to myself: I am going to add something to his royalties." A short laugh shook Haas followed immediately by a groan of pain. Then he raised himself on his elbow: "Bless you," he said almost solemnly.

The elephant was lying on its flank, and on the other there was still the fine red dust from the desert untouched by the water, and two herons were wading between its legs. At first Morel thought it was dead, but when he emerged from the reeds, he caught a slight twitch of its ear, the beginning of a reflex of alarm, and he saw its eye move and stare at him. He touched the dust with his finger: the animal had not even the strength left to spray itself. There were only a few inches of water in the pool, and its muddy surface bubbled all over; the drying marshes resounded with an incessant beat, like the pounding of millions of hearts: the mudfish were leaving the vanishing lake, bouncing along on their fins. This was the first time he had heard them move during the day; generally they waited for night before undertaking their mysterious migration. He wondered where they hoped to go and why they had waited so long. They could cover many miles by hopping in this way and he had rarely come across a dead mudfish. He sat down on a rock with his rifle on his knees, his nostrils full of the smell of mud and rotting plants; before his eyes were the zigzagging insects that sometimes hit his face; his ears were full of their incessant drone. He had already caught the Kaï villagers cutting the tendons of elephants isolated and prostrate like the one before him. After the punishment he had administered, he did not think the fishermen would try again, but their children were still on the prowl among the rushes, and he had nothing to do except mount guard, and anyway that was what he had come for. And he liked the company. After half an hour the elephant raised its trunk and squirted itself limply. Morel winked at it.

"That's it, old man," he said. "Never say die. You have to be mad, it's true, to keep going and hope, but the first reptile who dragged his belly out of the water a million years ago to live on land without lungs and tried to breathe all the same—he too was mad. In the end the reptile became a man. We must always try to do the best we can—perhaps one day we'll become human, who knows."

He wondered if he had been merely thinking or if he had spoken out loud, and he turned toward Youssef, but they had been together for a year and no doubt nothing now surprised him.

"Youssef!"

The boy came out of the reeds slowly.

"Yes, *missié*."

"When you're master here—and soon you will be—you must look after the elephants . . ."

"Yes, *missié*."

But he was not interested in the herds. He was not even looking at them. Morel even had the impression that he despised them. And yet it was of his own accord that he had joined this campaign for the protection of the African fauna. One day, right at the beginning of the struggle, he had emerged from the bush without a word, and he had followed him everywhere ever since, with a tommy gun in his hand, a sort of black guardian angel. For some time now, Morel had known who he was and why he was with him, but he took good care not to betray his knowledge. He looked at him again with a slightly ironic but friendly gaze. The face was without a trace of servility and the eyes had a depth of passion and gravity it was impossible to mistake. They had been together for nearly a year now, eating and sleeping side by side, and once Morel had heard the boy talking in his sleep. It was a bright Sahara night and he had taken a turn in the blue moonlight and come to a stop close by Youssef, who was lying on his side with his face to the ground. The boy had suddenly uttered a few words, and Morel overheard his dream: those few seconds had been enough to show him the forces that were struggling for the soul of Africa, and without hesitation he had placed his trust in the best of them. Since then Youssef's presence had reminded him constantly of the stake—something more than his own life.

"Don't you get tired of always following me?"

"No, *missié*."

Morel couldn't resist an ironic grin, and he pushed his little felt hat back on his head and asked, "You really care what happens to me, don't you?"

A sign of uneasiness, quickly repressed. Morel was on the point of saying at last what he had guessed, what he had known for so long now, but he stopped in time. It would have done no good. There was no short cut. This young African must be left to take his chances, he must carry out his own education as a human being and succeed or fail. He trusted him. There was no reason why he should fail.

"Afraid something might happen to me, eh?"

The boy lowered his eyes. A trace of inner struggle showed on that face in which only the width of the nostrils spoke of the blood of the first Arab conquerors.

"Me go everywhere with you."

Peer Qvist had called it the last trust of Africa. Waïtari had another name for it: paternalism. The servant's loyalty to his master. The Frenchman's ironic eye met that of the elephant among its reeds.

"Don't worry, we'll beat the lot of them," he told him. "Whites, blacks, grays, yellows, we'll beat 'em all. The mud doesn't last forever. We'll crawl out of it like other prehistoric beasts. In the end we'll have lungs to breathe with and we'll become men; we'll become a human species at last."

## XXXV

FIELDS SPENT HIS second night in the hut, rolled up in the blanket Minna had given him. He slept badly and his ribs hurt; twice he had to go out and be sick. He was awakened a third time by a feminine presence at his side. He sat up, but it was only the African night, with its air of a veiled woman. He tried to calm his

pounding heart: it was an old yearning and yet he never got used
to it. When he was very tired or sick it became almost physical; his
whole body ached with longing. Sitting there in the darkness he
smoked a cigarette, trying to convince himself that it was a mere
reproductive instinct, a trick nature played on you, a simple physical urge. But this need for another company was such that all the
reasoning in the world could only emphasize his loneliness and the
hopelessness of the struggle he had been carrying on for so long
against it. It was ridiculous to think that a woman would be an
answer to such a need, ridiculous to imagine that a pair of arms
around your shoulders could rescue you. Besides, he had slept with
a good number of women in his life: it had nothing to do with that
need for company. He stubbed out his cigarette in the sand: What
he needed was a good dog who would come and offer his paw from
time to time.

It was two in the morning. Elephants were trumpeting in the
dark, tumultuous and quite close—it occurred to him that there was
nothing to prevent these giants from knocking over the huts, and
crushing them.

He dozed off again, to be awakened, it seemed, almost at once—
he had really slept deeply for three hours—by the sound of shots.
He listened for a moment, thinking that he was the victim of his
usual recurring dreams: it was the same staccato yet dense firing he
had heard at the Anzio bridgehead on the fifth day after the landing,
or on the Normandy beaches, or when the French troops advanced
through rice paddies in Indochina. But he wasn't dreaming. The
only possible explanation was that Morel had been surprised by
troops—and was defending himself. But that did not account for such
a density of fire.

He seized his camera and a bag of films, and ran out onto the
dune. He still had one film unused, and half another in the Rolleiflex.
But he was not relying on the reserve film: it was a principle with
him always to leave a margin of safety of one spare roll, whatever
the pressure of events. This enabled him in all circumstances to keep
his peace of mind. (Fields was strangely haunted by the idea that
some sensational, fantastic, unheard-of event, a miracle in fact,
would occur just as he ran out of film.) His eyes were still gummy

with a mixture of sleep and lack of it, but he took his first picture before he even knew what was happening.

In a clear, serene light, like some total lucidity of earth and sky, the whole landscape seemed to have moved nearer; and on every rock, on every island of grass and reeds, standing, kneeling or prone, men in khaki were firing at the elephants.

The shots seemed to come from all sides at once, and a single glance was enough to show Fields that the same massacre was going on over the whole expanse of the Kuru, as far as the marshes to the north, where all the birds in the world seemed to have suddenly blackened the sky, while thousands of buffalo moved like a black landslide toward the western cliff. The trumpeting of the terrified beasts rose in a monstrous din, so that finally no sound of firing was heard, while the soldiers, upright on the rocks, took aim again and again, silhouetted against the sky, the sun gleaming on their yellow headdresses.

A compact gray mass of about two hundred elephants stood in the middle of the lake, huddled together against the bullets, and big white splashes of water were rising above them: lying flat on the rocks, soldiers were throwing sticks of dynamite at their legs. (Fields said later that his first impression was that a battalion of troops had taken up position on the Kuru during the night.)

He took half a dozen photographs from where he was, then tried to go down into the water to take a close-up of a group of seven elephants slowly collapsing under a continuous squall from automatic weapons fired at less than five yards' range, but he heard a bullet whistle past his ears and decided not to take the risk with his precious films on him—they might easily end up in the water. He therefore retired to the top of the dune and tried to get his bearings and decide what pictures to take.

It was typical of Fields that he wasted no time asking himself *why* this systematic massacre of the exhausted elephants; he confined himself to registering it coldly on his film. (Fields was later to publish one of these photographs with a caption quoting the explanation given him by Waïtari: "We did it to get some money from ivory, but above all to dispose of the Morel legend. People are trying to conceal our struggle for independence under the smoke screen of a so-called 'humanitarian' campaign for the protection of the African fauna. It is a classical maneuver to try and conceal under big words and big humanitarian principles the ugly realities of colonialism. We had to put an end to those tactics.")

After a few more shots, Fields let his camera drop to his chest and began running toward Morel's hut. It was then that he missed a unique photograph. As he ran he caught sight of a magnificent bull with its enormous tusks raised toward the sky, lifting itself halfway up a rock in spite of the bullets fired at it almost point-blank; as Fields took aim with his lens the animal succeeded in seizing the hunter with its trunk and rolled down into the water with him. Fields missed the scene only by half a second and then only because during the fall the hunter's body was hidden from him by the elephant. Through the din, he had distinctly heard the man's cry of terror.

(Fields was completely wrong in his estimate of the number of animals killed in the Kuru basin. On his return to Fort Lamy he gave an approximate figure of four hundred elephants killed in the two days' massacre. The official figure communicated by the Chad authorities and reproduced in the press was two hundred and seventy animals killed, two hundred of them with tusks. Fields was probably mistaken because he concentrated more on each photograph than on the general scene; also, he had based his estimate for the whole expanse of the Kuru basin on what was happening in its central part. The figures he gave, and even those quoted by the official communiqué, met with incredulity from all specialists in big game hunting. Even admitting that De Vries had managed to place his thirty-five or forty men quietly during the night along the Kuru cliffs, taking advantage of the prostration of the herds, an average of more than seven animals per gun was barely believable. The greatest slaughter of elephants recorded, that of 1910 in the Ubangi, was seventy animals to twenty men, and that was a herd bogged down in the Bandu marshes and hardly moving, leaving the hunters all the time they needed. The experts also threw doubt on Fields's statement that during the two days the operations lasted a great number of animals returned to the water after having escaped at the beginning of the massacre. The figures were discussed even

after Schölscher's return and in spite of the irrefutable proof he
brought with him. Fields at first threw doubt on Schölscher's figures,
which were based on the number of tusks brought in and took no
account of wounded animals that had moved away from the lake to
die. These must have been many, since those who did the shooting
relied much more on the density of fire than on its accuracy. The
qualities that make a good soldier are not necessarily those of a
good hunter, and Habib had recruited the majority of his men
among the deserters from the Sudanese units which had revolted
in April, and were later collected in small, carefully camouflaged
groups by their leaders and held ready in the cities for the time of
the referendum on independence or union with Egypt. There were
also a few deserters from the Foreign Legion. The whole expedition had indeed been run as a military operation. Not only were all
the men in uniform, khaki shorts and yellow Arab headdress, but
many animals had been killed by machine-gun fire and many had
their heads smashed in by explosives. As Fields was to put it, the
only thing lacking was dive-bombers.)

Fields found Morel in his hut sitting on the ground with his companions, his hands tied behind his back and his face covered with
blood. He found out later that as soon as the shots had awakened
him, Morel had seized his Sten gun and rushed out toward the lake,
stopping for a second to shoot from the dune; he then dashed into
the water and continued to shoot with the water up to his chest,
standing there among the elephants which were rushing about him
in all directions. He had got his hunter at the third shot and was
taking aim again, when a blow from a rifle butt on the back of the
neck knocked him unconscious. Shortly before, Forsythe and Minna
had been awakened by Habib and his men, but they had not managed to find Morel, who slept in the open at the other end of the
dune, rolled up in a blanket, nearer to the stars and to the herds.
Habib had sought for him vainly, until he suddenly saw him in the
water among the elephants, firing at the hunters.

Except for Minna, they all had their hands bound behind their
backs; two Sudanese held them covered with tommy guns, and between the two grinning soldiers stood a man whom Fields had never
seen before, who impressed him immediately with his extraordinary

good looks and an air of true nobility. He was a Negro and his face was charcoal-black, and this gave his features, delicate and of an almost classic severity, a virile beauty hard to forget. He was powerfully built, of statuesque carriage, and he held his head back with an almost royal disdain. (Fields's first reaction was a feeling of inferiority.) And yet it was not the good looks of the man that fascinated him. Fields could not take his eyes off this black Caesar's kepi. It was a French cavalry officer's kepi, with the five stars of a full general, but these stars were not gold; they were black. Fields stared at them, gaping. The thing was both frightening and pathetic —one of the noblest cases of schizophrenia it had ever been granted him to observe. The kepi was French, but the stars had another story to tell. Instinctively his hands moved to his camera and he took a photograph, at the same time shouting: "American journalist, American journalist . . ." wondering, nevertheless, if he wasn't taking the last picture of his life. (A year earlier, in New York, Fields had met the colored writer George Penn, who was just back from Accra. Penn had told him: "There are several politicians of importance in Africa. There's N'Krumah of Accra, Azikwé of Nigeria, Awoluwa of the Iambas, and Kenyatta of Kenya, now in prison in Tanganyika. But there's also one of the most extraordinary men I have ever met, white or black: Waïtari of French Equatorial Africa. When Africa really raises its voice, that's the name that will be heard. Unless the French meanwhile make him their own Prime Minister: they're quite capable of that.")

Behind Waïtari was a man who seemed to be enjoying the scene at least as much as he did the dead cheroot clamped between his teeth. He was wearing a white yachtsman's cap, blue canvas shirt and trousers and dirty black-and-white shoes, and with his expression of good-natured rascality he suggested some small Mediterranean port where a little smuggling affair was just being nicely settled far more than the heart of Africa and the oldest struggle of all.

Peer Qvist was sitting beside Idriss in a corner of the hut, his chin on his chest. Johnny Forsythe must have offered serious resistance; although he was smiling, blood was running from his lips. He had at first been misled by the military appearance of the men who

had kicked him awake. He had thought that they were a regular
police force from the Sudan, come to arrest them, acting in liaison
with the French Equatorial African authorities. He offered no resistance and did not understand what was happening until he saw
Waïtari and Habib—even then he had had to wait until he was out
in the open and could see the massacre on the lake before being
completely enlightened. Then he charged the soldiers who were
taking him away, and was badly beaten up. Youssef was not there;
Minna, with her blouse torn, her face distorted by hatred, was
sobbing and screaming hysterically, and struggling to free herself
from a laughing Sudanese who held her firmly by the shoulders.

Fields, when he entered the hut, was welcomed by the two Sten
guns, which turned toward him with impressive reflex action. But
in spite of a second's painful anticipation, he had clutched his
camera and taken a picture, while reciting his sacred status of
American journalist. (Fields was not really scared. He had a very
clear idea of his destiny. His deep conviction that he was to die one
day of cancer of the prostate or the anus was largely responsible for
his cold-blooded courage and the reputation for total indifference to
danger which he enjoyed in his profession.) His only real worry at
that moment was his camera and films: he expected to have them
confiscated. But Waïtari appeared, on the contrary, delighted by his
presence. His whole attitude was one of courtesy and eagerness, and
he hardly bothered to conceal his satisfaction at seeing an American
journalist. Fields had a veteran's eye for politicians, and he at once
sniffed out Waïtari's motives. He understood perfectly well the interest which the former deputy for the Oulés might have in publicity, especially in the United States. In any case, at the journalist's
appearance, Waïtari appeared to forget about Morel altogether, and
began to converse with Fields with a courtesy and an effort to
please which clearly showed the importance he attached to his profession. (Fields was to say later that he had, all along, the impression
that he was chatting with a French intellectual.)

"I hope you will be fair to us in what you write," Waïtari said.

(Fields noted that at first he spoke in a rather high-flown manner,
but that this soon vanished, giving place to a muffled violence, that
of conviction. From the beginning, Fields felt sure that he was

perfectly sincere and believed in himself. He had the art of commanding attention in that indefinable way which is the secret of both great demagogues and true popular leaders. Fields was not taken in by the purely oratorical part of the performance—he had never yet met a politician who could forget the public when he was addressing a journalist—but he knew a great personality when he came across it, and the strong impression made immediately by Waïtari was in addition based on a certain physical dignity and even nobility which irritated him and made him slightly jealous.)

"Your presence here will enable the truth to be heard at last. I can't tell you how angry and indignant those who are fighting for independence have been at the efforts of the colonialist press to camouflage the real object of our struggle, which is liberty for Africa, and to substitute for it this scandalous, absurd and insulting version which Morel has been specially paid to foist upon public opinion. We know who is paying him, and why he has been able to escape the authorities for so long. He has served as a humanitarian smoke screen behind which they want to hide our legitimate aspirations. We are all the more indignant and outraged because we have had enough of being used by the whole world as its zoo, as a repose for the eyes of tourists tired of their skyscrapers and motorcars, who come here to relax in the primitive, to relax at the sight of our nakedness and our herds. We have had enough of it—more than enough—and we intend to rescue Africa from its savage past; and I can tell you that in our eyes factory chimneys are a thousand times more beautiful than the necks of giraffes which your tourists so much admire. We are here to put an end to this sentimental nonsense about elephants and about Africa, 'the last garden of Eden.' We are not interested in the preservation of savage animals but in the birth of new Africa. For this we need modern weapons and the ivory will pay for them, at least for some of them. I've never had any taste for hunting. I should even like to see our people forget they were ever a people of hunters. Hunting is one more link with primitive times—with an archaic age from which we shall rescue our people, whatever the cost. But our movement needs money. Our presence here proves that we are in nobody's pay. I was offered aid from Cairo; I refused. But the arms merchants do not give their goods for nothing. They have to be paid. Your public opinion is full of sentiment about the elephants: the fate of the African peoples is unimportant to it or unknown. My aim is to awaken its attention, and I am relying on your professional ethics to tell the truth about us. If we had to sacrifice all the elephants in Africa to attain our aims, we should do so without hesitation."

Fields had lived in Paris for several years, but he had never heard anyone speak French with such talent and such power. He wondered in what language Waïtari had addressed the tribes of French Equatorial Africa during his official campaign tours.

(Later on he tried to find out. The only dialect Waïtari knew perfectly was Oulé. The twenty-seven or so other dialects of the territory were completely foreign to him. He was one of those Negro politicians who had, since 1945, carried on most energetically the campaign for teaching French to the tribes and for progressively eliminating the African dialects. The reason was easy to guess. The witch doctors and tribal chieftains retained their power behind the barrier of dialects. To Waïtari the use of French was the principal weapon of emancipation, unification and political education, the best way to carry out the fight against the primitive past. The Oulé dialect contained no word for "nation," no word for "country," no word for "politics," no word for "worker," "working-class," "proletariat," "Marxism" or "socialism"—all were quite beyond its vocabulary, and indeed the expression "the right of peoples to self-determination" became "victory of the Oulés over their enemies." The apparent paradox which had made a nationalist like Waïtari an intransigent champion of the French language had thus a simple explanation.)

While Waïtari was speaking, the firing by the lake continued. Fields thought that it made a good background, a sort of practical demonstration of what he was saying.

Like many of his compatriots, Fields did not have a particularly philosophical turn of mind and, particularly since his naturalization, took good care not to let himself be too much drawn toward abstractions. He was more sensitive to the practical means used to reach a goal, to tangibles, things one could photograph—there would be plenty of those by the lake—than to the loftiness of the aims pursued.

While the black leader was conjuring before him in vibrant tones the image of a future Africa, industrialized, electrified and cleared of its jungles and its primitive conditions, Fields was above all conscious of the shooting outside and could not restrain himself from mentally estimating the number of elephants slaughtered. He quickly exaggerated this number out of all proportion.

He took another photograph of Morel, Forsythe, Peer Qvist and Idriss sitting there with crossed legs and bowed heads, with their hands tied behind their backs in the hut; this posture of defeated men had about it an indefinable tang of the eternal. Beside them Minna, disheveled, her blouse torn, was now crying quietly, sometimes wiping her tears with the back of her hand. (Fields was later to say, as he sat in a small Paris café where he used to meet some of his compatriots: "The only revolution I still believe in is biological revolution. One day man will become possible. Progress can only come from the biological laboratories.")

Somewhat to Fields's surprise, Morel seemed the calmest of them all—neither shocked nor indignant. It was obvious that he had met with all this long ago, that he had always known what he was up against, and also that he was not easily discouraged. Questioned later by Fields, who asked him rather peevishly what he had been thinking of during the massacre, he answered quietly, "About Youssef. It's in his hands. It's up to him to understand. To lose the fight or to win it. He's the one who'll make the choice."

(As he came and went, Fields saw Youssef several times with the horses he looked after. The boy was squatting on the sand. He must have hidden his weapon, or perhaps it had been taken away from him; but, no doubt on account of his youth, Habib's men had left him alone. When the journalist spoke a few words to him, the boy raised his eyes and looked at him without answering—perhaps without seeing him—and Fields was struck by the extraordinary expression of suffering which came to him from that generally impassive face. The lips were trembling, the eyes were pained, and the features had lost their firmness, revealing a distress, a hesitation, an inner conflict whose causes the journalist could not understand. The boy slowly lowered his head without reacting or responding to Fields's friendly question.)

While Waïtari made his political speech—it was hard to regard his passionate torrent of words as anything else—Morel only once emerged from his apparent indifference. He smiled bitterly and nodded ironic approval when the former deputy for the Oulés made this angry thrust:

"Of course I am accused of being a Communist sympathizer. That's an easy way out. But it wasn't the Communists, it was a French writer of the extreme right wing, Charles Maurras, who said that the most precious of all human liberties is the independence of one's country . . ."

The only person who gave Fields any relief during this interview was the man in the yachting cap, whose cheroot, stuck in the middle of an obviously dyed jet-black beard, had something both obscene and cheerful about it, and who seemed to be savoring the scene with extreme pleasure, sometimes shaking with silent laughter. Forsythe listened with a mocking smile, sometimes looking with pity at Minna, and spitting blood. Peer Qvist was the only one who tried to interrupt. Several times he gave Waïtari an impatient glance and finally in a voice deepened by rage, with his beard shaking and in his drawling Scandinavian accent, he thundered:

"The tens of thousands of Negroes who died building the Congo-Océan railway are nothing in terms of human suffering compared to what you plan for Africa. You'll be one of the cruelest of colonizers and conquerors—one of those most foreign to Africa—the color of your skin makes no difference: you are a typical product of the West, one of our finest products. The tribes have known the slave traders, cannibalism, disease and colonization, but that's nothing compared with what they'll be up against when you start building a new Africa, and my heart bleeds for the survivors."

Waïtari shrugged. "Pity there are no white men like you left in Africa, Peer Qvist. Our task would have been easier. The most dangerous to us are the Europeans trying to do something new, not those who are content with natural splendor. You yourself are an anachronism, even in Europe, and it would be no use trying to convince you—you're the past, you don't count any longer. As for Morel, his exquisite misanthropy, his disgust for human hands because they are not clean enough for his taste—that's a typical bourgeois neurosis which leaves me indifferent. I have long ceased to consider, as our witch doctors do, mental sickness as the sign of a supernatural presence. Our friend Forsythe is here for reasons of his own. Idriss is defending the most backward past of Africa—that of savage tribes, of lions and leopards raiding the villages, of elephants and buffalo as far as the horizon. This young woman, for whom I have the friendliest feelings, is here, let's say, because of a certain experience of men: she should have been content with the company of a dog. All of you are typical products of an unbalanced and doomed society. I am not talking to you now, but to a representative of American public opinion whom our good luck brought here and who can do a great deal for African freedom. As for you, Peer Qvist, once again, I like you because you amuse me, and I know the secret dream that torments you. I myself was brought up in the missionary's schools. Allow me to tell you that the Garden of Eden is closed for good. The black peoples have suffered much too much from their own superstitions and their need for miracles for you to be allowed to add your own. You still dream of mystic shepherds—at night you look for the Star of Bethlehem; every time a woman goes past on a donkey in the desert, you wonder if she is hiding a new-born child under her veil. No wonder that when you're confronted with the hard realities of economics, of political progress, of the proletariat and workers' wages, you go mad with rage and take refuge, like our friend Saint-Denis, in the heart of 'magic' Africa, the Africa of mysterious rites and witch doctors, or among the herds which help you to dream of Biblical times. You'll never forgive us for trying to deprive you of your opium dream. But do you know what the cost of it is, old man? It is ignorance, leprosy, starvation, elephantiasis, filariasis, it's all part of the 'magic'—it's infant mortality and chronic undernourishment of two hundred million people. That's the price our people are paying for your nostalgic dream, for those herds of elephants and the so-called 'natural splendor' by which you set such store. I advise you, Peer Qvist, to go back to your dear Copenhagen Museum. As a rare specimen. That's where you belong."

He turned to Fields.

"I'll talk to you later. Please try to remember that we are doing all this to gain our freedom. We'll take the ivory to Khartoum and buy arms for the money it brings us. We are very few, and you can help us by doing your job as a reporter honestly."

The voice was hard and almost commanding, yet it was impossible not to feel the anxiety and the desperate sincerity of the man. But the cries of the wounded or dying elephants echoing from the lake amid the sound of firing were enough to bring back to Abe Fields all that he had learned in the twenty years he had spent behind his camera recording history in the making. This African revolutionary was no different from all the other revolutionaries who inscribed the words "liberty," "justice" and "progress" on their flags and then went on to kill, to torture and to suppress all living liberty in the name of their noble and human goal. The contradiction was a human one and no political revolution could solve it. It was something in the nature of man himself. So he remained unmoved by the plea addressed to him in such deep and burning accents of sincerity, and he tried also to remain unperturbed by the sound of death coming from the lake. The only thing that mattered was to take good pictures. He took another of Waïtari who was staring at him in silent intensity; the charcoal-black face under the blue French kepi had an expression of dignity, of nobility which it was difficult to dismiss, although Fields knew of course that this was nothing but sheer physical beauty. Now he had to go easy on film; he was beginning to feel the terror of running out.

When Waïtari had left the hut, the man in the yachting cap— Fields learned later that he was a Lebanese adventurer called Habib —went over to Morel, took the pack of *Gauloises* from his pocket, put one between Morel's lips and offered him a light. Morel accepted it, and inhaled the smoke. He seemed to have some sympathy for this man, perhaps because he was obviously no more than a mercenary rascal, totally devoid of ideology or any disinterested motive.

"It's not one of your lucky days, I'm afraid, my friend," the Lebanese said to him in an almost gentle tone. "I don't know if Your Human Highness has been keeping up with the news, but the Bukavu Conference adjourned three days ago without deciding anything about Her elephants. The present law on hunting has been modified in details, but there's no real change."

The Frenchman seemed profoundly affected by this news. His face became deeply furrowed, the eyes took on an expression of distress, and for one brief moment he looked almost defeated. Fields realized how much he had been counting on the good sense and generosity of the very people he had been fighting and defying.

(Later Fields had an opportunity to talk with some of the delegates to the Bukavu Conference. One of them gave him the following explanation:

"Our instructions were to re-examine the law relating to the protection of the African fauna, particularly as regards the species menaced with extinction. We were not called upon either to express an opinion on the moral aspect of big game hunting, or to deal with Morel and his obsession. It is true that in certain districts the number of African elephants is diminishing, but that corresponds to the general reduction of the forest area and the advance of cultivation. Generally speaking, and taking Africa as a whole, it is completely untrue to say that the elephants are in danger of becoming extinct. They are diminishing in numbers—which is not the same thing. There will always be time to modify the law and to protect enough of them to ensure the preservation of the species. For the moment they are numerous enough to constitute a serious threat to cultivation. The moment will of course inevitably come when the number of elephants, which require great open spaces and limitless freedom, will have to be severely reduced. This moment has not yet arrived, but it will. Imagine what it would be like if vast herds were left to roam freely in one of our industrialized countries, such as Belgium. God knows the price Nehru would be willing to pay to rid India of the sacred cows. We do not, after all, intend to sanctify the African elephants at the request of a maniac.")

Morel's companions also seemed stunned by the news, except Forsythe, who later told Fields that he had never had any illusions about the results of the Bukavu Conference.

(A little later, perhaps to defend himself against the cries of dying elephants, which sounded like calls for help—as if the murdered giants were calling to their rescue the man who loved them so much and cared so deeply about them, some of the screams rising in deafening anger to stop abruptly under the impact of yet another bullet

—Forsythe attempted cynicism again. He repeated to Fields, in a broken voice and with a disillusioned smile: "It doesn't matter to me. There's nothing one can do about it. I give up. All I want is to go home. When all's said and done the best way to turn your back on the lot of them is to stay quietly at home watching television." But that only lasted a few hours, and he was not long in recovering that angry and fierce expression of his which was a sign of health.)

Habib observed Morel's reaction with obvious delight: it looked to Fields as if he enjoyed rubbing it in. He lit his cheroot which had gone out, inhaled the smoke, and watched the man he called "His Human Highness" with a knowing eye.

Morel abruptly raised his head and looked at Forsythe: "Jack, that fellow on the cliff. Do you know if I got him?"

"You did, all right. I saw him fall into the lake. He didn't get up again. Besides, the elephants went over him."

"Good." He turned to Habib: "I was sure from the first that it was one of your friend De Vries's ideas," he said. "He's that sort of man. Remember, in Fort Lamy, some months ago, I warned him. I warned you too. I told him that if I caught him again anywhere near a herd, I'd kill him. Now I have."

For a moment, Habib was out of countenance. His face had gone gray, and his teeth bit deep into his cheroot. Then his features relaxed, and he recovered his mocking smile. He shook his head and grabbed the cheroot between his fat fingers.

"So the poor young man's escaped me, in spite of everything," he said almost gaily. "I managed to hold him back two or three times, but it was bound to happen. I shall have to find another companion of misfortune."

He spat out the cigar-butt and for a while looked rather thoughtful. Then he threw his head back and laughed a good, big, unforced laugh.

"*Inch' Allah!* It'll take more than that to stop an old buccaneer!"

When Fields later learned the nature of the relationship that had bound Habib to his young protégé, he could not help admiring the good cheer and robustness of this sturdy scoundrel, about whose great earthly qualities he no longer had any doubts.

(Fields was to run into Habib again one day, at Istanbul, in the bar of a hotel. He was brooding over a Martini when he heard a hearty laugh, and an enormous paw descended on his shoulder. It was Habib, with his black beard freshly dyed, very much at ease in the uniform of a Merchant Marine captain of one of the Central American republics. "A cargo of oranges, sir, would you believe it? Genuine oranges this time, I swear! I never thought I'd come to that!" Fields had flown to Istanbul because there was tension between Greece and Turkey. The blockade of Cyprus by British warships had not put a stop to the traffic in arms and he suddenly thought that, oranges or not, Habib might give him some interesting sidelines. Habib did seem remarkably well informed. Then they got on to Morel and their meeting at Lake Kuru. "Do you remember when you turned to the Frenchman and asked him if you could do anything for him? That was a good one. Why? Because you had already saved his life without even knowing it. Yes, I can explain: Waïtari's three young disciples—Madjumba, N'Dolo and . . . I can't remember the name of the third, but he was very beautiful—well anyhow, they had decided to execute him as a traitor. They had even sat as a tribunal of three at Khartoum, and had judged him and condemned him as a traitor to the cause of African independence, after the raid on Sionville. Apparently in the manifesto he had published there Morel had denied that his action had a political motive, stating firmly that all he cared for was the protection of elephants, not nationalism. As soon as they arrived at Lake Kuru they had pressed Waïtari to let them carry out their sentence. If you had not been there, Morel would have been killed like a rat—but with a famous American journalist on the spot, Waïtari had no trouble explaining that it was out of the question. And you asking Morel what you could do for him . . . it was too funny! Ah! those were the days. Unfortunately idealists like Morel, good for a real laugh, aren't met with every day. Pity. Well, one has to take it as it comes, *inch'Allah!*" He concluded a shade regretfully. He picked his teeth for a moment in silence. "And do you know, my friend, what the last word about His Human Highness will always be?" Fields silently shook his head. "You remember that briefcase full of proclamations and petitions that he was forever carrying with him?" Fields nodded. Habib's chest began to shake, he pressed his paw against it, his head thrown back, his eyes closed, and his whole face a mask of cruel mirth. "It was made of animal leather . . .")

Fields remained for a little longer in the hut, where no one said a word. He tried to find something encouraging to say. All he could think of were a few vague and not very convincing remarks about the reaction of American public opinion "which had taken this campaign for the protection of elephants to heart and would certainly do something about it"—which earned him an ironic look from Forsythe. Morel paid him not the slightest attention; Minna sighed deeply and wiped her eyes.

"We'll go on as long as is necessary," said Peer Qvist briefly.

Morel turned to Fields. "You asked me just now what you could do for us. You might try and persuade Waïtari to leave us some arms and ammunition. After all, if the only thing that interests him is to get people talking about terrorism in Africa, I don't see why he should refuse."

Fields suddenly realized that, ever since the news of the failure at Bukavu, Morel had not ceased for an instant to make plans for future campaigns. He was relieved to find something he could try to do for him, and he left the hut at once with the firm intention of obtaining arms and ammunition for Morel even if it meant stealing them during the night.

He found Waïtari a little lower down on the dune, under the darkening sky, in heated discussion with two young black men, who argued bitterly in French. The third was standing a little way off and looked sad and embarrassed. At Fields's approach the argument immediately stopped and the two young men looked at him unpleasantly. Waïtari seemed surprised by the journalist's request, but after an instant's reflection he agreed to leave Morel with some arms and ammunition to carry on his campaign. He then dismissed the matter with a shrug and appeared curious about Fields's reaction to his speech and the massacre. Fields muttered something indistinct, and then went off to take a few pictures by the lake, where the shooting, though now less dense, was still going on in outer creeks and among the reeds.

He also tried to find out what kind of men Waïtari had with him. He found that they were practically all southern Sudanese. They all seemed to have some rudiments of English, and called him "sir," standing instinctively to attention in a way that had something clearly military about it. But to all his questions they showed their teeth in a huge smile and refused to reply. He was rather surprised to find among them four white men: two Germans, one Slovak and one from the Baltic states, all deserters from the Foreign Legion who had jumped ship at Suez. All four had long ago achieved indifference to what side they were fighting on, provided that their professional services were properly paid for—which apparently was not the case in the Foreign Legion; this, together with the length of contract, was one of the things they had against it. They let themselves be photographed while they were having a rest, like people with no ties anywhere who didn't care if their faces remained anonymous or not. They complained about the Sudanese, who shot like conscripts; which, on the lips of the fair-haired solidly built Slovak sounded like a professional's supreme insult. They reckoned that with well-trained shots, they might have bagged seven to ten elephants per man. They were much more discreet when Fields tried to find out why they had come to Khartoum; one of the Germans in the end merely said that they were "waiting for orders." Fields noticed that the whole expedition bore the marks of good military organization, and the only concern he heard them express was the fear of being interrupted by the Sudanese police on the return journey "although they have other fish to fry."

The heat was at its peak.

Flocking in from all directions, vultures wheeled over the lake. Fields was surprised to see a whole black population in the water, men, women and children: they had rushed up from heaven knew where, and were attacking the meat with their knives.

Fields tried to calculate the number of elephants killed this first day, but his reckonings varied considerably. He was particularly interested by this, because he was trying to estimate, at least approximately, the money Waïtari might expect to realize from the ivory, and the quantity of arms which it represented. At the end of the second day he had arrived at the following figures (but the next morning he doubled them, and before he got back to Fort Lamy he made them even higher): 150 animals killed, 84 of them with tusks; taking a pair of tusks as worth on the average £40, that would make 3,500 Egyptian pounds at the most. A Thompson machine gun was worth £50 at that moment in the Middle East; a case of twenty-four grenades £100; a revolver £10-15 depending on condition; an Italian Beretta rifle £20; and these were figures that often varied by 50 per cent in the fluctuation of the market and the political situation. A deserter from the Foreign Legion could be enrolled at £50 a month. Fields estimated that even at the most optimistic figures, Waïtari could equip and pay about twenty "volunteers" for three months. That certainly was not on the scale of his ambitions, nor was it even enough to start some real trouble in what was one of the most peaceful and best-run territories of Africa. In the end he put this question to Waïtari, rather bluntly. Waïtari nodded, showing that he had considered the question.

"Believe me, Monsieur Fields, I have no illusions. The tribes are, alas, far from being ready to follow me, thanks to the primitive condition in which their chieftains, sultans, kings and witch doctors keep them—with the blessing of the French, who are so anxious to safeguard their 'customs.' For the moment, to be quite frank with you, my chief purpose is to reach international public opinion, which indeed is ready to listen to us. People must know that there is such a thing as an African revolt. Two or three armed raids into the territory will do precisely that. I don't mind going to a French jail: on the contrary, I am looking forward to it. Kenyatta, of Kenya, is in prison, N'Krumah, of the Gold Coast, only came out of prison to assume power. Today colonialist prisons are waiting rooms for office."

Fields made a sign that he understood, but although he was not exactly in the habit of showing his feelings when he was on a job, his face must have registered a trace of silent disapproval. Waïtari stared at him for a moment.

"I feel I am shocking you," he said almost sadly, "and perhaps you think I am trying to play the part of a Negro Machiavelli; but, Monsieur Fields, you don't know how it feels to be a fully civilized Negro in this land—a land which is still at that stage . . . Look."

He pointed toward the carcass of an elephant in the water about twenty yards away: two completely naked men were sitting in the animal's open and bloody belly biting at its guts . . .

"Yes, you may well reach for your camera. But for us that's an everyday sight."

He stood for a moment still pointing to the scene, then turned his back on Fields and moved away, with a dignity that made his figure look even more lonely under the sky.

A little later, Waïtari was to return to the subject once more. The shooting had ceased: Habib hoped thus to encourage the herds to return after a quiet night. But the sound of dying still came from the lake, where the wounded animals were trying to find a refuge among the reeds. Fields had sat down on the sand by the edge of the water, completely exhausted and only half breathing, so as to lessen the pain from his ribs. He had very little physical resistance. He sometimes displayed an athlete's endurance when he was on a job, but it was entirely based on nervous tension—a sort of second wind which took charge of him whenever he got hold of a good story. It was a mysterious source of energy, which he lacked completely in everyday life—he always ran out of breath climbing the five floors to his Paris apartment. All day long he had been rushing over the dunes and into the water with his camera and his case of films, from which, more than anything else, he was afraid to be separated. He had now only half a roll of film left. He could feel the coming of that brutal moment of nervous collapse which would stretch him flat on his back—unless some new story suddenly turned up. It was the moment when above all things he needed a drink and a fresh pack of cigarettes.

It was now very cool, almost cold, and this violent change of temperature after the burning heat made him completely groggy. So there he sat in the twilight, in the sand, with his head lowered, and every time he raised his eyes the sky had changed color, altering from pale blue to yellow and then to mauve, and at length plunging into a darkness which reminded him of the Gulf of Mexico with the milky phosphorescent plankton in the water all round his boat. He tried vaguely to remember what he had been doing in a boat in the middle of the Gulf of Mexico, and recalled that he had gone there to do a story on the life of marine creatures for a magazine which never tired of publishing special numbers about the earth, the sky, the sea, animals and men, and of which it was said that one day it would bring out a special number about God, complete with photographs in color. He tried not to hear the trumpeting of the wounded and dying animals, of which the night was full. The last picture he had taken before darkness was of a pile of ivory which the men from the village were transporting tusk by tusk to the trucks. The roots were still covered with blood. (Fields had no more color film left.) He tried to tell himself that there was nothing in that very different from what happened in all the slaughterhouses of the world, and the fact that these were elephants instead of cattle did not really make much difference.

Perhaps because he was very tired, Fields's thoughts then took a turn which he was accustomed to call "useless." One of his first childhood memories was his mother's smile, and it happened that it was a smile that gleamed with the gold of her many gold teeth, which fascinated the child. Every time he was depressed this memory returned, together with that of a pile of gold teeth "recovered" by the Nazis from the Jewish victims of the gas chambers. Fields had spent hours staring at the photographs of this pile published by the newspapers of the time: he was looking for his mother's smile.

He had reached this point in his reflections when he saw a silhouette coming toward him in the blue light. It was Waïtari. They exchanged a few words. Fields made some remark about the extraordinary variety of cries and sounds coming from the lake, and particularly a dull, almost continuous pounding which arose from all sides. Waïtari told him that the noise was made by the mudfish trying to leave the drying marshes and to reach water: one sometimes found them many miles away from any water, still leaping forward on their fins.

"Wonderful country," said Fields.

Waïtari remained silent for a moment. "Yes. And yet it's about time to put an end to that wonder. To put an end to prehistory. Do you know what I feel when I see, along our few roads, those herds your tourists come here to admire? Shame. Shame, because I know that that 'beauty' goes together with the bare behinds of our natives, with smallpox, people living in trees, superstitions and crass ignorance. Every lion, every elephant at liberty, means still more waiting, still more savagery and primitivism, and the superior smile of the white technicians who pat us on the shoulder and tell us: 'You can see for yourself, old man, you can't do without us yet.' "

His voice trembled with anger and he made a gesture toward the stars.

"Africa will never awaken to her destiny until she has stopped being the world's zoo. America emerged from limbo with the disappearance of the bison; as long as wolves pursued the sledges on the Russian steppes, the Russian peasant died of squalor and ignorance; and the day when there are no more lions or elephants in Africa there will be a people master at last of its own destiny. For our educated youth, for our students, big herds at liberty are simply a measure of our people's backwardness. We are ready to try and surmount this backwardness, not merely at the price of the elephants but at that of our own lives . . ."

In spite of his fatigue, the pain in his left side, and his general state of exhaustion, Fields was perfectly conscious of the anxiety with which this African colossus with a voice of thunder was endeavoring to convince him. He had often been subjected to eloquence, but never with such fervor, such suppressed violence, never in a voice so overwhelming in its virile beauty. In addition he was embarrassed by the thought of a misunderstanding, which he now tried to dispel.

"You know," he said, "I'm only a cameraman and I've never published anything in my life—I mean not anything written . . . I let my camera do the talking. I can understand your motives very well, but I shall never be able to explain them as clearly as you have done."

He hesitated. He wanted to say: "That requires a professional politician," but he said, "That requires a professional writer."

Waïtari remained silent for a while. "Listen, Monsieur Fields," he said at last. "You must help us. You have no idea of the conspiracy of silence to which I am being subjected. Even the Arab press and radio never mention me except when they have nothing else to say. Your duty as a journalist and as an American is to tell the world about us."

"Give me a written statement. I'll do what I can. I've no talent for words. I've an eye for a picture, that's all. You need a lot of talent with words to . . ."

He was about to say "to justify all this," but he stopped short.

"I'll give you all the documentation you require before you leave. Why don't you come with me to Khartoum? That would enable you to get your story off by the first plane."

"No. I think I'll stay with Morel."

"You seem more interested in that madman and his elephants than in the fate of the peoples of Africa . . ."

"I can't see what I should find to photograph in Khartoum. I've got a good half a roll of film left. Morel won't go very far, and I want to be there . . . when the inevitable happens."

Waïtari got up. In the night and against its lights—he blacked out the stars with his shoulders—he appeared to Abe Fields, who remained seated, almost a giant.

"I see. You, Monsieur Fields, are a hardened professional."

"A professional, yes."

"I'll give you my biography and a statement about our movement tomorrow morning. Don't forget you have there a first-rate story for your country, which has been a colony itself."

He moved away with that supple stride of his which was perhaps the most African thing left about him. Fields followed him with his eyes, rubbing his aching side. He thought suddenly that Waïtari was perhaps less of an African nationalist than another example of French factionalism and of their quarrels among themselves.

Even the biography which he handed to him next day, together with the outline of his political aims, was profoundly French, with its lycées, its scholarships all proudly set out, the Doctorate of Law, the books he had published, the various French political groups and parties to which he had belonged, the Parliamentary committees he had sat on—there was nothing missing. Waïtari was a French product, and its one defect was that it had been too successful, and that it was isolated: his ambition was only a measure of his loneliness. Fields remembered once again what his friend the Negro writer Georgie Penn had said about him: "When Africa really raises its voice, that is the name that will be chiefly heard . . . unless the French make him their own Prime Minister."

(Fields kept his word and gave Waïtari's statement and explanations all the publicity he could. But the results were somewhat limited. The American public as a rule reacted much more to what touched its emotions than to what appealed to ideological considerations, and Fields's story of Lake Kuru, with his pictures of slaughtered elephants, touched people's emotions much more directly than did the political motives behind it. The sympathy and immediate interest aroused in the public by anything that concerned animals was something well known to newspaper editors, who always relied on it in a pinch. In this connection, Fields enjoyed telling the following anecdote. Before the war he had published in a magazine of large circulation a picture story showing giant turtles lying on their backs before being thrown alive into vats of boiling water and transformed into canned turtle soup. After that issue, the magazine's sales had gone up by 5 per cent. Fields never knew what effect his story had had on the sale of canned turtle soup. He presumed that it had not changed.)

## XXXVI

ABE FIELDS PUT UP a vigorous fight to get better treatment for Morel and his companions, protesting against the privations to which they were subjected with such indignation that Waïtari told him, rather contemptuously, that Americans were too apt to describe as "torture" any extreme lack of comfort.

"When your prisoners came back from Korea, what they called Communist 'tortures' were the conditions of life of the great mass of Asiatic peoples for centuries, which they had been made to share for a few months . . ."

"That may be," said Abe Fields, "but the question is, do you want to gain the sympathies of the American public, or are its reactions unimportant to you? At present that public knows nothing about you but is passionately interested in Morel's adventure, and what are you doing? In the name of liberty and of the right of peoples to self-determination, you start by massacring the elephants for reasons that are, let's say, a bit too theoretical and ideological for the average reader, and as for Morel, whom the press has made an almost legendary hero, you keep him and his companions bound hand and foot for the last twenty-four hours in a murderous heat. . . . I know it's stupid, but the people in my country react much more to basic human decency than to ideologies."

Waïtari interrupted him almost brutally. "I think I'd better ask you one or two questions before we go any further."

"Go ahead."

"Are you—yes or no—in favor of liberty for the African peoples? Are you for or against colonialism? You are the only journalist here, and it will be easy for you to present what we are doing in a tendentious light."

Abe Fields's nose began to emit angry sounds. "I'm against colonialism. I'm for liberty for everyone. Even for the French, and I'm not mad for the French—they've been throwing too many big words at us. I've been taking photographs of History with a capital *H* for a quarter of a century, and in the end I seem to have a great deal of sympathy for the elephants. Call it misanthropy if you like, but I don't think I'm far wrong when I say that millions of people in the world have much more sympathy for Morel than you seem to realize."

"You are truly a spokesman for the Western world, Monsieur Fields," said Waïtari.

A touch of sarcasm here, but Fields was used to French intellectuals. "I don't know. I don't know how far the Soviet public, for instance, is aware of Morel's adventure. If it is, it seems to me that a Russian worker, who slaves for eight hours a day screwing up bolts and spends the rest of his time listening to speeches about the necessity for screwing up more bolts, more quickly, with more enthusiasm—I think that that Soviet worker would have a lot of sympathy for Morel and his elephants, for what he's trying to save . . ."

The conversation took place in one of the huts. Waïtari was sitting in front of an ammunition case which served as his desk. There was a map open under his hand, and beside it, a pack of cigarettes, a lighter and his sky-blue kepi with the five black stars. A Sudanese in a yellow headdress stood guard before the hut. At the right hand of the black leader, one of the young men who accompanied him everywhere stood in a stiff military pose, with one hand on the revolver attached to his leather belt.

Fields glanced from time to time sideways at that carefully polished belt. He loathed leather belts—indeed leather in general: there was a close association, from the beginning of time, between leather and brutality. Abe Fields was certainly the most anti-leather man in the world. Since he had entered the hut, he had been struggling against an animosity. Again the French and their big words, he thought. This African had been brought up on the traditions of French military greatness and now he was trying to emulate it. The blue kepi with the black stars was a last tragic homage to France. It's astonishing, thought Fields, how completely the French have brought off their colonial conquests. That black man would at any moment quote as his authority Joan of Arc or Lafayette, the Resistance, Charles de Gaulle, Lyautey, Napoleon, and the Revolution.

"You don't understand," said Waïtari.

He took a cigarette from the pack. He wore on his wrist an extremely complicated gold watch with three concentric dials. It was obviously the last word in modern precision. Fields was also sensitive to the beauty of Waïtari's hands. It's strange, he thought, how beautiful human hands can be in spite of what they do.

"I'm only too anxious to understand."

"The French are great experts with the smoke screen. Their smoke screen is the fine phrase, the great rhetorical slogan: liberty, equality, fraternity, protect the African fauna. Morel's elephants are just that, just such a smoke screen. It's very clever, very convenient, to shove a 'popular hero'—to use your expression—in our way, to pretend that the disorders in French Equatorial Africa are due solely to an eccentric whose one preoccupation is to defend the elephants

against the hunters. A pretty legend, astutely fabricated for the purpose of putting opinion to sleep. But reality is refusing to conform.
We refuse to remain hidden by these clouds of the legendary and
the fabulous. The world has got to see us, people have got to see
the reality of Africa, with all its wounds. Anyhow, your 'legendary
hero' has probably been paid a fat sum by the colonialists to sow
confusion."

"Do you really believe so?"

"How else do you explain the, to say the least, odd leniency of the
authorities toward him? However, let's admit that he's a visionary
who really believes in what he's doing. My duty is to dispel all misunderstandings about this. What matters is African independence.
Not the elephants."

He moved his hand in a stern gesture.

"I'm not saying that Morel is a French agent, I'm saying that he
might as well be. We are busy dispelling the smoke screen. People
don't want to see us; they are going to see us."

Fields wondered how much "I" there was in that "we."

"For all that, and out of my personal regard for your scruples, if
your 'legendary hero' gives me his word that he will stay quiet and
do nothing as long as we are here, I'm ready to let him free. I can't
afford the luxury of immobilizing three men to guard him—I need
them elsewhere."

Abe Fields noticed that the word of the Frenchman was obviously enough for him. He did not for a moment think that Morel
would accept this condition, but to his surprise he did so without
objecting. Clearly he considered this new lost battle as merely one
more passing phase in the struggle he had undertaken. He did not
seem dejected, still less discouraged. Incredibly dirty as he was, his
cheeks black with stubble, his hands bound behind his back, sitting
there under the tommy-gun barrel of an uneasy Sudanese, he still
seemed to be upheld by some improbable, calm, total confidence,
an invincible obstinacy. His madness must consist in just that: a
certain basic inability to be discouraged, or to despair. *Un con,*
thought Abe Fields in French: it was the only word to fit him. A
happy idiot who refuses to give in to the evidence of hopelessness.
And yet there was no lack of evidence: there were not only the

trumpetings of the elephants as they died on the lake, but also the
failure of the Conference on the protection of the African fauna,
which had adjourned once more without managing to change the
law. Elephants would be shot as before: in the name of progress,
of intensive industrialization, of the need for meat, or of the fine art
of shooting. But Morel was behaving just as if he had not been informed of all this. Manifestly life never managed to teach him anything. There was, true enough, a shade of sadness in his voice, but it
was only a trace, hardly perceptible.

"Someone will have to invent a special injection," he was saying.
"Or pills. They're sure to stumble on it one of these days. I've always
been a confident sort. I believe in progress. They're sure to market
dignity pills, humanity pills, one of these days. People will take one
every morning, in a glass of water, before work. Then things will
become interesting all of a sudden, and even politics will become
possible. He wants my word that I won't budge from the hut if he
unties us, does he? I give it willingly. On one condition: that he
leave us weapons and our horses when he goes."

"He's promised that."

"Good. What does he expect us to do? We're disarmed anyhow.
Of course we might spit in their faces, but that's ineffective. I'm
for what's effective. I like clear-cut, limited, possible jobs. I'm no
dreamer. That's why I'm here."

He was almost laughing. Fields noticed for the first time that he
wore a small Cross of Lorraine pinned to his shirt. It was a badge
adopted during the last war by a handful of Frenchmen who refused to accept defeat and had rallied round a general, now vanished, called Charles de Gaulle, another man who believed in
elephants. That small badge explained a good deal—or at least it
explained the air of confidence he had.

His companions seemed to have caught his mood. He was contagious. Abe Fields had no doubt about that. He was beginning to
feel a touch of it himself: his heart pounded almost indecently, he
felt elated, and he was aware that he had a particularly idiotic smile
on his lips. Peer Qvist, with one thick gray eyebrow drooping over
one eyelid and the other raised above a malicious blue icicle, was
observing the reporter with interest, but it was said of the old ad-

venturer that under that patriarchal expression of his he concealed a particularly fierce kind of humor, together with a marked urge to get himself talked about.

But what was one to say of that girl, that German, who stood now at Morel's side with an expression of pride, exaltation, almost happiness, as though she had at last attained something that no one now would ever be able to take away from her? After all, she was a poor second-rate tart; it was hard to understand how she got herself mixed up in this adventure, this display of man's deep-rooted confidence in his chance to prevail. How could she have emerged from Nazi Germany, the ruins of Berlin and the hands of conquering soldiers, with all her illusions intact and an almost limitless faith in the splendors of nature? It was easier to suppose that she had come there as a mere camp follower—Morel was handsome enough.

(Fields always had to defend himself against a restrospective sympathy when he discussed Morel with his compatriots in the small American bar in Paris. "Somebody found a good nickname for Morel: an *esperado:* a new species of men that had arisen victoriously from the depths of ignominy. Of course I didn't fall for it.")

Forsythe himself had been touched no less than the others by this ironic contagion, by this extremism of hope, which no contrary evidence seemed able to destroy. On his swollen face the freckles still found room enough among the blue to create a grimace of cheerfulness, and he winked at Fields.

"Things will straighten out," he told Fields. "The free world is already behind us, according to what you told me yourself. All we can do now is wait for the Communist countries. Any minute now I should have a telegram from my 'interrogators' in China, something like this: 'REGRET SINCERELY PAST MISUNDERSTANDINGS STOP TAKING IMMEDIATE STEPS ASSURE PROTECTION ELEPHANTS AND OTHER FRIENDS OF MAN STOP COMMISSION OF SCIENTISTS HAVING STATED FALSELY BACTERIOLOGICAL WARFARE USED BY OUR AMERICAN BROTHERS HAS JUST CONFESSED SABOTAGE AND PROVOCATIVE ACTION IN LEAGUE WITH BERIA STOP ITS MEMBERS CONDEMNED FORCED LABOR PERPETUITY STOP WARM GREETINGS TO ALL PEOPLES FRATERNALLY UNITED FOR DEFENSE NATURAL SPLENDOR.' I tell you, there's no reason to be discouraged."

Abe Fields adjusted his camera and took a good picture of him with his red hair caught in the streaks of light that filtered through the grass roof of the hut, his red bandanna around his neck, his swollen, smiling face and his naked torso—he took refuge behind his camera, in self-defense against that wave of hope breaking over him.

"So you can give him my word," Morel repeated, "as long as he leaves us some arms and our horses to go on with the fight . . ."

He followed Abe Fields with a friendly stare. A decent creature, that little cameraman. Brave and anxious to help, boiling with sympathy underneath his apparent indifference. A frail man, short-sighted, with his curly hair and long nose—certainly more shaken up by his plane crash than he cared to admit. But ready to leave his camera and rush to the help of threatened giants. It was a stroke of luck that he was there and it was important that he should take good pictures: they would stir up public indignation, there was never enough indignation around. The whole world must be made aware that a handful of men were unshaken and as confident as ever that they would prevail. It was only a matter of courage and of patience. From Moscow to Madrid and from Peking to the Chad, the hidden springtime of humanity living its subterranean life in darkness would burst into the open with all the irresistible power of its millions of weak and groping shoots. He could almost hear their slow movement toward the sky and the light, toward dignity and freedom, that whisper of hope, that clandestine rustling. A slowly rising murmur, hard to detect, but the roots were strong and deep in the heart of man and the shoots were breaking their slow way into the open and his ear was keen and as he lay there on his back he could almost hear them and his laughing eyes could almost see, in the deepest recesses of the earth, the slow thrust of that ancient and difficult spring.

Riley, of the *London News*, lifted his pale, infected eyes over the cans of beer and stared angrily at Ole Olsen, from *Politiken*. A dozen journalists had been waiting for the last eight hours on the terrace of the Tchadien for an "important announcement" regarding Morel, promised by Government House.

"A case of impotence, that's what it is," Riley said. "The man is impotent, so he chooses the biggest, strongest animal there is to compensate for his lost virility. A dream of infinite strength, of magnificent power, of the strongest possible back to be able to bear it all."

"You keep your dirty confessions for your readers," Olsen said. "I'm not interested."

"He's just unable to endure his weakness any longer," Riley said.

The rumor that Morel's arrest was imminent had somehow spread at Fort Lamy and had been immediately taken up by newspapers everywhere. All those who thought of him with a secret satisfaction, as if they had tacitly appointed him to represent them, their secret longings, their indignation, their resentment, all those who had had enough of "it," without exactly realizing the limitless greatness which that small pronoun took on in the world as it was; all those who felt themselves avenged by his refusal to acquiesce and to submit, made in their name, and were secretly flattered by it—as they were personally flattered when Captain Carlsen remained clinging for three days to his piece of wreckage on the high seas; all those who attributed to their own small personal worries a rancor that went much deeper and flowed in their veins with the very blood of the species, felt angry and balked at the thought that the man who so well expressed their impossible dream of dignity, their yearning to be treated with respect at last, their aspiration to be men at last, was about to be brought in handcuffed between two policemen like any common thief.

In Haute-Savoie, in the sanatorium of Sarcelles, every item of news published by the press or radio about the man who was demanding an elementary respect for nature, was put up on the blackboard in the entrance hall. When the AFP dispatch announcing that the arrest of the outlaw was expected at any moment appeared on the blackboard, there was such depression and consternation among the patients that the head doctor prohibited the posting of further news. Most of the sick were young people and had been stricken when life and hope were at the full. A girl with one lung just removed and half of the second lung affected looked at the blackboard and burst into tears: it was the first time she had wept since she had been in the sanatorium. The decision to put up the news about Morel's crusade had been made by the patients' committee, and the head doctor had trouble making them go back on it. A student hurled at him a phrase whose connection with the Morel affair seemed to the doctor decidedly enigmatic. The dying boy said: "There's no reason why we should accept our fate without a fight."

At about the same moment, a fourteen-year-old black boy was having his head smashed in because he had given a whistle of admiration as a white woman went by; the dove-fancier Russians were exploding a hydrogen bomb and preparing a transcontinental rocket capable of transporting it and of rendering uninhabitable a territory larger than Great Britain; the Mau-Mau were mixing the brains of a new-born baby into the potion they were drinking as they swore fidelity to the cause of the right of peoples to self-determination; and the French Minister of Housing was attending the funeral and shaking hands with the parents of the child who had died of cold in a slum dwelling a short while before. In the name of liberty certain North African tribes were raping six-year-old children, castrating men and opening the wombs of French women with their knives when their virility could no longer manifest itself in any other way, while the scientists were gravely discussing whether the quantities of radioactive dust and strontium 90 contaminating the atmosphere after atomic experiments would end by creating a generation of geniuses or idiots, while in France the only solution that ancient home of culture seemed able to offer the world was to increase its production of alcohol. All those who found such items in the papers every morning and experienced a sharp moment of satisfaction, a feeling of revenge, when they heard from the man who refused to give up and was carrying on his fierce campaign for the protection of nature, were upset, and some almost enraged, by the news of his imminent arrest—in which indeed they still refused to believe.

On June 22, as the last journalists left at Fort Lamy were awaiting the fruit of their long patience—they had been told confidentially that the arrest of Morel and his companions was imminent—a group of horsemen, two of them Africans and three of them white men, was moving slowly through the thorny thin bush country southeast of Gola, where even the pale shade of the *mimosées* seemed to lie dying on the ground and the whole countryside, with its rare twisted trees, its ant-hills, and scorched grasses, seemed about to vanish in the blinding light.

For a month now, in French Equatorial Africa, in the Sudan, in Uganda and in certain districts of the Congo, Kenya and Tanganyika, all hunting for sport had been forbidden; it was reckoned that the drought would decimate the herds, and that it would take ten to fifteen years to offset it; the losses of cattle and crops everywhere made government help necessary; in the South witch doctors were threatening to make the drought go on until they were restored to their ancient position in the councils of the tribes; whole populations were leaving the stricken districts; and the loss of the cotton harvest was ruining the majority of planters.

The air no longer smelled of the jungle but of the desert, and in an atmosphere from which the last traces of humidity had vanished, Haas recognized once more in his nostrils a dryness almost identical to that of the *khamsin*.* He was deeply impressed by the tragic spectacle he had never seen before, even in the Tibesti region, where living things had long been used to the desert's barren dryness and conditioned to subsist in good harmony with it. Remembering the fetid humidity of the Chad, he had at first chewed his cigar with a certain satisfaction, filling his lungs with the healthy air totally devoid of miasmas, but little by little, struck by the almost total absence of life, by the agony of thirst of the few animals in sight, and by the stricken appearance of people in the rare villages they passed through, he finally fell silent, only swearing between his teeth at every new humming of the flies, and soon began thinking of the Lake Chad and his mosquitoes with real homesickness.

His companion, Jean de Fonsalbert, the special correspondent of a big Paris weekly, was less sensitive to that tragic landscape: it was his first visit to Central Africa and he lacked a basis for comparison. He had only one worry: to be the first journalist to meet Morel.

Haas had lived for twenty-five years among the elephants of the

* *Khamsin:* a desert sand wind.

Chad, which he captured for the zoos; in fact ever since the First World War, during which he had been gassed. He had arranged this expedition for the purpose of finding Morel and escorting him to a safe place. He had no doubt of Morel's sincerity but he was nevertheless determined to learn the truth for himself. If the adventurer was sincere, if he was hiding no ulterior motive, if a love for animals was his only magnificent obsession, he was determined to help him, and to escort him to a hiding-place where he would be safe from all pursuit. If not, if there was another piece of human filthiness, political or other, behind it, just another propaganda trick, he would spit in his face and go back to his reed beds, his mosquitoes, back among the last elephants of Lake Chad.

As for Verdier, who was accompanying them, Haas had recruited him because he had announced his sympathy for Morel, and also because he owned an abandoned plantation in the Cameroons, which would be an ideal refuge for Morel, provided they could get there. He paid no attention to his chatter. The man had long been a laughingstock in French Equatorial Africa. Having founded the Association of Free Frenchmen in the Chad and played a part in rallying the territory to the Allies during the war, he was a fanatical follower of General de Gaulle, for whom he had something of the same attachment that Haas had for the elephants. Right now this big man, now growing stout and paunchy, was busy painting a picture of Morel which was merely a picture of his own outmoded and pathetic obsessions.

"Let me tell you," he perorated, addressing the journalist in a tone of condescension, "if you'll take the trouble to consult the writings of General de Gaulle you'll find in them the key to our adventurer. I know the passage by heart: 'All my life I have had a certain idea of France. It is inspired by sentiment as well as by reason. The emotional side of me naturally imagines France as the princess in the fairy tales, or the Madonna in the frescoes, vowed to an eminent and exceptional destiny. I have an instinctive feeling that Providence created her either for complete success or for exemplary misfortunes. If ever, nonetheless, mediocrity stains her actions, I feel that there is some absurd anomaly, to be imputed to the faults of Frenchmen, not to the genius of the land . . .' Well, sir, replace the word 'France' with the word 'humanity,' and there's your Morel. He sees the human species like a princess in the fairy tales or the Madonna in the frescoes, vowed to an exemplary destiny. If it disappoints him he feels that there is there some absurd anomaly, to be imputed to the faults of men, not to the genius of the species. Then he gets angry and tries to extract from men some sort of response in the way of generosity and dignity, some sort of respect for elephants. That's your man. A delayed Gaullist. It seems obvious."

The face of Haas as he listened had on it all the expression of contempt that his beard allowed him to show. Decidedly, human beings were so imbued with themselves as to be absolutely incapable of understanding that anyone could have enough of them, of the sight of them, the smell of them, and could decide to go and live among the elephants because there was no better company in the world.

<center>~~~ XXXVII ~~~</center>

WHEN FIELDS EMERGED from the huts, he saw great black clouds massing in the east, and he was struck by that inky weight on the horizon which seemed to announce some imminent and monstrous explosion of the skies; and even Habib, pacing to and fro on the dune like a captain on the bridge of a threatened ship, was visibly impressed by that swollen horizon and gazed at it with all the respect of an old seaman for the elements.

"It's the last time I shall ever believe in anything, even if it's only the weather report," he said to Fields. "I hope all the same we'll have time to get through before the ground is soaked."

He shouted in Arabic and gave several kicks to the grinning Kaï fishermen who were carrying the ivory to the trucks which he had brought forward as far as the edge of the dried marsh. If the rains came, the trucks and their ivory would be stuck in the mud till next year, and Abe Fields was willing to pay a high price for a picture of that very moral sight. But the Lebanese remained firmly optimistic. He moved up and down the dune on his stocky legs, his dirty white cap over one ear revealing part of his bald pate, and the stump of a cheroot protruding from his pitch-black beard—he never took it out except to hurl a few oaths at the porters, who replied with huge happy grins. Seeing that Fields was observing him with interest, he winked. "You see I can take command of land operations as well when I have to."

He gave the American a friendly tap on the shoulder and moved off in company with the tall fair-haired legionnaire with whom he seemed to have struck up a pleasant relationship. (Besides his protégé, De Vries, Habib had lost two more men during the operations; one of them had been lifted from his rock and crushed by an elephant and the other killed by a stray bullet during the disordered firing at dawn of the first day.)

Fields sat down on the sand to catch his breath. His ribs hurt more and more, and he was beginning to wonder if he would be able to go with Morel. In the lake, standing on the flanks of the slaughtered animals, the birds of prey pecked rapidly at the carrion, then raised their heads and looked attentively round them, then returned to their feast. Fields did not know which he hated the more, their rounded backs or that way they had of bending their heads to one side and looking at him. The slaughtered elephants were like gray funeral cairns over the whole expanse of the lake, each one with its great hunchbacked sentinels. Laughter and cries rose from the water: the women and children of the village were cutting up the meat and throwing it into baskets on their backs; when they drew near, the birds of prey raised their beaks, ran to the other end of the animal and only gave up their places at the last moment, rising in heavy, lazy flight, only to settle immediately on the next cairn. A few live elephants had already returned to the water, and the air was full of distant trumpetings among which Fields kept trying to recognize those of wounded animals.

Caught in the last rays of the sun over the reeds, a flotilla of horns was moving like masts: the antelopes were coming back to the water. A long way off, to the west, a cloud of red dust touched by the sun announced the coming of fresh herds.

At dawn on the first day Fields had seen a packed mass of buffalo raising a spiked forest of horns where, the day before, there
had been nothing but birds. (At Fort Lamy, when Fields spoke
of buffalo at Lake Kuru, there was a unanimous cry of protest: no
such thing had even been seen before. But there were buffalo there
—thousands of them. Fields was able to supply photographs in
proof.)

At about four o'clock Waïtari prepared to leave the lake, and sent
word to Fields that he would like to speak to him. Fields saw his
silhouette a long way off high on the dune under the stormy sky,
above the marsh where the birds were, at the very place where he
had had his first conversation with Peer Qvist. He was flanked by
the three young men who had not spoken a single word to the
journalist all the time they had been there. He had donned his sky-
blue kepi with the black stars, and surrounded by his aides-de-camp
in khaki uniforms, with their belts and buckles and revolvers, standing there at the top of the dune under the immense sky, he gave
Abe Fields a vivid impression of something all too familiar. It was
one of the most thoroughly outworn clichés of history. He took a
picture, nevertheless, out of sheer courtesy. (Fields had always
claimed that the profound tragedy of Caesar's life was not Brutus'
dagger thrust: it was the absence of a photographer. Of course, the
sculptors had made up for it, but that was not the same thing and,
essentially, Caesar's career had been wasted.) The three young men
were standing stiffly in an attitude of hostility, but Waïtari extended his hand.

"I wanted to say goodbye."

"I'm sure it's only *au revoir,*" said Fields politely. "I'm convinced
we shall hear a lot more about you."

"We shall see. I have every hope that there will be a clash, on our
way back, with the French forces of repression. You must tell the
world that you saw us ready to be killed, or to go to a colonialist
prison. The public opinion of your country is the only force we
have."

"I think we shall meet again," Fields repeated.

"Perhaps. In any case I am relying on you and on American public opinion. Tell them to help me. Tell them that we are alone. That we need a friendly hand."

Fields said a few appropriate words. To his surprise he felt more moved than he would have thought possible. However great this man's ambition, his loneliness was even greater. He had taken the photograph when he was still at the foot of the dune, and at that angle, with the immensity of the sky all around, it would be, once again, more eloquent than any accompanying text: a study in loneliness. That was his trade: to beat the text and render it superfluous.

He was relieved when Waïtari moved off at last toward the trucks, followed by the three young men who did not even nod goodbye. It is always pathetic to watch the efforts a man makes to cling to a straw, especially when one is oneself the straw. And so he followed him with his eyes with a certain sympathy and no little sadness. He did not, however, forget to take a picture of the group as it moved away.

A silhouette detached itself from the retreating column and stood for a second on the dune, then raised an arm against the lowering sky and waved a white yachting cap: Habib.

Fields remembered the parting words of the privateering captain: "Please give my love to His Human Highness! There will never be another like him!"

He waved back.

When he returned to the huts, he found Morel on the dune in animated argument with Peer Qvist and Forsythe. He was trying to persuade his companions to go back to Khartoum and from there to their respective countries, to give a fresh impulse to the campaign. Minna was sitting on the sand with her chin in her hands, looking toward the lake and apparently not listening.

"Anyway, the rains are here, and there's nothing we can do while they last. You will be much more useful in Europe and America. Give lectures, hold meetings, speak on the radio. Make a hell of a row. You'll be listened to, after all this publicity. I mean to lie low for six months in the hills. Tell them I'm still there and shall be back. They must force the governments to call a new conference, not in the Congo this time, but somewhere more conspicuous—at

Geneva, for instance, where they'll really be in the public eye."

They spent the rest of the day, part of the night and the next morning trying to find and finish off the wounded animals who were dying in agony among the rushes. Morel only once appeared discouraged. As he was padding about with Fields behind him, in the stench of carrion and the buzzing of the flies, among the vultures who left the gray funeral cairns only at the last moment, he said, "My God, won't they ever change? The time it's been going on! Sometimes I feel like giving up the whole damn thing and going to live in Germany."

"What the hell do you want to do in Germany?" shouted Peer Qvist, who was wading at his side, with his trousers rolled up to his bony knees and his rifle held well above the water.

"Soak myself in my memories. Perhaps that'll cure me. Maybe the Nazis told the truth about us. Maybe the Nazis *were* the truth. We shouldn't forget that: perhaps they were the truth. The rest, just beautiful lies. We've sung many beautiful lies about ourselves. Perhaps that's what I'm trying to do—to sing another beautiful lie."

"Pooh!" spat the Dane, indignantly.

When he heard him talking like this, Abe Fields felt very unhappy. He liked to see his Frenchman with anger in his eyes and a rifle in his fist, not waiting for the dignity pills, the decency pills, to make their appearance on the market. (It was probable, besides, that the human organism would not be able to stand them.) But whatever mood he was in, Abe Fields felt happy only when he was walking at Morel's side with his camera. Then he forgot his injured ribs, his weariness, his long direct experience of the human species and everything he already knew about lost causes. He even came to believe that something could really be done about it all. He tried to tell himself that this was a purely professional enthusiasm: he still had a good half-roll of film left, and that was the only reason why he was determined to stick to Morel. True, that wasn't enough if he was going to spend six months with the Frenchman in some cave in the Oulé hills. And yet he felt happy only when he heard Morel making plans for future campaigns.

"I think, with a little perseverance and a well-arranged press campaign, we shall get results. That's why it's important that you two should be out there to get things done. They'll listen to you now, with all this publicity. They'll bring pressure to bear on their governments . . ."

Finally Fields asked Morel for permission to accompany him as far as the Chad. His intention was to go to Fort Lamy and send his photographs from there; they might as well, he said, rather lamely, do part of the way together. (Fields always defended himself indignantly against the charge of having wanted to follow Morel for other than professional motives. Perhaps he had some misanthropic streak in him, he admitted, but not to the point of preferring elephants to men. During his difficulties with the Chad authorities, who refused at first to believe his story of a plane accident and had spoken of aiding and abetting criminals, he owed his liberty to the indignant protests of the journalists who were still at Fort Lamy. This accusation on the part of the French authorities had provoked prolonged laughter at the expense of Fields among all the journalists who knew him. The idea of an Abe Fields in the *maquis,* an Abe Fields run amok, weapon in hand, defending the splendors of nature, an Abe Fields idealistic and disinterested—that was one of the best jokes of the year, and every time he appeared on the terrace of the Tchadien during the inquiry he was greeted with acclamations from all sides. Fields took it rather badly—which naturally increased the dose he was given. During his interrogation by the police, he defended himself angrily against the accusation that he had joined Morel out of sympathy for him and for his cause. He quoted all the professional precedents that came to his mind—Thomson following Zapata and Strauss following Pancho Villa in Mexico, and all the journalists who had visited Giuliano when he was terrorizing Sicily. It was only the return of Schölscher, who had seen the crashed airplane in Lake Kuru, that cleared him completely in the eyes of the police. Incidentally, it was only a few days after his return to Fort Lamy that Fields remembered a detail which had gone completely out of his mind. It concerned Squadron Leader Davis, his pilot. He remembered for the first time that Forsythe, to counteract the swift effects of the heat, had wedged the body between two rocks under the water until they should be able to give it a Christian burial. Afterward, with the events that followed, no one had given it another thought. The poor chap must still be stuck there among the elephants. Fields consoled himself by telling himself that, to a hero of the Battle of Britain, this would surely not be disagreeable company.)

Morel smiled ironically when Fields asked permission to come with him. "You want to be there to take a picture when they kill me?" And before Fields could think of an answer, he added: "They say you big reporters end by acquiring a special flair for being on the spot at the right moment."

Fields was struck by a trace of sadness in his tone. He wondered if the Frenchman was not attributing to him a premonition he himself perhaps felt.

(Fields did not believe in premonitions and felt none at that moment. Nor did he believe in the journalist's special flair "for being there at the right moment," as Morel had put it. His own best picture stories had been, for the most part, the result of chance. On the day Gandhi was assassinated he had happened to be there waiting for an airplane, on his way to photograph a tiger hunt with a maharajah; the three photographs he had managed to take a few seconds after the murder had brought him $15,000. He had placed himself on the road simply because he had nothing else to do. He had been on holiday in Haiti when a hurricane destroyed the town of Jeremie, which not only covered his expenses handsomely but paid his rent in Paris for a year. As far as Morel was concerned he had merely decided that, practically alone and disarmed as he was, the man could not get very far; and naturally he was rather anxious to be on the spot at the moment when an adventure in which the American public took so passionate an interest would come to an end.)

Morel had decided that they should leave at sunset, to get as far as possible during the night. Idriss and Youssef had brought the horses to the dune. Morel was intently examining the motionless sky; the clouds rose over the desert like a pile of black rocks. He turned to Idriss.

"Well? What do you say? Is it going to rain or not?"

Idriss shook his head. With his blue burnous, his white head-

dress, the two fierce furrows from the nostrils to the lips, and the
sparse gray hair on his chin, he inspired in Fields quite as much
confidence in his forecasts as did the New York meteorological office. (Fields had spent sleepless nights with his camera in the pre-
dicted path of hurricanes which went calmly off and devastated
regions where they were not expected.) But Morel seemed reassured.

"Let's hope not. We need at least two days to get across."

Fields spent the last moments before their departure with Peer
Qvist, who had been anxious to make a farewell round of the
marshes among the birds.

"I shall never see such a sight again," he said.

Abe Fields had never been particularly drawn to the contempla-
tion of nature, but this was a sight it was really difficult not to
admire.

The extraordinary, thrilling vegetation of feathers covered the
marsh as far as the eye could see, and under the heavy motionless
clouds there was a second sky, a closer one, living and innumerable,
which seemed to have triumphed over all the emptiness of the
other. And so the birds created, quite close to the earth, a heaven at
arm's length, at last accessible. Some of the species were so well
known to Fields that their presence on the confines of the African
desert troubled him; it seemed the consequence of some tragic
mistake. Swallows, storks, herons, the whole of ancient winged
Europe seemed to have come to take refuge here among the
huge jabirus, marabous, storks, pelicans, and the white eagles of
Bahr el Gazal, and all the other species whose names he did not
know. Peer Qvist told him that this living carpet, over fifty square
miles, which kept changing color, rising and falling again, scattering and reforming like some dazzling tapestry ceaselessly woven
and rewoven under his gaze, was only a tiny part, fallen by the wayside, of the thousands of millions of migrating birds on their way
toward the valley of the Nile and the marshes of Bahr el Gazal in
the Sudan. The Dane spoke of them with a fervor which was almost that of prayer, and when at last he turned away Fields saw
that the old naturalist's eyes were wet. Out of tact he pretended to
take a picture of the marshes, although he already had a whole set

in color, and Peer Qvist reminded him of his promise to send him copies.

(Fields kept his promise. He sent a complete collection to Peer Qvist, care of the Natural History Museum in Copenhagen. The packet was returned to him with this one word: *Unknown*. Fields found that this reply had a certain grandeur. He readdressed the parcel care of the International Committee for the Defense of Fauna and Flora at Geneva. It came back to him again, this time with the inscription: *Present address unknown*. Fields then had an inspiration. He sent it off addressed simply to *Peer Qvist, Denmark*. A few days later he received a letter of thanks.)

When they got back to the dune the others were ready. Fields approached his horse apprehensively; he wondered if he would be able to stand the journey. The lake was now silent. The women and children had gone back to their villages with the twilight, carrying the precious baskets of meat on their backs or heads. With the smell of mud there now mingled, more and more strongly, another smell which Fields could not ignore. Elephants were again coming to the water, others were wandering among the reeds, their trumpetings rose in all directions, and Fields's ear seemed still able to distinguish among them those of wounded animals. Morel attached his briefcase to his saddle. He was lighting a cigarette from his tinder. He had just shaved; his khaki scarf, freshly washed, dangled about his neck, and he had his little Cross of Lorraine pinned on his chest. He looked calm and ready to go on as long as might be necessary.

(Fields did not really understand the secret strength that dwelt in him till several years later, at the time of his meeting with Peer Qvist at the University of Uppsala, where the old naturalist was giving what was to be his last lecture on the preservation of species. With his memories crowding in on him, the old man spent half the night going over his past, and thus it was that he came at length to the story of Morel and the may-beetles. It was only then that Abe Fields really got to the heart of the matter. He listened without a word, and when he emerged into the snowy silent night in which even the stars were shivering, he walked with a new lightness and confidence, and he would have given a great deal to be able to see

Morel again and to tell him that he too, Abe Fields, believed whole-heartedly.)

For the moment he felt rather unhappy as he sat on his horse with his eyes and face burned scarlet by the sun, a handkerchief tied over his head with the four corners sticking up, wondering why he insisted on following the outlaw over miles and miles of desert country to end up in prison or in danger of death by sunstroke, when he had practically no film left.

Forsythe was already at the other end of the dune, holding his horse by the bridle, no doubt to avoid the goodbyes. He had done all he could to dissuade Minna from going with Morel.

"You'll never be able to make it."

"I've already done it once."

"Not under these conditions. The horses can barely stand up. Even if you reach the Chad, you'll be arrested. A man by himself might just manage, but a woman . . ."

"You ought to find out what women can stand, Major Forsythe. I could tell you something about that."

"Don't be stubborn. We've succeeded beyond all hope. People have understood. Public opinion is with us. The moment's come to carry on the campaign in other ways, taking advantage of their attention and sympathy. We can't waste the audience we've acquired. For Morel it isn't the same thing: even if he's arrested, his trial will attract enormous attention and give a fresh impulse to popular sympathy. No doubt he'll be triumphantly acquitted. But meanwhile he's risking his life, and so are you. It's madness."

"And what's made you suddenly so reasonable, Major Forsythe? Was it perhaps when you heard that you could at last go home and had even become almost popular in your country, or at least understood and forgiven, and that perhaps—who knows?—the American Army might honor you with a parade?"

He could not help laughing. "That would be a great day for the elephants . . . You're wonderfully well informed about our military traditions!"

"I've slept with a few American officers."

"If you don't want to come with me, go to Denmark with Peer Qvist."

She shook her head. "I must stay with him."

"You don't understand that there are other ways of helping him now, much more effective, even more urgent. That's just what we're going to do. We're not deserting him."

"I don't care. I don't even want to help him. How could I? I just want to be with him, that's all."

"Why?"

She smiled. "After all, there's got to be someone from Berlin with him, don't you think, Major Forsythe?"

She turned her back to him and moved off along the dune with a gait which the trousers she wore rendered both clumsy and even more feminine. He followed her with his eyes, a slight trace of cynicism on his lips. He was sure he would meet her again. He had only to wait. One day he would have his chance. The bond of memories in common, failing anything else, would be enough to bring her back to him. Unless, of course, Morel were to yield at last to so much abnegation and marry her when they came out of prison; unless they had children, set up house together in some African town and opened a little ivory shop for the tourists. "You can also go and see Morel, he's a local curiosity, you know; he had his moment of celebrity; now he keeps a shop with ivory souvenirs for tourists. Well, what d'you expect? He has to live; it always ends that way. He's quite willing to be photographed, especially if you buy something from him."

He raised his arm in a gesture of farewell. She answered it. Then he waited for the Dane to join him and they set their horses' heads towards the Gfat track. They had to cross the marsh, and the birds flew about them as they passed: the white wings of the marabous, storks and herons waved in the twilight like goodbyes. Peer Qvist pulled his hat brim low over his face and did not once turn back to look at the five silhouettes growing smaller against the sky. He was already reproaching himself for what seemed to him in spite of everything a desertion. Especially if Morel were going to be arrested and tried, as was almost inevitable, it was essential to be there rousing a general hue and cry, to assure his acquittal under pressure of public opinion. But he felt tired and unhappy, and to calm his regrets and forget his weariness he began planning aloud for future campaigns.

"We shall have to start up the committees and appeals all over again. It's an old story to me. We must get some of the names that matter, people who stand for decency and generosity. Pity old King Gustave of Sweden is dead. He was a friend. He would have helped us. And Pastor Kaj Munk, whom the Germans shot, in Norway. He was a great writer. And Bernadotte. And Axel Munthe. When you live too long you end up knowing nobody."

Forsythe said nothing and rode with bowed head. It was difficult to make plans for the future when one was leaving it behind.

XXXVIII

FOR THE FIRST FEW HOURS Fields thought his injured ribs would not survive his horse's jolting; during the hours that followed, it seemed to him impossible to stand up against the heat, the blinding reflection of light from the rocks, the crimson earth and the dust raised by the horses—each tuft of grass was like barbed wire tearing at his eyes.

But he bore it all with the tenfold, almost monstrous energy of people possessed: his fixed idea was to follow Morel as far as the denouement of his adventure and take a picture of it.

With both hands he clung to the pommel of his Arab saddle, his sweat-soaked handkerchief with its four horns still spread out on his head—he used it from time to time to wipe his neck, his face, his eyes and his camera lens, as well as to blow his nose and to fan himself. He dragged along on his horse—like the rest, it was caparisoned from head to foot in bright cotton cloth in the style of all Foulbé horses, which made their little band look like some belated crusaders, some errant knights. He dragged along over the desert plain, over escarpments, over rocks from which clouds of red dust rose, thirsty, furious, with clenched teeth, behind Morel, his camera

slung around his neck, with an obstinacy which amused the French
man and even seemed to fill him with a certain admiration.

"Well, shutterbug, do you think you'll be able to hold out?"

"Listen," answered Fields rather belligerently, "I've been in Libya,
Anzio, at Leyte, on the Normandy and Corregidor beaches, and I
was made Chevalier of the Legion of Honor by the French during
the liberation of Paris, if that means anything to you."

"All right, all right. And you've done all that just to take pictures?"

"Yep."

"And you don't give a damn about the rest?"

"Not a damn."

Morel's eyes were smiling. With his small bush hat scorched by
the sun, his dark cheerful gaze, his Cross of Lorraine, and the
khaki *chech* coated with red dust tied round his neck, which gave
him a somewhat military appearance, both dashing and untidy, and
that French mouth of his, and the old briefcase stuffed with petitions, manifestoes, proclamations and appeals, he looked so different from everything that the newspapers had been saying about
him that Abe Fields felt that his strictest duty was to bring back
some good pictures of the Frenchman, pictures with no captions, no
write-up, no explanation, just showing him as he was—perfectly
balanced, sure of himself, without a trace of hatred or rancor, making fun of you and your doubts with all the seriousness required, and
going on with his job. He took another picture of him. He could not
resist it, though now he had to husband his film seriously; they were
to remain together for a long time.

"Shutterbug . . ."

"Yes."

"You seem very determined. You wouldn't be interested in the
protection of elephants, by any chance?"

"I don't give a damn for your elephants. I'm doing my job, that's
all."

"Don't get angry. It's not nice. Do I ever get angry?"

"No, no, of course you don't. Everyone knows that."

"Did you say you'd done the liberation of Paris as well?"

"Yes."

"Was it fun?"

"I'll show you some photographs."

"Did you say you began it all during the Spanish War?"

"Yes."

"Me too. There were some fine elephants there."

"Yeah."

"And have you been in Russia?"

"Not yet."

"Oh! How come?"

"No visa."

"You'll get one. As soon as they have any elephants to show you, you'll get your visa. They'll lay out a red carpet for you. For the time being they're saying that to build a new world with the elephants in the way is impossible. You've first got to dispose of them for the sake of progress and efficiency. They say the elephants are a luxury they can't afford. They even suggest that man himself is a luxury, that he too is in the way. Total efficiency, you know. That's why what you and I are doing is so important."

"Not I. You. I just take pictures."

"Doesn't the fate of the elephants worry you?"

"Don't you ever think of anything else?"

"Yes. But it's very depressing. And besides, I'm mad, didn't they tell you?"

"Sure you're mad."

And on he went, haggard, clenching his teeth, his eyelids burning, his lips swollen, the red dust getting up his nose into his throat, into his ears, and even—he was sure of it—into his prostate gland, treacherously scraping away at his very foundation. From time to time he swept a glance around him, and saw red antelope lying by the hundreds, their horns motionless, like thousands of abandoned lyres—with the gray sentinel birds of prey on their flanks; whole hordes of buffalo prostrate, their powerful mass incongruous in such distress, some of them still striving spasmodically to get up at their approach; far off to the east, motionless, black clouds blocking the horizon; dust filling the nostrils together with the smell of carrion; dead baby elephants; the zigzagging of the gorged bottle-green flies, the slinking of the hyenas, more dust, more rocks, termitaries under thorn trees, Churchill's face in 1940 shouting into the microphone his determination to go on fighting alone, while he,

Fields, waited in the next room with his camera—and once his horse struck against the gaping carcass of a lion with its buzzing entrails, in front of which Idriss, like an impassive blue phantom, had long stood incredulously in the silent respect he accorded only to his oldest enemies; the sight of that dead lion almost made Abe Fields weep with self-pity.

Idriss seemed indeed to have taken a dislike to him and his camera: the great tracker kept glancing askance at him, and spat ostentatiously every time the reporter aimed his lens at Morel. Several times he called him "*oudjanga ga*" and "*oudjanga baga*" which—as Morel obligingly translated—meant "bird of ill omen" and "bird of the dark." Morel laughed. But in his state of nervous exhaustion Fields felt hurt beyond all measure, outraged, humiliated and indignant. With bowed head he brooded at great length over this, deciding in the end that Idriss was an anti-Semite. Once, when he saw a vulture standing wings open and spread out on a half-rotted carcass, he meditated that he himself was neither more nor less than that—a vulture ready to throw himself with his camera upon every fresh victim; and he even found in himself a certain physical resemblance to the bird. He tried to explain all this in broken French to Idriss, pointing to the sky where his colleagues were circling slowly, each one of them trying to be quicker than he, to snatch the bread from his mouth: it wasn't his fault, he explained, you had to get there first to take a picture, that was the job. Idriss spat, looked scandalized and went to warn Morel, pointing to the gesticulating and muttering reporter.

They stretched him out under a blanket spread tentlike over a thorn tree and Minna sat by him, wiping his forehead with a wet handkerchief. He recovered his wits somewhat and stared fixedly at the exhausted face of this German girl—at this feminine shape and the soft, gentle hands, so unexpected, so improbable in that land of universal persecution; a face with features so drawn that it was almost unrecognizable: only the fair hair under the wide felt hat held back by a chin-strap, and the innocent gray-blue eyes, were still unchanged in their kindness.

"Why didn't you go to the Sudan with the others? Are you in love with him, or what?"

"Try and get a little sleep, Monsieur Fields . . ."

"Do you love him as much as all that?"

"We'll talk of that another time, when we both feel better . . .
I'm almost beat, too, you know, and I've got dysentery."

In her face the shadows were more marked than the features.
That's what love is, thought Fields—with the profound knowledge
of love of a person who has never been loved. Really she doesn't
care two hoots about the elephants. A woman doesn't go through all
this for the sake of ideas, in the name of some absurd dream of universal decency. But they would go through anything for a man they
love. I know women, Fields told himself triumphantly. I've slept
with a great number of them. Panting dismally under the improvised
tent, he reckoned up the number of elephants he was prepared to
sacrifice in order to inspire a woman with such love, such devotion,
and he very soon reached the point of sacrificing the entire species.

She was leaning over him, with a slight smile that was victorious
over everything: victorious over her sickness, over the incandescent
air, over her exhaustion, the dust, the stench, the merciless heat.
Lying flat under the bush, his eyes bloodshot and his nose bleeding,
Fields told himself that he would particularly have liked to inspire
such love and devotion in a German woman—he, the son of parents
who had been gassed by the Germans at Auschwitz: it would have
proved that to be a man was after all not hopeless. To fall in love
with a German girl, he a Jew, that would show the Germans how
he felt about it. But perhaps it was merely lust.

"Don't tell me you're doing this for the sake of animals."

"I'm not telling you anything, Monsieur Fields. Try and get a little sleep. I'll put your handkerchief over your eyes."

Nihilists—that's what they were—nihilists and subversives, the sort
of people who would want to overthrow the government of the
United States by force. Never, never would Abe Fields give them an
American visa, that visa which he himself in his time had had so
much trouble in obtaining. The whole business was typical of European decadence, of anarchy, a subversive enterprise inconceivable
in the United States, where the dignity of the human individual was
assured on every front, before, behind and on the flanks, so that the
problem did not even arise. He had only one desire—to go back to
America, publish his story and denounce the moral nihilism of the

French and German intellectuals; but for the moment he was caught in an improvised tent between a cactus and a thorn tree, stuffed full of dust, unable to see anything between his aching eyelids but a sort of still life composed of stone, thorns, sand, and his feet, the feet of Abe Fields, globe-trotter, whose intention was, on his return, to make this campaign for the preservation of the elephants his life's aim. It was indeed his last story. He would give up his profession, and no one could make him go back on this decision. (Later, Fields often quoted this irrevocable resolution as a significant sign of his state of physical and moral prostration at that moment.)

Fields did the last twelve hours of the desert journey in a condition of almost happy stupor, subject to erotic visions caused partly by the friction of the saddle and partly by his determination to cling to life in spite of everything and so to find in it some tangible attraction. On the third day they entered the short brush country of the Chad; the brush covered the ground with its stunted and shadeless nudity; it was a land of such dryness that even the ant-hills shattered into dust at the slightest touch of a hoof.

Morel made no effort to pass unnoticed and rode through the Gola villages openly. The women drying manioc on broad palm leaves raised their heads to watch them pass; an impotent centenarian chieftain appeared, supported by two men, at the door of his mud hut, his face scarcely visible under a pile of white draperies, and followed them with his eyes for a long time; the naked children ran after him; the potters abandoned their red amphorae and rushed to catch a glimpse of him; and the draped blue horsemen drew aside on the road to let him pass. It was there that Fields heard for the first time the nickname by which Morel was known throughout the Chad: Ubaba-Giva—which meant, as Morel told him with obvious satisfaction—"ancestor of the elephants." It was clear that people attributed to him some sort of holy or supernatural quality, and that he inspired in them a respectful fear, perhaps merely a fear of contagion: the demon inhabiting him was said to be one of those who sometimes emerged from the ear and slipped into you through your nostrils, if you came too close.

"Aren't you afraid of being arrested?"

"The authorities aren't so anxious to arrest me. If they did arrest me, they'd have to try me, and it would be a fine thing for French justice and a French court to try a man because he defends elephants. What sort of France would that be?"

The man seemed sincerely confident and carefree, and Fields took his favorite picture of him as he stood laughing and joking with the blacksmith who was shoeing their horses. (As far as Fields could remember later, two of their seven horses had to be shot during the crossing of the desert, and when they reached the first Gola village the remaining five were in such a state that they had to let them rest every two hours. Idriss spent a day negotiating the purchase of fresh animals.)

He wondered where the Frenchman was finding his reserves of strength, but then he remembered what was always said about people animated by a strong faith; and he knew from personal experience to what lengths he himself could go for a good picture. It was a matter of inner compulsion. But the girl was exhausted. Under that big bush-hat of hers, her face seemed every day smaller, more furrowed, both pale and sun-scorched: its features had changed shape, had become sharp; and one night, when the pain from his broken ribs made sleep impossible, as he left his hut to seek cool air—in spite of his certainty that the points of his ribs were digging into his left lung, he found her leaning against a tree, being sick.

"Don't tell him, Monsieur Fields."

"It's no use pretending. You're in no condition to go on. Neither am I. We're both of us ready for a hospital. Maybe I could hold out another day or two, but you . . ."

"I'm going to try again tomorrow. I can't leave him alone, Monsieur Fields."

"But why?"

"You know why . . . I'll stay with him as long as I can . . ."

"You can love a man without dying of dysentery for him."

She shook her head obstinately. "You don't understand at all. Just because I'm a tart . . . I'm here on my own, Monsieur Fields. My parents were killed in an air raid when I was sixteen; I was raped by the soldiers, and then . . ."

"They were Russian soldiers. And it was war. That's no reason to go and die for animals."

"They weren't *Russian* soldiers, Monsieur Fields. The uniform makes no difference. They were men . . . You should know. You should be the first to understand why a man sets out to defend nature so fiercely. You told me the other day that your family was gassed at Auschwitz."

"Yes. So what? That's why I try to take good pictures of it all. The thing is to get together first-rate documentation—that's all you can do."

She was not listening. Her voice had an almost hysterical tone now, but it was difficult to know if this was due to exhaustion, or to her sickness, or if it had always been there; or if that incredible girl had really, as she claimed, acted "on her own," because she understood the demonstration, the protest, and had charged to the rescue of a completely unrealistic, exaggerated, absurd and even unacceptable notion of human decency and dignity. She must have understood it all instinctively; she was neither very bright nor educated, and her fate was to possess a body and a face that made men less anxious to understand her than to undress her. Her action must have been a protest against that too. As for intelligence, Abe Fields had his own idea about that: a certain extreme form of femininity, with all it involves in the way of intuition and sympathy, was the nearest thing he knew to real genius. He had never indeed met with it in a woman. He sometimes had the impression that he possessed it himself, in the form of a terrifying need.

Leaning against the acacia, with her face shining in the moonlight, molten in its sweat and tears, exhausted, emptied of all substance except her will to hold out, she stood there, so very serious, so painfully devoid of humor, as Germans often are, and as far removed as possible from Morel's angry mockery—and yet surely no one understood the ironic Frenchman better than she.

"I'll try to stick it out another day. I don't care if it kills me. I want to be with him if something happens. I don't know what he's hoping for, but that doesn't matter. The cave where we were before, in the hills, where we stocked all our medical supplies and ammunition, has been found by the troops. If tomorrow I feel I'm becoming a dead weight on him, I'll stop. I'll tell him to go on alone; he's already been taking the easiest way, because of me. He's just following the track. Yesterday Idriss wanted him to avoid this village because they watch out for him here, but he wouldn't pay any attention, simply so that I should get a night's rest."

"It isn't because of you," said Fields. "He's sincerely convinced that nothing can happen to him. His real madness is to think himself surrounded by universal sympathy and approval. Not only in Africa: everywhere. It wouldn't surprise me if he believed that the Russian workers pray for him in their factories . . . That's where his madness lies: in his incredible confidence, his total optimism. He's persuaded himself that the French authorities are secretly protecting him, that they're proud of him. He believes in France, just to add to the absurdity. He's like that, there's nothing to be done about it. That's his real folly. In India perhaps it would have earned him a kind of holiness . . . I also think that if he goes on much longer, he'll get shot. When it happens, and it won't be long, I mean to be there, I mean to be there to get the picture. That's all there is in it for me."

And it was true that Morel seemed to be borne forward by a bewildering, almost contagious, confidence. Fields was beginning to be affected by it in spite of himself, and to feel that nothing would ever happen to his Frenchman.

"Well, shutterbug, tired?"

"Tired."

"Don't exert yourself too much. The job isn't done. This job is never done. You'll have more pictures to take."

"I hope so."

"Save your film."

Wrinkles of laughter leaped into sight on his face, like small friendly insects running all over it, then back on both sides of his brown, youthful, warm eyes. But he made an effort to remain serious.

"Remember, we're after something very hard to catch. No one's yet managed a good picture of it."

Fields nearly said that he had managed all right, once or twice. Snapshots lasting a ten-thousandth of a second, a flash—and sometimes the camera caught a gleam of human dignity that lingered for a moment on a man's face when life itself had just left it. There were even faces that had remained fixed forever in that expression, so that it became intimately mingled with the earth. But he refused to fall into the trap. He observed Morel with a cameraman's cold, professional stare, trying to decide why he found the man so French; he decided that it was a certain dark cheerfulness, a mixture of anger and irony, the voice and its drawling Parisian accent, and the line of the mouth which somehow always seemed to call for a *Gauloise bleue.*

"Tell me, have you still got a lot of them in America—elephants, I mean?"

"There have been no elephants in America since the Miocene age."

"So there are none any longer?"

Fields clenched his teeth. "Yeah. There are still some."

"Alive? Or on paper?"

"Alive."

"How's that?"

"We have a President who's interested in the question."

"Doesn't he do anything for them?"

"Yeah. For instance, he's abolished segreg . . ."

He broke off. He was not going to let himself be drawn. He was not going to rise. Morel was laughing, erect in the saddle, with his head thrown back and all the light of Africa gleaming on his face. "That's good. In France we've done a lot for the elephants. In fact, we've done so much that France has ended up by becoming an elephant herself and is now threatened, like them, with extinction. Tell me, shutterbug, do you still believe I'm mad?"

"Yes."

"You're right. One has to be mad. Are you well educated?"

"Yes."

"Do you remember about the prehistoric reptile, the ancestor of man, the first to emerge from the mud in early Paleozoic times, a milliard years ago, who set out to live in the air and to breathe, even though he had no lungs?"

"I don't remember. I wasn't there. But I read something about it somewhere."

"Good. Well, he was mad too. Absolutely bats. That's why he

tried. He's the ancestor of us all, and we shouldn't forget it. But for him we wouldn't be here. He was as crazy as they come. We too have got to try. That's what progress is. By trying, like him, perhaps we'll wind up with the necessary organs, the organ of dignity, of decency, or of fraternity. That would really be worth photographing, an organ like that. That's why I tell you to save some film. One never knows."

"I always save some, just in case," said Fields.

He made some efforts at conversation with Youssef, but met an almost hostile silence. Ever since they had left Lake Kuru, the boy had seemed tortured by some secret suffering. He watched over Morel with a strange nervousness, following him like a white shadow, never put down his weapon, and during the night squatted beside the Frenchman and watched him for hours by starlight. He seemed to be struggling against a profound dread, a repulsion, whose reason the journalist tried in vain to discover; he concluded that the boy had understood that their adventure was nearing its end, and that soon he would have to part forever from his friend.

Fields tried also to question Idriss, to find out why the great tracker had sided with Morel: his whole life had been one long journey through the bush, and it was difficult to suspect him of any secret ideological motive. He had taken some excellent pictures of him, with that wild head of his, the snub nose with nostrils shivering in the wind, the furrows that ran down like two fine cuts into the sparse gray hairs on his chin, and those attentive yellow eyes that watched no track but those that ran on earth. All he got from him was a few monosyllabic grunts; but suddenly, just as he was giving up, the man who had spent his whole life in the bush among the herds threw at him, almost negligently, in that guttural voice of his: "Where there are elephants, there I go free."

But no doubt he was merely trying to please the white man who was his employer, and Fields energetically refused to believe that this noble, primitive creature might also be contaminated by abstractions like liberty, or dignity, or humanity. And yet he could not forget that this was French Africa, and that the French were perfectly capable of having stuffed his head with their own ideas. Colonialists respect nothing. They would take creatures royal in their primitive beauty, serene in their ignorance, and noble in their naked simplicity, and would twist them out of shape, distort their minds, contaminate them with their own ideologies and abstractions. Colonialism must be finished with, once for all, and Africa be given back its innocence again. It really took a Frenchman to be stupid enough to believe that mankind could simultaneously achieve progress and burden itself with elephants. There was an obvious incompatibility there. No wonder French industry and economy were still in an archaic condition.

Abe Fields sat sweating on his horse, gesticulating feverishly and sometimes making remarks aloud which amused Morel. The moment came when he lost his head completely, stopped and addressed a summons to the elephants to appear before him that he might photograph them, and then accused them of not existing, of being a myth, an abstraction, a new trick of the liberals and intellectuals, a mere excuse for bringing Abe Fields to his death, to the great joy of his competitors.

They dismounted him, helped him to lie down full length under the trees, and Minna tried to make him swallow some pills.

"Ha, ha!" said Abe Fields, "dignity pills!"

He protested against the revolting insinuation. He told them he was an American who had emerged from the mud twenty years ago —the date of his naturalization—and had thus acquired lungs with which to breathe calmly.

He slept for an hour, then mounted again, wondering bitterly how that German girl managed to put up with what he, Abe Fields, the great reporter, could not endure. Every time he emerged from his torpor he saw her riding beside Morel, sustained by her ridiculous but tremendous love for elephants. And yet, when they stopped to rest and Abe Fields, having been carefully taken off his mount by Idriss and Youssef, took a few steps with his legs apart, feeling as though he had a fifty-pound weight where his prostate gland should be, he could see quite clearly, as he came up with her, that the girl had reached the end of the road. Her face was gray under the sweat, and her eyes had an expression of physical suffering—the only kind that is really unbearable, as Fields had decided long ago, whatever they might say. She had abandoned all pretense at femininity, even the most elementary modesty, and when she stopped, twenty times a day, and dismounted with Idriss' help, one had to turn away not to see her—she had not even the strength to go apart. That poor female reptile had crawled bravely to the side of Morel out of the mud and ruins of Berlin, but her body, which had already caused her so much trouble, once more had the last word.

(Fields had always been of the opinion that governments did not do enough for biological research: they took too much interest in politics and not enough in biochemical progress. A thousand generations of Einsteins of biology could easily get us out of the mess, he thought. He felt full of hope and began to hum a tune. He distinctly saw the reptiles round about him wagging their heads with approval. Fields later said that at that time he had all the symptoms of *delirium tremens,* due to the drought and to being deprived of alcohol, and that he saw himself surrounded by a brotherly circle of reptiles of his own size, with their scaly maws wide open, busy doing breathing exercises under his direction. He himself did his best, but his broken ribs stuck into his lungs each time, and his one dream was to be able to return to his native mud, to crawl through his delicious pool of nice fresh mud, roll himself up in a coil and stay there, abandoning once for all his dreams of human dignity. And yet Abe Fields the precursor, Abe Fields the first really human being, Abe Fields the first human reptile to emerge from the mud to the triumphal conquest of dignity—that was a picture! His competitors would kill themselves for it . . . Pulitzer Prize, Pulitzer Prize . . . He began to weep with hope and excitement.)

But when the fever left him, he could not help being touched by Minna's face, by the effort the girl was making, by her eyes big with suffering.

"If only I could find some Vioform . . ."

"You can't go on in that condition," stammered Fields, who was himself at that moment standing by the side of the road, clasping a tree trunk in his arms, with his legs wide apart as they had been when he was helped from his horse, and convinced that his prostate gland would burst or simply fall out if he made the slightest movement. "You must let him go on alone. It's absurd. It makes no sense."

"I'd like to hold out just as far as the hills . . ."

"And then what?"

"I don't care. If I'm going to die I'd rather it was there—" a faint smile—"among the elephants."

"And what then?" Fields asked soberly. "What then, after you've died?"

She looked surprised at first, then pondered, searching for some answer, and of course, thought Fields with satisfaction, found none except that absurd, obstinate courage of hers which never left her, a real Boche obstinacy.

"That's true," she said. "But it doesn't matter. I have to try."

"But try what?" shouted Fields, utterly exasperated by her stupid obstinacy and refusal to acknowledge reality. "In the name of what? For the sake of what? What the hell can it all add up to, anyway?"

She was sitting against a tree, her face running with sweat, her hat on her knees with her inert hands on top of it. She raised her eyes to him, and he saw there something which always infuriated him, a tiny spark of defiance and even gaiety, which she had no doubt picked up in the company of that madman Morel—and in that emptied face, with the jutting cheekbones accentuating its thinness, in that face reduced to its simplest expression, the spark of gaiety was all the more intolerable, and he heard himself laugh, a croaking, broken laugh, but a laugh all the same.

"All right," he said. "All right. You win. And I know the story. But all the same you can love the elephants without letting yourself die idiotically of dysentery for them."

She shook her head. "I believe in it, you see."

"In what?" Fields shouted.

She closed her eyes, shook her head, and rested her back against the tree, smiling.

Clutching the pommel of his saddle with both hands to avoid bearing too heavily on his prostate, Fields told himself furiously that the humanists and humanitarians of all casts were undoubtedly the last and most arrogant aristocrats, that they never learned anything and always forgot everything. They still went into ecstasies over the splendor of nature, refused to be discouraged or to give up, and went on believing in liberty and humanity in spite of the evidence of forced labor camps and nationalistic hatred, of fear and cruelty and betrayal around them. They went on dreaming of freedom and of the rights of man, refusing to face the fact that their disappearance, like the disappearance of the elephants, was an irreversible process, the price paid by mankind for a new, modern and ruthlessly efficient world. The only thing that could save us, he reflected again, was a biological revolution, but unfortunately scientific research was straying in other directions, it was more interested in nuclear explosions. It was a pity. For there was no lack of courage in the species, no lack of an extraordinary determination. To convince oneself of that one had only to look at that girl refusing to give in to her physiological wretchedness and who was still there at every halt. In the clouds of dust, with that fair hair of hers and the curves of her body whose gentleness and softness no exhaustion could make less apparent, she was a sight he would have liked to have forever before him.

Fields saw those two sometimes turn toward each other not to speak, but only to exchange those smiling and secret glances which filled him with indignation. That was not obstinacy, it was more; it was really a sign of some sort of congenital and infectious madness. You would have said they were really sure, sure of victory, tranquilly convinced they were advancing toward some radiant and triumphant future. And as they went along, they even had the impudence and the strength to admire the landscape.

"Look, that's the plain of the Ogo and beyond it, the first hills. How beautiful! You ought to take that one in color."

"I have no intention of wasting my last film," Fields growled. "To hell with landscapes. Besides, I haven't any more color film."

"Pity. What are you keeping your scrap of film for exactly? My arrest?" He was laughing. "You're fooling yourself, shutterbug. Nothing is going to happen to me."

They stopped in a village only a few miles from the first spurs of the Oulé hills, where the bamboo forest began. The whole population watched them pass. Idriss had a long consultation with a little shriveled man whose arms were furrowed with scars and whom he had known for thirty years—since the last great days of ivory hunting. His fingers were dead, and the scars on his arms and hands had been made by the claws of the lion that killed Bruneau de Laboré at Ouadaï in 1936. From him they learned that, since the discovery of the cave containing their arms and reserves of food and ammunition, a military detachment of fifty men with two lorries and a jeep had been combing the Oulé hills and was now looking for them somewhere along the road. Idriss renewed his efforts to persuade Morel to leave the road, give up for the time being the idea of making directly for the hills, and lie low in the bush for several days. Fields saw him arguing animatedly, sometimes pointing at the road ahead of them. They had stopped under the big tree in the square, where the meetings of the village elders must have been held for centuries, surrounded by the wretched yellow curs, the eternal pariahs of all African villages, who ran round them yapping, while the few inhabitants who had emerged from their huts held their children tight and watched them from a distance. Youssef sat motionless on his horse with his face expressionless, gripping his tommy gun and saying nothing. The shadows of the branches and the rays of sun played over them. Idriss was insisting, gesticulating violently, talking volubly, with his ample blue sleeves falling down his arm at every gesture of his raised hand. Morel listened to him attentively but kept shaking his head. Once or twice, as Idriss went on, Fields saw the Frenchman glance quickly toward Minna. She was sitting on the ground, her knees up against her chin. Her shrunken skull-like face, her huge eyes reflected utmost misery. The drops of sweat about her lips were not those of heat but those of exhaustion. Fields himself felt like a warm, wet rag, but he knew that he could hold out as long as he had a scrap of film left. But it was impossible to expect the wretched girl, in the condition she was in, to leave the road and to go climbing on foot for hours among the rocks of the bamboo forest. At last Idriss fell silent, after pointing angrily one last time along the road. Morel nodded approval.

"I know we're going straight into them," he said calmly. "But either I'm much mistaken, or they'll move discreetly off the road so as not to run into us. They'll let us through. Hell, they're French soldiers, after all."

Fields found himself gaping in astonishment. This was far worse than madness, it was a sort of wild disdainful provocation, bent on engulfing everything in its contempt. Unless, on the contrary, he was perfectly serious, convinced of what he was saying—a blind confidence that would be even more appalling. There was indeed that spark of gaiety in his brown eyes, but that seemed to have been there always and was perhaps no more than some spot of lighter color in his pupils. Fields decided to put off all idea of understanding the man until later. For the moment he was too tired to be able to do anything but try to remain in the saddle.

He saw Minna get up, and they took their places once more in the small group behind Youssef.

The boy kept so close to Morel that the flanks of their horses sometimes touched, and on his sweaty face there were now gleams of anguish and fear as his eyes swept the straight and empty road that extended before them between the trees; he held his tommy gun ready, pressed tight against his elbow.

The student felt rebellion growing in his heart, and it was a rebellion that had now only a distant relation to that which had once driven him to join Waïtari.

At some point in front of them, on that track stretching between the first trees of the equatorial forest, there would appear the soldiers whose orders were, whatever Morel might say, to arrest the Frenchman at all costs. But the boy's rebellion did not spring from fear.

He had been attached to Morel by Waïtari from the start, to keep a watch on his slightest movement and above all to prevent him from falling into the hands of the authorities alive. It was essential to prevent this humanitarian madman from appearing at a trial, when the whole world would be listening to him, and from proclaiming that the disorders he had provoked had really no aim other than the protection of the African fauna. If he were to fall into the hands of the police alive, nothing could keep him from crying out his essential truth for all to hear. The only solution was to suppress him in time and afterward to present him to the world as a hero of African nationalism struck down by colonialist murderers in

a dark corner of the forest. That was the task entrusted to Youssef
from the very start of the campaign. The instructions he had received were explicit, but the presence of the American journalist on
the Kuru and now here had complicated matters. Instead of returning to Fort Lamy, his declared intention, the reporter was obstinately following Morel as if he meant never to leave him.

But even this complication was nothing beside the student's own
torturing confusion.

What was growing in him was something like a plain refusal
to carry out his orders. Disguised as a mere servant, he had been
living in Morel's company for more than a year. He was a
nationalist, he was ready to die for African independence, but
there were moments when he let himself be overcome by that contagious confidence and hope that emanated from the Frenchman;
and in the very idea of a new and free and proud Africa there was
something impossible to reconcile with a burst of submachine-gun
fire in the man's back.

Yet that was what the movement demanded of him, in the name
of ends justifying the means, that indisputable logic of imperious
necessity. And what right had he to be thinking of anything but the
historic need of the African people? What right had he to indulge
in his humanitarian weakness? His only excuse was the presence
of the journalist, an embarrassing witness to say the least; but
if the detachment of soldiers appeared at the end of the track he
would no longer have a choice.

So he held his weapon ready but with a total lack of resolution,
his face impassive but his heart overwhelmed, doing his best to
struggle against this impulse of sympathy for the Frenchman whom
he had followed for so long and who seemed eternally condemned
to sweat between two fires, and who yet continued to defend with
so much optimism and such a contagious confidence something
with which the modern world had no longer any intention of bur-
dening itself.

The track unrolled before them, between the trees, rising slightly
and ending in the sky.

They had left the short scrub country, and the first tall equatorial trees stood on both sides of the road, packed beyond the banks on both sides, closer and closer together; and Fields, perhaps from his past experience with patrols in Korea and Malaya, was struggling against the fear that the silence and emptiness around them concealed a human presence—there was nothing like it to make the bush silent.

He was ready to bet anything that they were running straight into an ambush.

But the silence continued and the track remained empty. Occasionally bands of baboons started from the thickets and set off shouting and bouncing along the road in front of them. Whole clusters of them were found drowned at the bottom of wells, or stifled in the big jars of millet whose lids had trapped them when they were trying to pillage.

The sky was dull and fleecy, and Fields checked his lens, measured the light and altered shutter speed. Several times he had noticed the glances of barely disguised panic which Youssef was throwing in all directions. He was watching Morel, tensely. He was practically touching him with the muzzle of the Sten gun, and Fields observed that the young man held a finger on the trigger, and that the weapon was cocked.

Lieutenant Sandien's detachment, which was moving along the track from the opposite direction, was at that moment about twenty-five miles ahead of them.

Youssef kept a few feet behind Morel with his finger on the trigger, and Fields was to remember to the end of his days the white-clad figure on the nervous horse, the flowing white draperies and the young black face where the sweat of fear and nervous tension rose in great drops, and where every feature bore the mark of some deep anguish.

And yet the track remained silent and empty between the trees and Fields could hear no sound except the throbbing of the blood in his ears. But his old professional instinct continued to cry out to him that danger was near, that the end was imminent, and every few seconds he nervously checked the lens of his camera, feeling with more certainty that the end of their adventure was there, a few steps ahead of them.

Schölscher had been waiting for Waïtari's trucks about thirty miles from the Sudanese frontier among the granite boulders of the El Garajat gorge, at the precise spot where, more than half a century ago, Captain Gentil's topographical expedition had been cut to pieces by Nubian horsemen. He had been on the march for the Kuru to arrest Morel when he was informed by a wire from Gfat, retransmitted by Fort Lamy, of the crossing of the frontier by a group of Sudanese rebels. He had only twenty men with him, and he decided to intercept the band on their way back, at the only point where the rocks made it possible for him to conceal his men and their camels. He was in touch by radio with Lieutenant Dulud, who had remained on the Gfat track with a dozen men, and he kept wondering what the deserters from the Sudanese regiments could be looking for in the Kuru basin. No doubt these were just a few gunrunners operating farther south than usual.

On June 23 at three in the afternoon he saw columns of dust rising far to the west; the visibility was so clear that he had to wait half an hour before he could make out the three trucks and another quarter of an hour before giving the order to open fire at their tires. The trucks stopped at once, except the last one, which swerved off to the left and, careening wildly over the boulders, overturned under the weight of its cargo of ivory, which spilled out before the astonished Schölscher. A burst of tommy-gun fire came from the cab of the second truck; men leaped out and took cover behind stones, more for self-protection than for resistance, but the bursts of firing continued from the second lorry and peppered the rocks blindly.

Then there was a moment of complete silence, and then three young men in khaki, armed with submachine guns, leaped down and charged the rocks, firing as they came. One of them gave, as he charged, a long strident yell in which Schölscher recognized at once the old battle cry of the Oulés: the student who had uttered it was returning instinctively to the oldest tradition of the warriors of his tribe. It was obvious that the three young nationalists wanted

to die, but behind the boulders Schölscher's experienced Camel
Corps men exchanged grins and held their fire. The rejected heroes
emptied their magazines, then let their arms fall to their sides, condemned once more to the banality of existing and the loneliness of
wondering why.

The door of the lead truck opened abruptly and a hand waved a
yachtsman's cap whose dirty crown was probably intended to pass
for a white flag. Habib got down, with his hands up and his teeth
still nervously clenched on a squashed cheroot, his nose bleeding as
a result of a brutal jolt against the windshield. Behind him there
appeared, slowly, a fine African head under a sky-blue kepi.

Schölscher rounded up the Sudanese, who had thrown down their
weapons and raised their hands and were grinning. There were
three white men among them—but he left that problem for later and
walked toward Waïtari and Habib. The Lebanese, though rather
gray in the face, quickly regained his composure.

"It has nothing to do with me; I was just passing by, hitchhiking,
and they picked me up, on my word of honor!" he said.

Waïtari gave him a contemptuous look. "We are soldiers in uniform," he said, "and we expect to be treated as such."

It cost Schölscher an effort to take his eyes off the sky-blue kepi
with its black stars. In all the firmament there might well be no
stars more lost and lonely than those.

"*Bonjour, Monsieur le député,*" he said.

"I left all that behind me long ago, as you know very well," said
Waïtari. "I'm here as a fighter in the army of African independence.
Do your duty."

Schölscher glanced at the three young men who stood behind
their leader: one of them had a fine intellectual's face, another was
chiefly remarkable for his clenched fists, and the face of the third
was so gentle and sad that it made him turn away with anger and
depression. Perhaps, he thought, the right thing is to educate the
masses before creating the elite; otherwise you only make desperate
and lonely men.

"How many young people like this can you rely on among the
Oulés? How many are ready to follow you?"

"I'm appealing to world public opinion," said Waïtari. "I'm not

yet appealing to the Oulés. World public opinion is my army. Do
your duty, Schölscher—but don't preach to me. I think I can claim
to have more solid political experience than a little Camel Corps
officer who spends his time among the stars of the desert. I know
what I'm doing. Tomorrow your own press will be forced to tell
the world that the African independence army has had its first
skirmish and that its leader is in prison. That's enough for me—for
the moment."

"I'm afraid there's some misunderstanding," said Schölscher. "No
doubt you don't know that your lorries are literally stuffed with
ivory." In spite of himself he could not help smiling. "So that I'm
afraid my report will merely speak of ivory smugglers caught on
their way back from a poaching raid—something not very different
from what our old friends the Kreichs tribesmen are doing, a little
farther south, it's true, with much less elaborate equipment. A pity
to have got your name mixed up in that.

"I admit I've none of your knowledge of political expediency,"
said Schölscher, "but I suggest to you that you might say also that
the trucks and ivory were planted in your path by the French authorities in an effort to discredit you."

Waïtari shrugged his shoulders and turned his back on him. As
for Habib, he had recovered all his cockiness.

"Word of honor," he said. "I was simply hitchhiking through the
desert and they picked me up."

From him Schölscher got all the information he wanted about
Morel and his intentions. He got in touch with Lieutenant Dulud by
wireless, who told him that Forsythe and Peer Qvist had been
arrested as they were about to cross the Sudan frontier. He gave
over the command to his Number Two, took six men and started off
immediately in one of Habib's trucks. He stopped by Lake Kuru for
a few hours only and continued westward in a desperate effort to
catch up with Morel, whose tracks he had no difficulty in picking
up at Gola: he missed him by only half an hour.

At Fort Lamy the Governor shifted in his chair and tried to think
of something to say. He had now been waiting twelve hours for a
radio message.

"I don't understand. Schölscher must have been at the Kuru since this morning. Anyhow it can't be long now. I hope they'll bring him back alive."

"I doubt it," said Herbier.

He had come to report on the situation among the Oulés, but the Governor had been detaining him on one pretext or another for the last three days. They were friends of thirty years' standing whom chance and promotion had separated: one of them had reached the top of the ladder, while the other had stopped short en route, no doubt forever. But Herbier was much too fond of Africa and its people to feel sorry that he had never been able to contemplate them from the administrative heights: a fine view, perhaps, but a distant one. He had long ago chosen the bush, the black peasants, and there he had remained all his life.

"You doubt it?"

"I doubt that Morel would let himself be taken alive. I don't think he would accept living under *our* conditions."

"What the hell do you mean by that? Are you turning metaphysician in your old age?"

"Morel is afflicted with too noble a conception of a man. He demands too much of human beings, and he refuses to compromise. You can't live with that inside you. It becomes almost a question of physiology. What he calls for is not even moral progress; it's really a biological mutation. He can't accept the very biological limitations which make us what we are—weak, crawling in our mud, and totally devoid of dignity. That's the iron law he's protesting, the law he refuses to submit to. I doubt very much that he'll let himself be taken alive."

On the terrace of the Tchadien there was only Joubert. He had gone there to sit after sending off his latest dispatch on the Morel affair, perhaps because he needed to soak himself again in a landscape which expressed so clearly what it was all about. To understand, one had only to look around. Beyond the parapet the lassitude of the river—shivering slightly under its glittering scales, between the two banks of sand and petrified grass—seemed to be slowing down time itself, and the single palm tree of Fort Foureau, in

the midst of the total emptiness of the sky, drooped as if it had had
many bereavements in its family. What fascinated him about Morel's
revolt was that it was not the first one of that nature; they went very
far back in history. In Egypt, for instance, at the time of the Lower
Kingdom, the mob had once invaded the temples, threatening the
terrified priests. That Egyptian mob four thousand years ago was
not demanding bread, or peace, or liberty. It was demanding immortality. It stoned the priests and demanded immortality with
anger, indignation and clenched fists. Morel's demonstration was of
the same order and had about as much chance of succeeding. Standing on the hills of Africa, he brandished his fists, raised his voice,
protested and made signals that were doomed to remain unan-
swered. Essentially, the human riddle was not susceptible of solution—the injustice was such that there was no human revolution
capable of redressing it.

The horse Butor was having the roughest time of his life. He had
been left in peace by his master at the White Fathers' Mission at
Nguélé, and was enjoying a well-deserved rest, when the Franciscan
reappeared in a state of fury and excitement whose immediate effect
was to make his weight seem even greater, perhaps because he
never stopped shifting impatiently about in his saddle. Father
Fargue's face was purple with consternation, and as usual when he
was stirred, he puffed, groaned, sighed and sweated as if he were
already on the point of coming face to face with the One Who
would, in spite of everything, certainly have some questions to ask
him. He was not alone. Behind him, bony and nervous on their
mules, two White Fathers whom he had torn away from the peace
of their prayers were following with apprehension—but also with a
resolution which was not entirely due to the disagreeable words the
missionary to the lepers had thrown at them that very morning.
"You concealed some pro-Nazi traitors during the war," Fargue had
yelled as he pushed them energetically toward the door of the mission; "well, you can now conceal a man from the Resistance. All
right, all right, keep quiet, you can't teach me my Catechism. Of
course he's a man of pride and a blasphemer, someone who ought
to go down on his knees and pray instead of showing his fists. But

it isn't entirely his fault. His heart's so full that he couldn't take a long enough run, it's too heavy. So he stopped short, he stopped at the elephants. But perhaps a good kick in the ass will give him just the run he needs. Meanwhile I don't want him to get himself killed halfway, where he got stuck, like a mad dog, without having had time to understand and to address himself and his petitions to the Right Quarter. You will therefore keep him concealed for me at the mission as long as is necessary, and you will leave it to me to give him the run he needs. I'll teach him to raise his sights! I know my business! Come on."

"Up to now the mission has never had any trouble with the authorities," said the youngest of the Fathers, in a slightly peevish tone.

"No," said Fargue happily, "but it's none too soon to begin."

She did not know whether it was a passing moment of faintness, due to fever and exhaustion, or something deeper, a truth that she had refused to face and that was at last overcoming her because she no longer had the courage or the strength to resist it—but there were moments when the only thing that mattered was that he should put his arm round her shoulders and stroke her face and draw her close. Everything else then ceased to exist. She still tried to think that it was only a moment of weakness and that it would pass, and that the longing, the need for affection was due only to her physical condition, a mere need for repose. But perhaps what most helped her to hold on, when the branches of the trees were beginning to spin above her head and she had to close her eyes to stop the dizziness, was the fear of displeasing him, of not appearing as confident and as strong in her belief as he thought she was. Every time he questioned her, anxiously, as their horses rode on side by side at the same slow pace between the trees and toward the hills, she found enough courage to answer him with a semblance of cheerfulness.

"How goes it?"

"Don't worry about me, Monsieur Morel. I'm a solid German girl of good peasant stock."

"In two hours' time we shall be in the hills. There's a cave or two in the district, and we've prepared them for just this sort of occasion. Of course there's no medicine. But we'll get some somehow."

"Please, don't worry about me. I'll manage."

He kept telling himself that he needed her simply and solely because she was a German, and because her presence at his side proved that it was not possible to despair. It was certainly the Germans' turn to do something for the elephants. It was time that they too demonstrate their love of nature, that they too come to its help and take up that defense of all its menaced roots which had nearly cost him his life in Nazi prisons. He felt that he was on the point of succeeding, of gaining at least partial results. A little more perseverance and there was no reason why a new conference should not meet, under the pressure of public opinion, and reach at least some degree of agreement about the protection of species. Afterward . . . He could not help turning toward her again.

"Look, you can see the hills already."

"Yes, we're almost there."

"A little more and we'll be out of danger. We'll be able to rest awhile."

Youssef raised his sleeve and wiped the sweat from his face. There was still no trace of the troops at the end of the track, but he was taking a great risk by waiting till the last moment. And yet he still had a good excuse: the presence of the American journalist. It was impossible to kill Morel under his eyes. That might well do a great deal of harm to the movement. The reporter was now only just able to keep in the saddle, and even so Idriss had to support him to prevent him from falling off. Any second now he would stop, sit down by the side of the road and give up. Then he would be able to carry out his orders. It was no good telling oneself that the end does not justify the means: that was just a form of weakness. That particular dialectic problem had long ago been settled by the political thinkers as part of the movement's doctrine, and on that ground at least there was no hesitation possible. If he did not press the trigger, even if only at the last moment, he would be breaking the only brotherhood he knew—that of the Negro race—and would become a pariah like Morel, condemned to wander between two camps, forever caught between two fires.

He could hardly hold the weapon because of the sweat on his hand, which he had to wipe incessantly.

He stared at the track ahead with such attention that he began to see spots before his eyes; and he took them, each time, for the military convoy he was watching for.

At that moment Lieutenant Sandien's detachment was still about six miles ahead along the road—about a quarter of an hour away.

The Governor of the Oulés had left Sionville in haste, driving his car himself, as soon as he received the first reports from Gola about Morel's presence on the track leading to the Oulé hills. The military convoy must have left the hills that very morning, and if there was one thing the Governor was firmly determined to prevent, it was Morel's death in a skirmish with French soldiers. That would have been against nature—as much against nature as if Morel had been killed by the elephants. The Governor had received a telegram the night before confirming him in his post, and he was ready to throw all his recovered authority into the balance to save the Frenchman who refused to give in.

The only white man who saw them pass—some eighteen miles south of Gola, where the track cuts across the cotton plantations to make directly for the Oulé foothills—was a uranium prospector named Jonquet, who had arrived from Europe six weeks before and was driving back in a jeep from a visit to a local cotton planter, whom he had tried in vain to interest in his researches; in his own words, "he needed some financial support." He had just left the path from the plantation where it joined the main track and he had to jam on his brakes to avoid running into the horsemen. He stared at them as they went by, ignoring him. Jonquet's account of this unexpected meeting was eloquent in its simplicity.

"I thought the time for this sort of adventure was over—or if you prefer, hadn't begun—in French Equatorial Africa. Morel wasn't armed. But behind him there was a young black who was armed enough for two, if I may put it that way. I've just arrived in Africa, I'm not yet blasé, and that boy with his tommy gun—he stared at me

—and the other black man, much older, with his blue burnous and his white turban—he had a really savage expression, the kind that wishes you no good—it really did something to me. There were also the village urchins running behind them at a respectful distance. Morel was leading the way, covered with dust, wearing a European felt hat and a sort of dirty khaki scarf round his neck; and, contrary to everything I expected, he didn't look mad or even excited. But mad he must have been; otherwise he wouldn't have been there in broad daylight, on that track which even at that season is used by lorries, right in the middle of the plantation district. Either he didn't give a damn about being killed, or we must believe that he was protected from very high up. I don't say he was, I'm raising the question, that's all. What struck me most was the girl. She looked really frightful, though one could see she must have been pretty—but her eyes were all sunken, with blue rings around them, and there was nothing left of her face but tight skin covered with dirt and sweat, and I'd have sworn she wouldn't be able to do another yard. There was also that American journalist with cameras slung around his neck and a leather case over his shoulder; he looked absolutely mad at that moment, with a handkerchief knotted over his head, the four corners sticking out like horns. He was haggard, and his eyes were popping out of his head. And all that for the sake of elephants! I've seen some liberty-loving maniacs and anarchists in my time, but this—this went beyond everything! You really need to loathe mankind, want to spit in its face, to go to that length. I can't get over it. And mind you. I can understand it to some extent. We've all got something of that in us. Take me—I've got my hope of finding uranium to console me. After all, we've got to believe in something, haven't we . . . I went back to the plantation at once to warn them. I found Roubaud and told him. I don't know what I expected him to do exactly, but I wanted to share it with someone. He listened to me calmly. You know him: a great big, rather gloomy chap. 'Right,' he said. 'Morel's passed that way. Right. So what? I don't care: I've got nothing against him. I advise you to keep your mouth shut.' That's what we've come to, sir. I call that misanthropy. No wonder he didn't want to take a share in my prospecting, that

man Roubaud: he's another of those fellows who believe in nothing
—in uranium any more than in anything else. If I found Morel
hidden at his plantation, I wouldn't be at all surprised."

Jonquet had been mistaken when he said that Minna was not
capable of doing another yard. She did another three miles, although she had to stop several times. She gave up only when she
fainted dead away and, on opening her eyes, saw Morel's face bent
over her with a friendly and worried expression. She tried to smile.
   He answered: "My poor friend, this time you've had it."
   *"Ich kann ja nicht mehr . . ."*
   He was holding her in his arms. She raised a face covered with
tears toward him, with a smile still trembling through the dirt and
sweat, but he could see the unmistakable signs of total exhaustion
which he knew so well from his experience in the camps—a fly running over her forehead and cheek, and she without the strength to
brush it away, not feeling it probably. It was a thing he knew so
well—the fly that begins to feel at home. He removed her chin-strap,
took off her felt hat and took her head in his hands. Even her lips
had lost their contours; they were almost gray and lifeless. And yet
he had taken every risk to shorten the journey, keeping to the main
road, moving straight ahead when soldiers were no doubt moving
to meet them, relying, it was true, on sympathy from some, on
understanding from others, and on the loyalty of the French to their
traditions; but the fact was that she could not go on any farther. He
himself had no idea where to go. Their cave in the Oulé country
had been discovered. There were others, but they had no medical
supplies, and there was no ammunition but what Waïtari had left
them—which would be enough for a few more days at the most.
And yet he had to go on. People had to know that he was still there,
alive, present somewhere in Africa: they needed him.
   "Suppose you rest for an hour or two? We could stop for that
long."
   She said nothing, and he did not even try to convince her.
   "Right. I'll take you back to the village. There may be a first-aid
post. Anyhow there's a plantation over there. I'll see if I can find
the people."

"I'll go by myself."

"No, you won't."

"I can't have you arrested because of me. Please, don't be arrested. Please go . . . go on. Do it for my sake."

"And leave you here by the roadside?"

"I don't want anything to happen to you because of me. Please, don't let anybody stop you."

He hesitated for a second, but it was hard to mistake the meaning of that supplicating yet determined gaze of hers. To go on was the only thing he could do for her. For her and for some millions of other people. He must be crafty, hide, unrestingly defend the margin of humanity in the midst of our worst troubles, keep out of reach somewhere deep in the jungle, among the last of the great elephants; people must know that he was still there, as a consolation, a promise, an irreducible sign of confidence. First and foremost he must keep out of reach; if he got hit he must drag himself away to die in some obscure hole in the bush, so that he would never be found and those who had need of him could still believe him alive. If he was destined to end his days with a bullet in the back in the classic tradition of the end justifying the means, it was essential that this not be known, so that legend might lay hands on him and his adventure and proclaim his invincible presence everywhere at once, so that people might believe he was only hiding, ready to rise once more to defend the threatened giants.

"All right. I'll leave you now."

"Nothing must happen to you . . ."

"Nothing will happen to me," he promised gravely. "I have friends. I haven't told you everything, but I'll get help, don't you worry. It's all been arranged . . ."

He did not know whether she believed him or not, but it was essential to reassure her—reassure them all. It was very important that people believe he was still alive, still present.

"If you hear defeatist rumors, don't believe them. That I've been killed, anything like that . . . Tell them not to believe it; they'll never get me."

He almost believed it himself. He did not know what to do, or where to go, almost without arms and ammunition as he was, but he was sure he would find friends.

"Perhaps you'll hear no more of me for some time, but I'll be hiding in there . . ." He pointed toward the forest. "And I'll come back. We'll force them to call another conference, and another and another . . . till the work is done. I may even be asked to attend it. I tell you, in the end they'll give us the margin we need. *On les aura.*"*

Abe Fields yelped in contempt. "*On les aura . . .*" He had a violent loathing for that cocky expression, having heard it a thousand times from French soldiers who never came back. Abe Fields, in spite of his fever, felt pride in being a realistic American with the highest national income per head of population in the world, and the most comfortable standard of living since the beginning of evolution; the reptiles of the primeval sea could be proud of America, and the ancestor who had first crawled out of his native mud, in a desperate effort to become a man, might now sleep in peace—he had succeeded. His name should be venerated in every American school; he was the real pioneer, the father of free enterprise, of the spirit of initiative, of all those who dared, who risked, of all that had led to the stupendous material progress of the United States. He swept them with a triumphant glance, and the lizards seated about him applauded. Abe Fields tried to salute them, and only the swift intervention of Idriss prevented him from falling from his horse.

"Do you think you can hold out as far as the plantation? It's about six miles."

"Monsieur Fields will help me."

"No, he won't. Just look at him—his eyes are starting out of his head. He doesn't know what he's doing. Hey, shutterbug."

Fields grabbed his camera.

"Can you go with her?"

"I want to go on with you."

"Listen to him. I thought you had no more film?"

"That doesn't matter. I'll manage."

"How do you propose to take pictures?"

* We'll get them.

"I want to help you."

"Well! I thought you didn't give a damn about the elephants."

"I had all my family gassed at Auschwitz."

"I see. You should have said so. But I can't take you with me."

"Why not?"

"It wouldn't be fair. You no longer know what you're doing."

"I'm an American citizen, and I've a right to defend the elephants wherever they're threatened," yelled Abe Fields. "Jefferson, Lincoln, Eisen—"

"Yes, yes, I know."

"I've the right to defend the elephants like anyone else."

"That's right, you go and defend them like everyone else."

"I want to give my life for the elephants!" yelled Abe Fields.

"You're really in trouble."

"The American GIs came to Europe to defend your damned elephants!" Fields yelled. "Without us . . ."

A particularly violent pain in his left side sobered him somewhat. He put both hands on his side, his face twisted in pain, and he looked around him.

"The two of you will turn back. There's a plantation a few miles off over there. Do you hear me?"

"I don't know if I can hold out as far as that. My ribs are jabbing into my lungs."

"You'll try. What's the matter?" Morel looked up.

"A jeep and some lorries," shouted Youssef.

The student could feel hot sweat running over his face and neck: it was as if he were bleeding. He had pressed the weapon under his elbow so hard that his arm was now locked and he could not move it. He took a deep breath, his eyes staring fixedly at the black specks that were growing bigger on the horizon. Twenty minutes or half an hour after leaving the track they would reach the foot of the Oulé hills where the thick bamboo forest filled the space between the rocks. There he would be alone with Morel and Idriss, and there would be no embarrassing witness. He mopped his face with his sleeve, trying almost violently to believe that he had taken his decision and that it would be quite simple: a burst of tommy-gun fire and Morel would be a legend forever. He would go down

in history as the first white man to give his life for black nationalism. No longer would he be able to protest, to stand before public
opinion and voice his obstinate truth. It would be at last possible to
make full use of him for a precise political end, to give his name
all the publicity desired without any fear that the confident fool
would turn up somewhere in his clumsy fury with his briefcase
stuffed with petitions and appeals and with that disheveled look of
the perpetual militant, and bang the table with his fist and undo
all the efforts to make use of him: "I want you to stop hunting elephants, damn you!" But the most irritating thing of all was that
sometimes when Morel turned back and saw the barrel of the
weapon aimed at him and ready, the student had the conviction
that he was not deceived, that he *knew*. At those moments there was
a gleam of mockery in his eyes, almost of challenge, so typical of
his deep, confident madness, as if he were saying: "I dare you!" It
was intolerable: the man seemed to have embarked on a secret
struggle with you, which he felt sure of winning because he believed in you. Youssef longed to insult him, even to strike him,
to wrench out of him once and for all that absurd confidence in
humanity, to shout at him that he himself put nothing above African
independence—no other care, no other human consideration, no
other dignity, and that all means were good if they attained that
end. But he also felt that if he had to strike down a man who put
such trust in him and believed so obstinately in the dignity of the
human hand, it was better that he know nothing of it, that he at
least be able to die instantly, shot in the back, and so with his
confidence intact.

The struggle Youssef was carrying on with himself was so painful
that there were moments when he longed to charge the approaching
convoy at a gallop, fire on them and be killed. His horse felt his
nervousness and reared, raising a cloud of dust which must have
been visible from where the French were.

Idriss began speaking furiously, gesticulating with energy and
waving his forefinger toward the convoy. Morel made up his mind
at last.

"All right, all right. It's now or never."

"Where do you intend to go?" cried Fields.

Abe Fields took a last look at him—with his scorched hat over his curly hair and his youthful look, the little Cross of Lorraine on his chest, that spark of gaiety deep down in his brown eyes, the ironical curve of those lips, and, attached to his saddle, that absurdly fat briefcase of his, emblem of the perpetual believer, stuffed with tracts, manifestoes and petitions. Abe Fields had a sudden inspiration.

"Wait," he shouted to him. "What will you do with all that stuff in the jungle? Pin it up on the trees? Give it to me. I'll look after it."

"You're right," said Morel. He undid the briefcase and threw it to the track.

"Take good care of it. Go on with the job. I'll be back one day, and I'll ask what you've done. It's up to you now. Goodbye and good luck!"

He turned his horse toward the bank, and Idriss and Youssef followed him. They left the track and disappeared among the trees. Six or seven miles farther south, thick bamboo forests would replace the trees where the first gray crags of the Oulé country began, a stony soil with sparse scraggy tufts, with villages crouching among the heaps of boulders under their pointed roofs, and again the bamboos and the yellow savanna over the hills, elephant grass stretching for fifty thousand square miles, higher than horse and rider, in which no posse could find them. Still farther south they would find Father Tassin and his excavation site, and although the work must have stopped with the coming of the rains, he would certainly not refuse them the hospitality of his empty huts. Perhaps he would even agree to help them more actively. He was a man who was said to take a keen interest in everything that had to do with the beginnings of man. In any case he felt sure there would be plenty of outstretched hands. For the moment he had to get as far away, as quickly as possible, from the track—it was the same track on which, ten months before, he had come face to face with Administrator Herbier, and he remembered with pleasure that honest, outraged face, the face of a man who had always done his best.

Fatigue was deadening his body, and he carried its weight with greater and greater effort, and as always when the limit of his strength made itself felt, his memories became more vivid and more insistent. He thought of all that the newspapers were printing about him. Each man attributed to him his own hopes, his own motives and rancors, and his own secret misanthropy: it was in vain that he stated his own aims clearly; there was nothing he could do about it.

And yet the truth was clear; it could hardly be clearer.

He loved all those free roots that gave their beauty to the earth and to man's life on it.

He loved nature, and he had always done his best to defend it.

The hardest fight he had ever put up had been in defense of may-beetles.

A smile—the smile Abe Fields mistrusted so—appeared on his lips and remained there. He remembered that fight with an astonishing accuracy, as if he were still carrying it on—and of course he was. He always remembered it vividly when he was in physical pain and when the limit of his strength seemed to have been reached, and it was a memory that helped him every time to hold out and to go on.

It had happened in May, after his first year in the forced labor camp, and he was the ringleader.

They were working then in the quarry at Eupen on the Baltic, carrying sacks of cement on their backs for the gigantic constructions of the new Pharaohs who were building for the next thousand years. They moved slowly in single file, taking care to avoid stumbling: to lose balance under the weight could be fatal.

They included both political prisoners and common criminals, all subject to the same system of re-education by forced labor—the custom of the twentieth century; and meanwhile the S.S. men, their faces already hot from the early sunshine, took their ease in the grass, flowers between their teeth.

There was Rotstein, the Polish pianist; Revel, the French publisher, whose beard grew so fast that he sometimes seemed full of hair inside, like a mattress, and who used to recite Mallarmé's poetry aloud in order to combat the stench during latrine duty; Szwabek, another Pole—he always carried a crumpled photograph of his sow, which had taken first prize at an agricultural show, and he showed it proudly to prove that he had been somebody; Prévost, known as Emile, a French railwayman who once burst into tears when he heard a locomotive whistle.

There was Julien, the chaplain, who hardly got any thinner during his two years at the camp, so that he was even accused of being fed secretly by God when no one was looking.

There were others, many others, who fell by the wayside and whose names no longer meant anything. And so there they were, marching, bent double under their loads, while the guards lay in the grass, relishing the first warmth of spring with their trousers open to the first caresses of the sun.

Suddenly Morel had felt something strike against his cheek and fall at his feet. He lowered his eyes cautiously, taking care not to lose his balance. It was a may-beetle.

It had fallen on its back and was waving its legs, trying in vain to turn over. Morel stopped and stared fixedly at the insect at his feet. He had been at the camp a year, and for the last three weeks he had been carrying the sacks of cement for eight hours a day on an empty stomach. But this was something impossible to let pass.

He bent his knee, keeping the sacks balanced on his shoulder, and with a movement of his forefinger placed the insect on its feet again. He did so twice more in the course of that journey. The man marching in front of him, Revel the publisher, was the first to understand. He growled approval and immediately helped the first may-beetle that fell at his feet. Then came the turn of Rotstein the pianist, although he was so thin that it seemed as if his body was envious of the fineness of his fingers.

From that moment practically all the political prisoners assisted the insects, while the common criminals passed by with curses. During the twenty minutes' break they were allowed, not one of the political prisoners gave way to exhaustion, and yet that was when they usually threw themselves to the ground and lay without stirring till the next whistle. But this time they seemed to have found new strength. They wandered about with their eyes fixed on the ground in search of insects to help.

It did not last long, of course. Sergeant Grüber arrived on the scene. He was not a mere brute. He had some education. He had been a schoolteacher in Schleswig-Holstein before the war. Immediately he had understood what was happening. He had recognized the enemy. He had known immediately that he was face to face with a scandalous provocation, an affirmation of unbroken spirit and faith, a proclamation of dignity, totally inadmissible in men reduced to zero. Yes, he had needed no more than a second to sum up the situation, to feel the full gravity of the challenge which had been flung at the builders of a new world.

He rushed into the fray.

To begin with he threw himself upon the prisoners, seconded by the guards who had no very clear idea of what was up but who were always on hand when it was a question of beating somebody. They distributed kicks and blows with their rifle butts.

But Sergeant Grüber very soon understood that this was not what was needed in order to touch the demonstrators where they were most sensitive.

He therefore did something which was perhaps loathsome, but also almost pathetic in its impotence: he began running through the grass with his eyes cast down, and every time he saw a may-beetle he stamped on it. He ran in circles, jumping, raising his foot high in the air and bringing his heel down on the ground and jumping again, in a sort of ridiculous Cossack dance, almost touching in its futility. For he could strike down the prisoners and he could stamp on the may-beetles, but what he was aiming at was out of reach and could not be killed.

At last he understood.

He had undertaken the task which no army, no police force, no militia, no party, no organization could successfully carry out. It would have been necessary to kill all human beings down to the very last, and even then it was possible, yes, it was probable that their imperishable spirit would remain behind them like a smile of heaven over the face of earth.

Of course he made them pay heavily for his defeat. He made them toil two hours longer that day, and those two hours were the difference between the final limit of human strength and what was beyond it.

That evening they wondered if such exhaustion was possible, if there would still remain to them a little strength for the next day.

Rotstein was particularly affected. He stretched himself out across

his mattress, just where he had fallen. Morel longed to bend over
him and turn him over on his legs again, like a fallen and abandoned
insect. To help him to fly away. But there was no need to help him.
He flew by himself every evening.

"Hey, Rotstein. Rotstein."

"Yes."

"Are you still alive?"

"Yes. Don't interrupt. I'm giving a concert."

"What are you playing?"

"Johann Sebastian Bach."

"Are you mad? A German?"

"Precisely. That's just the point. To restore the balance. You can't
leave Germany on its back forever. You've got to help it to its feet
again."

"We're all on our backs," growled Revel. "We were born that
way."

"Shut up. I can't hear what I'm playing."

"Big audience tonight?"

"Not bad."

"Any pretty girls?"

"Not this evening. This evening I'm playing for Sergeant Grüber."

Otto, the Silesian, groaned in his corner. He was having a dream.
They knew it. It was always the same one: he had killed a widow
in order to rob her, and every night he dreamed that she was putting
out her tongue at him. He woke up with a start.

"*Immer die alte Schickse,*" he growled.

"It's odd that she should always put out her tongue at you," said
Emile.

"It isn't odd. I strangled her."

"Oh, I see," said Emile. "So the day she shows you her ass it
will mean she's forgiven you."

Through the ventilator slit they could see the watchtower with
its slanting machine gun.

"Look here, what are we to do tomorrow if there are more of
them?"

"We must hope and pray there won't be any more," said Father
Julien.

"Oh no," said Revel, "I hope there will be. That way we can at least say what we think. It does one good."

"You don't say so," said Emile. "Look at Rotstein."

"Hey, padre."

"Yes?"

"What's God think He's up to?"

"*Merde*," said Father Julien angrily. "Leave God out of this. What's He got to do with it?"

"Nothing, as usual."

"Perhaps He's fallen on His back. Perhaps He's waving His legs but can't get up."

"*Merde, merde* and *merde*," said the chaplain with feeling.

"That's no language for a priest."

"Well, we aren't among priests here."

"Emile . . ."

"Yes?"

"Are you a Communist?"

"Yes."

"Then what are you doing, bothering about may-beetles? It isn't the party line."

"A fellow has the right to let himself go from time to time," said Emile.

"Emile . . ."

"Yes."

"Are you a Communist?"

"Shut up. That's enough."

"Well, do you believe that in a forced labor camp in Russia they'd let you waste your time turning over may-beetles?"

"Certainly not."

"Well then?"

"There aren't any forced labor camps in Russia."

"Oh, I see."

"The hell there aren't."

"What I don't understand is why they always fall on their backs."

"It's the way nature works. Why are we here?"

"Then it's a thing that still needs to be put right."

"What is? What thing?"

"Nature."

"They'll put that right for you, don't you worry."

"Emile . . ."

"What is it now?"

"Why do you do that for the may-beetles, you, a Marxist?"

"Out of Christian charity."

"Bravo, well answered," said Father Julien.

"You padre, you'd better shut up. You're discredited. You've lost face. You can't talk any more."

"That's true," said someone. "Couldn't that merciful God of yours do a little something for us? He isn't exactly obliging."

"I'm really doing all I can," said Father Julien.

"Of course, of course."

"Don't you believe me?"

"Yes, yes."

"He might all the same do a little something for us. We're on our backs, doesn't He see?"

"I'm doing my best, I tell you," said Father Julien. "I pray and I pray and I pray . . ."

"Even *we* find a way of doing something for the may-beetles."

"You don't give a damn about the may-beetles, you bastards," said Father Julien. "You do it out of pride. If you weren't in a forced labor camp you'd step on may-beetles without even noticing their existence. This is something that happens in the head, not in the heart. You're bursting with pride, that's what it is."

"It isn't pride," someone protested weakly. "It's something else . . ."

They were holding their horses by the bridles, alone now, in the thick undergrowth of thorns that covered them with tattered shadows, deep in the yellow bamboo forest, one standing, holding his Sten gun ready, the other sitting on a rock with his back turned, lost in his memories, and smiling, either contemptuous of death or incredibly sure of himself. The sound of the moving trucks receded in the distance, and Youssef now heard nothing but the panic of insects around them, while he stood there, his finger on the trigger, staring at the man who was so tranquilly turning his back on him and seemed to be waiting patiently for the burst of tommy-gun fire; and sometimes, when he moved his head slightly, the student could see his ironic profile under the scorched felt hat. Idriss had gone ahead of them trying to find a passage through the entanglement of jungle and rocks and they were alone now in the yellowness of the bamboos.

"Well, what're you waiting for? Let me have it. Shoot!"

The student's face was empty and almost hollow under its sweat. He had to make a violent effort to swallow, to unlock his throat. "How did you know?"

. . . In the desert night, the white form lying under the stars had stirred in the sand and Morel had stopped and leaned for a second over the sleeping youth. The face with the closed eyes was serious and almost sad under the blue light. And it was then that the lips trembled suddenly and murmured a few words and Morel stood there for a long while, motionless, his hand touching that proud and rebellious head. . . .

"I overheard you dream aloud, in French. You were talking in your sleep."

"And what was I saying?"

Morel looked away. "You were mumbling something about human dignity." He turned toward the student, with that serious, humorous smile of his, a smile that had in it much more of the kindness of the eyes than of the irony of the lips.

"Well, who are you exactly? It's about time I knew."

"My name is Youssef Lanoto and I did two years' study at the Paris University of Law."

"And then?"

"Then I joined the C.L.A. Waïtari attached me to you. I was to keep an eye on you . . ."

"Very thoughtful of him."

"The movement couldn't afford to let you be captured alive. You would've protested to the end that the only thing you cared about was elephants."

"That's right. That's the only thing I do care about."

"After Sionville, we sentenced you to death. But we couldn't carry out the sentence because of the American journalist."

"I see."

"I was to get rid of you the moment he had left us. Or when we were alone."

"Now, in fact."

"Yes, now."

A trace of bitterness . . .

"Then they would have presented you to the world as a hero of African independence."

"That would've been nice. And they weren't far wrong, you know. Only, you see, that's not enough for me. National independence, I wouldn't settle for that only. That's an old, old trick, and it doesn't work any more. Nine tenths of the world is made up of independent nations and look at them. No, my friend, that's not enough for me. I want more. I'm asking them for more. I'm asking them to become human at last, and I shan't settle for less. But if you feel that you can do what we didn't manage so well, if you feel you can insure the protection of elephants, you can have all the independence you wish, I'll come along with you. It suits me fine. Liberty always suits me fine. But on one condition: do the job. I don't give a damn who does it: you or us, the whites or the yellows, the reds or the blacks, I don't give a damn. I'll come along, but on one condition. Do the job. Because for me there's only one thing that matters."

The voice suddenly regained all its angry thunder.

"Respect the elephants. I won't settle for less."

"I know," said Youssef gently.

Morel looked once more into the barrel of the Sten gun aimed at him. Almost with longing: he wouldn't have minded a little rest, before carrying on.

"So you were to shoot me," he said, almost regretfully. "I wonder what prevented you. However, you can still do it. I should even say this is the best moment and the right place."

"I have no intention of doing it."

"And why, may I ask?"

Youssef looked at him almost with a paternal feeling. This crazy, lonely white man had to be defended, protected; it was essential to the African fighters for independence, and to the whole species, to justify his incredible confidence, the unbroken, indestructible hope that dwelt in him.

"Why don't you kill me?"

"I think we can still go a long way together," Youssef said.

Abe Fields stood in the middle of the track, looking down at the briefcase. It lay in the dust of the road, stuffed with proclamations, manifestoes, petitions, appeals; heavy with disappointed hopes. He stooped painfully and picked it up, clutched the briefcase firmly and turned to the German girl. She was sobbing now as she stared at the place where Morel and his two companions had disappeared among the trees. Abe Fields took her gently by the hand.

"*Weint nischt,*" he said to her in Yiddish, convinced that he was speaking good German. "Nothing can happen to him."

Ever since dawn the Jesuit had been following the path along the hillside, going home with a light heart, looking forward to another season on the site of his excavations, alone with his thoughts and his manuscripts: his Order liked to know that he was in the depths of the African forest rather than in Europe. This exile bothered him very little; from his wilderness he carried on a correspondence with the half-dozen men whose names were like beacons in the darkness of the century, and whose thinking, often very different from his own, supplied him with the valuable stimulus of contradiction. He was tired after a sleepless night, but he also felt the weight of another fatigue, a deeper, more irremediable lassitude, and this saddened him a little. He felt a most lively curiosity, together with a certain irritation at the idea of having soon to part from the human adventure without having been able to foresee more distinctly the fresh forms it would take, forms as changing and mysterious as the hills through which he had been journeying since the first light of dawn. He was human enough to regret it, and as he swayed in his saddle to the pace of his horse, he felt sorry that he would have to give up before he could witness its most interesting phases. He tried not to yield too much to this rather authoritarian curiosity, of which he himself disapproved for its excess and lack of humility, but which only increased with age—perhaps because with the approach of the end every factor that came under observation took on an increased importance. He was sorry not to be bringing back more cheerful news from his expedition, but he was used to patience. He kept thinking of the last words Saint-Denis had said to him as they parted, standing there beside his horse and looking up at him, with eyes in which the last glow of the night seemed still to be burning. "They say, Father, that you hid our friend at one of your excavation sites, and that he's merely getting his breath before he goes on, but I can't see very clearly why you should show so much sympathy for a man whose aim after all was to take the protection of nature into his own hands. That seems to me to go against what one has heard about your Order—and even about your writings. If I have understood them, you don't seem to expect much from our efforts, and it might be said that you consider even Grace as a biological mutation which will in the end give man the organic means to make himself what he wants himself to be. If that's so, Morel's struggle must appear to you both comic and futile. And perhaps all you've been trying to get from my company and from these memories we have invoked together, is a brief moment of amusement. With his petitions, his manifestoes, his defense committees, and finally, his organized *maquis,* it must seem to you that he's after something that's not yet possible, and won't be for a long time, except as a hymn of hope. But I can't resign myself to such skepticism, and I prefer to believe that you are not untouched by a certain secret sympathy for that rebel, whose idea is to extract from Heaven itself this minimum of respect for our condition. After all, we emerged from the mud some millions of years ago, and although we got rid of our scales, there is still a long way to go before we become really human—but one of these days we shall triumph over our limitations, over the harsh biological law which has been imposed upon us. Our friend was right: it's an inhuman law, and it's high time to change it. Then all that will be left of the infirmity and the challenge of being a man will be one more cast skin by the side of our track."

The Jesuit nodded abruptly—it might as well have been a sudden jolt of his horse as a sign of assent. With those thin, though not dry, lips, always softened by two small lines of compassion, and with his narrow piercing eyes and great bony nose, he had the profile of a

Breton sailor accustomed to watching the horizon. His enemies liked
to recall that he had famous buccaneers among his ancestors, and
he did not dislike these allusions to his adventurous blood. He had
himself lived one of the finest and most interesting spiritual adventures a creature can have on earth, in the absence of doubt and in
the certainty of a final discovery. He swayed slightly in his saddle to
the pace of his horse, turning his conquistador's profile toward the
hills, or toward the silhouette of a tree whose infinite complexity of
branches his eye followed with delight: for a long time now the tree
had been his favorite sign on earth, before even the sign of the
Cross. He was smiling.

## ABOUT THE AUTHOR

ROMAIN GARY *has had three careers: as writer, soldier and diplomat. His first novel,* Éducation Européenne, *won the Prix des Critiques in 1945 and was a sensational best seller throughout Europe. The Roots of Heaven, his fifth novel, has won him the highest French literary honor—the Prix Goncourt—and has sold 300,000 copies in France.*

*M. Gary began his military career in 1937, when he enlisted in the French Air Force. He served in France until it fell to Hitler, then joined the R. A. F. and finally fought with the Free French. He received the Croix de la Libération, the Croix de Guerre, and was made a Chevalier of the Légion d'Honneur.*

*He is now a career diplomat and has served France in her embassies in England, Bulgaria and Switzerland, and as First Secretary of the French delegation to the United Nations. At present he is French Consul-General in Los Angeles. He was born in 1914, received a law degree, speaks and writes English, Russian and Polish in addition to French. He is married to the English writer, Lesley Blanch. He is now at work on his autobiography.*